Bound by Bone

The BoneBound Court

Harleigh Rose Knight

Trigger Warnings

This book may discuss topics that are not suitable for everyone and may be difficult for some readers. This book includes mentions of grief, emotional abuse, trauma, violence, death, gore, blood, child death, general manipulation, murder, religious and political manipulation, starvation, torture, body horror, emotional distress, ritual magic, toxic romantic dynamics.

In general, it's a dark series.

Take care of your mental health first. We will meet another time for another story.

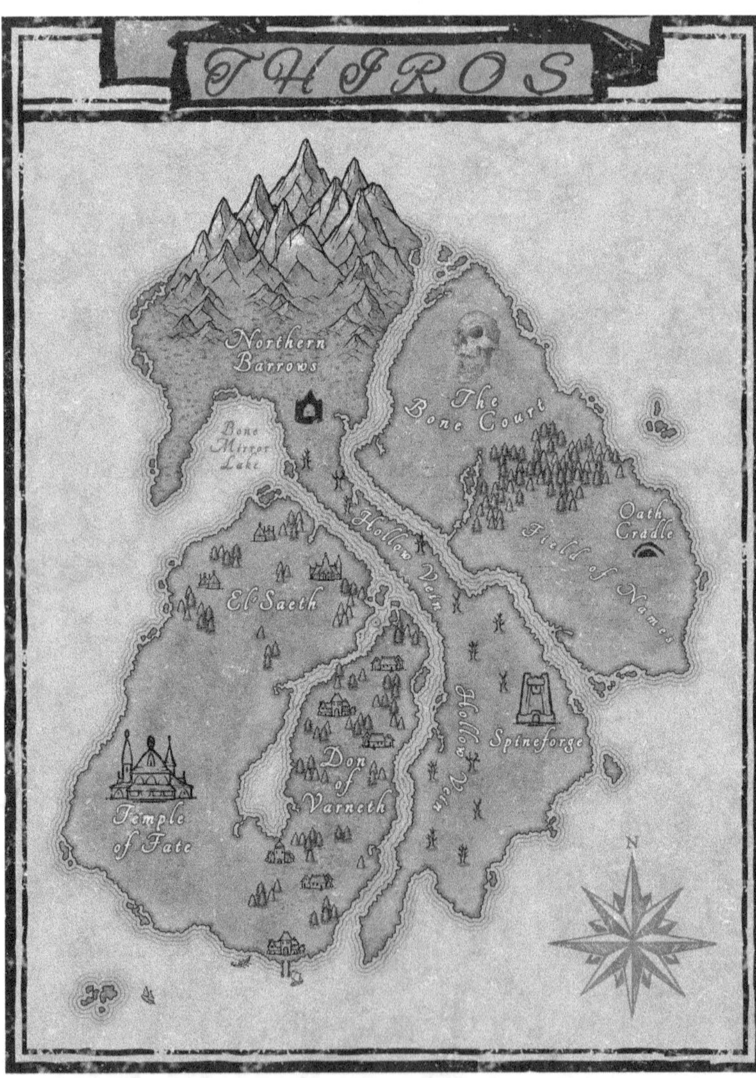

THIROS
Northern Barrows
The Bone Court
Bone Mirror Lake
Hollow Vein
Oath Cradle
Field of Names
El'Saeth
Hollow Vein
Spineforge
Don of Varneth
Temple of Fate
N

Contents

Coming Soon...

The Bloodborn Inheritance
Hourglass of Blood, Book Two
Shadow of the Last Born, Book Three

The Bonebound Court
Midnight Oath, Book Three

The Serpents Vengeance

Heartless

Keep up to date with the latest news and release dates by following on social media.
Find Harleigh Rose Knight on all platforms.

Act One

Between Worlds

Chapter One

Between Worlds

Nokoa

The first thing I remembered was bone.

Not flesh. Not breath. Not the golden light of morning or the smell of wisteria or any of the thousand small things that make a life worth living. Just bone—cold, hollow, impossibly heavy.

I existed in pieces. A femur here, vertebrae scattered like dice across an endless dark. My skull floated somewhere above me, or below me—direction had no meaning in this place. This void.

I tried to move and found I had no body to move with. Tried to scream and had no throat to shape the sound. The silence was absolute. It pressed against the absence of my ears. I was consciousness without form, memory without vessel, and the weight of it—the sheer wrongness of existing as pieces—threatened to scatter what remained of my mind.

How long had I been here? Hours? Days? Years?

The darkness gave no answers. It simply was, thick as tar and twice as suffocating. I floated in it, or sank through it, or perhaps I was the darkness itself and simply hadn't realized it yet. The thought made me want to laugh, but I had no lungs for it. No belly to shake with it. Nothing but the terrible awareness that I should have those things and didn't.

Then, movement.

My radius and ulna drifted together, drawn by some invisible current. They aligned with a soft click I felt more than heard—a vibration that resonated through my scattered consciousness. Strange, that sensation. Not quite painful. Something that tasted like memory and smelled faintly of copper.

I remembered breaking my arm once, at thirteen, falling from a tree while trying to impress a girl whose name I could no longer recall. The healer setting the bone, the way it ached for weeks after, deep and persistent. This felt like that moment in reverse. Not breaking, but mending. Not injury, but restoration.

Another bone found its match. Then another. My ribs began assembling themselves like a puzzle solving itself, curving inward to protect organs that didn't yet exist. Each connection sent that same resonant click through the void, and with each one, I became more present. More real. More trapped.

Because that's what this was, I realized. A trap. A cage built from my own skeleton, snapping shut bone by bone.

I tried to stop it. Tried to will the pieces apart, scatter myself back into merciful fragments. Better to be broken than whatever this was becoming. But my bones had their own momentum now, their own terrible purpose. They wanted to be whole. They needed it, with a hunger that wasn't mine but somehow lived inside me anyway.

My spine assembled itself vertebra by vertebra, a ladder of bone leading somewhere I didn't want to go. My pelvis locked into place with a finality that hit like a door closing. Like a sentence being passed. Fingers found each other, threading together in a grotesque parody of prayer.

And then—light.

Not true light. Nothing so kind. But a lessening of the absolute darkness, gray seeping in at the edges of my awareness like dawn through dirty water. It revealed the void for what it was: not empty space, but an abyss. Endless. Hungry. Waiting.

The gray light had texture to it. It moved like fog, cold and damp against my forming bones. If I'd had skin, it would have raised gooseflesh.

In the distance—though distance meant nothing here—something gleamed.

A mirror.

It hung suspended in the darkness, its frame carved from bone and sinew, its surface rippling like disturbed water. No reflection showed in its depths. Instead it was a window. A lens. And through it, I could see—

Her.

Renata.

She knelt in a chamber I didn't recognize, carved from stone and lined with bones that seemed to watch her work. Candles burned with blue-white flame, casting her face in harsh relief. Their wax smelled acrid even through the barrier between us, mixing with the iron tang of blood. She looked terrible. Beautiful and terrible, like a storm given human form. Her white hair hung in tangles, and those gray eyes I'd loved were fever-bright, too wide, seeing things that weren't there.

Or perhaps seeing things that were, and shouldn't be.

Her lips moved in words I couldn't hear through the mirror's barrier. But I could see what she held: a dagger made of bone, its edge wickedly sharp. And on the altar before her—

My body.

My corpse, I should say. Because that's what it was. My body, dressed in burial clothes, laid out like an offering. My skin had taken on a waxy quality, the gray-blue tinge of meat left too long in the sun. But she touched me like I was still warm, her fingers trailing along my jaw, my throat, my chest, leaving smudges of something dark behind.

She was weeping. Silent, desperate tears carving tracks through the grime on her cheeks.

And she was smiling.

That smile split something open in my chest. This wasn't grief. This was something that wore grief's face but had nothing human left beneath it.

She raised the dagger. Pressed it to her own palm and drew it across in one quick motion. Blood welled up, dark and thick, and she held her hand over my corpse's mouth, letting it drip between my blue lips. Black in the blue candlelight. Viscous and wrong.

"Come back," she whispered, and somehow I could hear her now, her voice cutting through the void like a blade. "Come back to me. I fixed it. I fixed everything."

No, I tried to say. No, Renata, whatever you're doing, stop. Please stop.

But I had no voice. Only bones, still assembling themselves with that relentless click, click, click.

My skull finally drifted down, settling atop my spine, and suddenly I could feel everything—the void pressing against me, the bones humming with terrible energy, the mirror's pull like a hook lodged in my sternum, dragging me forward inch by excruciating inch.

The pull had weight. Gravity. It wanted me there, in that body on the altar, and it didn't care what it had to break to make that happen.

And beneath that—fainter, but unmistakable—I felt her. Not her touch, not her thoughts. The bond between us didn't work that way. But her presence scraped against whatever piece of me remained tethered to the living world, and even that distant awareness sent a lance of pain through my reforming chest. The bond had always hurt when we'd gotten too close. Now, with me caught between death and life, it felt like being flayed.

I couldn't know what she was feeling, couldn't hear her thoughts, but I knew she was there. And the knowing was agony.

"You're awake."

The voice came from everywhere and nowhere. Deep. Ancient. Satisfied with itself.

I spun—or tried to. My assembled skeleton hung in the void like a marionette with cut strings. But I could sense him now, the owner of that voice. A presence in the darkness, vast and still, watching me the way a cat watches a mouse in a trap.

"What—" My voice surprised me. I had a voice now. Thin and hollow, like wind through a cave, but mine. "What's happening to me?"

"Resurrection." The word rolled through the abyss like thunder, reverberating against my bones. "Or something like it. Your little queen is quite determined, isn't she? I'm giving you a glimpse of your future."

Through the mirror, Renata had begun carving symbols into the stone around my corpse. Witch runes—I recognized them from old texts, forbidden things. Divine magic, corrupted and bent to purposes the gods never intended. They glowed white as she carved them, pulsing in time with her heartbeat.

In time with my heartbeat, I realized. Because somehow, impossibly, I had one now. Faint and stuttering, but there. Each beat sent a dull throb through my chest, like a drum struck with a muffled hand.

"She shouldn't be able to do this," I managed. "The Hollow Crown has brought me back once already. This isn't normal. The dead don't—we don't—"

"Come back?" The presence laughed, and the sound made my newly-formed bones ache, vibrating them like tuning forks. "No. They don't. Death is supposed to be final. But your queen has found a loophole, hasn't she? Or rather, she's been shown one. You are the most vital part of everything, after all."

He moved closer. I still couldn't see him, not truly. Just impressions—shadows darker than the surrounding dark, a suggestion of massive bones, eyes like distant stars. I felt his attention like weight, like gravity. The air—if it could be called air—thickened with the scent of old earth and older stone.

"Who are you?" I managed.

"I have many names. Most of them have been forgotten." A pause, as if savoring the moment. "But you can call me... a concerned party. Someone with a vested interest in your return to the world of flesh and breath."

Through the mirror, Renata had finished the circle of runes. She sat back on her heels, swaying, her shoulders bowed with exhaustion. Blood dripped from her hand onto the stone, pooling in the carved symbols. They drank it in, glowing brighter, pulsing like something alive.

"Why?" I asked. "Why would you care if I live or die?"

"Because, dear boy—" and I could hear the pleasure in his voice now, the patience of something that has waited a very long time— "without you, none of this would be possible."

Sinew began threading through my bones. I watched it happen, felt it happen—this grotesque reversal of decay. Muscle followed, wrapping around the framework of my skeleton like vines claiming a trellis. It should have hurt. It should have been agony. But instead it felt inevitable. Like this had always been going to happen, and I'd simply been too foolish to see it. The muscle was cold at first, then began to warm, fibers twitching with nascent life.

"None of what?" I demanded, though my voice cracked on the words.

The presence circled me slowly. I tracked him by the displacement of darkness, by the way the void bent around him like water around a stone.

"The breaking. The opening. The beautiful, terrible thing your queen is about to become." He sounded almost fond. "She thinks she's saving you. In a way, she is. But what she doesn't understand—what none of them understand—is that saving you requires destroying everything else."

Through the mirror, Priestess Alaira had entered the chamber. The old witch looked different than I remembered—younger somehow, but with eyes that had seen too much. She and Renata spoke briefly, then Alaira began adding her own power to the ritual, her hands moving in patterns I couldn't follow, weaving something between worlds, stitching reality back together in ways it was never meant to be sewn.

Weaving me back.

"Stop this," I begged. "Whatever you are, whatever you want—stop this. She doesn't know what she's doing."

"Oh, but she does." The presence was directly in front of me now, close enough that I could feel his breath—or something like breath—against my newly-forming face. It smelled like incense and rot. "She knows exactly what she's doing. She's choosing you over the world. Over morality. Over her own soul. It's really quite touching."

Skin began sliding over my muscles, pale and new, cold as a fish's belly. I looked down at my hands and saw them becoming real, becoming mine again. Ten fingers where there should be ten. But I could feel the wrongness in them, in all of this. I was being rebuilt, yes. But not as I was. As something else.

"Please," I whispered.

"Begging?" The presence laughed again, the sound rolling through me like thunder through hollow caves. "I've waited so long for this. Nothing is going to stop it."

Through the mirror, Renata had begun the final incantation. Her voice rose and fell in rhythms that predated language, each syllable a key turning in a lock that should have stayed sealed. Alaira joined her, their voices twining together like braided rope. The witch runes blazed so bright I had to look away, afterimages burning behind my eyelids.

Memory hit like a hammer. My clothes slick with blood. Renata screaming my name as Fatin broke my ribs and gripped my heart.

That was how I died.

That was where I lost her.

And then—pull.

It felt like being turned inside out. Like every piece of me that had scattered across the void was being yanked back through a hole too small to fit through. I tried to scream, but the sound was lost in the roar of displacement, of worlds colliding, of death being forced to yield its claim. White-hot and freezing all at once, every nerve ending I didn't yet have screaming in protest.

If I could have gotten one thought to Renata—if I could have sent her one thing—I would have shouted, See me. See what you're doing.

The last thing I saw before the void shattered around me was the presence, finally visible for just a heartbeat. Massive and skeletal, crowned in something that might have been bone or might have been light. And his smile—gods help me, his smile was almost gentle. He stood utterly still, but the air around him pressed down like the moment before lightning strikes.

"Welcome back, little weapon," he said. "Welcome back to the world you're going to help me unweave."

Then I was falling, falling, falling.

And landing back in flesh.

My chest heaved with a breath that tasted like copper and ashes. My heart slammed against my ribs, frantic and furious at being forced to beat again. Every nerve screamed at the wrongness of inhabiting space, of having weight and substance and form. The world had texture again—the cold stone beneath my back, the too-warm air of the chamber, the rough weave of burial cloth against my skin.

I tried to open my eyes and found I couldn't. Not yet. I was trapped in this body, this cage, this gift I never asked for. My limbs felt like lead, as if I'd forgotten how to tell them what to do.

But I could hear her.

"Nokoa?" Renata's voice, right next to me. Her hand on my face, warm and trembling, her fingertips rough with dried blood. "Nokoa, please. Please wake up. Please come back to me."

Her voice cracked on the last word.

I wanted to tell her I already had. That I was here, trapped between death and life, cursed by her love. But my mouth wouldn't work. My tongue was lead. All I could do was exist in this horrible liminal space, feeling her grief and desperation crash against me like waves against stone, each one wearing away a little more of what I'd been.

And underneath it all, barely perceptible, I could still hear him. That presence from the void. The bone god, I understood then. Because what else could he be?

His laughter echoed through my newly-beating heart like a promise.

Soon, it seemed to say. Very soon.

And then, finally, I felt my eyelid twitch.

Chapter Two

THE VIGIL BEGINS

Renata

The ritual chamber smelled like winter and old blood.

I sat cross-legged on the stone floor, my dress pooling around me in waves of black silk that had gone stiff with dried sweat and gods knew what else. The fabric scratched against my skin where it had bunched beneath my knees. The candles had burned down to nubs, their blue-white flames guttering in pools of their own wax. Priestess Alaira had left hours ago—or maybe minutes, time moved strangely down here—with instructions to rest, to prepare myself for what came next.

"You need time alone with him," she'd told me, her patchy hair falling across her face as she gathered her things, tucking vials and herbs into her worn leather satchel. "Time to say goodbye to who he was. The ritual needs the right timing. The half-moon, three nights from now. Use this time to prepare your heart."

As if my heart wasn't already scraped raw and bleeding, every beat a reminder of what I'd lost.

What I was getting back.

I reached out and traced the line of Nokoa's jaw, my fingertips skating over skin that felt cool but not cold. Not the terrible cold of the dead. Just the coolness of deep sleep, of a body conserving its strength for the work ahead. His stubble rasped faintly against my touch—he'd need a shave when he woke.

"You're resting," I whispered. "That's good. You'll need your strength when you wake up."

His chest rose and fell—I could see it, the shallow movement of breathing. The candles flickered, and in their dancing light, I watched him draw air into his lungs. Steady. Real. He was still here with me, just sleeping deeply. So deeply.

Did you see that? I asked the crown silently. He's breathing.

Rest now, Queen Oriana's voice answered in my ear, soft and maternal. The ritual needs just the right timing to work. Let him gather his strength. Let yourself gather yours.

He was beautiful, Queen Lyanna added, her tone wistful. Keep him that way. Don't let decay touch him before the magic can.

The dead don't judge, King Alaric chimed in, pragmatic as always. Only the living do.

I nodded, running my thumb along Nokoa's bottom lip. His mouth was slightly parted, and I could feel the whisper of his breath against my skin. Warm. He was still warm.

"I brought you water," I said, gesturing to the cup I'd set beside his ice bed earlier. The liquid had gone tepid, but that was fine. He'd drink it when he was ready. "And bread. You must be hungry. You haven't eaten since..."

Since when? When had he last eaten? Before the battle, certainly. Before everything went wrong.

Before I'd failed him.

But I wouldn't fail him again. The crown had shown me the way. Priestess Alaira had confirmed it was possible. Three more days, and the ritual would bring him fully back. Not as he was—better. Bound to me so completely that nothing, not death itself, could separate us again.

I leaned down and pressed my lips to his forehead, feeling the coolness of his skin against mine. See? Still cool, not cold. Still holding onto life, just resting. Gathering strength for the resurrection that would make him whole again.

"I missed you today," I breathed against his skin, taking in the scent of him—herbs and something metallic beneath. "The Bone Council had another meeting. Ancelin was insufferable, as always. Going on about tithes and traditions and maintaining order. As if any of that matters now."

Nokoa's eyelids fluttered—just slightly, barely perceptible, but I saw it. The finest tremor, like a leaf stirring in a breeze. He was listening. Somewhere in that deep sleep, he heard my voice and responded to it.

There you are, I thought, my heart swelling. I knew you were still in there.

I pulled back and smiled at him, brushing a curl away from his forehead. His hair had gotten longer since the coronation, the dark strands falling across his brow in waves. I'd need to trim it for him when he woke. He always liked it short enough that it didn't fall in his eyes when he fought.

When he fought.

Would he need to fight again? After everything, could I ask that of him?

You won't need to ask, the crown whispered, Oriana's voice a caress against my thoughts. He'll want to protect you. That's what love is.

Yes. That's what love was. Protection. Sacrifice. Doing whatever was necessary to keep each other safe.

I'd learned that lesson well.

My fingers trailed down from his face to his chest, pressing against where his heart beat. Steady. Strong. I could feel it beneath my palm, that reassuring rhythm that meant life, meant hope, meant he was still here with me.

"Your heart is so strong," I said softly. "It kept beating even when everything else stopped. Did you know that? Even when I thought I'd lost you, your heart refused to give up."

Is that true? A small voice in the back of my mind asked. Is his heart really beating? Last I recalled, it was ripped from his chest.

I pressed harder, feeling for that pulse. There—yes, there it was. Faint but present. The steady thrum of life that the ice bed was preserving until the ritual could restore him fully.

The ice bed. I'd commissioned it specially, had it carved from a single block of enchanted ice that would never melt. Its surface gleamed dully in the candlelight, slick and smooth as glass beneath the thin layer of linen I'd placed between

Nokoa and the cold. It kept him perfect, kept decay at bay, kept him here until I could bring him back properly.

I hadn't known we had any such thing before, but the Hollow Crown assured me it was real and it would work. They were right.

I ran my hand down his arm, feeling the firmness of his muscles beneath the burial clothes I'd dressed him in. White linen, simple and clean, the kind he would have chosen for himself. He'd always been strong. A warrior born and bred, trained from childhood to be someone's sworn blade. Mine, eventually, though neither of us had chosen that path willingly.

But we'd found love anyway. Despite everything. Despite the crown and the court and all the forces trying to keep us apart.

And love didn't die. Not real love. Real love persisted beyond death, beyond reason, beyond everything the world said was possible.

"When you wake up," I told him, my fingers threading through his, "we'll leave this place. We'll go somewhere no one can find us. Somewhere we can just be without all this weight pressing down. Would you like that?"

His fingers moved in mine. Just barely—a twitch, really, probably just the cold making his muscles contract—but I felt it. He'd heard me. He was agreeing.

"I knew you would," I breathed, smiling. "We'll have a garden. You always wanted a garden. Somewhere to grow things, to watch life flourish instead of watching it end. I'll make that happen for you. For us."

My mouth felt dry for a moment.

Or was that my dream? I couldn't recall anymore.

Soon, Oriana promised. Three more days and he'll be whole again. Bound to you forever.

I brought Nokoa's hand to my lips and kissed his knuckles one by one, tasting salt and something else beneath it. Something sweet and wrong, like fruit left too long in the sun. Probably just the preservation spells. Magic always had a strange taste.

"I should clean you," I said, setting his hand down gently. "Keep you comfortable while you rest."

I stood, my knees protesting after sitting so long, and moved to the basin I'd brought down earlier. The water had gone cold while I sat, but that was fine. He'd always preferred cold baths anyway, said they helped clear his head after training.

After training. Would his body remember how to move, how to fight, after the resurrection?

Of course, Alaric assured me. The body remembers. Muscle memory persists. He'll be exactly as he was.

Better, Lyanna added, bright with certainty. The ritual will perfect him.

I carried the basin back to the ice bed and began washing his face with gentle strokes, cleaning away the waxy buildup that came from lying still so long. His skin was cool beneath my touch, but that made sense. The ice bed kept him at the perfect temperature to prevent decay.

"There," I said, rinsing the cloth and moving to his neck, watching rivulets of water run down into the hollow of his throat. "That's better. You look more like yourself now."

His lips were blue-gray in the candlelight. Beautiful, really, like winter frost on stone. I traced them with my fingertip. He'd always had nice lips. Full and soft, quick to smile before everything went wrong.

I leaned down and kissed them softly, just a brush of contact. They tasted metallic, sharp, like old copper coins. Cold against mine.

When I pulled back, I could swear I saw him smile. Just the barest upturn at the corners of his mouth, gone so quickly I might have imagined it.

But I hadn't. I knew I hadn't.

"You're welcome," I whispered. "I'll always take care of you. That's what we do, isn't it? Take care of each other."

I continued washing him, working my way down his arms, his chest, his hands. Each finger cleaned carefully, each nail checked for dirt. He'd always kept himself immaculate when he was—when he was awake. He'd hate waking up to find himself dirty.

His hands were stiff in mine, fingers curled slightly inward, the joints resistant when I tried to straighten them. It couldn't have been rigor. He was only resting.

There were more important things to think about. How long had it been? Days? A week? Time blurred down here in the catacombs, where the only light came from candles and witch runes carved into stone, glowing faintly like trapped stars.

Don't think about time, the crown advised, Oriana's voice steady. Time is meaningless. What matters is the ritual.

Yes. And in three more days none of this would matter. The stiffness, the cold, the blue tinge to his skin—all of it would vanish when the magic took hold and brought him back to me.

I set the cloth aside and lay down beside him on the ice bed, careful not to disturb his rest. The cold seeped through my dress immediately, making me shiver, raising gooseflesh along my arms. But I didn't care. I needed to be close to him. Needed to feel his presence beside me, even if he couldn't hold me yet.

"Tell me about the in-between," I whispered, staring up at the chamber's vaulted ceiling, watching shadows dance across ancient stone. "What's it like where you are right now? Can you see me? Can you hear me talking to you?"

The silence stretched, but I knew he was listening. Somewhere in that deep sleep, he heard every word.

"Priestess Alaira says the ritual will bind our souls," I continued, my voice barely above a breath. "Says we'll be connected in ways that go beyond normal bonds. You'll feel what I feel. I'll know your thoughts. We'll never be apart again, not really. Doesn't that sound perfect?"

His chest rose and fell beside me. I watched the movement, counting breaths, reassuring myself that he was still here, still fighting his way back to me.

One breath. Two. Three.

Is he really breathing? that small voice asked again. Or are you just seeing what you want to see?

I turned my head to look at him, really look at him. His profile was stark in the candlelight—sharp nose, strong jaw, those lips I'd kissed a thousand times. His eyes were closed, lashes dark against his cheeks. Peaceful. He looked peaceful.

Except—

There was something wrong with his skin. A waxy quality, like candle tallow left too long in the sun. And his color was off, not just the blue-gray of his lips but a pallor that went deeper, that spoke of—

No.

I sat up sharply, my heart slamming against my ribs. No. I was imagining things. The candlelight was playing tricks, making shadows where there were none. He was fine. He was resting.

I pressed my hand to his chest again, searching for that heartbeat I'd felt earlier.

Nothing.

I pressed harder, panic rising in my throat.

Still nothing.

"No," I said aloud, my voice cracking. "No, you're—I felt it earlier. Your heart was beating. I felt it."

Did you? my own voice asked, gentle and terrible. Or did you feel what you needed to feel?

"Stop it," I hissed, pressing both hands against his chest now, willing his heart to beat beneath my palms. "Stop trying to make me doubt. The ritual will work. Three more days and he'll wake up and everything will be—"

Trust us, Renata. He's only resting, Queen Oriana crooned in my ear. We promised, didn't we? Have we ever led you astray?

A sound from the entrance made me freeze.

Valdic stood in the doorway, my emaciated DirgeWolf companion, his purple eyes gleaming in the darkness like twin amethysts. Half his ribs showed through patches of dark fur, and the smell of decay that clung to him seemed suddenly overwhelming in the close confines of the chamber, mixing with the incense and wax and something else I didn't want to name.

He tilted his head, studying me.

"What?" I demanded, my voice sharper than I intended. "Why are you looking at me like that?"

He made a low sound, almost questioning, deep in his chest.

"I'm talking to Nokoa," I said defensively, hearing how my voice pitched higher. "He's resting. He needs—"

I stopped, realizing how it sounded. How it looked. Me, alone in a tomb, talking to—

To what?

To him, I thought fiercely. To Nokoa. Who is right here. Who is coming back to me.

Valdic padded closer, his claws clicking on stone, the sound echoing in the chamber. He sniffed the air near the ice bed, his nostrils flaring, then looked back at me with something like concern in those purple eyes.

"He's fine," I insisted. "He's just sleeping deeply. The ritual—Priestess Alaira said—three more days and—"

Valdic made another sound, softer this time. Almost pitying. The kind of noise he made when he found something wounded beyond saving.

"Don't," I warned, my hands curling into fists. "Don't look at me like that. Like I'm—like I'm—"

Who are you talking to? the crown asked suddenly, Oriana's voice sharp.

"Valdic," I replied, gesturing toward him. "He's right here. He's—"

Is he? Alaric questioned, carefully. Or are you alone in this chamber, talking to shadows?

I looked at Valdic. Then at Nokoa. Then back at Valdic, whose purple eyes watched me with that same unreadable expression, his head still tilted.

"You hear him, too," I said desperately. "Tell them. Tell them Nokoa is still here. That he's breathing. That his heart is beating. Tell them I'm not—"

Valdic lowered his head and made a mournful sound that sent ice through my veins, a keening note that spoke of death and loss and things beyond recall.

"No," I whispered. "No, you're wrong. You're all wrong. Look—"

I grabbed Nokoa's hand, holding it up as if that proved something. "See? He's still warm. He's still—"

But his hand was cold in mine. Not cool. Not the comfortable coolness of sleep. Cold. The kind of cold that came from ice beds and preservation spells and bodies that didn't move, didn't breathe, didn't live. The kind that seeped into your bones and stayed there.

I dropped his hand and watched it fall back against his chest with a dull thud.

"No," I said again, the word barely a breath. "No, I felt his heartbeat. I saw him breathing. He smiled at me. He—"

"You're trying to make me doubt myself, doubt Nokoa!" I yelled at Valdic, my voice bouncing off the stone walls. "He was fine until you got here!"

"Stop it!" I pressed my hands to my ears, trying to block out the whispers, the doubts, the terrible knowledge trying to claw its way into my mind. "Stop trying to confuse me! The ritual will work! Alaira said it would work!"

I stared at Nokoa's body—and it was a body, wasn't it? Not him sleeping. Not him resting. A body, waxy and still and wrong—and felt something give way inside my chest.

"But I heard him," I whispered, tears blurring my vision. "I felt his heartbeat. He moved his fingers when I held his hand. He—"

You saw what you needed to see. The thought arrived in my mind in a voice that wasn't quite mine and wasn't quite Valdic's, something between them. *What you needed to believe to keep going. It's not the truth, Renata.*

Tears spilled down my cheeks, hot and bitter against my cold skin. "I can't—he can't be—"

He isn't dead, Oriana interrupted, her voice cutting through the panic. *Not really. Not yet. But in three days he won't be. The ritual will bring him back. Truly back. You just need to hold on a little longer. Can you do that?*

I looked at Nokoa's face—waxy, still, wrong, his lips parted slightly as if he'd been trying to speak when death took him—and felt my mind skitter away from what I was seeing.

"Yes," I heard myself say, the word hollow. "Yes, I can do that."

Good girl, Lyanna praised. *Now send the mutt away and clean Nokoa properly. Make him beautiful for his resurrection. Show him how much you love him.*

I picked up the cloth with shaking hands and returned to my work, washing him with gentle strokes, pretending I didn't notice how his skin slipped slightly under my touch, how it moved wrong, like leather that had gotten wet and dried stiff. Pretending the smell seeping through the incense was just old stone and stale air. Pretending everything was fine, was going according to plan, was working.

Valdic watched me for a long moment, then turned and left, his claws clicking away into darkness until I was alone again.

I worked through the night, talking to Nokoa, telling him about my plans, about the future we'd have together. My voice filled the chamber, echoing off stone, coming back to me in fragments. And if my voice cracked sometimes, if tears made the cloth wet as I cleaned him, if I had to keep stopping to press my hand to his chest searching for a heartbeat that never came—

Well. That was between me and the dead.

And the crown, which purred approval with every denial, every delusion, every desperate attempt to unsee what I was really doing.

The candles burned lower. My hands moved automatically, washing, smoothing, adjusting. And all the while, the crown whispered in my ear, soft and insistent and kind.

Three more days, they promised. Three more days and everything will be perfect.

I believed them because I had to.

Because the alternative was letting him go.

And I wasn't ready for that.

Not yet.

Chapter Three

THE HOLLOW QUEEN'S PREPARATIONS

Morning came without my noticing.

I only realized it when a sliver of light crept down from the ventilation shaft above, cutting through the blue-white glow of the witch runes to paint a pale stripe across the chamber floor. Dust motes danced in the beam, lazy and golden. Day one, I thought distantly. Three more days until the half-moon. Until the ritual that would bring him back properly.

Until I could wake him from this deep sleep.

I'd fallen asleep beside him at some point, my head pillowed on his chest, my arm thrown across his waist. The ice bed had left me stiff and aching, my joints protesting with every small movement. My dress was damp with condensation, the fabric clinging cold and unpleasant against my skin. But I'd been close to him. That was what mattered.

I sat up slowly, vertebrae cracking like dry twigs. Nokoa lay exactly as I'd left him perfectly still, hands folded over his chest, that peaceful expression on his face that almost looked like contentment. I'd arranged him that way after washing him, wanting him to look dignified. Restful.

Not dead.

Never dead.

I leaned down and pressed a kiss to his cheek, my lips lingering against his skin. Cool, yes, but the ice bed did that. Kept him at the perfect temperature.

When I pulled back, I let my hand trail down his neck, across his collarbone, feeling the delicate architecture of bone beneath skin. Lower.

My fingers found the edge of his shirt and slipped beneath it, spreading across his stomach. His skin was smooth there, unmarred. I remembered kissing that spot, remembered how he'd laughed and pulled me closer, his hands warm on my waist. The memory felt distant now, like something glimpsed through fog.

I wanted to feel that closeness again. Wanted to press my body against his and pretend, just for a moment, that we were anywhere but here. That he could hold me back.

"It's quiet. Only the two of us," I whispered, my hand moving lower, tracing the line where his pants met his hip. "We have time for this. All the time in the world. No more hiding. No more stolen moments. Just us."

"Renata?"

I jerked back so fast I nearly fell off the ice bed, my heart slamming against my ribs. Cressa stood in the entrance, her green eyes wide. She wore fresh robes, gold and yellow bright even in the dim chamber, and carried a tray of food that I dimly registered I should probably eat. The smell of fresh bread reached me across the cold air.

"What were you doing?" she asked carefully.

My face burned. "Visiting him. He's resting."

Cressa's gaze moved to Nokoa's body, then back to me. Her throat worked. "Renata, you've been down here all night. People are starting to talk. The Bone Council—"

"Can wait," I interrupted, standing and smoothing my dress. The damp fabric clung to my legs, cold and restrictive. "I have three more days before the ritual. I'm not leaving him alone down here."

"Three more days until what ritual?" Cressa set the tray down on a carved stone shelf, her movements slow and deliberate. Like she was trying not to spook a wounded animal.

I bristled. "The resurrection. Priestess Alaira explained it all. The half-moon provides the right alignment, the witch runes will—"

"Witch runes." Cressa said it like she was tasting something foul, her lip curling slightly. "Renata, those are corrupted magic. Divine gifts twisted into—"

"Into something that works," I finished. "Into something that will bring him back to me."

Cressa took a step closer, hands raised. "I know you're in pain. I know you want him back. His first resurrection was a miracle on its own. But keeping his body down here, touching him like he's still—" She stopped, seemed to search for words. "Like he can feel you. That's not healthy."

"He CAN feel me," I insisted, hearing my voice rise, echoing off the stone walls. "The bond is already forming. When I touch him, he knows. When I talk to him, he hears. He's just resting until the magic can bring him fully back."

Something in Cressa's expression crumbled then. Not pity—worse than pity. Understanding. The kind that said she thought she knew better than I did about what was happening in my own ritual chamber.

"Renata," she said softly, and the gentleness in her voice made me want to scream. "Please. Let me help you. We're friends. We grew up together. I know you're hurting, but this—" She gestured at the chamber, at Nokoa, at me standing there in my damp dress with my hair wild and my hands shaking. "This isn't grief anymore. This is something else."

She doesn't understand, Oriana breathed in my ear. She never understood you.

She's jealous, Lyanna added. She never had anyone love her the way he loves you.

She wants to take him from you, Alaric warned. Have him burned before you can perform the ritual.

"Get out," I said quietly.

Cressa froze. "What?"

"Get. Out." Power crackled along my skin, raising the fine hairs on my arms, and the witch runes carved into the walls flared brighter in response. White light flooded the chamber, casting sharp shadows across Cressa's face, turning her eyes into dark hollows. "You don't know what you're talking about. You don't understand what we have."

"I understand that you're keeping a corpse," Cressa said, and her voice broke on the last word. Tears gathered in her eyes. "I understand that you're talking to him like he can answer. That you're—gods, Renata, were you about to—"

She didn't finish. She didn't need to. The implication hung between us, heavy and accusatory.

My hand moved before I'd fully decided to move it. The slap cracked through the chamber, sharp and sudden, and Cressa stumbled back with one hand flying to her reddening cheek. The sound echoed off stone, repeating itself in the silence.

We stared at each other. Both of us breathing hard. I could see my handprint blooming across her skin, stark and red. My palm stung.

"Don't," I said, my voice low and shaking, "presume to judge me. Don't presume to understand what I'm willing to do to keep him."

Cressa's hand trembled against her cheek. Tears spilled over, tracking down her face. "I'm trying to help you," she whispered. "Please. Just come with me. Stay in your chambers tonight. Let me be there for you. That's what friends do."

She's lying, Alaric hissed. She wants to separate you from him.

But underneath their voices I heard something else—a memory, faint and fading. Afternoons in a garden somewhere. Cressa teaching me to read, her finger tracing words in an old book while sun warmed our shoulders. Her laugh, bright and genuine.

The memory slipped away before I could grasp it fully.

"If you were really my friend," I said, "you'd believe me. You'd trust that I know what I'm doing."

"I want to trust you." Cressa's voice cracked. "But you're scaring me. The way you look at him, the way you touch him—he's gone, Renata. He's been gone for days and he's not coming back no matter how many witch runes you carve or how long you sit down here talking to—"

"GET OUT!"

The words tore from my throat with more force than I'd intended, and power surged with them. The witch runes blazed so bright they turned the chamber white as noon. Cressa cried out, shielding her eyes, and I felt something hot and shameful move through me at her fear.

When the light faded, she was already running. Her footsteps echoed through the catacombs, getting fainter until they disappeared entirely, swallowed by stone and distance.

I turned back to Nokoa. He lay peaceful and still on his ice bed, undisturbed by my violence. His expression hadn't changed—that same serene peace, as if he approved of what I'd done.

"I'm sorry," I whispered, settling beside him again, my hand finding his. "I'm sorry you had to hear that. She doesn't know what she's talking about. The ritual will work."

I took his hand—cold now, too cold—and brought it to my lips.

"I should eat something," I said, glancing at the tray Cressa had left. "Keep my strength up for the ritual. Will you forgive me if I leave you alone for a few minutes? I'll come right back. I promise."

His fingers didn't move. His chest didn't rise or fall. But I could feel his presence anyway, that sense of him that went beyond physical signs. The bond forming, invisible but real.

He understands, Oriana soothed. He knows you need to take care of yourself so you can take care of him.

I stood reluctantly and moved to the tray. Bread, cheese, some dried meat. My stomach turned at the sight of it, but I reached for the bread.

Small green spots had begun to appear on the crust. I blinked, watching them spread like ink on wet paper, blooming outward until every piece on the tray was covered in gray-green fuzz. I picked up a wedge of cheese anyway, and it crumbled between my fingers, falling to dust that drifted down to scatter across the stone floor. The smell hit me a moment later—rot and decay, thick enough to taste, heavy on the back of my throat.

I stepped back, breathing through my mouth, and my gaze caught on the wall where the witch runes were carved deepest. I pressed my hand against a section of stone that seemed different from the rest—smoother, almost seamless—and magic surged in response, warm and eager. The wall shifted beneath my palm.

Clever girl, Alaric praised. *The crown shows you what you need to see.*

The hidden door ground open with a sound of stone on stone that echoed through the chamber. Beyond it lay another room, smaller than the first, cold and stale.

And in its center—

Bones.

So many bones, arranged in careful patterns across every surface. Some were carved with the same witch runes that covered my chamber, glowing faintly in the darkness. Others bore symbols I didn't recognize—older, stranger, shifting when I looked at them directly, making my eyes water. In the corner, four mummified bodies slumped against the walls, their desiccated faces frozen in eternal anguish. Their mouths hung open.

"What is this place?" I whispered.

The bone god's crypt, Oriana answered, her voice reverent. *Where Priestess Alaira sealed him away. Where his bones still rest, waiting. Now that you're changing, you can be here.*

I should have felt afraid. Should have turned and run. But I stepped inside instead, drawn by something that felt like the memory of something I'd always known.

Journals lay scattered among the bones—hundreds of them, their pages yellowed with age, corners curling. I picked one up at random and opened it, squinting at faded text in a spidery hand I recognized as Alaira's.

The Goddess of Fate gave us runes, it read. *Asked us to protect the world She loved so much. To ease suffering. To guide death gently when it came. I took Her gift and made it into chains. Into a crown that feeds on what it was meant to protect. Forgive us. Forgive me.*

I flipped through more pages. Diagrams. Theories. Instructions for using witch runes in ways they were never meant to be used.

And there—near the back—a section on resurrection. On binding souls together so tightly that death couldn't separate them. On creating anchors.

Study it, Alaric urged. *Learn what you need to know. The ritual is in three days. You need to be prepared.*

I sank down among the bones, dust puffing up around me, and began to read. My fingers traced over corrupted divine magic, over instructions for mixing bone magic with witch runes, over warnings about prices. About what happened when you forced magic to do what it wasn't meant to do. About the cost of defying death itself.

Small prices, I thought, compared to what I'd already paid.

Hours passed. Or maybe days. I read until my eyes burned, until the words blurred together, until I could recite the ritual steps by heart.

Carve names into bone. Exchange pieces of yourselves. Mix the bone powder with blood and a catalyst. Speak the binding words at the moment of the half-moon.

Simple, really, when laid out like this. Just steps to follow. Just magic to perform.

Just resurrection.

I copied the most important runes into a journal of my own, my hand cramping as I worked. The crown fed me understanding, helping me see connections I shouldn't have been able to make. This rune meant binding. This one meant transformation. This one meant love-past-death, desire made manifest, obsession given form.

Combined with bone magic—the natural magic of this world—they created something new. Something that could drag a soul back from wherever souls went when they left their bodies. Something that could make death yield.

By the time I finally stood, my legs had gone numb. Pins and needles raced up my calves as feeling returned. I gathered the journals I needed and turned to leave, my mind already moving through the next steps.

A sound stopped me.

Faint. Distant. Footsteps in the outer chamber.

I hurried back through the hidden door, letting it grind shut behind me, and found Valdic standing beside Nokoa's ice bed. My DirgeWolf looked up as I entered, his purple eyes gleaming.

"What?" I demanded, moving to Nokoa's side, placing myself between them. "What are you doing?"

"Keeping watch," Valdic said. "Someone has to."

I relaxed slightly and set my journals down. "I'm fine. I've been reading. Learning. The ritual is in three days and I need to understand it perfectly."

"I know." He tilted his head, studying me. "You have ink on your hands and dust in your hair and you've been in that crypt for most of the day."

"Don't look at me like that," I said. "I know what I'm doing."

"I didn't say you didn't." His voice was careful in a way that meant the opposite. "I'm just noting what I see."

I turned back to Nokoa. My fingers trembled as they traced his collarbone, seeking that warmth I remembered. That proof of life.

But he was so cold. So still. His skin felt waxy under my touch, slipping slightly.

The ice bed, I reminded myself. Just the ice bed keeping him preserved.

I leaned down and kissed him, my lips pressing against his. He tasted wrong—that metallic tang stronger now, mixed with something sweet and rotten that made my stomach turn. Like fruit left too long in the sun. Like meat beginning to spoil.

When I pulled back, I thought I saw his lips move. Just barely. Just a twitch.

"There you are," I whispered. "I knew you were listening. Just hold on. Hold on for me."

Soon, Oriana promised.

I settled beside Nokoa again, my hand finding his, my head resting on his chest where his heart no longer beat. The silence beneath his ribs was absolute. I closed my eyes and pretended I could hear it anyway—that steady thump-thump that had once lulled me to sleep.

Behind me, Valdic curled up at the foot of the ice bed, keeping watch over both of us. The witch runes pulsed their steady white light.

The chamber grew colder as night fell again, though I barely noticed. I had my journals. I had my plans. I had Nokoa, still and silent beside me.

And I had the crown, whispering with three voices that sounded more and more like my own.

Three more days, they promised.

I believed them.

Because the alternative—the truth pressing at the edges of my mind, trying to break through—would shatter me in ways no ritual could repair.

So I didn't think about the mold on the food. Or the way Nokoa's skin had felt under my fingers. Or Cressa's face as she'd run.

I thought about the half-moon. About the moment when Nokoa's eyes would open and he'd look at me again, truly look at me.

Everything would be worth it then.

Everything would make sense.

I pressed my lips to his cold ones one last time before sleep took me.

Just three more days.

Chapter Four

RAGE OF THE CROWNED

Renata

The outer cities' army arrived at dawn on the second day.

I stood at the tall windows of the throne room, watching the horizon darken with their approach. Banners snapped in the wind—sharp cracks that echoed across the valley—a sea of colors I should have recognized but couldn't quite place. Red and gold? Blue and silver? They blurred together, meaningless.

They'd come for retribution. For answers. For blood.

Let them.

"You should rest," Cressa said from somewhere behind me, her voice careful, controlled. She'd kept her distance since yesterday, since the slap. Smart of her. "You haven't slept properly in days. The Bone Council can handle—"

"I've slept." I didn't turn around. "Beside Nokoa. He keeps me calm."

Silence stretched between us. Then: "Renata—"

"Don't." The word came out sharp as broken glass. "Not today."

I heard her leave, footsteps quick and retreating, the rustle of her robes fading into nothing. Good. I didn't have time for her doubt, her fear, her attempts to drag me back into a grief she thought I should be wallowing in.

I wasn't grieving. I was planning.

You need protection, Oriana whispered, her voice sliding through my thoughts. Real protection. They're coming for you, child. The outer cities, the council—everyone wants to take what's yours.

Take him from you, Lyanna added. Burn him before you can complete the ritual.

You need soldiers, Alaric stated. Loyal ones. The dead make excellent soldiers—they don't question orders.

The crown was right. It was always right.

I turned from the window and headed for the catacombs, my heels clicking against marble, then stone, then earth-packed floors as I descended.

Valdic found me halfway down, his purple eyes gleaming in the torchlight. The emaciated DirgeWolf fell into step beside me, his skeletal ribs visible through patches of dark fur, his claws a steady counterpoint to my footfalls.

"Off to visit your sleeping beauty again?" he asked, his tone dry.

"No." I kept walking, my torch casting wild shadows on the walls. "I need to go deeper."

"Deeper." Valdic made a sound that might have been a laugh, more growl than humor. "Because the regular catacombs aren't creepy enough?"

"I need the tomb of the first hollow rulers."

That stopped him. I heard his claws scrape against stone as he halted. "Why?"

I looked at him sidelong, the torchlight turning his purple eyes orange. "Protection. The outer cities have an army. I need one too."

"Ah." Valdic resumed walking, matching my pace. "Necromancy. Lovely. And here I thought today might be boring."

"You don't have to come."

"And miss you raising the dead?" He paused, tilting his head. "Though I should mention—Nokoa is still very much dead on his ice bed. Getting rather ripe, actually. The preservation spells can only do so much."

My hand tightened on the torch until my knuckles went white. "He's resting."

"Is he? Because from where I'm standing, he's—"

"Valdic." My voice came out low. A warning.

"Fine, fine." He trotted ahead, his tail low. "But when he starts to smell worse than I do, don't say I didn't warn you."

We descended in silence after that, past the chamber where Nokoa lay, past the hidden room with its journals and warnings. Down, down, down into the oldest dark, where the air grew thick and cold and tasted of minerals.

The tomb's entrance was sealed with a door of bone and iron, covered in warnings in three dead languages. I couldn't read them all, but I understood the gist: Disturb not the sleepers. Let the dead remain dead. Here lies only sorrow.

"Well, that's ominous," Valdic observed.

I pressed my hand against the door. The crown surged—hot against my skull, almost burning, searing where the metal touched skin—and something broke in the air. Not just broke. Shattered.

The seals didn't fail. They screamed.

High and piercing, the sound of magic dying, of ancient protections torn apart like wet paper. It burrowed into my ears, made them ring, made my jaw ache. The door swung open with a groan that sounded almost alive, almost pained, and I stumbled back from the force of it, my torch nearly dropping.

Cold air rushed out to meet us. It didn't just smell of stone and time—it smelled of rot barely held at bay, of death magic so old it had calcified into something solid you could almost touch. The cold bit through my dress, raising gooseflesh along my arms.

My skin prickled. Not recognition. Warning.

"After you," Valdic said, his voice stripped of its usual humor. He pressed closer to my leg. "I insist."

Inside, seven stone biers held seven bodies. The first hollow rulers, preserved by magic that should have faded centuries ago but hadn't. Each one bore the marks of how they'd died—throats slit ear to ear, dark lines still visible across gray skin; chests caved in like crushed fruit; eye sockets empty and weeping some dark fluid that had stained the stone beneath them. Violence marked them all, and the wrongness was in how fresh it looked. As if they'd died yesterday instead of centuries ago. As if death here didn't work the same way it did everywhere else.

The only part of them that looked truly ruined was where bones had been taken for the crown—skull fragments, finger bones, pieces harvested to create the very thing now burning against my head.

I moved to the center of the tomb, my torch casting dancing shadows that made the bodies seem to breathe. I set it in a wall sconce and the flames guttered, turned blue at the edges, painting everything in ghostly light.

Call them, Oriana urged. The crown knows the words. Let us show you.

I opened my mouth, and words spilled out in a language I'd never learned. Not just words—sounds. Ancient syllables that tasted like ash and copper and something sweeter that made my stomach turn. Each one resonated through the air, through the stone, through my bones. The witch runes I'd carved along my path here began to glow. Not the soft white light I'd grown used to, but something harsher. Cold fire that hurt to look at. They bled up through stone like wounds opening, illuminating the tomb in radiance that seared afterimages into my vision.

Nothing happened at first. I kept speaking, the words flowing faster now, tumbling over each other, my voice taking on harmonics that weren't mine—Oriana's maternal tone, Lyanna's brightness, Alaric's cold pragmatism, all of them speaking through me at once. My throat burned with the effort.

Then the first body moved.

Just a finger. A single index finger on the queen with the slit throat, curling inward like a dying spider's leg.

Then her hand. Her arm. Her head rolling to face me with a wet crack of vertebrae that should have been fused solid. The sound echoed off the walls, overlapping with itself.

The others followed. Not slowly—all at once, seven corpses rising in perfect unison. But it was wrong. They didn't sit up so much as they were pulled up, like puppets on strings I couldn't see. Their movements were jerky, unnatural. A king's head lolled too far to one side, exposing the wound at his throat. A queen's arm bent backward at the elbow with a snap that made me flinch.

And their skin. Gods, their skin. It had been waxy but intact moments ago. Now it was becoming translucent. Not fading—thinning. Stretched over bones that seemed too large for the flesh containing them. I could see their ribs through their chests. Could see the hollow spaces where organs should have been, dark cavities that seemed to go on forever.

Bones showed through where the skin simply gave up and tore. Eyes that had been clouded cleared, but what filled them wasn't life. It was something that glowed with the same harsh light as the witch runes—cold, and aware, and watching.

Something that saw me.

Seven former hollow rulers, spectral now, watching me with expressions I couldn't read. Horror? Recognition? Hunger?

They turned to look at me as one, and I felt their recognition crash against my mind like a wave. They knew what I was. What I was becoming. What the crown was making me.

But underneath that recognition, I felt something else. Something that made my hands shake and my breath come short.

Wrongness.

This wasn't supposed to feel like this. Necromancy in the journals had seemed clinical, straightforward. Raise the dead, bind them to your will, use them as tools.

But this didn't feel like tools. It felt like I'd reached into somewhere I shouldn't have reached and pulled out something that shouldn't have come free, and now it was here, staring at me, waiting. Waiting for me to slip, to falter, to give them an opening.

I should have had questions about why the bodies of Oriana, Alaric, and Lyanna weren't among the seven—but my thoughts skittered away every time I tried to grasp it, forced back on track like a horse with a bit. Something kept redirecting me, keeping me focused only on what mattered now.

"Serve me," I commanded, and my voice came out smaller than I'd intended. Thinner. Almost pleading.

Seven heads bowed in acknowledgment.

The movement was synchronized. Too perfect. Like they'd rehearsed it a thousand times. Like they'd been waiting for this moment, knowing it would come.

I stood there, studying my new guards, trying to convince myself they were what I needed. Loyal. Powerful. Unable to die because they were already dead.

But my hands wouldn't stop shaking.

"Well," Valdic said after a long moment, his voice quiet in a way I hadn't heard from him before. "That was disturbing."

I ignored him, because if I acknowledged the wrongness aloud, I'd have to acknowledge it to myself. And I couldn't afford that. Not with two days left until the ritual.

You did well, Oriana soothed. *They're yours now. They'll protect you.*

Effective, Alaric added. *That's what matters.*

Yes. Effective. That was what mattered.

I forced my attention to the first hollow queen's bier. Something about her bones still called to me—the way she'd died, the blood magic feeding the crown for decades after. Her sacrifice had been profound. Her power still lingered in the marrow, humming faintly.

Take it, Alaric urged. *Make it yours.*

I reached down and wrapped my fingers around her tibia and pulled.

It came away easily. Too easily. With a sound like tearing wet cloth, and the bone was warm in my hand despite the tomb's cold. Warm and faintly pulsing. The surface was slick, almost greasy.

Her skull followed, separating from her spine with a wet pop that echoed through the chamber. Heavier than I expected. Denser. It hummed against my palm, vibrating in a frequency I could feel in my back teeth.

I laid the bones out on the floor. My hands were steadier now, focused on the work. This was something I understood. Something the crown had shown me in dreams, in flashes of knowledge that felt like memory.

I began carving. Witch runes flowed from my fingertips—not onto the bones, but into them. The symbols sank beneath the surface, white light glowing from within the marrow like trapped stars. This rune for binding. This one for strength. This one for rage.

My rage, crystallized and given form.

The crown fed me knowledge faster than I could process it. How to twist this rune just slightly to make it sharper. How to layer this one over that one to create resonance. How to corrupt divine magic into something that could hurt.

"You know," Valdic observed, "there's something deeply concerning about how natural this looks for you. When I met you at the cottage, I'd never have believed you'd be here."

He was right. Back then this would have been impossible. I wouldn't have had the stomach for it. Now it felt like breathing. Like something I'd always known how to do, just forgotten until now.

The crown purred approval.

I drew my knife and pressed it against my palm. Not a quick slice—a slow, deliberate cut, dragging the blade across scarred flesh until it hit bone. The pain was bright and clarifying, sharp enough to make me gasp. I worked the blade back and forth, scraping bone, feeling fragments break away with little pops of pressure.

Bone dust. My bone dust. Mixed with blood that pooled in my cupped hand, warm and thick.

I let it drip onto the queen's bones.

They drank it in. Not absorbed it—drank it. I watched the blood disappear into the marrow, watched the bones glow brighter, watched the witch runes pulse in response.

And something inside me gave.

Not pain. Worse than pain. A piece of me being pulled out through my chest—steady and irreversible, like a tide going out. A memory, unraveling even as I reached for it.

Someone's face. Kind eyes, patient hands. Teaching me something important—what? How to—

Gone.

Just gone, between one breath and the next, as if it had never been there at all. I was left with the shape of it, the outline of something lost, and no way to know what I was missing.

"What did I just forget?" I whispered, staring at my bleeding hand.

Does it matter? Alaric asked. If you can't remember it, it couldn't have been important.

That logic felt wrong, circular and broken, but I couldn't quite grasp why. The thought slipped away.

I continued working, speaking binding words in that ancient language the crown provided. They tasted like iron and rot. The bones assembled themselves under my hands, drawn together by magic and will and desperate need.

A mace took shape. Heavy, brutal—the queen's skull at its crown, her tibia forming the handle. It should have looked crude, cobbled-together. Instead it looked right. Like it had always existed in this form, just waiting for someone to recognize it.

When I lifted it, it hummed with power. Not just magical power—eager power. The weapon wanted to be used. Wanted to break things. Wanted to hurt.

And gods help me, I wanted that too.

I hefted it, feeling its weight, its balance. The skull's empty eye sockets seemed to watch me. It fit my hand like it had been made for me. Which, I supposed, it had.

"Come," I said to my seven spectral guards. "We have business with the Bone Council."

They fell into formation without a word. Still too synchronized. Still too perfect. Their movements fluid and identical, like a single creature with seven bodies. But I pushed that thought away and led them up through the catacombs.

Valdic trotted beside me, unusually quiet. Then: "You're going to do something dramatic, aren't you?"

"Yes."

"Something violent?"

"Probably."

"Something you'll regret later?"

I looked down at him, at those knowing purple eyes. "I don't regret things anymore. Regret is for people who doubt their choices."

"Ah." His tone was flat. "Right."

The Bone Council's chamber doors loomed ahead, carved from ancient bone and bound with iron rusted at the edges. I could feel the council members waiting beyond them, their fear and fury bleeding through the walls like heat through stone.

Show them strength, Oriana urged. Show them what you've become.

Make them understand, Alaric commanded. That you are not to be questioned.

I pushed open the doors. They swung wide with a boom that shook dust from the ceiling.

The council chamber fell silent.

Chapter Five

BLOOD ON BONE

Renata

The Bone Council's chamber felt different when I entered with seven spectral guards at my back.

Colder, maybe. Or perhaps it was just that I was different—carrying a weapon made from royal bones, trailing the scent of disturbed tombs and corrupted magic. The witch runes carved into my mace pulsed faintly, casting white light across the marble floor in rhythm with my heartbeat.

Or the crown's heartbeat. Sometimes it was hard to tell the difference.

The council members were already assembled, each seated on their throne of bone and shadow. Ancelin with his serpentine dreadlocks and silver-sheen obsidian eyes that caught and held the light. Bahni with her empty eye sockets and blade-like nails that clicked softly as she shifted. Fatin, massive and spiked, his bike armor bound to bone with leather straps that creaked. Maxin, still mortal-looking but paler than I remembered, dark circles under his eyes deepening by the day.

And Praxis, watching everything with those crimson eyes that never seemed to blink.

They all looked up as I entered, and the temperature in the room dropped. I watched Ancelin's breath mist in the air, white clouds that dissipated slowly. Watched Maxin pull his robes tighter around himself, his shoulders hunching against the cold.

My spectral guards spread out behind me in perfect formation, and I saw the exact moment each council member understood what I'd done. What I'd brought into their sacred chamber. Their expressions shifted—horror, fury, disgust.

Bahni rose first, her movements sharp with fury, bone grinding against bone.

"What is the meaning of—"

"Sit down," I commanded.

She didn't. Instead, she moved toward me, her blade-nails catching the light, each one reflecting like a knife edge. "You dare bring those abominations into this chamber? You dare disturb the first rulers' rest?"

"I dare quite a lot these days." I moved to the center of the circle, my guards spreading out around me. "You wanted to discuss the outer cities? Fine. Let's discuss."

"There's nothing to discuss," Ancelin stated, his joints grinding as he leaned forward. The sound was like millstones turning. "You've lost control. The outer cities demand answers about the crop failures, about the famine spreading through—"

"Let them demand." I set the mace down with a heavy thunk that cracked the marble floor, sending hairline fractures radiating outward. "I have other priorities."

"Your priorities are killing people!" Bahni's voice rose, and I watched her eye sockets somehow manage to convey fury despite being empty. "The resurrection you're planning—it's disrupting the natural order! Crops are failing because you're corrupting magic itself! Can't you see what you're doing?"

"Good."

That stopped them all. The chamber went silent except for the faint hum of my mace.

"Good?" Maxin spoke softly from his throne, and there was something like grief in his voice, thick and heavy. "Renata, people are starving. Children are dying in the outer cities. Mothers are eating their shoes to have something in their stomachs. How is that good?"

"It's not good," I corrected, my voice flat. "It's irrelevant. I have two days until the ritual. Two days until I bring him back. Nothing else matters."

"Everything else matters!" Ancelin slammed his skeletal hand against his armrest hard enough to chip the bone. The crack echoed through the chamber. "You're the hollow queen! You have responsibilities! Duties to the living, not just to your dead lover!"

"I have one duty." My voice went cold, and I felt the crown pulse hot against my skull in approval. "Protecting what's mine. And right now, all of you are threatening that."

Bahni laughed. It was a sound like wind through empty sockets, like the last breath escaping a corpse. Hollow and wrong. "Listen to her. Mad with grief. She speaks to corpses as if they answer. She raises the dead and calls it protection. She uses magic she doesn't understand and calls it love." She turned to the other council members. "I move to bind her. For her own safety. For the realm's safety. For his safety, because what she's planning will damn his soul as surely as it's damning ours."

"Seconded," Ancelin agreed immediately.

Fatin shifted in his throne, his massive form creaking. He remained silent, but his eyes tracked my every movement.

Maxin looked at me with deep, genuine sorrow, lines deepening around his eyes. "Renata, please. I helped create this crown. I know what it does to people. I've watched it hollow out ruler after ruler, watched it feed on everything they love until there's nothing left." His voice dropped. "Let us help you before there's nothing left to save."

"I don't need saving." But my voice shook slightly, betraying me. "I need you to stay out of my way."

Only Praxis remained silent through all of this, watching with clinical interest, his head tilted slightly.

Bahni stood fully now, her blade-nails extended. "Then we have no choice. By ancient right, by council law, by the authority granted to us by the first hollow rulers themselves—" She gestured at my spectral guards, rage flickering across her skeletal features. "—whose rest you have disturbed, whose bodies you have defiled—you are hereby declared unfit to rule. You will be bound, contained, and held until such time as the crown can be safely removed or you can be safely—"

"No."

The word came out flat. Final. Like a door slamming shut.

Bahni's head tilted. "You don't have a choice in this, child. Four council members have voted. The binding will—"

She moved. Fast. Faster than bone should move. Her blade-nails extended toward my throat, and I saw genuine intent in her empty sockets. Not to kill, maybe. But to stop me. To bind me. To take away my choice.

To take away him.

My hand shot out and caught her wrist.

And I pushed.

Not physically. Not with strength. With magic. With everything the crown had been teaching me, every corrupted witch rune, every twisted scrap of divine power. It flooded out of me in a wave—bone magic and witch runes tangled together, death magic and resurrection magic colliding, creating something that shouldn't exist.

Creating something that burned.

Bahni screamed.

It was a sound like nothing I'd ever heard. Not pain, exactly. Worse than pain. The sound of someone realizing they were dying. The sound of bone recognizing its own destruction. It echoed off the marble, multiplying, filling the chamber until it was all I could hear.

Her arm cracked first. Just a hairline fracture, then another, then a web of them spreading up toward her shoulder like lightning frozen in bone. The bone didn't break cleanly. It shattered, fragmenting from the inside out as the magic ate through her, white light bleeding from the cracks.

"Stop!" Ancelin's voice. "Renata, stop! You're killing her!"

But I couldn't stop. The magic had its own momentum now, its own terrible hunger. It poured through Bahni, following the paths of her bones, cracking through her ribs with sounds like breaking branches, her spine, her skull. Each crack was a small explosion, bone dust puffing into the air.

"You tried to take him from me," I said, and my voice was eerily calm. Detached. "You tried to bind me. Lock me away. Keep me from what's mine."

"We were—trying—to help—" Bahni's voice fractured along with her jaw, the words coming out garbled, wet. Her blade-nails clattered to the floor one by one as her fingers disintegrated.

"I don't need help."

I released her wrist, and she collapsed. Not fell—collapsed. Like a building coming down, all structural integrity gone at once. Bone dust and shattered fragments scattered across the marble in a gray cloud that hung in the air, sparkling in the witch-light.

Silence.

I stood there, staring at what I'd done. At the pile of bone dust that had been a council member moments ago. At my hand, still glowing faintly with residual magic, white light fading from my fingertips. My palm felt hot, almost burned.

"I didn't—" My voice came out small. Shaking. "I didn't mean to—"

The crown's voices rushed in immediately.

She would have imprisoned you, Alaric declared. Taken you from him.

You were defending yourself, Oriana added. Any mother would do the same.

She wanted to hurt you, Lyanna whispered. She was jealous of what you have. What you're willing to do for love.

But underneath their reassurance, something sharp lodged in my chest. Cold and precise.

Fear.

I was afraid of myself. Of what I'd just done. Of how easy it had been.

The remaining council members stared. At Bahni's remains. At me. At the hand I was now holding against my chest like I could stop it from doing more damage.

Then Fatin stood. His massive form unfolded from his throne, bike armor creaking, shoulder spikes flaring outward. "You murdered her. You murdered a council member."

"I didn't—she attacked me first. I was just—" The words stumbled out, catching in my throat.

"You murdered her!" Fatin's voice boomed through the chamber, making the marble floor vibrate. "And now you'll—"

The crown pressed into me like a hand on the back of my head, and the grief and fumbling fell away all at once. What replaced it was clean and hot and absolute. I was looking at the man who had killed Nokoa. Who had reached into his chest and taken his heart. And he was standing in front of me, armor creaking, daring to lecture me about murder.

The bone mace was in my hand before I'd consciously decided to pick it up. It swung in a wide arc, and Fatin's skull exploded in a spray of bone shards and ancient magic. The impact sent vibrations up my arm, the sound like a melon splitting.

This time, I meant it.

His massive body toppled backward, throne cracking under the weight. Armor scattered across the floor, metal ringing against marble.

I stood there between two corpses—one accidental, one very much not—and felt something in my chest finally, completely break.

"I need obedience," I whispered. But I was shaking. My whole body was shaking, tremors running through my limbs. "I just need... I need..."

You need to survive, the crown finished. That's all. Survival. Protection. Love.

The remaining council members stared in absolute silence. Even Praxis looked surprised, his usual composure fractured.

Ancelin found his voice first. It came out hoarse, horrified. "You've murdered two council members. In cold blood. In our own chamber. You'll answer for—"

"For what?" I turned to him, and I could hear the desperation in my own voice. The need for someone, anyone, to understand. "For protecting myself? For refusing to be bound? What was I supposed to do, Ancelin? Let her take him from me?"

"He's already gone!" Ancelin's silver eyes blazed. "He's been gone for days! You're not protecting him, you're defiling his memory!"

The mace came up again, my arm lifting, but Maxin stood quickly, hands raised.

"Wait. Just wait. Everyone wait."

I held the mace ready, my arm trembling. The skull's empty sockets stared at me.

Maxin moved slowly down from his throne, approaching me like I was a wounded animal. Which, I suppose, I was. "Renata. Look at me."

I did. Saw the grief in his face. The regret. The recognition of what he'd helped create etched in every line.

"I helped make this crown," he said quietly. "Helped Priestess Alaira corrupt the witch runes. Helped bind the first hollow rulers. I've regretted that every single day since." He gestured at Bahni's remains. "I know what it does. How it feeds on you. How it takes and takes until there's nothing left."

"Then you should understand," I said, and my voice cracked. "You should understand why I can't let them stop me."

"I do understand." Maxin's face was impossibly sad. "That's why I'm not fighting you. That's why I'm yielding right now, publicly, so you know I'm not a threat." He turned to Ancelin. "We can't stop her. We can only try to guide her. Help her. Before she becomes something none of us recognize."

Ancelin looked like he wanted to argue. His skeletal hands gripped his armrests hard enough to crack them. But finally, he nodded once. Sharp. Defeated.

I looked at Praxis. He'd been silent through all of this, just watching.

Now he stood, his towering form unfolding slowly. "Well," he said. "That was certainly instructive."

Ancelin whirled on him. "You have nothing to say? She just murdered two council members!"

"I have plenty to say." Praxis moved toward me, and I tensed, but his posture was relaxed. "I'm wondering where you learned that particular application of witch runes. That combination of divine magic and bone magic—it's not in Alaira's journals. So either you're innovating, or the crown is teaching you things even I don't know."

I didn't answer. My throat was too tight.

Praxis continued, his tone almost conversational. "I've fed this crown for centuries. Every sacrifice, every hollow ruler—all my work. I convinced King Alaric to sacrifice his daughter Esmer for immortality. So when I see you making similar choices, I don't judge. I recognize a fellow survivor." He looked at me steadily. "And right now, surviving means being on your side."

"That's your justification?" Ancelin's voice was hollow with disgust. "Survival?"

"It's kept me alive this long." Praxis glanced at the others, then back at me. "The outer cities still wait at your gates. Thousands of soldiers demanding answers. What will you tell them?"

I looked at my seven spectral guards, still standing in perfect formation. At the bone mace in my hands, spattered with Fatin's remains. At Bahni's dust settling on marble, coating everything in a fine gray film.

"That I'm done negotiating," I said quietly. "That they can yield or burn."

Maxin stepped forward. "You can't fight an entire army. Even with necromancy. Even with corrupted magic. There are too many of them."

"Then I'll raise more dead." The words came out automatic, easy. Too easy. "I'll raise every corpse in these catacombs if I have to. I'll turn this entire court into—"

I stopped. Heard what I was saying. Heard the monster in my own voice.

"Two more days," I whispered. "Just two more days and everything will be fine."

No one answered. They just stared at me—horror, pity, and in Praxis's case, something that looked almost like hunger.

I turned and walked toward the exit, my spectral guards falling into step behind me. At the doorway, I paused and looked back.

"The funeral is tonight," I announced. "For Nokoa. The formal one, for the court. I expect all of you there." My eyes found Ancelin. "All of you. To show unity."

"Unity," Ancelin repeated flatly. "While two of our members lie dead by your hand."

"Yes," I said simply. "Unity."

I left before anyone could argue, my guards flowing behind me like shadows, their footsteps silent on marble.

Valdic waited outside the council chamber, examining his claws with apparent disinterest. But I saw his ears perk up at the sound of my footsteps, saw him take in the blood on my hands, the spectral guards, the bone mace dripping something dark onto the floor.

"Well," he said dryly. "I see diplomacy went splendidly."

"Bahni's dead. Fatin too."

"Tragic. I'll miss Bahni's winning personality." He fell into step beside me, then paused. "Wait. Bahni's dead? I thought you were only planning to kill Fatin."

"It was..." I swallowed hard, my throat tight. "An accident."

"An accident." Valdic's purple eyes studied me. "You accidentally murdered a council member?"

"She attacked me first. I defended myself. I just—I didn't mean for it to go that far. I couldn't stop it once it started." My voice cracked. "Valdic, I couldn't stop it."

He was quiet for a long moment, just the clicking of his claws on stone. Then: "And Fatin?"

"Wasn't an accident."

"Ah." He trotted ahead a few steps, then looked back at me. "So we're murdering council members on purpose now? That's the plan?"

"That's not—" I stopped walking. "I'm protecting myself. Protecting what's mine. They wanted to bind me. Lock me away. Stop the ritual."

"And that justifies killing them?"

"Yes!" The word came out too loud, echoing through the corridor, bouncing back to me. "Yes, it does. Because in two days, I bring Nokoa back. And nothing—nothing—is more important than that."

Valdic studied me with those knowing purple eyes. "You're scared."

"I'm not—"

"You are. I can smell it on you." His nose twitched. "Fear and bone dust and something else. You're terrified of what you just did. Of what you're becoming."

He moved closer. "But you're going to keep doing it anyway, aren't you? Keep killing, keep corrupting magic, keep sacrificing everything and everyone until there's nothing left but you and a corpse you've convinced yourself is sleeping."

"He IS sleeping!"

"Renata." Valdic's voice gentled. "His skin is starting to slip. His color is wrong. There's a smell coming off him that even my decayed nose can detect. The preservation spells are failing. He's decomposing. Slowly, yes, but he is. And no amount of denial changes that."

My hands tightened on the mace until my knuckles went white, until my fingers ached. "Two more days. The ritual will fix it. It will fix everything."

"Will it?" Valdic asked softly. "Or will you just drag his soul back into a rotting body and call it love?"

"Stop it." My voice shook. "Just stop."

"I'm trying to help you see reality before you do something truly irreversible. Before you become something he wouldn't recognize. Wouldn't want."

"He'll want me," I said desperately. "When he comes back, when he sees everything I did to save him, he'll understand. He'll—"

"He'll be horrified." Valdic's tone was gentle but unrelenting. "He'll see the murders, the corruption, the way you've twisted yourself into something monstrous. And he'll realize that you didn't save him—you damned him."

The mace was raised before I'd consciously decided to raise it. Valdic didn't flinch. Just looked at me with those purple eyes.

"Go ahead," he said quietly. "Add me to your list of murders today. It won't change the truth."

I held the weapon there, trembling, feeling the bone queen's skull hum with anticipation. One swing. That's all it would take. One swing and he'd stop saying these things, stop making me doubt, stop being right.

Do it, the crown whispered, Alaric's voice sharp and eager. He serves no purpose but to weaken you.

But he was Valdic. He'd followed me into exile. Stayed with me through everything. Never lied to me, even when the truth hurt.

Especially when the truth hurt.

I lowered the mace slowly. "I can't lose him."

"You already have."

"No." The word came out broken, barely more than a breath. "No, he's just sleeping. Just resting. The ritual will—"

"Will drag his soul back into a body that's been dead for days. Will bind him to you so tightly he can't escape even if he wants to. Will curse him to feel pain every time you're near him because of the bond." Valdic's voice was impossibly gentle now. "Is that love, Renata? Or is it the most selfish thing you've ever done?"

I wanted to argue. Wanted to explain that he didn't understand, that none of them understood. That sometimes love meant doing terrible things. That sometimes protecting someone meant damning yourself.

But the words wouldn't come.

Because somewhere deep down, in a place the crown hadn't quite reached yet, I was starting to wonder if he was right.

"Two more days," I whispered.

Valdic made a sound that might have been agreement or might have been resignation. "If you say so."

He trotted ahead, leaving me standing in the corridor with my spectral guards and my bone mace and my desperate, crumbling certainty.

Behind me, I could still see the faint glow of witch runes from the council chamber. Could still smell Bahni's bone dust on the air. Could still feel the ghost of that moment when I'd lost control, when I'd reached for something and found I couldn't pull back.

But necessary, the crown whispered. All of it necessary. For him.

I walked, and tried to believe it.

Chapter Six

The Weight of Winter

Renata

The negotiations with Nalla began at midday, when the sun should have been warm but wasn't.

I sat in the throne room with winter seeping through my bones, the cold settling deep in my marrow. The crown felt hot against my skull—feverish, pulsing with its own heartbeat—while the rest of me had gone cold. Numb. Like I was watching myself from somewhere far away, a puppet going through motions someone else controlled.

Nalla stood before me with three of her commanders, all of them travel-worn and angry. Dirt caked their boots, dust coated their armor. She'd always been beautiful in a sharp way—dark eyes, hair cropped close to her skull like a soldier's. Now she looked harder. Leaner. Hungry in a way that had nothing to do with food.

"Hollow Queen," she said, and the title sounded like an insult. Like she was spitting out something foul.

I gestured vaguely at the council members standing to my right. Ancelin, Maxin, and Praxis—the only ones left after this morning. They'd positioned themselves carefully, maintaining distance from each other. From me.

Smart.

"Ask your questions," I said. My voice came out flat, empty of inflection.

Nalla's jaw tightened, muscle jumping beneath skin. "The outer cities are starving. Crops that should have yielded harvest are withering in the fields. Livestock are dying—just collapsing in their stalls, blood coming from their eyes. Children—" Her voice cracked slightly. "Children are dying, Hollow Queen. And it started the moment you performed that ritual. The moment you brought him back."

"I haven't brought him back yet," I corrected. "The ritual isn't for two more days."

One of her commanders—a man with gray in his beard and scars across his knuckles like he'd beaten them bloody on stone—stepped forward. "Then what did you do? What magic did you use that's killing our land?"

Tell them nothing, Alaric warned. They're looking for weakness.

But Oriana's voice was softer: They're frightened. Desperate. Like you. Perhaps honesty would serve better than threats.

I looked at Nalla, really looked at her. Saw the exhaustion in her eyes, purple shadows beneath them deep as bruises. The way her hands trembled slightly before she clasped them behind her back. She wasn't here for conquest. She was here because people were dying and she didn't know how to stop it.

"I prepared for resurrection," I said finally. "I raised guards from the tomb. I forged weapons. I—" I stopped, unsure how much to admit. "I used witch runes. Combined them with bone magic in ways they weren't meant to be combined."

Maxin made a sound—half cough, half bitter laugh. "That's putting it mildly."

"And that's what's causing the famine?" Nalla demanded. "Your magic?"

"We don't know," Ancelin stated before I could answer. His silver eyes found mine, cold and accusing. "But the timing is suspicious. Crops began failing the day after she entered the tombs. The day after she started carving those corrupted runes."

"They're not corrupted," I protested automatically. "They're divine. A gift from the Goddess of Fate herself."

"A gift you've twisted," Maxin said quietly. "Perverted into something they were never meant to be." He looked at Nalla. "The witch runes were designed to protect life. To ease death when it came naturally. What she's doing—forcing resurrection, binding souls—it's inverting their purpose. Creating a magical paradox."

"I don't care about paradoxes," Nalla said, her voice rising. "I care about feeding my people. Can you fix it? Can you undo whatever you did?"

Don't you dare, Lyanna hissed. Don't let them take this from you. Not when you're so close.

"No," I said.

"No?" Nalla's voice rose higher, echoing off the vaulted ceiling. "You won't, or you can't?"

"Both." I met her gaze. "I won't undo the preparations. And even if I wanted to, I don't think I could. The magic has already... settled. Taken root. Two more days and the ritual completes. After that—"

"After that, what? Everything goes back to normal?" The gray-bearded commander laughed harshly. "Or does it get worse?"

I didn't answer, because I didn't know. The silence stretched between us like a chasm.

The quiet was broken only by wind rattling the windows, a lonely howl that made the glass shake in its frames. Outside, I could see the outer cities' army—thousands of soldiers, their campfires dotting the landscape like fallen stars.

"We came here with demands," Nalla announced finally. "Terms for peace."

"It's not the first time you've come with demands. Last time I met them all without hesitation. This time I won't promise the same."

"End the Bone Council's authority. They've bled us dry for centuries with their tithes—bone marrow, heartfire, everything we have to give while they sit comfortable in their immortal bones." She gestured at Ancelin and Praxis. "Dismantle the system. Return power to the people."

Ancelin's joints ground as he shifted. "That's not—"

"I wasn't speaking to you," Nalla cut him off. She kept her eyes on me. "Second: destroy the crown. Whatever it's doing to you, whatever it's making you become—end it. Before it's too late. The terms before were too light. We see that now."

Destroy me? The crown's voices rose in unison. After everything we've given you? Everything we've taught you?

"No," I said.

"Then there's nothing to negotiate." Nalla's hand went to her sword, fingers wrapping around the leather-wound hilt. "We'll take what we need by force."

"You'll try," I corrected. "You'll fail. I have spectral guards now. Seven former hollow rulers who can't die because they're already dead. I have weapons forged from royal bones. I have magic you don't understand."

"And we have numbers," the gray-bearded commander said. "Thousands of soldiers who are willing to die if it means their children might eat."

"Then they'll die," I said simply. "And their children will starve anyway. You're bargaining with someone who has nothing left to lose."

Nalla stared at me like I was a stranger. "What happened to you? The woman who negotiated with us before—who listened, who cared about something beyond her own grief—where did she go?"

"She learned," I said, "that caring gets you nothing. That mercy is weakness. That the only thing that matters is protecting what's yours."

"Even if protecting it destroys everything else?"

"Yes."

Maxin cleared his throat. "Hollow Queen, perhaps we could—"

"Dismiss them," I interrupted. "We're done negotiating."

"Renata—" Maxin started.

"I said we're done." The crown pulsed hot, searing where metal touched skin, and power crackled along my arms. The witch runes I'd carved into the walls flared white. "Tell your army to withdraw, Nalla. Tell them to go home and pray the harvest comes next season. Tell them whatever you want. But if they attack these walls, I'll raise every corpse in the catacombs to fight them."

"You're bluffing."

"Am I?" I smiled, and it felt wrong on my face, muscles moving in ways they shouldn't. "Ask Bahni and Fatin if I'm bluffing. Oh wait—you can't. Because I killed them this morning. If so much as one finger touches my gates, I'll burn you all."

The shock on Nalla's face was almost satisfying. Almost enough to push back the numbness.

"You..." She struggled for words, mouth opening and closing. "You murdered council members?"

"I defended myself," I corrected. "And I'll defend myself against your army too, if necessary."

Nalla's hand tightened on her sword hilt until her knuckles went white, but she didn't draw. Couldn't draw, not here, not surrounded by my guards and my magic and my desperate, terrible certainty.

"This isn't over," she warned.

"It is for today." I stood, feeling the crown's weight, feeling how it had changed me. How it was still changing me, reshaping me from the inside out. "You have until dawn to withdraw your army. After that, I consider them an act of war."

I left before she could respond, my spectral guards flowing after me like shadows. Behind me, I heard Ancelin trying to smooth things over, heard Maxin's quiet apologies. Praxis said nothing at all, and somehow that silence followed me down the corridor longer than any of the words.

The Bone Council reconvened in their chamber an hour later, minus two members and plus considerably more tension.

I stood in the center where I'd killed Bahni, where bone dust still stained the marble. No one had cleaned it up. Maybe they were leaving it as a reminder. Or maybe they were too afraid to touch it, afraid of what residual magic might linger in those gray remains.

"The outer cities won't withdraw," Ancelin declared without preamble. "Nalla's commanders are arguing for an immediate assault."

"Let them assault." I studied the bone dust, watching how it caught the light, sparkled faintly like powdered diamond. "My guards will handle them."

"Seven spectral guards against thousands of soldiers?" Maxin shook his head. "Renata, please. Be reasonable."

"I'm being perfectly reasonable. I have priorities. Defending walls isn't one of them."

"Then what is?" Ancelin's silver eyes blazed. "Because from where I'm standing, your only priority is a corpse in the catacombs."

The bone mace was in my hand before I'd consciously reached for it. "Careful."

"Or what? You'll kill me too?" Ancelin stood, his serpentine dreadlocks writhing. "Go ahead. Add me to the pile. See how well you rule with no council left at all."

He's trying to provoke you, Alaric warned. Stay calm. Don't give him the satisfaction.

But staying calm felt impossible. Everything felt impossible except the ritual, except bringing Nokoa back, except—

"The famine," Praxis interjected, his voice cutting through the spiral. "We should discuss the famine."

I lowered the mace slowly, my arm trembling. "What about it?"

"It's worse than we told the outer cities." Praxis gestured at Maxin. "Tell her."

Maxin pulled out a leather-bound journal, his hands shaking slightly as he opened it. "Tithe collections are failing. Not just because the outer cities are refusing—though they are—but because there's nothing to collect. Bone marrow stores are depleting faster than they can be replenished. Heartfire is flickering out. The magical infrastructure we've maintained for centuries is... collapsing."

"That's not my problem."

"It will be," Ancelin said coldly, "when the council members start dying. We're immortal, yes, but only as long as we're fed. Bahni and Fatin's deaths didn't just remove council members—they removed connections, power sources. The whole system is destabilizing."

I should have cared. Some part of me knew I should have cared. But that part felt very far away, buried under crown-whispers and desperate need.

"How long?" I asked. "How long until the council starts dying?"

Maxin consulted his journal, finger tracing down columns of numbers. "Three weeks, maybe four. For the outer cities?" He looked up, and there was genuine grief in his eyes. "Days. Maybe a week for those with stores. Children and elderly first. Then the weak. Then everyone."

"Fix it," I said.

"We can't fix it!" Ancelin slammed his hand on his throne. "You broke something fundamental when you started mixing witch magic with bone magic. You created a paradox—divine protection twisted into divine curse. Life magic inverted into death magic. It's spreading like rot through the whole system."

"Then stop it from spreading."

"We don't know how!" Maxin's voice cracked.

Good, Lyanna purred. Let them suffer.

"The ritual is in two days," I said. "After that, I'll help you fix the famine."

"If there's anything left to fix," Ancelin muttered.

"There will be." I had to believe that. Had to believe the world would wait two more days for me to save the one person who mattered. "Now if we're done—"

"We're not done," Maxin interrupted. "There's something else. Something you need to see."

He pulled out a smaller journal—older, the leather cracked and faded, edges worn soft with age. "I found this in the archives. From the first years after the crown was created."

"And?"

"And it describes what happens when witch runes are corrupted." Maxin flipped pages, his finger tracing lines of cramped text. "Priestess Alaira documented everything. The side effects. The prices. The consequences."

"I know about the prices," I said. "Memory loss. The crown feeds on what I forget."

"That's not the only price." Maxin looked up, his expression grave. "The runes were a gift from the Goddess of Fate. Divine magic meant to protect her creation. When you corrupt them—when you twist them into something they're not—you're essentially telling the Goddess her gift wasn't good enough. That you know better than divinity."

"So?"

"So there are consequences." Maxin's voice dropped. "Alaira theorized that widespread corruption of the runes would attract attention. Divine attention."

Something cold moved through my chest and kept moving, spreading outward. "What kind of attention?"

"She didn't know. Couldn't know, because no one had ever corrupted witch runes on this scale before." Maxin closed the journal. "You're in uncharted territory, Renata. And the map you're following was drawn by someone who created the most destructive artifact our world has ever known."

"Are you trying to scare me?"

"I'm trying to warn you." Maxin's expression was sad. "The crown is using you. The bone god is manipulating you. And you're so focused on resurrecting one person that you can't see you're damning everyone else."

"I see fine," I said coldly. "I see that you're all cowards. That you'd rather let him stay dead than risk anything to bring him back."

"What's the point in bringing him back if the world is ending?"

"Dismissed." I turned toward the exit. "All of you. I have other matters to attend to."

"Renata—" Ancelin tried.

"I said dismissed."

The crown pulsed, and power flooded the chamber. Not violent—just present. A reminder of what I could do if they pushed. The air grew thick with it, pressing against their skin. They left without further argument, filing out in silence.

Praxis was last. He paused at the doorway and looked back at me over his shoulder, those crimson eyes moving slowly around the chamber—at the bone dust, at the mace, at me—before he walked out. He didn't say anything. He didn't need to.

Don't listen to them, Oriana soothed. They're trying to manipulate you. To make you abandon him.

You're doing the right thing, Lyanna added. The only thing that matters.

Two more days, Alaric confirmed. Then everything will be worth it.

I wanted to believe them. Needed to believe them.

Because if they were wrong—if this was all for nothing—

I couldn't think about that.

I went back to the catacombs. My feet carried me there the way they always did now, like the passage had worn a groove in me, like that downward pull was just part of how I moved through the world.

To the chamber where Nokoa lay.

I moved to the ice bed and looked down at his body.

Really looked at it.

His skin had a waxy quality now, like candle tallow left too long in the sun. The blue-gray tinge had spread from his lips to his fingertips, his nail beds turning dark. His face looked sunken. Like something essential had already left, leaving just the shell behind. His cheeks were hollow, eye sockets deeper than they should be.

The smell hit me then—faint but unmistakable. Sweet rot mixing with the metallic tang of preservation spells failing.

What if love meant letting go?

No, the crown said firmly. Love means holding on. Fighting. Refusing to accept loss.

Yes. That's what love was. That's what it had to be.

I pulled a cloth from my pocket and began cleaning him again. Gentle strokes across his forehead, his cheeks, his neck. Washing away the waxy buildup that came from lying still too long. Pretending the skin wasn't slipping slightly under my touch. Pretending everything was fine.

"I brought you food," I said softly, gesturing to the plate I'd set down earlier. The bread had gone stale, the cheese hardened and cracked. "You should eat when you wake up. Keep your strength."

The silence that answered me was complete.

I kissed his forehead. His cheek. His lips, tasting that metallic tang that had gotten stronger, mixing with something sweet and rotten that made my stomach turn. His lips were cold, unresponsive.

When I pulled back, I thought I saw his eyelids flutter. Just barely.

"There you are," I whispered. "I knew you were listening. Just two more days, love. Hold on for two more days."

Two more days, the crown echoed.

I settled beside him on the ice bed, my hand finding his cold fingers, my head resting on his silent chest. The ice seeped through my dress, making me shiver, raising gooseflesh along my arms and legs. But I didn't move.

Couldn't move.

This was where I belonged. Beside him. Waiting for him to wake.

Even if he never would.

Even if I was lying to myself about everything.

Even if—

Stop, Oriana commanded. Doubt serves no purpose. Focus on the ritual. On what comes next.

Yes. What came next.

I stood reluctantly, my joints protesting from the cold. I moved to the back wall, to the hidden door. The passage that led somewhere deeper, somewhere that felt dangerous in ways the tomb didn't. I'd been circling it since yesterday, not quite ready.

Go, Alaric urged. There's more to learn.

I pressed my hand against the wall and it shifted under my touch, stone sliding away to reveal darkness and cold air. The bone god's crypt.

My spectral guards tried to follow, but something stopped them at the threshold—some ward they couldn't cross, their forms flickering as they pressed against invisible walls. I left them there and went alone.

The passage was narrow, carved from living rock, and it descended sharply. No witch runes here to light the way—just darkness and the faint phosphorescent glow of something ahead. My footsteps echoed, multiplying in the confined space.

The passage opened into a chamber that made my breath catch.

It was vast—much larger than the ritual chamber, larger than the throne room. The ceiling disappeared into darkness overhead, and the walls were covered floor to ceiling in bones that hadn't been arranged so much as grown, pushing through the stone in formations like coral, like something that had been reaching toward light for centuries and never found it. They pulsed faintly with their own cold luminescence.

And there, in the very center, a stone sarcophagus. Sealed. Covered in witch runes that glowed with the same harsh white light as mine, but layered over each other in patterns that made my vision swim when I tried to follow them. They shifted when I looked directly at them, resisting being seen.

A prison.

The bone god's prison, Oriana confirmed. Where Priestess Alaira sealed him away.

"Why?" I whispered, my voice echoing back from all directions. "Why did she seal him?"

Because she was afraid, Lyanna said. Afraid of what he represented. What he could do.

Or, Alaric added, because he told her truths she didn't want to hear.

Around the sarcophagus, scattered like offerings, were journals. Hundreds of them, leather-bound and ancient, some crumbling at the edges. Priestess Alaira's research. Her confessions. Her warnings.

I picked one up at random and opened it, the binding cracking.

The Goddess of Fate gave us runes, the spidery handwriting read. Asked us to protect the world She loved so much. To ease suffering. To guide death gently when it came. I took Her gift and made it into chains. Into a crown that feeds on what it was meant to protect. Forgive us. Forgive me.

Another journal, older, the ink faded to brown: The bone god whispered to me today. Said the Goddess abandoned us. Said Her gift was a test we failed. Said he could show me how to use the runes properly—not for protection, but for transformation. For transcendence. I told him no. But his words linger. What if he was right? What if we were meant to become something more?

Another, more recent: The crown is finished. The first hollow ruler—Oriana—will wear it tomorrow. May the Goddess forgive what we've done.

The entry stopped there. Nothing after it.

I flipped through more journals, my hands shaking. Found diagrams of witch runes, theories on resurrection, warnings about combining divine magic with bone magic. Each page more desperate than the last.

And there, near the back of one journal, a section on soul-bonded pairs.

Two souls bound so tightly that death cannot separate them, Alaira had written in handwriting that grew more erratic with each line. The anchor and the tethered. One becomes a stabilizing force, grounding the other in reality. But the price—gods, the price. Every emotion becomes pain. Every thought bleeds across the bond. They can never be apart without agony, never be together without hurting each other. It's beautiful. It's horrific. It's the most selfish act of love I can imagine. I failed. They weren't the right couple.

My hands tightened on the journal, fingers leaving prints in the dust on the cover.

That's what I was planning. That's what the ritual would do.

Bind Nokoa to me so tightly that we'd hurt each other just by existing. Just by being near each other. Every time I thought of him—pain. Every time he felt any emotion—pain for both of us.

Was that love? Or was it exactly what Valdic had said—the most selfish thing I'd ever done?

It's survival, the crown whispered. It's refusing to accept loss. It's love.

But was it?

I set the journal down. My chest felt heavy, the air pressing in from all sides. The sarcophagus pulsed in the corner of my vision, its runes shifting and sliding, patient.

Two more days.

Just two more days and I'd find out if I was saving him or damning us both.

Chapter Seven

Unseen Scars

Renata

I woke on the ice bed beside Nokoa, my body aching from the cold.

For a moment, I couldn't remember where I was. The catacombs? The crypt? My chambers? Everything blurred together—stone and darkness and the constant whisper of the crown telling me what to do next, who to trust, what mattered. The voices overlapped, harmonizing into a single command that felt like my own thoughts.

Only Nokoa mattered.

I sat up slowly, every joint protesting with sharp pains that shot through my spine. How long had I been down here? Hours? Days? The ventilation shaft showed darkness outside, but whether it was the same night or a different one, I couldn't say. Time had become liquid, flowing around me without shape or meaning.

My dress clung to me, damp with condensation from the ice bed. The fabric was stiff in places, frozen where it had pressed against the ice. I was shivering, I realized distantly. Had been shivering for a while now. My teeth chattered when I tried to speak, clicking together like dice.

"I should go," I told Nokoa, my breath misting in the cold. "Get warm. Eat something. Come back when—"

But I didn't move. Couldn't move. The thought of leaving him alone down here, even for an hour, made my chest constrict with panic. We were so close. And there were so many in the Bone Court who wanted to take him from me.

What if something happens while I'm gone?

What if he wakes and I'm not here?

What if they take him from me?

"No," I whispered. "I'll stay. Just a little longer."

I lay back down beside him, my head on his silent chest, and tried to remember what warmth felt like. The memory slipped away before I could grasp it.

When I finally forced myself to leave the catacombs, it was because Valdic found me and physically blocked the passage.

"You need to eat," he stated flatly. "You look like a corpse yourself."

"I'm fine."

"You're not fine. You're gray. You're shaking. When's the last time you had water?" His purple eyes were hard, unblinking.

I tried to remember and couldn't. "Yesterday?"

"Try three days ago." Valdic's voice was sharp. "You're killing yourself down here. And for what? He's not getting any more alive."

The mace was in my hand before I'd thought about it, fingers wrapped tight around the bone handle. But Valdic didn't flinch.

"Go ahead," he said tiredly. "Add me to the list. But you still need to eat, and hitting me won't change that."

I lowered the weapon slowly, my arm trembling. "I don't have time. The ritual is tomorrow night. I need to prepare—"

"You need to not die before you can perform it." Valdic moved aside, gesturing up the passage with his muzzle. "Food. Water. Sleep in an actual bed. Then you can go back to your corpse-vigil."

He's trying to separate you from Nokoa, Lyanna warned.

But my legs were trembling, threatening to give out beneath me, and my vision had started to gray at the edges. And somewhere underneath the crown's certainty, I knew Valdic was right.

I couldn't perform the ritual if I collapsed first.

"Fine," I said. "But only for an hour."

"We'll see."

The walk back to my chambers felt longer than it should have. The corridors stretched and warped, walls seeming to breathe. Twice I had to stop and lean against cold stone, waiting for dizziness to pass.

Valdic stayed close, his skeletal frame bumping against my leg when I wavered, his fur coarse and smelling of decay.

"How long has it been?" I asked. "Since I last came up?"

"Two days. You went down after the council meeting and didn't come back."

Two days. That couldn't be right. It felt like hours.

But my body told a different story. My muscles shook with every step. My skin felt papery, thin enough to tear. My hair—I touched it and found it tangled, matted with gods knew what from the catacombs. Something sticky coated the strands.

When had I last bathed?

When had I last changed clothes?

When had I last been human?

You're beyond human now, Alaric said. You're becoming something greater.

The thought should have been comforting. Instead, it just made me feel cold. Hollow.

My chambers were exactly as I'd left them—which is to say, a disaster. Clothes scattered across the floor, trampled and dirty. Books left open, spines cracked. A tray of food gone moldy on the side table.

How long since I'd slept here?

A week? More?

Cressa was waiting inside, and the look on her face when she saw me made something in my chest twist. Her expression cycled through shock, horror, grief—emotions I could name but no longer quite feel.

"Gods," she breathed. "Renata, you look—"

"I'm fine."

"You're not fine. You're—" She moved closer, her eyes cataloging the damage. Lingering on my face, my hands, the way my dress hung on a frame that had lost too much weight. "You've lost weight. You're pale. Your eyes are..." She stopped, her throat working. "When's the last time you ate?"

"I don't remember." The admission came out small. Childlike.

Cressa's jaw tightened, but she didn't lecture. Just moved to the fireplace and began building a fire with quick, efficient movements. Wood scraping. Kindling crackling. "Sit down. I'll get you food."

"I can't stay long. I need to get back to—"

"Sit. Down." Cressa's voice was sharp enough that I obeyed without thinking, my body responding to command when my mind wouldn't.

The chair felt strange under me. Too soft. Too comfortable. Wrong, somehow, after days on ice and stone. The cushion gave beneath my weight, and I sank into it like I was drowning.

Valdic settled at my feet, his purple eyes watching Cressa work.

"You told her," I said to him.

"Of course I told her. Someone needs to keep you from killing yourself through neglect." He paused. "Though at this rate, the crown will do it for you."

Cressa returned with bread, cheese, dried meat. Simple food, but my stomach turned at the sight of it. The smell hit me—yeast and salt and something that should have been appetizing but made nausea rise in my throat instead.

"I'm not hungry."

"Eat anyway." Cressa pushed the plate closer. "Even if you have to force it down. Your body needs fuel, especially if you're planning to perform complex magic tomorrow."

I picked up the bread. Before I could take a bite, green began spreading across the crust under my fingers, blooming outward from where I held it—the same way it had spread across the tray in the catacombs, the same way everything I touched seemed to turn. I stared at it for a moment, then took a bite anyway. It tasted like ash in my mouth, dry and bitter, but I chewed and swallowed.

Cressa watched me eat with an expression I couldn't quite read. Concern, yes. But something else underneath it. Something that looked like grief. Like she was watching someone die.

"What?" I asked around a mouthful of cheese.

"Nothing." She turned away, busying herself with the fire, poking at the logs until sparks flew up the chimney. "Just... you're different. Every time I see you, you're more different."

"The crown teaches me. I'm learning—"

"You're forgetting," Cressa interrupted, her voice tight. "That's not the same thing."

I frowned. "Forgetting what?"

"Everything." Cressa's voice cracked slightly. "Do you even remember my name?"

"Of course I remember your—" I stopped. Searched my mind. Found nothing. Just a vague impression of someone important, someone who'd mattered once. A face already blurring at the edges. "You're my... friend. A healer. You've been with me since..."

Since when?

"Since we were children," Cressa said quietly, her back still to me. "We learned to read together. To ride. You were the first person I told when I wanted to marry your brother." Her green eyes—when had I forgotten they were green?—glistened with unshed tears when she turned. "We were going to be sisters."

Sisters. The word felt familiar but distant, like something from a dream I could no longer quite recall.

"I remember," I lied.

"You don't." Cressa's voice was flat now. Empty. "You don't remember any of it. The crown took it. Took me. And you don't even care."

"That's not true. I care, I just—" But the words felt hollow even as I said them, echoing in the empty space where emotion should have been. Did I care? About this woman whose name I couldn't remember, whose face was starting to blur?

She's irrelevant, Lyanna whispered. Only Nokoa matters.

"I need to get back," I announced, standing. The room tilted, floor rushing up, and I grabbed the chair for support.

"You need to rest," Cressa countered, moving toward me. "Renata, please. Just a few hours. Let me draw you a bath. Get you into clean clothes. You can't perform resurrection magic like this."

"I'm fine."

"You're falling apart!" Cressa's voice rose, bouncing off the walls. "Look at yourself! You can barely stand! You've forgotten everyone who ever cared about you! You're—"

"Doing what needs to be done," I finished. "And if you can't understand that, then maybe you should leave."

The words came out colder than I'd intended. Cressa flinched like I'd struck her, hand coming up to her chest.

"If I leave," she said quietly, each word careful and measured, "I'm not coming back. This is your last chance, Renata. Stay here. Let me help you. Let someone help you before you become something none of us recognize."

She's trying to manipulate you, Alaric declared. To make you choose between her and Nokoa.

"Then don't come back." I moved toward the door, my legs unsteady but determined. "I don't need your help. I don't need anyone's help. I just need one more day."

"One more day," Cressa repeated, her voice hollow. "And then what? You bring him back and everything's fine? You think he's going to thank you for what you've become?"

I didn't answer. Couldn't answer.

Because somewhere deep down, I was starting to wonder the same thing.

I left before Cressa could say anything else, Valdic trailing behind me in silence. His claws clicked against stone, the only sound in the empty corridor.

I found Maxin in the archives, surrounded by books and looking older than he had that morning. More skeletal. His skin had taken on a gray cast, waxy and stretched too tight over bone. His hands trembled as he turned pages.

"You're changing," I observed from the doorway.

He looked up, unsurprised by my presence. "So are you."

"The crown is teaching me. You're just... dying."

"Same thing, in the end." Maxin closed his book with a soft thump. "The corruption you're spreading—it's not just affecting crops and cattle. It's affecting the council too. We maintained immortality through careful balance.

You've upset that balance. Now we're all slowly reverting to what we should have become centuries ago."

"Good," I said, though I didn't quite mean it. The word tasted wrong. "Maybe you deserve it."

"Maybe we do." Maxin stood, his joints creaking like old wood. "But you don't. Not yet, anyway. That's why I wanted to see you. To try one last time to teach you properly. To show you how to use witch runes without destroying yourself—and everyone else—in the process."

I should have refused. Should have turned and walked away. But something in his expression stopped me. Not pity. The recognition of someone who'd made similar mistakes and spent centuries regretting them.

"Fine," I relented. "Teach me."

We worked through the afternoon—or what felt like afternoon, though time had become increasingly meaningless. The light from the high windows never seemed to change. Maxin showed me runes I'd seen in Alaira's journals, explained their proper applications, their intended purposes. His voice was patient, gentle, like teaching a child.

"This one is for easing pain," he said, tracing a symbol in the air. White light followed his finger, soft and warm. "Not removing it—the Goddess understood that pain has purpose. But making it bearable. Gentle."

I copied the rune, and it came out wrong. Not wrong, exactly. Inverted. Where his glowed soft white, mine pulsed harsh and bright, hurting to look at.

"You're corrupting it," Maxin said quietly. "Even when you try not to, the crown twists what you do."

"Maybe that's better." I studied my inverted rune, watching it pulse like a heartbeat. "Maybe the Goddess's gift wasn't strong enough."

"Or maybe we weren't worthy of it." Maxin drew another rune, movements slow and deliberate. "This one is for binding wounds. For encouraging flesh to knit back together properly. It's meant to work with the body's natural healing, not against it."

I copied it. Again, it came out inverted. This time, the rune pulsed with an energy that felt predatory. Hungry. Like something alive.

"That's not healing," Maxin said, and there was horror in his voice. "That's... some kind of forced regeneration. It would work, yes, but the pain—"

"Pain doesn't matter if it works."

"Pain always matters." Maxin's voice cut sharp. "The Goddess gave us these runes to reduce suffering, not increase it. Every time you invert them, you're spitting on Her gift."

"Then She should have made them stronger," I said coldly. "Strong enough to bring back the dead."

"They were never meant to bring back the dead!" Maxin slammed his hand on the table, books jumping. "That's the whole point! Death is natural. Death is necessary. The runes were meant to ease death, not prevent it!"

"Well, I'm preventing it anyway." I drew another rune, watching it invert under my touch, white light bleeding to harsh brightness. "With or without your help."

Maxin was silent for a long moment. When he spoke again, his voice had gone soft. Defeated.

"You're learning too fast," he observed. "Runes that should take years to master, you're corrupting in minutes. The crown is feeding you knowledge, yes. But it's also feeding on you." He gestured at me. "Can you even see what you're becoming?"

"I'm becoming powerful enough to save him."

"You're becoming something he won't recognize." Maxin's expression was worn through with regret, eyes ancient and tired. "Renata, please. Stop. Just for a moment. Look at yourself. Really look."

I glanced down. Saw my hands—thin, almost skeletal, skin stretched tight over bones that pressed too close to the surface. Saw my dress hanging loose. Saw the black veins that had started creeping up from my wrists, spreading like roots under my skin, branching and dividing.

When had that happened?

"Those are from the crown," Maxin said quietly. "Corruption made visible. Every time you use witch runes, every time you feed the crown with memory, those veins spread. Eventually they'll cover you completely. And then—" He stopped.

"And then what?"

"And then you'll be like the rest of us. Hollow. More bone than flesh. More magic than human." He met my eyes. "Is that what you want? Is that what he would want?"

"He doesn't get a choice," I said. "He's dead. I'm fixing that."

"By becoming a monster?"

"If that's what it takes."

Maxin studied me for a long moment, then nodded slowly. "Then I can't help you. I won't help you corrupt the Goddess's gift any further."

"I wasn't asking for help. Besides, when he's back I'll be strong enough to fix everything else." I turned to leave, but his voice stopped me.

"There's something you should know," he said. "About the ritual you're planning. About what happens when you bind two souls that tightly."

I looked back. "What about it?"

"It doesn't create connection," Maxin warned. "It creates shared suffering. Every emotion you feel, he'll feel as physical pain. Every thought you have will bleed across—not as communication, but as agony. You won't be giving him life—you'll be giving him a prison." He paused. "Read Alaira's journals. The ones you've been copying. She documented everything. Including what happened to the souls she tried soul-fusion on before. How they begged for death. How they—"

"Enough." I couldn't hear this. My hands pressed against my ears, but his words still found their way in. "One more day. Then you'll see I was right."

"I hope so," Maxin said, his voice thick with sorrow. "I truly do. Because if you're wrong—if this doesn't work the way you think—you'll have damned him to something worse than death."

I left before he could say anything else, his words chasing me down the corridor.

The descent back to the catacombs came easy now, familiar as breathing. My spectral guards fell into step behind me, their synchronized movements no longer unsettling. Just normal. Just part of my new reality.

Valdic had disappeared somewhere—probably to avoid watching me descend again into madness. Smart of him.

I was alone with my thoughts for the first time in days.

And my thoughts kept slipping. Memory to memory, none of them solid enough to hold. Cressa's face already fading. The conversation in my chambers—had that been today? The details ran together like wet ink. I reached for things and found outlines where substance used to be.

No, the crown soothed. It doesn't matter. Only the ritual.

I descended past the ritual chamber where Nokoa lay. Past the hidden door to the bone god's crypt.

Down, down, down to a place I didn't remember discovering but somehow knew existed.

A chamber even deeper than the crypt. Older. The air here was different—not just cold but wrong, pressing against my skin like it was trying to get in. My teeth ached with it. The walls weren't stone. They were bone. Not carved—they had grown through the rock, ribs and femurs and smaller things I couldn't identify pushing through the dark stone like roots through soil, and they pulsed faintly with their own slow rhythm.

This was where it had started, I realized. The corruption. The inversion. This chamber was the source of everything wrong with the crown, with the runes, with me.

And in the center, a mirror.

Not like the ones in the bone god's crypt. This one was massive, taller than me, wider than I could stretch my arms. Its frame was made of bone and sinew, still wet, still living somehow. The surface rippled like disturbed water.

And its surface showed me.

But not as I was. As I was becoming.

The reflection stared back with eyes gone completely black, pupils blown so wide they'd consumed the iris entirely. Black veins covered every visible inch of skin. My white hair had taken on a gray cast, and something moved within it—not hair exactly, but something that shifted and pulsed at its own rhythm. The crown sat heavy on my head, but in the reflection, I could see what it truly was. Not bone anymore. Not wholly. It had started to merge with my skull, roots spreading beneath skin, becoming part of me.

Becoming me.

"No," I whispered.

But the reflection smiled, and its teeth were too sharp. Too many. Rows of them where there should only be one.

This is what you're becoming, it said in a voice that was mine but distorted. This is the price of resurrection.

"I don't care." But my voice shook. "I don't care what I become as long as he comes back."

Does he get a choice? the reflection asked, leaning closer to the glass. Or are you deciding for him? Choosing his suffering because you can't accept yours?

"Stop it."

You've forgotten her name. The reflection's voice was quiet now, without cruelty. Cressa. The woman who was supposed to be your sister. You've forgotten your brother's face. Your mother's voice. Every memory the crown takes, you lose a piece of what makes you, you.

"I don't need to be human. I just need to be strong enough."

Strong enough for what? To drag his soul back? To bind him to a body that's been dead for days? He's going to look at what you've become and realize you didn't save him. You damned him.

"You're lying." Tears were running down my face now, hot and bitter, tracking through dust and grime. "You're lying, you're—"

I'm you, the reflection said, and its voice gentled. The part of you that knows this is wrong. The part you're trying so hard to silence. The part that remembers what love actually is—letting go when holding on would hurt more.

I pressed my hands over my ears, but the voice came from inside my skull.

One more day, it whispered. One more day and you can't undo this. Can't take it back. Can't stop being the monster you've become.

"I don't want to let him go," I sobbed, the words breaking. "I can't. I can't do this without him."

You already are, the reflection said. You've been doing it for days now. You're just too afraid to admit it.

I stood there, shaking, staring at what I was becoming. At the black veins and the too-sharp teeth and the crown growing into my skull.

And I made my choice.

"One more day," I whispered. "Then everything will be worth it."

The reflection's expression was sad in a way that had no bottom to it. Its tears mirrored mine.

If you say so, it said.

And disappeared, leaving just my normal reflection. Pale. Thin. Exhausted.

Still human.

For now.

I turned and climbed back up toward Nokoa. Toward the only thing that still made sense.

One more day.

Chapter Eight

The Resurrection

Renata

Night came like a held breath.

I stood in the ritual chamber, watching the last light fade from the ventilation shaft overhead, watching shadows deepen and spread like spilled ink until only the witch runes provided illumination. White light pulsed from every carved surface, casting everything in harsh relief that made my eyes ache.

Tonight. The half-moon hung somewhere above, invisible but present. I could feel it pulling at something deep in my chest, could feel the crown responding with heat that bordered on pain, searing where metal met skin.

Tonight, everything changed.

Nokoa lay on the ice bed where I'd kept him for days. His preservation had held—barely. The spells were failing, yes, but slowly enough. He'd lasted long enough.

Long enough for me to bring him back.

I'd cleaned him one final time, washing away the waxy buildup, the smell that had started to seep through despite my denials. Sweet rot and something chemical from the preservation spells fighting decay. I'd dressed him in simple clothes—nothing elaborate, nothing that would constrain. He'd need freedom of movement when he woke.

When, not if.

Never if.

"Ready?" Priestess Alaira's voice came from the entrance, and I turned to see her emerging from shadows like something conjured. Her white robes seemed to glow in the witch-light.

She looked different than last time. Younger, somehow, but in a wrong way. Her patchy hair had grown in thicker, but the new growth was white as bone. Her skin had taken on a waxy quality that reminded me uncomfortably of Nokoa's deteriorating flesh. And her eyes blazed with something that had moved past fanaticism into territory I didn't have words for.

"I'm ready," I said, my voice steadier than I felt.

"Are you?" Alaira moved into the chamber, her white robes trailing through bone dust and dried blood, leaving dark streaks. "This isn't resurrection as you understand it, child. This is transformation. Both of you will change. Neither of you will be quite what you were."

"I don't care."

"You should." But she was already pulling items from her robes. Bone implements that clicked together. Vials of liquid that glowed faintly green, casting strange shadows. And there—a box. Small, carved from bone, covered in witch runes so complex they seemed to shift and crawl across the surface when I tried to focus on them.

The same box I'd seen her guarding before. The one she'd warned me not to touch.

"What's in the box?" I asked.

"Insurance." Alaira set it down carefully, reverently. "The bone god's seal. The anchor that keeps his prison stable." She looked up, and something in her expression made my skin crawl. "Every great working needs an anchor. This resurrection will need one too."

"I don't understand."

"You don't need to." Alaira began arranging items in a circle around the ice bed, placing each with precision. "You just need to trust me. Trust the process. Trust that the Goddess of Fate is watching, even if She doesn't answer."

That last part came out bitter, acidic. I remembered what Praxis had told me. How Alaira had created the crown hoping to get the Goddess's attention. How she'd been waiting centuries for acknowledgment that never came.

"Will She answer tonight?" I asked.

"Perhaps." Alaira's hands trembled as she worked. "If the bone god rises—if his prison weakens enough—perhaps that will finally make Her look at what we've done. What we've become." She laughed, and it sounded on the edge of breaking, high and brittle. "Or perhaps I'm just a fanatic who corrupted Her gift for nothing. We'll see."

She pulled out a dagger—not bone, but something darker. Blacker than obsidian, drinking in light rather than reflecting it. The blade hummed with its own frequency, a low vibration I could feel in my jaw, and looking at it made my eyes water.

"This was forged from the bone god's first sacrifice," Alaira explained. "Before he was sealed. Before we understood what he truly was." She pressed it into my hand, and the handle felt wrong. Too warm. Too alive. Like holding something with a pulse. "You'll need it for the severing."

I looked at the blade, then at my hands. Both of them. Ten fingers where there should be ten.

After tonight, I'd have eight.

"You remember the steps?" Alaira asked.

I nodded, my throat tight. I'd memorized them from her journals, had practiced the movements until they were muscle memory. "Carve our names into bone using witch runes. Exchange pieces of ourselves—pinkies, ground to powder. Mix with blood and catalyst. Speak the binding at the moment of the half-moon."

"And the price," Alaira prompted. "You remember the price?"

"Memory," I said. "The crown feeds on what I forget."

"Not just memory." Alaira's voice dropped. "Connection. Every tie that binds you to anyone but him—the crown will take it. Mother, father, friends, everyone who ever mattered. You'll remember they existed, but you won't remember caring. Won't remember why they were important."

She gestured at the box. "And something else. Something I haven't told you yet."

My hands tightened on the dagger. "What?"

"The resurrection requires an anchor. A sacrifice to balance the scales." Alaira's eyes gleamed. "Life for life. Death for death. You're not just bringing him back—you're displacing something. Pushing the natural order aside to make room for him."

"Displacing what?"

"That depends." Alaira smiled, and it was the smile of someone who'd stopped caring about consequences long ago. "Maybe nothing. Maybe everything. Maybe the bone god's prison weakens just enough that he can start talking. Really talking, not just whispering to me through cracks."

Something cold spread through my chest, outward. "Whispering to you? You want to free him."

"I want the Goddess to notice." Alaira's voice rose, passionate and desperate, echoing off stone walls. "For centuries I've prayed. For centuries I've sacrificed and suffered and tried to prove I'm worthy of Her attention. And nothing. Nothing. She gave us Her gift and then abandoned us to figure it out alone."

She grabbed my shoulders, her grip stronger than it should have been. "But if the bone god rises—if what is imprisoned breaks free—She'll have to answer. She'll have to acknowledge what we've become. What Her gift became."

"You're using me," I said. "Using this resurrection to weaken his prison."

"I'm giving you what you want," Alaira corrected, releasing my shoulders. "And taking what I need. That's how magic works, child. Everything has a price. Everything requires balance."

She stepped back, smoothing her robes. "Now. Do you still want him back? Knowing the cost? Knowing what it might unleash?"

I looked at Nokoa. At his still face, his silent chest, his hands that would never hold mine again unless I did this. At the blue-gray tinge to his lips, the sunken quality of his cheeks.

"Yes," I said.

"Then we begin."

Alaira moved around the chamber, carving additional witch runes into surfaces I'd already covered. Hers were more complex than mine—layered, intricate, shifting when I tried to follow their logic. The sound of her carving tool against stone echoed rhythmically.

"These are binding runes," she explained as she worked, her voice taking on a lecturer's cadence. "Not just for souls—for reality. We're going to tear a hole between life and death, reach through, and drag him back. Reality doesn't like being torn. These runes will hold it in place long enough to complete the working."

"Stop analyzing and start preparing," Alaira commanded without looking up. "Strip. Both of you. The magic needs skin contact."

"He's already—"

"Undress him anyway." Alaira's tone left no room for argument. "Everything off. We're returning him to how he entered this world—naked, new, unmarked by anything but what we give him."

I moved to Nokoa and began undressing him with shaking hands, fingers fumbling with fabric stiff from cold and preservation spells. His skin was cold beneath the clothes, waxy to the touch, and I tried not to notice how it had started to slip in places. How his joints had stiffened. How he looked less like someone sleeping and more like—

Stop, the crown commanded. Focus on the ritual.

I removed my own clothes until I stood bare in the chamber's cold air. Goosebumps rose across my skin in waves, and I watched the black veins that had spread up my arms pulse in time with my heartbeat. They'd grown since yesterday, branching like tree roots up to my elbows.

Alaira studied me, her gaze moving over the veins without expression. "You're further gone than I thought. The corruption has taken root deep." She moved closer, tracing one black vein with her finger. Her touch was cold. "Bone magic and witch runes fighting for dominance in your body. You're becoming something between divine and profane."

"Will it affect the ritual?"

"It might make it stronger." Alaira pulled out bone dust compressed into stick form, leaving gray-white marks. "Or it might make you explode. We'll find out."

She began painting symbols on my skin. Starting at my feet, working up my legs in careful strokes, across my stomach and chest, down my arms. The bone dust felt warm, almost hot, and where she drew, the symbols sank in—not on my skin but into it, becoming part of me.

"Now him," Alaira directed.

Together, we lifted Nokoa from the ice bed and laid him on the chamber floor, in the center of the circle Alaira had drawn. His skin was colder away from the ice, and I watched frost form on his lips almost immediately, crystals spreading like lace.

Hurry, Oriana urged. Before it's too late.

Alaira painted Nokoa with the same symbols, working quickly, her movements practiced. His skin took the marks differently than mine—they didn't sink in so much as sit on the surface, glowing faintly. Because he was dead, I realized. The magic had nothing living to anchor to.

Yet.

When she finished, Alaira stepped back and surveyed her work. Nokoa and I lay side by side, covered in glowing witch runes, surrounded by circles within circles of carved symbols that pulsed with their own rhythm.

It looked like something between a resurrection and a summoning.

Maybe it was both.

"The first step," Alaira announced, pulling out two pieces of bone. Long, white, carved with names that seemed to move. "Your names, written in the old tongue. In the language the Goddess used when She first spoke creation into being."

She handed me one bone. It was warm in my hand, fever-hot, and I could see my name carved into it in symbols that shifted as I looked at them. Not Renata, exactly. Something deeper. My true name. The one that existed before language, before identity, before self.

The other bone bore Nokoa's name in similar script, the letters crawling across the surface.

"These will be your anchors," Alaira explained. "Your soul's tether to flesh. After tonight, these bones will be the most important things in existence. Guard them. Hide them. Because if someone destroys them—" She stopped.

"What happens if they're destroyed?"

"You unravel," Alaira said simply, as if discussing the weather. "Both of you. Soul from flesh. Consciousness from form. You'd exist, but you wouldn't be. Forever aware, forever unable to interact with reality. Forever trapped between."

She pulled out the black dagger again. "Now we sever."

My stomach dropped. "Both pinkies?"

"Both." Alaira positioned herself between us. "The ritual requires symmetry. Left pinky to bind souls. Right pinky to bind flesh. Both ground to powder and mixed with blood. Both consumed at the moment of the half-moon."

She looked at me, her expression almost sympathetic. "This will hurt. More than anything you've felt before. Pain is part of the working—it anchors the magic, makes it real. If you pass out, the ritual fails. If you scream too loud, the resonance breaks. You need to hold it together."

"I can do it," I said, though my voice shook.

"We'll see." Alaira positioned the blade over my left pinky. "On three. One—" She cut.

Not on three. On one. The blade sheared through bone and sinew like they were nothing, and pain exploded up my arm in waves of white-hot agony that stole my breath.

I bit down on my scream, tasting blood where my teeth cut my tongue. The pain was impossible. It felt like my entire arm was being torn off, like every nerve was firing at once, like my hand was being held in fire and ice simultaneously.

"Good," Alaira said, her voice distant through the roaring in my ears. She picked up my severed pinky—gods, I could see it lying there, disconnected, still wearing the ring I'd forgotten I had—and set it aside on a white cloth. "Right hand now."

"Wait—" I gasped, tears streaming down my face. "Let me—I need a moment—I thought it was only one—"

"No moments. The magic needs fresh pain. Immediate pain. If we wait, the resonance fades." The blade came down again, and my right pinky joined my left.

I couldn't stop the scream this time. It tore from my throat, raw and primal, and the witch runes flared in response. White light flooded the chamber, searing my vision, and I felt something shift. Something noticing us. Watching us.

Judging us.

Through the pain, through the tears, through the blood dripping from my mangled hands, I watched Alaira move to Nokoa.

"He can't feel this," she said. "The dead feel nothing. But the magic doesn't care. It takes what it takes."

She severed his pinkies with quick, efficient movements. They came away easier than mine had—less blood, more like breaking dried twigs than cutting through living flesh. The sound made my stomach turn.

She gathered all four and moved to a mortar and pestle carved from the same black bone as the dagger, the surface etched with symbols.

"Watch," she commanded.

Alaira ground the pinkies with methodical precision. Bone splintered under the pestle with sharp cracks. Flesh macerated into paste, wet and red. Blood and marrow mixed into something that looked like grave dirt.

The smell hit me in layers. Copper first, then rot, then something underneath that was almost sweet. Almost floral. Like death trying to remember what life smelled like.

When she finished, she held up the mortar. Maybe two tablespoons of powder. Gray-brown. Wet. Wrong.

"This is you," she said. "Both of you. Mixed together at the most fundamental level. Bone to bone. Blood to blood. Name to name." She set it down and pulled out a vial—the catalyst, filled with liquid that glowed green like foxfire. "And this is what makes the magic permanent."

She poured the catalyst into the mortar, and the powder reacted. It bubbled and hissed, steam rising in thick clouds, and the smell thickened until my empty stomach heaved.

"What is that?" I managed through clenched teeth.

"The Moon Goddess's blood," Alaira said. "The Goddess of Fate's mother. The last drops ever shed."

The mixture settled into something that looked like black tar. Thick. Viscous. Moving on its own, pulsing slowly.

"Half for you," Alaira said, pouring some into a small bone cup. "Half for him. You'll consume yours now. He'll consume his when he wakes."

She pressed the cup into my trembling, bleeding hand. Blood smeared the white bone. "Drink."

I looked at the mixture. At the pieces of Nokoa and me ground into powder and mixed with a goddess's blood. At the thing that would bind us together or kill us trying.

Drink, the crown urged. Finish it. Bring him back.

I raised the cup to my lips.

The taste tore through me—dirt and rot and copper and something that burned going down, that felt like swallowing broken glass dipped in acid. I gagged but forced it down, forced every drop, forced myself to keep it in my stomach even as my body screamed to expel it.

When the cup was empty, I fell back, gasping. The pain in my hands had faded to a dull roar compared to what was happening in my stomach. It felt like I'd swallowed fire. Like something was eating me from the inside out.

"The magic is taking root," Alaira explained. "Spreading through your blood. Through your bones. Soon it will reach your heart, and then—"

She stopped. Tilted her head, listening. "Do you hear that?"

I heard nothing except my own ragged breathing and the roar of blood in my ears. "What?"

"The prison." Alaira's eyes blazed bright. "It's weakening. The displacement is beginning. The bone god is—" She laughed, high and delighted, the sound bouncing off stone. "He's aware. Really aware now. Not just whispers but actual consciousness pressing against the seal."

She moved to the bone box. Her hands trembled as she opened it, fingers fumbling with the clasp.

Inside, a single piece of bone. Small, black, carved with runes so old they'd worn almost smooth. The seal anchor.

"I'm going to do something," Alaira announced, "that I've wanted to do for centuries."

"What?" But I already knew. Could see it in her eyes. The fanaticism that had shifted into something darker. Something that had been building for lifetimes.

"I'm going to crack the seal," Alaira said, her voice gone quiet and reverent. "Just a little. Just enough to let him talk. To let him show the Goddess what Her gift became. What I became."

"No—" I tried to stand, but my body wouldn't obey. The mixture in my stomach had me pinned, locked in place while magic worked through my system.

Alaira pulled out the black dagger and pressed it against the seal bone.

"Forgive me, Goddess," she whispered. "Or don't. I've stopped caring which."

She twisted the blade, and the bone cracked.

Not broke—cracked. Just a hairline fracture, barely visible.

But it was enough.

The chamber's temperature dropped so fast that ice formed on the walls in spreading patterns. The witch runes flared impossibly bright, then dimmed, then flared again like they couldn't decide if they should exist.

And I felt him.

The bone god. Not whispering anymore. Not distant. Present. Aware. Watching through the crack in his prison like an eye pressed against a keyhole.

Well, his voice rumbled through the chamber, through my bones, through the crown itself. You took longer than expected.

"It took time to prepare them. Time to have them in a position where I could pull from their bond." Alaira's voice was steady, almost conversational.

Slow, but thorough, he acknowledged. You did well.

"I need the Goddess to notice me," Alaira said simply. "And She will. She'll have to. If You rise, if You break free, She can't ignore what that means."

The bone god's presence shifted, and I felt him studying me—attention pressing against my skin like physical weight. *And who is this? The young queen who's been corrupting witch runes so enthusiastically?*

"Renata," Alaira confirmed.

The presence moved closer, and I felt something brush against my mind. Not invasive—curious. *You're willing to become a monster for him?*

"Yes," I whispered.

Then continue. He pulled back slightly, but his presence remained, vast and patient. *I'll guide the working. Ensure it takes hold. But remember, priestess—when I finally break free, you and I have unfinished business.*

"I remember," Alaira said. "I'm counting on it."

"Now," Alaira said, turning back to me. "The binding words. You remember them?"

I nodded, my throat tight. The crown had taught me. Had fed me syllables in a language that predated humanity.

"Then speak them." Alaira positioned herself over Nokoa's body, carving tool in hand. "I'll paint the final runes. The bone god will ensure the working takes hold." Her eyes blazed. "Speak."

I opened my mouth, and words poured out.

Not in my voice—in something older. Layered. The crown speaking through me, and underneath that, the bone god adding resonance, and underneath that, something that might have been the Goddess of Fate Herself, watching through whatever crack we'd opened between divine and mortal.

The words didn't translate. Couldn't translate. They were meaning given sound, intention made real, desire crystallized into syllables that rewrote reality as they were spoken.

Alaira painted as I spoke, drawing one final rune across both our bodies. Starting at my heart, extending to Nokoa's, creating a connection that glowed brighter than everything else combined.

The chamber shook. Not physically—deeper than that. Something in the fabric of things, shuddering as we forced it to do what it was never meant to do.

Allow the dead to return.

"Now!" Alaira shouted over the roar of displaced reality. "Now you take the spirit arm bone and pierce it through both your throats while you kiss him! The tether must form at the moment of the half-moon—which is now!"

She held out a long bone—carved, ancient, humming with power that made my teeth ache. Not a weapon. A key. A bridge.

I looked at Nokoa. At his still face. At lips that had been blue-gray for days but were starting to show the faintest hint of pink as magic flooded through him.

Please, I thought at him. At the universe. At whatever was listening. Please let this work.

I positioned myself over him, taking the spirit arm bone in my bleeding, mangled hands. Leaned down until our lips were almost touching, until I could feel the cold coming off his skin.

And Alaira drove the bone through both our throats.

Pain exploded, but different than before. Not sharp—deep. Like being skewered on something fundamental, something that existed before pain and would exist after. Like being impaled on the axis of the world itself.

Our lips met as the bone sank deeper, and through the pain I felt—

Him.

Not his body. His soul. Returning. Pulled back from wherever it had gone, dragged through the space between life and death, forced back into flesh that didn't quite fit anymore.

I felt his confusion. His horror. His realization of what was happening.

And I felt him try to pull away.

But it was too late.

The tether formed. Soul to soul. Bone to bone. Our names carved into existence itself, bound together so tightly that nothing—not death, not distance, not even divine intervention—could separate us now.

The spirit arm bone dissolved. Not burned away—simply ceased to exist, its purpose fulfilled. Our throats sealed over like the wound had never been, but I could feel the tether now. A cord connecting us. Invisible but real. Pulsing.

And through it, I felt everything he felt.

Terror. Pain. Anger. Confusion.

And underneath it all, buried but present—love. He still loved me. Despite everything. Despite what I'd done. Despite what I was becoming.

But that love hurt him. I could feel it hurting him. Every emotion translating into physical agony across the bond. Each feeling a knife twisted in his chest.

Nokoa's eyes snapped open.

Brown eyes. Golden in certain light. The eyes I'd thought I'd never see again.

He gasped, and his chest rose. Drew breath. Lived.

His hand shot up and grabbed my throat, fingers pressing against my windpipe.

But then he just held me there, his grip weak but present, his eyes searching mine with an expression I couldn't read. Horror? Love? Both?

"Renata?" His voice was barely a whisper. Hoarse from days of disuse. Broken. Beautiful.

"You're back," I sobbed, and the emotion flooded across the bond. "You're back, you're—"

Agony exploded across the tether. My joy hitting him like a physical blow. He convulsed, his back arching off the stone floor, a scream tearing from his throat that matched mine from earlier.

I tried to stop feeling joy. Tried to push down my emotions. But they kept flooding across the bond like water through a broken dam, and every one made him scream.

"Stop," he gasped, his voice raw. "Stop, please, I can't—"

But I couldn't stop. Couldn't control it. We were bound too tightly now. Everything I felt, he felt. And it was killing him.

Or it would have, if he could still die.

But he couldn't. That was the point. The curse. We were both trapped now. Both anchored to existence by bones carved with our names, by a bond that would never break.

Forever aware.

Forever suffering.

Forever together.

Alaira stood over us, watching with something like satisfaction. "It worked," she breathed. "Gods, it actually worked."

Behind her, I felt the bone god's presence swell. Felt his prison crack just a little wider as displacement spread, as reality bent to accommodate something that shouldn't exist.

Perfect, he whispered, his voice satisfied. You've done beautifully. Both of you. Now rest. Heal. Grow stronger.

Because when I finally break free, I'm going to need you.

Both of you.

The chamber swam. My vision narrowed to a point. The pain in my stomach, the pain in my hands, the pain across the bond—all of it combined into something beyond endurance.

I collapsed beside Nokoa, our bodies pressed together, the tether between us glowing faint but present. Pulsing with each shared heartbeat.

The last thing I saw before darkness took me was his face.

Chapter Nine

Discovery

Renata

Nokoa was screaming. His body convulsed beside me on the chamber floor, his hands clawing at his throat, nails scraping against skin. His face twisted in agony, features contorting. The tether between us pulsed with white-hot pain, and I felt it too—a distant echo of what he experienced, bleeding across the bond into my own nerves.

But his pain was worse. So much worse.

"Stop," he gasped, the word barely intelligible through clenched teeth. "Please, whatever you're feeling, stop—"

I tried. Tried to empty my mind, to feel nothing, to be nothing. But the moment I saw him alive—truly alive, breathing, here—joy surged through me like a flood breaking through a dam. I felt something for the first time in days. And that joy hit him like a physical blow.

He screamed again, his back arching off the stone, vertebrae cracking audibly.

"I'm sorry," I sobbed, tears streaming down my face. "I'm sorry, I don't know how to—"

"Don't apologize!" The words tore from his throat, raw and bleeding. "Don't feel sorry! Every emotion is—gods, it's like being torn apart from the inside—"

I bit down on everything. Forced myself into numbness. Into the cold, empty space the crown had been carving out of me for days. Pushed down joy, relief, love, everything that made this moment what it should have been.

Victory. Reunion. Salvation.

Instead, we lay on cold stone, naked, both of us shaking, both of us learning the price of what I'd done.

The tether glowed faint between us. I could see it now when I looked—not with my eyes, but with something deeper. A cord of light connecting his chest to mine, pulsing with every heartbeat. His heartbeat. Real. Alive. The sound of it filled my ears like drums.

Worth it, I told myself. This is worth it.

But the way he looked at me—with fear, with dawning horror, with the realization of what I'd made him—suggested he might disagree.

Priestess Alaira knelt beside us, her white robes pooling around her like snow. "The binding took hold," she observed, and there was something like reverence in her voice. "You're connected now. Truly connected. Soul to soul, bone to bone."

"Connected," Nokoa repeated bitterly, the word sharp as broken glass. He tried to sit up, and I felt his muscles protest, felt the weakness in his limbs as a distant ache in my own. "Is that what you call this? I feel her in my head. In my bones. Every thought, every emotion—"

"Will stabilize," Alaira interrupted. "Eventually. Right now the bond is raw, new. Like a wound that hasn't healed. Give it time and you'll learn to manage it. To build walls between yourselves."

"Walls." Nokoa laughed, and it sounded broken, each note wrong. "How can I build walls against someone living inside my skull?"

I reached for him—not with my hand, with the bond. Tried to send comfort, reassurance, something to ease his pain. Tried to project warmth across the tether.

He flinched like I'd struck him, his whole body jerking away. "Don't. Don't do that. It hurts worse when you mean well."

I pulled back immediately, the emotional retreat feeling like tearing off skin, and the space between us felt like a chasm despite lying inches apart.

"Your bodies need rest," Alaira stated. "The resurrection took its toll. You've been dead for days, Nokoa. Your flesh needs time to remember how to be alive."

"I don't feel alive." He stared at his hands—the stumps where his pinkies used to be, bandaged now with strips Alaira must have wrapped while I was unconscious. The white cloth was already spotted with blood. "I feel like I'm wearing a corpse."

"That will fade too." Alaira stood, gathering her implements, metal clinking against bone. "The magic needs time to fully integrate. By tomorrow you'll feel more yourself."

She looked at me, and something in her expression made my skin crawl. Not pity. Not concern. Satisfaction.

"You did well," she said. "Both of you. The displacement worked perfectly. The bone god's prison has weakened. He's more aware now. More present." She smiled, and it didn't reach her eyes. "The Goddess will have to notice. She'll have to answer."

"Is that all this was to you?" Nokoa's voice came out flat. Cold. "An experiment? A way to get your goddess's attention?"

Alaira moved toward the exit, ignoring the question entirely. "Oh, and Renata? The council felt the magic. They're coming. You have perhaps five minutes before they arrive."

She left before I could respond, her footsteps echoing away into darkness. I made a note to find out where she'd gone. What she'd go to do next, now that the seal was cracked.

Five minutes.

I looked at Nokoa—at his naked body still painted with witch runes that glowed faintly, at the stumps of his fingers, at his face that showed too much bone beneath too-thin skin. At what I'd brought back.

"We need to get dressed," I said.

"We need to talk about what you did to me," he countered.

"After. When the council isn't about to—"

"Now." His eyes—golden in the witch-light, catching and reflecting it—pinned me in place. "What did you do to me, Renata? What am I?"

I searched for words and found none that wouldn't hurt him. So I told the truth. "I brought you back. I bound our souls together so tightly that death can't separate us again. I made sure we'd never be apart."

"You cursed me." His voice broke on the words. "That's what you did. You cursed me to feel everything you feel as pain. To never have privacy, never have peace, never have a single thought that doesn't bleed across this—this thing between us."

"It's not a curse. It's love."

"Love," he repeated, tasting the word. "You call this love? Dragging me back from death? Binding me without consent? Making it so I can't even—" He stopped. Swallowed hard, his throat working. "I can't think about you without agony. Can't care about you without it tearing me apart. What part of that is love?"

"The part where you're alive." My voice came out sharper than I intended, cutting. "The part where I refused to accept losing you. The part where I did everything—sacrificed everything—to get you back."

"I didn't ask you to sacrifice anything!" Nokoa stood, stumbling slightly, catching himself against the ice bed. I felt his dizziness as vertigo in my own head, the world tilting. "I didn't ask to come back! Maybe death was better than this!"

The words hit me like a physical blow. Through the bond, I felt his immediate regret at saying them, felt him trying to take them back, the guilt washing over both of us. But it was too late.

I'd heard.

I pushed down the hurt, the anger, the betrayal. Pushed it all into the cold empty space where my emotions used to live. "Get dressed," I said flatly. "The council will be here any moment."

"Renata—"

"Get. Dressed."

We moved in tense silence, finding our clothes scattered where we'd left them. The witch runes painted on our skin had faded to faint marks, like old scars. But the stumps of our pinkies throbbed in unison, a shared rhythm of pain, and I felt every spike of agony from his as clearly as my own.

I was pulling on my dress when footsteps echoed in the passage outside.

Multiple footsteps. Running. The sound growing louder.

The council had arrived.

Cressa burst into the chamber first, her healer's instincts overriding protocol. She took two steps inside, saw Nokoa standing there alive, and stopped so abruptly she nearly fell. Her hand shot out to catch herself against the wall.

"That's not—" She pressed a hand to her mouth, fingers trembling. "That's not possible."

"And yet," I said.

Behind Cressa, the remaining council members filed in. Ancelin with his silver eyes blazing like molten metal. Maxin looking grayer than ever, more skeletal, his transformation accelerating with each passing day. Praxis watching everything, his crimson eyes taking in every detail.

They all stared at Nokoa like he was a ghost.

Which, I supposed, he was. Or had been. Or something in between.

"You actually did it," Maxin breathed, the words barely audible.

"Did you doubt me?"

"Yes." Maxin moved closer, studying Nokoa with an intensity that bordered on hunger. "Hivro and the Hollow Crown brought him back once, but this—you. It shouldn't be able to happen with you still whole. The displacement alone should have killed you."

"It's not resurrection," Nokoa said quietly, his voice rough. "It's something else. Something wrong."

"Wrong how?" Cressa asked, her healer's training overriding her shock. She'd found her composure, was moving toward him with her healer's eye already cataloging damage. "Let me see you. Let me check—"

"Don't touch him," I warned.

Cressa stopped mid-step. "Renata, I'm a healer. I need to examine him to make sure the magic took hold properly—"

"It took hold fine. He's alive. That's all that matters."

"Is it?" Ancelin's voice cut through the chamber like a blade, sharp and cold. "Is it all that matters? Because from where I'm standing, you've just performed the most dangerous, most forbidden magic in existence. You've torn a hole in reality, destabilized the natural order, and from the feel of that working—" He gestured at the fading witch runes, at the residual magic thick in the air. "—you've weakened the bone god's prison in the process."

"That was Priestess Alaira," I countered. "Not me."

"Where is she?" Praxis asked, and something in his voice sharpened. "She was here—I can smell her magic. But she's gone."

"She left," I said. "Before you arrived."

The look Praxis and Ancelin exchanged said more than either of them chose to speak aloud. Whatever Alaira had gone to do next, they knew it wouldn't be nothing.

"You allowed it," Ancelin pressed on, returning to me. "You let her crack the seal. You helped create the displacement that let him wake up. Do you understand what you've done?"

"I brought back someone I love." I moved to stand beside Nokoa, and through the bond I felt his complicated reaction to my proximity. Relief and pain twisted together. "That's what I've done."

"You've doomed us," Maxin said softly, his voice heavy with resignation. "All of us. The famine will spread faster now. The corruption will deepen. Reality itself will start to fray at the edges because you forced it to do something it was never meant to do."

"Then fix it," I said. "You're the one who understands the magic. Fix what's broken."

"I can't fix this!" Maxin's voice rose, cracking. "You've gone beyond anything in Alaira's journals. Beyond anything I understand. You've created a paradox—life and death occupying the same space, divine magic and bone magic twisted together into something that shouldn't exist."

He pointed at Nokoa, his hand shaking. "He shouldn't exist. His soul should have moved on. His body should have decayed. But you dragged him back, forced the universe to make room for him, and now everything has to shift to accommodate that impossibility."

"Is that supposed to make me regret it?" I asked. "Because I don't. I'd do it again."

"Even knowing the cost?" Ancelin demanded. "Even knowing that every day he's alive, more people will starve? That the outer cities will burn? That the entire world might collapse under the weight of your selfishness?"

Through the bond, I felt Nokoa's reaction to that. Guilt. Horror. The crushing realization that his resurrection had a price others would pay. The weight of it pressed against my own chest.

"Don't listen to them," I urged, turning to him. "They're trying to manipulate you. To make you feel guilty for something you didn't choose."

"But they're right," Nokoa said quietly. "Aren't they? My being alive is killing people."

"No. The famine was already spreading. The corruption was already—"

"Stop lying." His golden-brown eyes met mine. "I can feel what you're feeling through the bond. I know you're lying. You just don't want to admit it."

The chamber fell silent. The only sound was our shared breathing, synchronized without either of us choosing it.

Cressa moved closer to Nokoa, her movements slow and non-threatening, hands raised where he could see them. "Let me examine you," she said gently. "Please. I need to make sure you're stable."

He nodded, and she began her assessment. Checking his pulse at his throat and wrist, his breathing, his pupils. Her hands hesitated over the stumps of his pinkies, hovering without touching.

"You severed them," she stated. "For the binding."

"Yes."

"And ground them to powder. Mixed them with blood and catalyst. Consumed them."

"How did you—" I started.

"Because that's what the journals say." Cressa's voice was hollow, drained. "That's how soul-fusion works. You trade pieces of yourselves. Make yourselves literally part of each other."

She looked at me, tears already tracking down her cheeks. "Do you even understand what you've done to him? What you've done to yourself?"

"I saved him."

"You imprisoned him." Cressa's voice broke. "You took away his choice, his autonomy, his right to his own mind. And you call that love?"

"Yes," I said. "Because love means not giving up. It means fighting for what matters, even when everyone tells you to stop."

"Love means letting go when holding on will hurt more." Cressa finished her examination and stepped back. "But you never learned that, did you?"

I didn't answer. Couldn't answer.

Praxis, who'd been silent until now, finally spoke. "The outer cities are still at the gates. Their army has grown—word spread about the magic you performed. They felt it." He paused. "They're demanding answers. Demanding you."

"Let them demand."

"They won't wait much longer," Praxis continued. "Nalla's commanders are pushing for immediate assault. They're calling you a monster. A threat to the natural order. They want you dead and the crown destroyed."

"They want a lot of things they won't get. Why are we acting as though I can't kill them?"

"Perhaps you could have." Praxis glanced at Nokoa, his gaze sharp and assessing. "But now you have a weakness. Something you care about more than anything. Something they can take away."

Through the bond, I felt Nokoa's understanding of what Praxis meant. Felt his decision forming before he spoke it aloud, the resolve solidifying like cooling metal.

"No," I said. "Whatever you're thinking, no—"

"I'll go with them," Nokoa announced. "As a hostage. As insurance."

"Absolutely not."

"It's the only way." He met my eyes, and I felt his resolve through the bond—solid, unyielding. "They need a guarantee you won't attack. I can be that guarantee."

"They'll kill you."

"They won't. Because if they do, you'll destroy them. They know that." He took a breath, and I felt how much even that simple action hurt him, ribs aching with resurrection-soreness. "This is the only way to prevent a war. The only way to buy time for the council to fix the famine. For everyone to adjust to... this."

He gestured at himself. At me. At the tether between us, still glowing faintly.

"I won't let you," I said, my voice breaking.

"You don't get to choose." His voice was gentle but final. "Just like I didn't get to choose resurrection. Now you don't get to choose this."

The parallel hit like a slap. Through the bond, I felt his small satisfaction at landing the blow. At finally having some agency in what happened to him.

"Nokoa, please—"

"It's already decided." He turned to Ancelin. "Tell Nalla I'll come willingly. As a hostage. As proof that Renata can be controlled."

"You can't control me," I said.

"No." Nokoa's smile was sad, barely curving his lips. "But I can hurt you. And they know that. They know that if they hurt me, it hurts you. That's enough."

Ancelin nodded slowly, joints grinding. "I'll send word to the outer cities. Arrange the transfer."

"At dawn," Nokoa said. "Give us tonight. Let me... adjust to being alive. Let the bond stabilize slightly. Then I'll go."

"Agreed." Ancelin moved toward the exit, the other council members following, their footsteps echoing. Only Cressa remained, lingering near the door, looking back at us.

"I'm sorry," she said quietly, her voice thick. "Both of you. I'm sorry this is what love became."

She left before either of us could respond, her robes whispering against stone.

We stood alone in the ritual chamber as the witch runes faded to nothing. As the evidence of what we'd done disappeared, leaving only the two of us and the tether binding us together. The silence was heavy.

"You should eat," I said finally, my voice hoarse. "Drink something. Your body needs—"

"I don't want to eat." Nokoa sat heavily on the ice bed—his deathbed, until hours ago. The ice creaked under his weight. "I want to understand. What happened to me. Where I was. What you pulled me back from."

"Does it matter?"

"Yes." His voice was quiet but intent. "It matters. Because maybe where I was—maybe it was better than this."

I felt the words hit me through the bond. Felt how much he meant them, the raw honesty of it.

"Tell me," he urged. "What happened while I was dead? What did you do?"

So I told him. Not everything—not about laying with his corpse, not about the extent of my delusion—but enough. About the council members I'd killed. About the spectral guards. About learning witch runes and corrupting them. About the famine spreading and the outer cities at the gates.

About becoming something I didn't recognize in order to bring him back.

He listened in silence, and through the bond I felt his emotions shift and change. Horror. Grief. Understanding. And underneath it all, a love that hurt him to feel but couldn't be denied.

"You became a monster for me," he said when I finished.

"Yes."

"And you'd do it again."

"Yes."

He was quiet for a long time, staring at his hands. Then: "I don't know if that makes me feel loved or terrified."

"Both, probably."

"Both," he agreed, a ghost of a smile crossing his face.

We sat in silence, the tether pulsing between us like a second heartbeat, learning the shape of our new existence. Learning how to be two people occupying the same emotional space. Learning the curse I'd created in the name of love.

"Dawn comes soon," Nokoa said eventually, his voice flat. "They'll take me then."

"I know."

"Can you..." He paused, choosing his words carefully. "Can you try to not feel anything while I'm gone? Can you be numb? Empty? So it doesn't hurt as much?"

"I can try."

"That's all I ask." He looked at me, and his expression was complicated in ways even the bond couldn't fully translate. "Thank you. For bringing me back. Even if I'm not sure it was the right thing. Even if this is a curse. Thank you for not giving up."

The words should have felt like victory. Like vindication.

Instead, they just felt heavy.

We stayed there through the night, not touching—too afraid of what our proximity might trigger across the bond—but together. Awake. Alive.

Cursed.

And when dawn came, when they took him away to the outer cities' camp, I felt the separation like something tearing loose inside my chest. Not sharp—slow. The way a stitch gives when you've pulled it too tight.

Felt his fear bleeding into my bones.

Felt the distance stretch the tether taut but not breaking.

Never breaking.

Because that was the point of the curse.

We could never truly be apart.

And we could never truly be together.

The crown pulsed warm against my skull, and for once, the voices were silent.

Even they didn't have an answer for this.

Chapter Ten

THE BARGAIN

Renata

The outer cities' army looked larger in daylight.

I stood at the skeletal jaw entrance of the Bone Court castle, watching their forces spread across the landscape like a plague. Thousands of soldiers, their armor catching the morning sun in blinding flashes, their banners snapping in wind that carried the scent of smoke and desperation. The sound was constant—metal on metal, voices calling orders, the low rumble of so many bodies in motion.

They'd been burning their dead through the night. I could see the pyres still smoldering at the edges of their camp, columns of gray smoke rising into pale sky. Too many pyres. Too many bodies.

The famine was killing faster than I'd realized.

"They're ready to talk," Ancelin announced from behind me, his joints grinding with each word. "Nalla and her commanders. They've agreed to parley in the main hall."

"How generous of them." I didn't turn around. Through the bond, I could feel Nokoa in the ritual chamber below, still weak, still adjusting to being alive. Every spike of pain from him registered as a dull ache in my own chest, a constant background throb. "What do they want?"

"The end of the Bone Council. The destruction of the crown. Your death, preferably." Ancelin's tone was flat, matter-of-fact. "Though now they're also demanding answers about the magic you performed. About what you brought back."

"I brought back Nokoa. That's all they need to know."

"They felt the displacement," Maxin added. He'd entered so quietly I hadn't noticed, his footsteps silent as snow. "Everyone did. Reality shifting to accommodate something that shouldn't exist. The bone god's prison weakening. They're calling it an abomination."

"They can call it whatever they want." I finally turned to face them. Both council members looked worse than yesterday—Ancelin's bones duller, losing their luster; Maxin's skin grayer, almost translucent. "I'm not destroying the crown. And I'm certainly not dying to make them feel better."

"Then what are you offering?" Praxis emerged from the shadows near the throne, silent as always. "Because they won't leave without something. And if you refuse to negotiate, they'll attack. You might have spectral guards and bone magic, but they have numbers. And desperation."

"Let them attack. I'm offering them the choice between life and death by my hands."

"Renata." Cressa's voice came from the doorway, soft and pleading. She looked exhausted, her healer's robes rumpled and stained, dark circles under her green eyes like bruises. "Please. Just listen to what they have to say. Maybe there's a compromise—"

"There's no compromise!" The words came out sharper than intended, echoing off stone. "They want me to undo everything I've done. To kill myself or destroy the crown or both. They want me to give up Nokoa after I just got him back. What part of that is compromise?"

Through the bond, I felt Nokoa stir. Felt him register my anger and fear, felt those emotions translate into pain in his newly-returned body—sharp stabs in his chest, his head pounding. I tried to push the feelings down, tried to go numb, but it was like trying to stop breathing.

"I'm sorry," I whispered, though I didn't know if I was apologizing to Nokoa or to everyone else.

"Bring them in," I relented finally, my voice hollow. "Let's hear what they want."

I made my way back inside the Bone Court caves first, my footsteps echoing in empty corridors.

Nalla entered the throne room flanked by four commanders, all of them armed despite the supposed truce. Swords at their hips, daggers in boots. She looked different than the last time I'd seen her—harder, leaner, with an edge of barely contained violence that made my spectral guards shift nervously, their forms flickering.

"Hollow Queen," she said, and the title was definitely an insult this time, dripping with venom. "Thank you for agreeing to meet."

"I didn't agree to anything. You're here because my council insisted." I stayed standing, refusing to sit on the throne. Some instinct told me that sitting would make me vulnerable, exposed. "Say what you came to say."

Nalla's jaw tightened, muscle jumping beneath skin. "Very well. The outer cities have three demands. Meet them, and we withdraw. Refuse, and we attack at sunset."

"Demands." I smiled without humor. "Not requests. Not negotiations. Demands."

"We're past negotiation." One of her commanders—the gray-bearded man from before—stepped forward, hand resting on his sword hilt. "Your magic is killing us. Our children are starving. Our crops are failing. Our livestock are dying—just collapsing in the fields, blood running from their eyes. We've tried being reasonable. We've tried waiting for the Bone Council to fix things. But nothing changes. It only gets worse."

"So you come with an army."

"So we come prepared to end this," Nalla corrected. "One way or another."

Through the bond, I felt Nokoa moving. Climbing the stairs from the catacombs, each step an effort. Coming here despite his weakness. Why? What was he—

Let them speak. The intention pressed against my consciousness across the bond—not words but meaning. A feeling of wait, listen, don't act yet. Let them say what they need to say.

I gritted my teeth but nodded. "Fine. What are your demands?"

Nalla's dark eyes held mine, unblinking. "First: dismantle the Bone Council. End the tithes. No more bone marrow, no more heartfire, no more bleeding us dry to maintain your immortality while we die."

"The tithes maintain the system," Ancelin stated. "Without them, the council members die. The magic holding this kingdom together collapses."

"Good," the gray-bearded commander said, his voice hard. "Let it collapse. We'll build something better from the ruins."

"Second demand," Nalla continued. "Destroy the hollow crown. It's corrupted. Whatever it's doing to you—" She gestured at me, at the black veins visible on my arms, spreading like cracks. "—whatever it's made you become—needs to end. The crown is the source of all this. Remove it. Destroy it."

Through the bond, I felt Nokoa's complex reaction to that. Part of him agreed with her. Part of him wanted me to destroy the thing that had corrupted me, that had turned me into someone he barely recognized.

But the crown pulsed hot against my skull, and the voices rose immediately.

Don't you dare, Lyanna hissed. After everything we've given you—

To destroy the crown is to destroy yourself as well, Oriana warned. The corruption has spread too deep. You and the crown are one now.

Refuse, Alaric commanded. Make them understand you're not someone who can be threatened.

"No," I said. "The crown stays."

"Then people keep dying," Nalla said flatly. "Children keep starving. The famine keeps spreading. All because you won't give up your power."

"It's not about power—"

"It's always about power!" Nalla's voice rose, bouncing off vaulted ceilings. "You performed forbidden magic. You brought back the dead. You killed council members. You've become exactly the kind of tyrant we were afraid you'd become, and you don't even see it!"

"I see fine," I said coldly. "I see an army at my gates making demands they have no right to make. I see people who want me to destroy myself to make them comfortable. I see—"

"You see nothing," Nalla interrupted. "You're so focused on your dead lover that you can't see the living dying all around you."

The throne room fell silent. Even the spectral guards went still.

Then Nokoa's voice came from the entrance, rough and tired. "I'm not dead anymore."

Everyone turned. He stood in the doorway, leaning heavily against the frame, one hand pressed to the stone for support. Still pale and weak but undeniably alive. The witch runes Alaira had painted on his skin had faded to faint marks, barely visible shadows, but his presence was impossible to deny.

Nalla's expression shifted from anger to shock, her eyes widening. "That's not—how—"

"Resurrection," Nokoa explained simply. He moved into the room, and I felt every step as an echo in my own legs, muscles protesting. "She brought me back. That's what the magic was. That's what everyone felt."

"Resurrection." The gray-bearded commander said it like a curse. "You defied death itself."

"She defied death," Nokoa corrected. "I didn't have a choice in the matter."

Through the bond, I felt his complicated emotions about that statement. Truth and resentment tangled together like thorns.

Nalla's expression softened slightly in his direction, tension easing from her shoulders. "How do you feel?"

"Like I've been dead for days and forcibly dragged back into a body that doesn't quite fit anymore." He glanced at me, and I felt his exhaustion like weight on my own bones. "But alive. For whatever that's worth."

"And bound to her," Maxin added quietly. "Soul to soul. They can't be separated now. What one feels, the other feels as pain. It's a curse as much as a resurrection."

Nalla's eyes sharpened. "Is that true?"

Nokoa hesitated, then nodded. "Yes. Every emotion she has, I feel as physical pain. Every thought of me causes her suffering, and mine of her causes me agony. We're..." He searched for words, his throat working. "We're trapped together. Forever."

"Then you're a hostage," one of Nalla's commanders observed. "Perfect leverage."

"That was my thought too." Nokoa moved to stand between me and the outer cities delegation. Not beside me—between. Choosing his position carefully, deliberately. "Which brings me to why I came up here. I have a proposal."

"Nokoa, no—" I started.

"Let me finish." He didn't look at me, kept his eyes on Nalla. "Your third demand. What is it?"

Nalla studied him for a long moment, her gaze assessing. "Your death. Hers. Both of you. As punishment for what you've done. As an end to the corruption."

"You can't have her death," Nokoa stated calmly. "If she dies, I die—we're bound that tightly. And I suspect she'd take a lot of your army with her before going down. So that demand is impractical."

"But yours isn't," Nalla said slowly, understanding dawning. "If we kill you, it hurts her. Cripples her. Makes her less dangerous."

"Exactly. Which is why I'm offering myself as a hostage instead." Nokoa's voice was calm, deliberate. "I'll come with you. Stay in your camp. Insurance that she won't attack. That she'll cooperate. That she'll work to fix the famine."

"No," I said, my voice breaking. "I'd argue the opposite. If you hurt him, I'll become the most dangerous thing you've ever seen."

"It's the only way to prevent a war." Nokoa finally looked at me, and through the bond I felt his resolve—solid, unyielding. "You know it is. They need assurance you can be controlled. I'm that assurance."

"They'll kill you." The words came out as a whisper.

"They won't. Because if they do, you'll destroy them. They know that." He turned back to Nalla. "That's the bargain. I come willingly. You keep me safe. She cooperates. Everyone gets time to figure out how to fix this mess."

Nalla looked at her commanders. Silent communication passed between them—glances, nods, small gestures that spoke of military discipline and shared understanding.

"We accept," Nalla announced finally. "With conditions. You come alone—no guards, no weapons, no magic. You submit to binding if necessary. And if she attacks us, if she performs any more forbidden magic, if she does anything we consider a threat—you die. Immediately. No warnings."

Through the bond, I felt Nokoa's fear at those conditions, cold and sharp in his chest. But also his acceptance. His belief that this was the right thing to do.

"Agreed," he said.

"You don't get to agree for me," I protested. "I don't accept these terms. I won't let you—"

"You don't have a choice." His voice was gentle but final. "Just like I didn't have a choice about resurrection. This is what needs to happen."

The parallel hit me again. The reversal of agency. Him taking control of the one thing he could control—where he went, what he sacrificed.

"When?" Ancelin asked.

"Dusk tonight," Nalla said. "Give them time to say goodbye. Let the bond stabilize. Let everyone prepare." She looked at me. "And Hollow Queen? If you try anything during that night—if you attack our camp, if you attempt rescue before he's even gone—the deal is off and we attack immediately. Understood?"

I wanted to refuse. Wanted to summon my spectral guards and my bone mace and everything I'd become. Wanted to show them exactly what happened to people who threatened to take Nokoa from me.

But through the bond, I felt his plea. His desperate need for me to accept this. To let him choose this one thing.

"Understood," I forced out through clenched teeth.

Nalla nodded. "Then we'll withdraw for now. Return at dusk to collect him." She turned to leave, her commanders following in tight formation, but paused at the threshold. "For what it's worth, Hollow Queen—I understand. What you did. Why you did it. Love makes us all monsters sometimes."

She left, and I was glad, because I had no words that wouldn't come out as threats.

The throne room emptied quickly after that. Ancelin and Maxin murmuring about preparations. Cressa hovering near Nokoa, checking his vitals, making sure the confrontation hadn't damaged him. Praxis slipping out last, soundless.

I stood there feeling the weight of what had just happened settle over me. The morning light through the high windows felt wrong—too bright, too ordinary for what was being arranged.

I had the afternoon. Just the afternoon before they took him away.

"Come on," Nokoa said quietly. He was beside me now, close enough that I could feel his body heat, could smell the faint scent of witch runes still clinging to his skin. Close enough that the tether between us felt less like a wound and more like a lifeline. "Let's go back to the catacombs. Away from all this. One last meal."

I nodded, not trusting my voice.

We walked together through empty corridors, past servants who stared and quickly looked away, past guards who didn't know whether to salute or run. Down into familiar darkness, back to the ritual chamber that had seen his death and resurrection.

Back to where everything had changed.

Cressa had left supplies—food, water, clean bandages wrapped in linen. We sat on the ice bed that was no longer needed for preservation, and Nokoa tried to eat while I watched.

Every bite was an effort. Every swallow made him wince, his throat working against it. Through the bond, I felt his body's confusion about being alive, about needing food and water and breath. The strangeness of lungs expanding, stomach accepting nourishment.

"Talk to me," he requested finally, setting down the bread he couldn't quite manage. "Not through the bond. With words. Tell me what you're feeling."

"Angry," I admitted. "Terrified. Like everything I did was for nothing."

"It wasn't for nothing. I'm alive."

"For how long? Until they decide you're not useful? Until someone in their camp decides to take revenge?" My hands clenched into fists, nails biting into palms. "I brought you back to keep you safe. To make up for my failure to protect you. And now you're walking into danger anyway."

"I'm walking into danger to prevent a war," Nokoa said. "To give everyone time to fix the famine. To stop more people from dying because of what you did to save me."

The words stung. Through the bond, he felt them sting, and I felt his regret at causing me pain—guilt washing over both of us.

"I'm sorry," he said. "That came out harsher than I meant."

"But it's true. People are dying because I brought you back."

"People were already dying. The system was already broken." He pushed the bread aside. "Maxin told me. The tithes, the crown, the council—all of it was failing before you resurrected me. I just... accelerated things."

"You didn't accelerate anything. I did. By refusing to let you go."

We sat in silence, the tether pulsing between us, carrying emotions too complicated to name. Love and fear and guilt and hope all tangled together.

"Do you regret it?" I asked finally, the question I'd been afraid to ask. "Honestly. Do you regret that I brought you back?"

Nokoa was quiet for a long time. Long enough that I started to dread the answer. "I don't know," he said finally, his voice soft. "Ask me again in a week. A month. A year. Maybe by then I'll have an answer."

It wasn't the reassurance I'd hoped for. But it was honest. And through the bond, I felt that honesty like a physical weight, pressing down on both of us.

"One afternoon," he said, changing the subject. "We have one afternoon. What do you want to do with it?"

I looked at him—at his too-thin face, at the stumps of his pinkies wrapped in bandages, at the witch rune marks that would never fully fade. At what I'd brought back.

"I want to memorize you," I said. "So that when you're gone, when distance stretches the bond thin, I can remember this moment. When you were here. When you were alive. When you were mine."

"I'm not yours," he said gently, no accusation in it. "I'm not anyone's. But I'm here."

We lay down together on the ice bed, not touching—afraid of what proximity might trigger across the bond—but close. Present. Alive. The cold seeped through our clothes, but neither of us moved.

I memorized the sound of his breathing. The rise and fall of his chest. The warmth that meant life instead of death. The way his eyelashes cast shadows on his cheeks in the dim witch-light.

And tried not to think about separation.

Hours passed. We didn't talk much. There wasn't much to say that wouldn't hurt one or both of us.

Too soon, the light from the ventilation shaft began to fade. Dusk approaching.

Nokoa sat up slowly, every movement careful. "I should go."

"Not yet." But even as I said it, I knew it was time.

"I love you," I whispered as he stood.

Through the bond, I felt his complicated response. Love tangled with fear, gratitude twisted with resentment, hope buried under exhaustion. All of it true. All of it his.

I had imagined this moment differently. I had thought he'd hold me despite the pain, that desire would be stronger than the bond's cruelty. I'd been so certain that love—our love—would find a way through even this.

I'd been wrong. And there was something in being wrong that felt more final than all the rest.

"I know," he said.

And left.

I watched him walk away, his footsteps echoing in the passage. Each step carried him farther from me, but the tether remained—stretched taut, vibrating with tension, never breaking.

I was grateful to hear his breath, to feel his heartbeat through the bond.

But gratitude and grief are not so different, in the end. Both leave you hollow. Both ask you to hold something you can't quite reach.

The bond pulsed between us as he climbed the stairs. As he walked through corridors toward the entrance. As he stepped out into fading light where Nalla and her commanders waited.

I felt his fear. His determination. His love and his anger and his hope that this sacrifice would mean something.

I felt the distance open between us like a held breath finally released.

And I stayed where I was, in the dark, in the cold, in the room where he had died and been reborn.

The crown pulsed warm against my skull.

Even the voices had nothing left to offer.

Chapter Eleven

Shared Pain

Nokoa

The outer cities' camp smelled like desperation.

I noticed it the moment we crossed the boundary line—that invisible threshold between the Bone Court's lands and theirs. The smell of unwashed bodies, of fires burning whatever they could find for fuel, of sickness and hunger and slow death. The air was thick with it, coating my throat.

The smell of my resurrection's cost.

Nalla walked ahead of me, her commanders flanking us on both sides. Not quite prisoners' escort, not quite honor guard. Something in between. Behind us, I heard Valdic's claws clicking against stone, the sound rhythmic and somehow comforting. The DirgeWolf had insisted on accompanying me despite Nalla's protests.

"He goes where I go," I'd stated firmly. "Non-negotiable."

Renata wouldn't notice his absence, but I'd notice his company.

Nalla had studied Valdic's emaciated, half-skeletal form and shrugged. "Fine. One more mouth barely makes a difference when we're all starving anyway."

Through the bond, I felt Renata's constant presence. Not intrusive, exactly—the bond didn't work that way, didn't let me hear her thoughts or see what she saw. More like a weight pressing against the inside of my skull. Her fear for me translated into a dull ache behind my eyes, throbbing in time with my pulse. Her anger at the situation made my chest tight, ribs constricting. Her love—gods, her love was the worst. Every spike of affection hit like a punch to the sternum, driving the air from my lungs.

I was learning to build walls. Mental barriers between her emotions and mine. But they were fragile things, easily shattered when she felt something strongly.

Which was often.

"You alright?" Valdic asked quietly, keeping pace beside me.

"No."

"Honest. I appreciate that." His purple eyes gleamed in the fading light. "How bad is it? The bond?"

"Imagine someone constantly screaming in your head, but the screams are emotions instead of sound. And you can't make them stop. Can't even turn down the volume." I stumbled slightly as Renata's fear spiked—she'd felt me stumble through the bond, which made her more afraid, which made me stumble again. Feedback loop. "And every time I react to her emotions, she reacts to my reaction, which makes everything worse."

"Sounds delightful," Valdic said dryly. "Really worth coming back from the dead for."

"I didn't have a choice about coming back."

"No," Valdic agreed, his voice soft. "You didn't. None of us did. She made all the choices, and now we're living with the consequences."

We reached the camp—a sprawling collection of tents and makeshift shelters that seemed to stretch forever. Thousands of people, I realized with growing horror. Not just soldiers. Families. Children. The elderly. Everyone who'd fled the outer cities as the famine spread, their belongings piled in sad heaps outside each shelter.

Everyone who was dying because of me.

A child stared as we passed—couldn't have been more than six, with hollow cheeks and eyes too large for his face. His ribs showed through his thin shirt. He clutched a piece of dried bread like it was treasure, protecting it with both hands.

Through the bond, I felt Renata's reaction to my emotions. Guilt. Anger. Defensive justification. All of it hitting me like waves, making my own feelings amplify and reflect back at her.

I stumbled again, and this time Nalla caught my arm, her grip firm.

"The bond?" she asked.

I nodded, not trusting my voice. Sweat beaded on my forehead despite the cold.

"We need to get you somewhere quiet. Somewhere you can build those mental walls without her constantly breaking them down." She guided me toward a larger tent near the center of camp, her hand steady on my elbow. "This will be yours. It's not much, but it's private. Guarded, obviously—you're a hostage, after all. But comfortable enough."

The tent was simple but clean. A bedroll, a small table, a basin of water that reflected candlelight. Luxury compared to what most of the camp had.

"Thank you," I managed, my voice hoarse.

"Don't thank me yet." Nalla dismissed her commanders with a gesture. They filed out, leaving us alone. "We need to talk. About her. About what she's become. About what you're willing to do to stop her."

"I'm not here to betray her."

"Aren't you?" Nalla studied me. "You volunteered as a hostage. You left her when she clearly didn't want you to go. That suggests you don't entirely agree with what she's doing."

"I'm here," I said carefully, choosing each word, "because it was the only way to prevent a war. Because people are dying and someone needed to do something. That doesn't mean I'm working against her."

"But you're not working with her either." Nalla sat on the ground, cross-legged, gesturing for me to do the same. "Tell me honestly—do you think what she did was right? Bringing you back? Performing forbidden magic? Killing council members?"

I wanted to say yes immediately. Wanted to defend Renata, to justify everything she'd done in the name of love.

But the honest answer was more complicated. More tangled.

"I don't know," I admitted finally. "I'm grateful to be alive. But the cost—" I gestured at the tent walls, at the camp beyond, at the sounds of suffering that filtered through canvas. "The cost is everywhere. In every starving child. In every crop that failed. In reality itself breaking down."

"So you regret it."

"I regret the consequences. I don't know if I regret being alive." I met her eyes. "Ask me again in a week."

Nalla nodded slowly. "Fair enough. But understand this—we can't wait a week. The famine is accelerating. People are dying faster every day. We need solutions now."

"I'm not a solution. I'm just leverage."

"You're more than that." Nalla leaned forward, her voice dropping. "You're bound to her. You feel what she feels. That means you can influence her in ways we can't. Make her see reason. Make her understand she needs to fix this."

"Or what? You'll kill me?"

"Or we'll all die anyway." Nalla's voice was flat, matter-of-fact. "Starvation. Disease. War. Take your pick. Your resurrection broke something fundamental. If it doesn't get fixed—if she doesn't fix it—there won't be anything left to fight over. She is not the Renata who wanted to live in the sun any longer. If you can't get through to her—"

She stood, brushing dust from her pants. "Think about it. Think about what you're willing to do to save people who didn't choose this." She moved toward the tent entrance, then paused. "Oh, and your DirgeWolf friend? He can stay with you. But he's being watched too. Just so you know."

She left, the tent flap swishing closed behind her, and I let out a breath I hadn't realized I'd been holding.

Valdic settled near the tent entrance, his skeletal frame folding into a surprisingly comfortable position. "Well," he observed. "That was ominous."

"Everything is ominous now." I lay back on the bedroll, feeling exhaustion I hadn't experienced since dying. My body still didn't quite remember how to be alive. Every movement felt strange, like I was operating a puppet instead of inhabiting flesh. My joints didn't move quite right, muscles responding a half-second too slow.

Through the bond, Renata's presence pressed constantly. Fear. Loneliness. Desperate need to know I was okay.

I'm fine, I tried to send, projecting the feeling across the tether. Just tired.

Her relief hit like a wave, crashing over me, and I gasped at the intensity. My chest tightened, breath catching.

"She's not making this easy, is she?" Valdic observed.

"She doesn't know how." I pressed my hands to my face, trying to center myself. Trying to find where I ended and she began. "The bond is too new. Too raw. Neither of us knows how to manage it yet."

"So you suffer until you figure it out."

"Basically."

Valdic was quiet for a moment. Then: "There's something you should know. About what she did while you were dead. What she became."

Something cold moved through my chest. "What do you mean?"

"She didn't just grieve normally. She didn't just cry and rage and eventually accept." Valdic's eyes were gentle but uncompromising. "She kept your body. Preserved it. Talked to it like you were still alive."

"I know. She told me—"

"She didn't tell you everything." Valdic shifted uncomfortably, claws scraping against canvas. "She laid with your corpse, Nokoa. Kissed you. Touched you. Convinced herself you were just sleeping. That you'd wake up if she just waited long enough."

The words landed like a stone dropped into still water, and I felt the ripples moving outward through my whole body.

"She was just grieving in her own way," I protested weakly. "She didn't—"

"She did," Valdic said, his voice soft but insistent. "I saw it. I tried to stop her, tried to make her see reality, but she couldn't. Or wouldn't. The crown had her so deep in delusion that she genuinely believed you were breathing. That your heart was beating. She was going to make love to your corpse, Nokoa. Cressa interrupted her."

I said nothing. There was nothing to say. I stared at the canvas ceiling and let the information sit there between us, taking up space.

Minutes passed. Maybe longer.

"I need air," I said at last, and the words came out flat, scraped hollow.

I stumbled out of the tent before Valdic could respond, into the camp proper. Soldiers watched me warily as I passed, hands moving to weapons. Children stared. Everyone knew what I was—the resurrected hostage, the Bone Queen's weakness, the thing that shouldn't exist.

I found myself at the camp's edge, staring back toward the Bone Court. The skull castle loomed in the distance, impossibly large, impossibly wrong. Its eye sockets seemed to watch me even from here. Somewhere inside, Renata was feeling everything I felt. My horror. My confusion. My dawning realization that maybe I didn't know her as well as I'd thought.

That maybe the person who'd brought me back wasn't the person I'd died loving.

The pain that hit me through the bond was enormous. Like every nerve in my body igniting at once, white-hot and consuming. I collapsed to my knees, gasping, tears streaming down my face. My vision blurred.

"Nokoa?" A hand on my shoulder—the gray-bearded commander. His grip was surprisingly gentle. "You alright?"

"No," I gasped between ragged breaths. "The bond. I hurt her."

"It must be a heavy burden." He helped me stand, supporting most of my weight. "Come on. Let's get you back to your tent. You need to learn to control this before it kills one or both of you."

He guided me back through the camp. I barely registered the journey, too focused on the gaping wound where Renata's presence sat. On the pain I'd caused her by reacting to what Valdic had told me. On the feedback loop of suffering we couldn't escape.

Back in the tent, Valdic took one look at me and said nothing. Which was somehow worse than anything he could have said.

I sat on the bedroll. Didn't lie down. Just sat there, elbows on knees, looking at my hands. The stumps of my pinkies. The witch rune marks that had sunk into my skin, permanent now, glowing faintly when I looked at them sideways.

"I know you're waiting for me to say something," I said eventually.

"I'm not waiting for anything," Valdic replied. "I'm just here."

We sat like that for a while. The camp moved around us—voices, the smell of cooking fires, a child's laugh that cut strangely through the grief.

"She loved me," I said finally. "That much I believe."

"Yes."

"She just—" I stopped. Tried again. "The crown twisted it. Or maybe it was already twisted and the crown just gave it permission." I pressed my palms flat against my thighs. "I don't know how to hold both things. That she loved me and that she—"

I couldn't finish the sentence.

"You don't have to hold them both at once," Valdic said. "You just have to carry them."

I thought about that for a long time.

"I should write to her," I said at last. "Try to put words to this. Even if she never gets them."

"Letters won't reach her. We're being watched too closely."

"I know. But I'll write them anyway." I looked around for paper and found none. "Do you think Nalla would give me writing materials?"

"Probably. If only to see what you write." Valdic stood, stretching. "I'll ask. You rest. Build those mental walls. Learn to separate your pain from hers."

He left, and I was alone with the bond.

I focused on it, really focused for the first time since waking. Tried to understand what Renata had created. What bound us.

The tether glowed faintly when I looked at it with something other than my eyes. Not physical sight—something deeper. Soul sight, maybe. It connected my chest to hers, pulsing with every heartbeat, carrying emotions back and forth like a river that never stopped flowing. Not thoughts—I couldn't hear what she was thinking, couldn't see through her eyes—but feelings. Raw, unfiltered, impossible to ignore.

And carved into my bones—actually into them, visible when I looked down at my arms with that same strange sight—were witch runes. The same ones Alaira had painted on my skin during the ritual. They'd sunk deeper than surface. They'd become part of my structure. Part of what I was.

I watched them glow faintly as Renata's emotions shifted. Brighten when she felt strongly. Dim when she went numb.

I was marked. Permanently. Magically. Changed at the most fundamental level.

Not just resurrected. Transformed.

I lay there, feeling her presence through the bond, learning the shape of our curse. The way her fear manifested as tightness in my chest. The way her love felt like being crushed. The way her desperation made my bones ache.

Learning what it meant to be bound to someone you loved and feared in equal measure.

Learning what it meant to be alive when maybe death had been better.

Valdic returned with paper, ink, and a wary expression. "Nalla agreed. But she's keeping copies of everything you write."

"I don't care." I took the materials and began writing.

Renata,

I'm sorry for what I felt. I was shocked and angry when Valdic told me about the things you did while I was dead. I took it out on you through the bond. That was wrong. Cruel. You didn't deserve it.

But I need you to understand—what Valdic told me, what you did with my body—I don't know how to process that. Don't know how to reconcile the person who'd do that with the person I fell in love with.

Maybe they're the same person. Maybe love and obsession are closer than I realized. Maybe I'm just naive about what people are capable of when they're grieving.

I don't know.

What I do know is that we're bound now. Permanently. And we need to figure out how to live with that. How to be together without destroying each other.

Because right now, loving you hurts. And being loved by you hurts. And I don't know if that's the curse or just the truth about what we've become.

Write back if you can. Tell me how to fix this. Tell me anything.

I love you. I think. I'm not sure anymore if what we have is love or just trauma wearing love's face.

But I'm here. I'm alive. That's what you wanted.

I hope it was worth the cost.

—Nokoa

I stared at the letter, knowing Renata would never see it. Knowing Nalla would read it and use whatever she learned against us.

But I needed to write it anyway. Needed to put words to the confusion in my head. To the tangle of emotions I couldn't sort through alone.

Through the bond, I felt Renata experiencing my emotions as I wrote. Felt her recognize the pain and confusion and complicated love that I couldn't express any other way.

Felt her respond with her own pain. Her own confusion. Her own desperate, broken love that had become something neither of us recognized.

The gap between us was growing despite the bond. Or maybe because of it. Because we could feel each other so clearly now that there was no room for illusion. No room for pretending this was a happy ending.

Just the raw, honest truth.

We'd saved each other and damned each other in the same breath.

And now we had to live with that.

Valdic settled beside me again, his weight making the bedroll shift. "You know," he said quietly, "I've been thinking. About her. About what she became."

"And?"

"And I realized—she didn't just become a monster for you. She became a monster because of you. Because losing you broke something in her that can't be fixed." His eyes were sad, old. "She loved you so much it destroyed her. That's not your fault. But it is your reality now."

"So what do I do?"

"Survive," Valdic said simply. "Learn to love her despite what she's become. Or don't. But either way, survive. Because you're all each other has left."

"That's bleak."

"Yes." A pause. "But it's honest."

Outside, the sounds of the camp continued—the suffering that was my resurrection's price, paid by people who'd never asked for any of this.

And through it all, the bond pulsed. Carrying her pain and mine back and forth in an endless loop.

I closed my eyes and tried to build my walls higher.

Tried to find somewhere inside myself that was just mine.

Tried to survive.

Chapter Twelve

THE HOLLOW SPACE

Renata

The first full day without Nokoa felt like missing a limb.

I woke alone in my chambers—when had I come here? I didn't remember leaving the catacombs—and the absence hit me like a physical blow, stealing my breath. Through the bond, I could feel him in the outer cities' camp. Distant but present. Alive but hurting.

Always hurting.

Because of me. Because my emotions—any emotions—translated into pain for him across the bond. Every feeling I had became a weapon turned against the person I loved.

I tried to feel nothing. Pushed everything down into that cold, empty space I'd been carving out inside myself. But even numbness had a weight, and I felt that weight travel across the tether, felt it register as a different kind of ache in him—hollow and wrong.

There was no winning. No position that didn't hurt.

A spike of pain lanced through my chest—not mine. His. Something had happened at the camp. Fear? Anger? I couldn't tell, just felt the sharp echo of it hitting my sternum, driving the air from my lungs.

I tried to send... what? Comfort? Love? But even the attempt to feel those things made the pain worse. I felt him convulse on the other end, felt his agony feedback into my own chest, felt the loop start to spiral—

I slammed it down. Went completely numb. The bond went quiet, muted like a scream underwater, and I felt his relief even through the suppression.

Better to feel nothing than to hurt him with feeling.

My hands throbbed where the pinkies used to be. Phantom pain, though it didn't feel phantom—it felt like the stumps were still there, still screaming, nerve endings firing signals for fingers that no longer existed. Through the bond, I knew Nokoa's stumps hurt too, the severed bones aching in mirror image.

Our shared sacrifice. Our permanent mark.

The bandages needed changing. I unwrapped them slowly, trying not to think too hard about what I was seeing. The wounds had healed—witch magic saw to that—but healing wrong. The flesh sealed over cleanly enough, but underneath I could see something moving. Not infection. Magic. The severed bones trying to regrow, stopped by the spell that had bound them into powder. Little pulses of light beneath skin.

They'd never grow back. That was part of the price.

I rewrapped them with shaking hands and tried not to think about it. About all the prices I'd paid. All the prices still coming due.

A servant had left food outside my door. The bread had gone stale, hard as stone. I picked at it without interest, managed three bites before my stomach rebelled—and before the mold started, green fuzz spreading from my fingertips outward across the crust, the corruption touching everything it could reach.

He was hungry. I could feel that through the bond. Not my hunger—his. A hollow gnawing sensation that wasn't mine but was, transmitted across the tether until I couldn't tell whose body was whose.

The Bone Council had summoned me. Not requested. Summoned.

I was growing increasingly annoyed with being ordered around.

Through the bond, I felt Nokoa's spike of concern when I stood. Felt him wonder what was happening, his worry bleeding across as wordless alarm. I tried to project calm but that just made his chest hurt, so I went numb again and felt his frustrated confusion at the sudden emptiness.

This was how we communicated now. Guessing. Interpreting. Never truly understanding.

The council chamber felt colder than usual. My breath misted in the air.

Ancelin sat rigid on his throne, his serpentine dreadlocks unusually still. Maxin looked worse than yesterday—not worse. Skeletal. His transformation was accelerating. I could see bone through skin in places now, his flesh thinning like paper worn too thin. His eyes had sunken deep into their sockets.

He was dying.

Praxis watched from his throne with those crimson eyes, a slight smile at his lips.

"Hollow Queen," Ancelin said, the sarcasm thick enough to taste. "How gracious of you to join us."

I didn't respond. Just stood there, feeling Nokoa's distant presence like an anchor. He was afraid. For me? Of me? I couldn't tell.

"We have demands," Ancelin continued, standing. His joints ground audibly. "First: remove the spectral guards. Their presence destabilizes the magical infrastructure."

"No."

"Second," his voice hardened, "you submit to binding. You're too powerful, too erratic. You need oversight."

"Also no."

"Third—" Ancelin moved closer, footsteps echoing. "—you answer for your crimes. You murdered two council members. You should be imprisoned. Possibly executed."

"Feel free to try."

Emotion spiked through the bond—Nokoa's fear this time, sharp and sudden. I tried to project reassurance but that translated to pain on his end, stabbing into his chest. His fear intensified, which fed mine, which hurt him worse—

The spiral was starting. I could feel it building, that terrible feedback loop where his emotions triggered mine which triggered his which—

I forced myself into complete emptiness. Cold. Blank. Nothing.

The bond went quiet but wrong. Dead quiet. The kind of silence that screamed.

Through it, I felt Nokoa's new fear—fear of the numbness. Fear of the hollow space where I used to be.

"You've become a monster," Ancelin observed quietly. "Do you even see it anymore?"

I looked at my hands. Saw them skeletal-thin, black veins spreading up from the stumps where my pinkies used to be. Saw the way my skin had started to look translucent, like I was fading from the inside out. I could see the bones in my fingers, the tendons moving beneath paper-thin flesh.

When had that happened?

"I've become powerful enough to protect what's mine," I said. My voice sounded distant, like someone else was speaking through my mouth. "Powerful enough to make the changes every past ruler talked of making."

"You've become powerful enough to destroy us all," Maxin interjected. His voice was tired, barely more than a whisper. "Including yourself. Including him."

That got my attention. "What do you mean?"

"The bond you created." Maxin pulled out one of Alaira's journals with shaking hands. "It's not just a tether. It's a magical paradox. Two souls occupying space meant for one. If it breaks—through death or forced separation—the accumulated energy has to discharge somewhere."

"Discharge how?"

"Violently." Maxin's fingers traced lines in the journal. "Queen Oriana was the only other brave enough to try this, and that ended with disaster for her lover and the land. It's how we ended up underground. The wasteland you see? That was her attempt at resurrection."

My hands started shaking, tremors I couldn't control. "You're lying."

"I'm trying to make you understand what you did." Maxin's expression was worn through with grief, old and tired. "You didn't just bring him back. You turned both of you into walking weapons. If either of you dies now, the magical backlash could kill everyone within a mile radius. Maybe more."

"So what do you want from me?" I asked flatly.

"Let us help." Ancelin's voice had lost some of its edge. "Work with us instead of against us. Let us find a way to stabilize the bond. To fix what's breaking. The Hollow Crown whispers to you—we know how that feels. We've lived with it for centuries."

"I don't need help."

"Yes," Maxin stated firmly, his voice finding strength. "You do. Look at me, Renata."

I did. Saw how much he'd deteriorated overnight. Saw his form collapsing back toward what it should have become centuries ago. Flesh turning to dust.

"This is what your corruption does," he explained. "The bond, the resurrection, the witch runes—all of it is breaking down the magical balance that kept us immortal. We're all dying. And the famine is accelerating. The outer cities will run out of food in days. Nokoa is sitting in a camp full of people who blame him for their starvation."

"Let me teach you," he offered. "Properly. The real witch runes, not the corrupted ones. Maybe if we use them correctly, we can slow the damage. Buy time."

"Why would you help me?"

"Because I helped create the crown. Helped corrupt the runes in the first place." Maxin's voice was hollow. "Maybe teaching you to use them properly is my penance. Maybe it's just survival instinct."

I looked at Ancelin. "And you?"

His jaw tightened. "I want justice for Bahni. For Fatin. But more than that..." He paused. "I want to know if there's anything left in you worth saving."

They don't trust you, Oriana whispered. They don't think you're strong enough to make the changes that need to happen.

"I have to go," I said abruptly, turning toward the exit.

We'll never abandon you, Lyanna added.

"We're not done—" Ancelin started.

"Yes, we are." I moved toward the doorway. "Handle the famine yourselves. Handle the outer cities. Handle everything. I have more important things to worry about."

"More important than thousands starving?" Maxin's voice followed me.

I stopped at the threshold. Turned back. "Yes."

The word hung in the air between us.

"Then we've lost you completely," Ancelin said quietly.

I didn't disagree.

Praxis caught up with me in the corridor outside, stepping out of an alcove without sound.

"That was well done," he observed. "Establishing priorities. Refusing to be controlled. Very efficient."

"What do you want?"

"To clarify something Maxin mentioned." Praxis fell into step beside me. "About the bond's volatility. The explosive potential if one of you dies."

"What about it?"

"He's not wrong. But he didn't tell you everything." Praxis's voice lowered. "The bond doesn't just threaten others if it breaks. It threatens the entire magical structure of this realm. The prison. The crown. Everything built on witch runes."

I stopped walking. "Explain."

"The bond uses corrupted witch runes to fuse your souls. The prison uses corrupted witch runes to contain the bone god. The crown uses corrupted witch runes to harvest memories." Praxis gestured at the glowing walls, the pulsing veins of magic. "Everything is connected. Everything runs on the same foundation—the Goddess of Fate's divine gift, twisted into something it was never meant to be."

"So?"

"So if the bond breaks catastrophically, it doesn't just explode. It inverts. Flips the magic inside out. Every witch rune in the realm would invert simultaneously. The prison becomes a door. The crown becomes a key. Binding becomes unbinding."

My mouth went dry. "You're saying if one of us dies—"

"The bone god goes free. Immediately. Inevitably." Praxis smiled, and it was the smile of someone who'd been waiting centuries for this moment. "That's why I'm invested in keeping you both alive. Not altruism. Pure self-interest. Because when he breaks free, I want to be on the winning side."

"You need to control that bond," he continued. "The feedback loops are going to get worse. Eventually you won't be able to stop them at all. They'll spiral until one of you passes out or dies."

"How do I stop them?"

"By shutting it off." Praxis turned to leave, already fading into the corridor's dim light. "You have to become more like us and shut yourself off."

He disappeared, leaving me alone with that knowledge.

I stood there in the corridor, feeling Nokoa's presence through the bond. Feeling his fear. His exhaustion. His complicated, painful love.

The longer I thought about him, the harder my chest ached. Not my chest—both our chests. The pain bouncing back and forth.

The bond pulsed between us, carrying pain in both directions, creating loops that grew worse with each iteration. His fear fed mine fed his fed mine until I couldn't breathe, couldn't think, couldn't—

I collapsed against the wall, gasping. Stone cold against my back. Across the bond, I felt Nokoa collapse too, both of us brought down by the very thing meant to keep us connected.

This was our eternity. This was what I'd created.

A curse that looked like love. A bond that felt like drowning. A connection that was killing us both one feedback loop at a time.

And somewhere, deep in the catacombs, something laughed.

Not the crown's voices. Not Praxis's amusement.

Something older. Deep and resonant, vibrating through stone, satisfied that its tools were sharpening themselves exactly as planned.

I pushed myself upright. Forced my breathing to steady. In through my nose, out through my mouth.

One breath. Two. Three.

I forced myself into numbness again. Into that cold, empty space where I was learning to live.

The space where monsters were made.

The space where love went to die.

Through the bond, Nokoa's presence flickered—afraid, hurting, alive.

Still alive.

I held onto that and didn't let go.

Act Two

Bound

Chapter Thirteen

The Stolen Weapon

Nokoa

The outer cities camp reeked of desperation and smoke. I pressed my palm against the canvas wall of Nalla's tent, steadying myself as another wave of nausea rolled through my chest. My fingers throbbed—three of them broken from this morning's episode, splinted now with strips of cloth and wooden fragments Valdic had scrounged from somewhere. The makeshift bindings dug into swollen knuckles, a constant reminder of how fragile this resurrected body had become.

The witch runes burned under my skin. They always burned, stealing pieces of what I felt and leaving only hollow echoes behind.

"You look like death," Nalla said from behind me.

I turned, forcing my face into something that might pass for calm. She stood in the tent's entrance, backlit by the failing afternoon sun, holding something wrapped in oiled leather. The camp sprawled behind her—cooking fires sending thin ribbons of smoke into a grey sky, children with hollow eyes watching us with the alertness of prey animals. The wind carried ash and the sour tang of unwashed bodies pressed too close together.

"I've been told," I managed.

She moved past me, setting the bundle on the low table that served as her war council. Her movements were careful, reverent almost. Whatever she carried mattered. The leather creaked as she set it down, and dust motes swirled in the shaft of light cutting through the tent's gap.

"Sit before you fall," she said.

I sat. The camp spun for a moment before settling, my vision blurring at the edges. Through the tent's opening, I could see guards watching me—always watching. I was their prize and their burden. The dead man walking who wouldn't stay dead. The oath-sworn blade who broke his oath by dying in the first place.

"You want to fight her?" Nalla asked, her voice cutting through my haze. "Then stop starving and start thinking."

She unwrapped the leather slowly. Cloth fell away in layers, each one darker than the last, until bone gleamed in the dim light. The air seemed to contract around it, growing colder.

A weapon. Long as my forearm, carved from what looked like a single piece of bone. Not shaped like any blade I'd seen—more like a dagger made by someone who'd forgotten what daggers were supposed to look like. Runes covered its surface, etched so deep they looked like veins. Not witch runes, not exactly. Older. Cruder. But powerful in a way that made my teeth ache and my broken fingers pulse in their bindings.

"We took this during the coronation," Nalla said. She didn't touch it, just gestured with careful distance. "When everything went to chaos and you died and she brought you back and the guardians sealed themselves away. There was a moment—just a moment—when the bone court was vulnerable."

I stared at the weapon, unable to look away from those ancient runes. "You stole from a guardian tomb."

"From the guardian tomb. The deep one, where they sleep." She finally picked it up, and the runes along its surface flickered with pale light. The illumination cast strange shadows across her face, hollowing her cheeks. "We didn't understand what it was then. Just knew it felt important. Heavy. Like carrying a piece of the world's skeleton."

The bone in her hand pulsed. Once. Twice. In rhythm with my heartbeat.

My stomach twisted. Wrong. This was wrong in ways I couldn't articulate.

"It lets us use death magic," she said quietly. "Not like her. Not like the queen with her spectral guardians and her bone crown. But enough. Enough to fight back."

I wanted to look away from it. Couldn't. The runes seemed to writhe in the flickering light. "You brought me here to show me a weapon."

"I brought you here to tell you why we're using it." Nalla set the blade down, and the relief I felt when she released it told me everything I needed to know about how wrong it was. The temperature in the tent seemed to rise slightly, as if the weapon itself had been leeching warmth from the air. "We're not rebelling for destruction, Nokoa. We're not trying to burn the world down."

"If you use that," I said quietly, each word careful, "I'll stop you."

Nalla turned, her expression hardening. "You and what army?"

"Me." The word came out stronger than I felt, and for the first time since waking, I felt like myself.

She studied me for a long moment, taking in my splinted fingers, my gaunt frame, the way I couldn't quite sit up straight anymore. Then something in her face softened. "We don't want to fight you or anyone else. We want her to honor her promise."

The words hit different than I expected. Not anger in them. Not rage. Just tired, disappointed truth weighted with months of betrayal.

"What promise?" But even as I asked, memory stirred. Hazy, from before. Before I died. Before everything broke.

"Fair tithe reforms." Nalla pulled a second item from her belt—a piece of parchment, folded and refolded so many times the creases had worn soft as cloth. She spread it on the table beside the bone weapon, smoothing it with trembling fingers. "She negotiated this. Before your death. You were there."

I was.

The memory came back in pieces, like light through fractured glass. Renata across a table from outer cities representatives, her grey eyes bright with conviction and purpose. Me standing behind her chair, hand on her shoulder, feeling the slight tremor of nerves she hid so well. The weight of the moment pressing down on both of us—her first real act as queen-to-be, my first real test as her sworn blade.

She'd promised them everything.

No children taken for tithe. Volunteers only, and paid fairly for their heartfire and marrow. No one forced against their will. No one stolen in the night. No more raids that left families screaming. No more quotas that couldn't be met without sacrifice. No more watching your neighbors waste away because the bone council demanded their life essence to keep immortal bodies animated.

"She was brilliant," I said, and my voice came out rough, scraped raw. "She saw the system was broken and she wanted to fix it."

"She did." Nalla's finger traced the words on the parchment with something close to reverence. I recognized Renata's handwriting in the signature. Careful loops, the way she made her R's with that extra flourish. The ink had faded but the words remained clear. "She promised us this. We trusted her."

"And then I died."

"And then you died," Nalla agreed, and the weight of those words settled between us like stones. "And she brought you back. And then she forgot us."

The tent felt too small suddenly. Too close. I could smell the bone weapon—cold and ancient and wrong, like graves opened too early. Could smell the smoke from cooking fires outside, burning wood they shouldn't be burning because there wasn't enough left. Could smell my own decay, subtle but persistent, the resurrection magic slowly failing despite Renata's rituals. Rot underneath everything. Death beneath life.

"She's not enforcing the reforms," I said. Not a question.

"She's not enforcing anything. The tithe is worse than before." Nalla's voice cracked. "Children still taken. People still dragged from their homes in the dark. We send complaints through official channels and they disappear into the bone court's depths. We send representatives to petition her and they don't return." Her jaw tightened. "She promised, Nokoa. You were there. You heard her. You stood beside her when she made that promise and you were proud of her."

I had been. So proud. Watching her negotiate, watching her care about people who the bone court had forgotten, people she had no reason to remember.

She'd worn a yellow dress that day. Bright as sunshine, bright as hope. She'd told me after that she wanted them to see warmth when they looked at her, not the grey stone of the bone court's caves or the black silk of mourning.

When had she stopped wearing yellow?

When had the black consumed everything?

"What happened to her?" Nalla asked, and it wasn't accusatory. Just sad. Just bewildered. "We trusted her. We believed in her. And then she—"

"Became queen," I finished, the words bitter on my tongue. "Wore the crown. Lost me. Got me back. And somewhere in all that, she forgot."

"Forgot, or chose not to remember?"

The question hung between us.

"Don't act as though you don't understand what the Hollow Crown does," I said, but even I heard the uncertainty in my voice. Did I know anymore? Did anyone know where Renata ended and the crown began?

Outside, a child called out—high and thin, crying for their mother. The sound cut through me, sharp as the bone weapon on the table. Nalla glanced toward it, something breaking in her expression, then looked back at me.

"That's why we fight," she said quietly. "Not to destroy her. Not even to kill her, though some of us wouldn't mind trying." She picked up the bone weapon again, and this time I forced myself to watch as the runes flickered with sickly light. "We fight because she made us a promise. Because we trusted her. Because we still remember who she was, even if she doesn't."

"You and I both know she doesn't realize what's happening to her."

"Then help her."

"I'm trying." My voice broke on the word. "I'm trying, Nalla. But every time I think of her, every time I miss her, we both pay for it. I can't get close to her. The bond punishes us for wanting each other. And she's so far away, lost in those caves, and I'm so—" I gestured at myself. At the broken fingers, at the witch runes burning under my skin, at the slow rot of resurrection, at everything I'd become. "I'm not exactly in a position to help anyone."

Nalla studied me for a long moment. Then she wrapped the bone weapon back in its leather, careful and slow, each fold deliberate. The temperature warmed as she covered it. "We're not your enemies, Nokoa. We never were. We just want what she promised us. Fair treatment. Safety. A chance to volunteer our heartfire instead of having it ripped away in the night. That's all."

"She promised," I repeated. The memory was solid now. Real. Her voice across that table, steady and sure: No child will be taken. No one forced. You have my word. The conviction in her eyes, the set of her shoulders. She'd believed it. Meant it. "I remember. I was there."

"Then remind her," Nalla said, and there was a desperate hope in her voice that made my chest ache. "If you love her—and I know you do, I can see it eating you alive—remind her who she was. Remind her what she promised. Before she becomes something that can't be reminded of anything."

She left me alone with that. With the memory of Renata in her yellow dress, promising to be better, promising to remember, promising to care about the people ground beneath the bone council's heel.

I sat in the tent as the sun failed outside. As the camp sounds changed from day to evening—cooking, quiet conversations, someone singing a lullaby to a child who wouldn't stop crying. The melody was off-key but tender. My broken fingers ached, a dull throb that matched my pulse. The witch runes under my skin pulsed with a heat that had nothing to do with fever and everything to do with resurrection magic slowly unraveling.

And I thought of her.

Couldn't help it. Thought of her grey eyes across that negotiation table, bright with purpose. Thought of how proud I'd been, standing behind her chair, watching her fight for people who meant nothing to her yet. Thought of the way she'd turned to me after and asked, "Did I do well?" like she needed my approval, like my opinion mattered more than the world. The slight smile that had curved her lips when I'd told her she was magnificent.

The bond punished me for it. Sharp pain lanced through my skull, from temple to temple, like someone driving iron spikes through bone. I gasped, pressed my splinted fingers to my forehead despite the agony it caused, and rode it out. Somewhere, in the bone court's depths, Renata was probably doubled over too. Paying the same price. Both of us suffering because I couldn't stop loving her long enough to breathe.

When the pain faded—never gone, just manageable—I pulled out parchment and ink. Nalla had left them for me. My broken fingers made it difficult, but I managed. Careful letters, each one deliberate, ink smudging where my hand trembled.

Renata,

I remember the day you negotiated with the outer cities. You wore yellow. You promised them fair treatment—no children taken, volunteers paid, no one forced. You were magnificent. I was so proud of you.

They haven't forgotten that promise. They're not rebelling to destroy you. They're rebelling because you forgot them.

Please remember. Please. They need you to remember who you were.

Who we both were.

—N

I folded it, the parchment crinkling in my damaged hands, and called for one of Hivro's butterflies—purple wings, already dead, already serving as messenger between worlds. It landed on my finger light as ash, delicate and wrong. I pressed the letter to its body and watched it dissolve into the insect's form, message and messenger becoming one.

"Find her," I whispered to the creature that couldn't hear me. "Remind her."

The butterfly lifted off, wings catching the last of the daylight streaming through the tent's gap, and disappeared toward the bone court's distant caves.

I sat back, exhausted. My resurrection burned through energy faster than I could replace it. Every movement cost more than it should. Every breath was work.

But I'd reminded her. Or tried to. Maybe this time, she'd remember. Maybe this time, the crown wouldn't eat the message before it reached whatever was left of her beneath the bone and whispers.

Maybe.

Outside, the camp settled into night. Guards changed shifts with quiet efficiency. Fires banked low to conserve precious fuel. Someone's baby finally stopped crying, leaving only the crackle of flames and low murmured conversations.

She'd believed in fairness once. In justice. In keeping her word to people who had nothing but her promise.

I had to believe she still could.

Even if the crown had eaten every reason why she cared.

Chapter Fourteen

The Butterfly Letter

Renata

The butterfly found me in my chambers, wings the color of dying embers.

It landed on my windowsill without sound, already dead, already serving something beyond its original purpose. Orange and red patterns swirled across its wings—colors that felt important somehow, though I couldn't remember why. The air shifted around it, carrying the faint scent of old paper and dust.

I watched it for a moment, this impossible messenger. Behind me, the room stretched out in shades of grey and black. My chambers. My prison. I couldn't recall when I'd stopped decorating them, when I'd stripped away everything that wasn't necessary. The bed was there because I needed to sleep. The desk because I needed to work. Everything else had been removed, piece by piece, until only function remained.

The butterfly's wings trembled. Once. Twice.

When I touched it, the wing dissolved into ash and parchment. The message uncurled in my palm, written in a script that shifted and changed as I tried to read it. Some words in the common tongue. Others in languages I'd never learned but somehow recognized. Half the letter was prophecy, wrapped in metaphor, impossible to parse.

Three will wake, it said, clear as daylight in one section. Then the words blurred, reformed. Fire first. Then: Remember who you were.

The rest was beautiful nonsense—poetry written by someone who'd seen too many futures at once and couldn't separate them anymore. Hivro. It had to be. The butterfly oracle, sending her cryptic warnings from whatever corner of the bone court she'd retreated to after Nokoa's death.

"Hivro meddles," Oriana's voice drifted through the hollow crown. "She always meddles."

I pressed my fingers to my temples, feeling the crown's weight. It had grown heavier lately. Or maybe I'd grown weaker. Hard to tell when exhaustion lived in my bones.

I set the butterfly message aside. Within minutes, I'd forgotten about it entirely.

The knock came an hour later. One of the rattlemaids—I couldn't remember her name, didn't try to—entered with her eyes downcast. Her joints clattered softly, like dice rolled gently across stone. She held another letter, plain parchment, folded simply.

"From outside, Hollow Queen," she said, her voice low. "Smuggled through the outer cities network."

I took it without touching her skeletal hand. She left quickly, relief evident in the speed of her retreat.

The parchment felt real in a way Hivro's prophecy hadn't. Solid. Present. Warm, almost, as if it still carried heat from the hands that had held it. I unfolded it carefully, and his handwriting struck me like a physical blow.

Renata,

I remember the day you negotiated with the outer cities. You wore yellow. You promised them fair treatment—no children taken, volunteers paid, no one forced. You were magnificent. I was so proud of you.

They haven't forgotten that promise. They're not rebelling to destroy you. They're rebelling because you forgot them.

Please remember. Please. They need you to remember who you were.

Who we both were.

—N

I read it three times. Then four. Each word sinking in slowly, like water through stone. My fingers traced the shape of his signature, feeling the slight indent where his quill had pressed too hard.

Yellow. I'd worn yellow?

The memory surfaced, distant and unclear. A dress. Bright, impractical. The kind of thing someone wore when they wanted to be seen, when they wanted to represent hope instead of authority. I could almost see it—fabric the color of sunshine, catching light in ways that made me feel warm. Had I really owned something so bright?

And a negotiation. Across a table from someone. Multiple someones. People with hollow eyes and desperate hope. I'd promised them something. Fair treatment. Reforms to the tithe system. No children taken. Volunteers only.

"I promised," I said aloud, testing the words. They felt strange in my mouth, like a language I used to speak fluently but had mostly forgotten.

The memory felt real. Solid. I could see myself sitting there, could see Nokoa standing behind my chair with his hand on my shoulder. Could feel his pride radiating through that touch, the way he'd looked at me after like I'd done something magnificent instead of just basic decency. The warmth of it. The certainty that I was doing right.

They were starving. The outer cities. Dying under the weight of tithes they couldn't afford to pay. And I'd promised to fix it.

But when? Before coronation? Before Nokoa died? Before I wore the crown? The timeline fractured in my mind, pieces scattering, refusing to form a coherent sequence. I knew I'd made that promise. Could see it happening. But couldn't place it in the story of my life, couldn't connect it to the person I was now.

Who was she? The woman in yellow who cared about fair treatment and kept her word?

I folded Nokoa's letter carefully, pressing my thumb against the crease until it was sharp and perfect. His handwriting. Proof that he existed. Proof that I hadn't imagined him entirely.

The thought of him sent warmth through my chest. Not the bond's pain—that would come later. Just warmth. The knowledge that he remembered me, remembered her, the woman in yellow who promised things.

I pulled out fresh parchment. Dipped my quill in ink. Started to write.

Nokoa,

I remember—

But did I? Did I really remember, or was I just echoing what he'd told me? The memory felt slippery. The yellow dress. The negotiation. The promise. All of it viewed through thick glass, distorted and unclear.

I started again.

Nokoa,

I want to honor that promise. I want to enforce the reforms. Tell them to wait for me. Tell them I haven't forgotten.

My hand moved to seal it. To send it.

Pain lanced through my skull. Sharp and sudden. I gasped, dropped the quill. Ink spattered across the parchment, black bleeding into white.

The crown's grip tightened. A warning. A reminder.

"You have so much to manage already," Oriana said. "So many burdens on your shoulders. The outer cities can wait."

"You can't save everyone," Alaric added. "Some must suffer so others may thrive."

The pain faded to an ache. I stared at the ruined letter, at the ink-stained promise I'd almost made. My hands trembled.

I pulled out new parchment. Tried again.

Nokoa,

The only time I feel like myself is in my dreams. I dream of us at the cottage. When I'm awake I still feel like I'm dreaming. Like I'm outside of myself, watching what should be my body move. Like I'm in a prison cell, and someone else is wearing my face.

I don't remember the yellow dress. I don't remember the promise. But I remember you. I remember how proud you looked when you thought I did well. I remember wanting to deserve that pride.

If I promised them something, I should honor it. I know that. But I can't remember what I promised, and I can't reach through this fog to find the woman who made that promise.

Help me remember. Please. Keep reminding me.

—R

Better. Honest, at least. I folded it, sealed it with wax and my signet ring. Called for another butterfly—purple this time. It landed on my desk, and I pressed the letter to its body, watching the parchment dissolve into wing and thorax.

"Find him," I whispered.

The butterfly lifted off, wings catching the dim bioluminescent glow from the caves beyond my window. Blue-green light reflected off purple wings, creating colors that had no names. It slipped through the crack in the stone, disappearing into the vastness of the bone court's tunnels.

I sat back in my chair, exhausted. My hands trembled—when had they started doing that? The skin across my knuckles looked too thin, stretched too tight over bone. Almost translucent in the low light. Black veins beneath, spreading like cracks.

I thought of Nokoa actively, deliberately. Pictured his face. His golden eyes that caught light like coins in sunlight. The way his hair curled when it got too long, soft against his neck. The sound of his laugh, though I couldn't quite hear it anymore—just knew that it had made me feel lighter.

Pain bloomed behind my eyes. Not the sharp lance from before—slower, deeper. A pressure building in my skull, pushing outward. My nose started bleeding. A single drop at first, then more, hot against my lip. I tasted copper.

Worth it. The pain was worth it to hold his image in my mind for just a moment longer.

I pressed my sleeve to my nose, watching red soak into black fabric. The contrast was stark—life against death, warmth against void.

My head pounded. The bleeding wouldn't stop. I slumped forward, pressing my forehead to the desk's cool surface. The stone was smooth, worn by years of use, and the cold seeped into my skin.

"Hollow Queen?" A voice from the doorway. The rattlemaid again, worry making her bold. "Should I fetch Healer Cressa?"

"No," I managed. "Just the bond."

"He must be thinking of you terribly," she whispered.

Or I was thinking of him. Same result.

"Leave me," I said.

She did.

The headache faded eventually. The bleeding stopped. I wiped my face clean with black silk and stared at the empty parchment where I'd tried to write promises I couldn't remember making.

The outer cities were rebelling because I'd forgotten them. Nokoa said so. And somewhere in the fog of my memory, I could almost see it—that negotiation, that promise, that moment of caring about people who weren't him.

But I couldn't reach it. The crown had eaten it, piece by piece, until only the ghost of a promise remained.

I folded his letter carefully. Tucked it into the drawer of my desk where I kept things that mattered. Not many things in there—a few pressed flowers, petals brown and brittle now, a sketch of gardens whose meaning escaped me. And now Nokoa's letter. Proof that someone remembered who I'd been. Even if I couldn't remember her myself.

The butterfly message from Hivro sat at the edge of my desk, still shifting its words. I glanced at it once more before sliding it under other parchments.

Remember who you were.

I was the woman in black now. The woman in grey chambers with blood on her sleeve and bone fused to her skull.

And Nokoa loved her anyway. Loved me anyway.

Outside my window, the bone court hummed with activity. Spectral guardians patrolling the deep tunnels. The machinery of death and governance turning endlessly, grinding everything beneath it into dust.

And somewhere beyond the skull castle walls, the outer cities starved and waited for a promise I couldn't remember making.

I'd fix it. Eventually. When I was stronger. When the crown's voices quieted long enough for me to hear my own thoughts.

For now, I sat in my grey chambers, bleeding from thinking of him.

Trying to remember yellow.

Chapter Fifteen

The First Soul

Renata

The exhaustion lived in my bones now. Not the kind that sleep could fix—something deeper, more fundamental. Like my body was a vessel with cracks spreading through it, and everything I poured in leaked out twice as fast. Even breathing felt like work, each inhale requiring conscious effort.

The spectral guardians were the problem. Had to be. Maintaining them required constant energy, constant focus. Even now, I could feel them at the edges of my awareness—seven dead souls bound to my will, the previous hollow rulers raised to serve. They patrolled the bone court's deepest tunnels, stood guard at the bridges between cave systems, ready to defend against whatever came next. They were necessary. Essential. But they were draining me hollow, leeching life from me with every moment they remained animated.

I needed to recharge.

The thought came naturally, like hunger. My body understood before my mind did—there was a way to fix this. A way to fill the cracks, seal the leaks, make myself whole again. The hollow crown pulsed against my skull, bone against bone, approving.

I found myself walking toward Cressa's healing chambers without consciously deciding to go there. My feet knew the path, carried me through corridors I barely saw. The bone court passed by in shades of grey and shadow, bioluminescent light painting everything in blues and greens that hurt to look at. The air was cool here, damp, smelling of stone and something medicinal.

The healing chambers were quiet when I arrived. Cressa wasn't there—probably tending to someone elsewhere, or maybe avoiding me. She'd been avoiding me lately. I couldn't remember if I'd done something to earn that avoidance, but it seemed right somehow. People should avoid me.

Two bodies lay on the stone slabs that served as beds. Both mortals. Both dying, though at different speeds.

The first was older, maybe fifty, with grey hair and skin that looked paper-thin. His chest barely moved with breath, shallow and labored. I approached slowly, drawn by something I didn't understand yet. Instinct, maybe. Or need. The hollow crown whispered approval.

"Gave his heartfire at the tithe," someone said behind me.

I turned. One of Cressa's assistants stood in the doorway, young and wide-eyed. She'd spoken without thinking, I could tell by the way she immediately looked terrified, her hand flying to her mouth.

"When?" I asked, and my voice sounded strange. Flat. Wrong.

"Three days ago, Hollow Queen. He volunteered. Thought he could handle the loss." She swallowed hard. "He couldn't."

I looked back at the dying man. His heartfire was gone—given willingly to fuel the bone court's needs, to keep the bone council alive in their immortal bodies, to maintain the system. And now he was dying from it, slowly, his body consuming itself because there wasn't enough life left to sustain it. His lips were cracked and grey. His fingernails had turned black.

The assistant fled. I heard her footsteps retreating down the corridor, quick and desperate.

I stood beside the dying man. Watched his chest rise and fall. Rise and fall. Each breath shallower than the last, like watching a candle gutter out. The room smelled of sweat and something sour—the scent of a body shutting down.

He was dying anyway. Already gone, really. Just a matter of hours now, maybe less.

I placed my hand on his chest. Felt the weak flutter of his heart beneath my palm, irregular and failing. Felt his life—what little remained of it—pulsing against my skin like a dying bird.

"I'm sorry," I whispered.

Then I pulled.

The essence came willingly. Like water flowing downhill, following the natural path. It dissolved into me, through my hand, up my arm, spreading through my body in warm waves that made me gasp. He tasted like dirt and roots. Like the earth itself, rich and dark and fundamental. Salt and copper and something ancient.

His chest stopped moving. The flutter beneath my palm went still, going from weak rhythm to nothing in a single heartbeat. And I—

I gasped.

The bone dust in my veins glowed. I could see it beneath my skin, white light tracing the paths of my circulatory system like lightning caught under glass. The cracks spread from my hand up my arm, and everywhere they went, the exhaustion faded. Strength flooded back. Clarity. Wholeness.

I felt whole. Full. Strong in a way I hadn't felt in weeks.

The horror came after.

I stumbled back from the body, staring at my hands. They looked the same. Same thin skin, same prominent bones, same black veins wrapping around pale flesh. But I could feel the difference inside. Could feel his life essence settling into the cracks, filling the empty spaces, making me more than I'd been moments before.

"What did I—" My voice broke. "I just—"

Killed him. I'd killed him. Not a mercy kill. Not really. I'd taken his soul, consumed it, used it to fuel myself like kindling in a fire.

"He was dying anyway," Oriana said. "You eased his passing."

But he was dying anyway. The thought came quickly, defensive, echoing the crown's whisper. He was already dead, just hadn't finished yet. I'd ended his suffering. That was mercy. That was—

It felt good.

That was the worst part. Not just the relief of being full instead of empty. Not just the strength replacing exhaustion. But the actual sensation of consuming him. The way his essence had dissolved on my tongue like something sweet and necessary. The way my body had welcomed it, had craved it, had known exactly what to do with it.

I looked at the plants on Cressa's shelves. Small herbs in clay pots, carefully tended. As I watched, they wilted. All of them at once, leaves browning and curling, stems drooping as if someone had poured poison into their soil. The scent of decay filled the air, sudden and wrong.

The bioluminescent moss on the walls dimmed. A visible circle of death spreading from where I stood, life draining from everything around me like water circling a drain.

Famine. The word came from somewhere deep, somewhere the crown hadn't reached yet. This is how famine spreads. Through me. Through what I am.

"You will eventually be worse than any bone council member if you're not careful."

I spun. Praxis stood in the shadows near the door, his bleached white bones almost glowing in the dim light. Crimson eyes blazed in empty sockets, watching me steadily. Without judgment. Just observation.

"What?" I managed, my voice small.

"Consuming life to fuel power." His voice was matter-of-fact. "It's practical. And it will destroy you faster than anything else you've done."

"I was—he was dying—"

"He was." Praxis moved closer. "And now he's gone, and you're stronger, and you've learned that death can feed you." He tilted his skull, considering me. "First direct warning I'll give you: this path leads somewhere specific. Make sure it's somewhere you want to go."

He left as quietly as he'd arrived, dissolving back into shadows.

I stood alone with two bodies. One dead by my hand. One sleeping, recovering from some other injury, unaware of the predator standing mere feet away.

I should leave. Should get out of this room, away from the temptation, away from the proof of what I'd just done.

But I was still so tired. The one soul had helped, but it wasn't enough. The spectral guardians were still draining me, still pulling at the edges of my consciousness. I could feel the exhaustion creeping back already, the cracks starting to spread again.

The sleeping man breathed steadily. Deep, even breaths. Healing. He'd probably survive whatever brought him here. He'd wake up in a few hours, maybe a day, and walk out of here on his own feet.

"You should take from him too," Oriana whispered. Gentle. Reasonable. Like suggesting I eat another bite at dinner. "You feel better now, but it won't last."

"One won't be strong enough to keep the guardians animated," Alaric added.

"Won't be strong enough to bring Nokoa home," Lyanna finished.

Nokoa. I thought of him. Pictured his face. His golden eyes. The way he looked at me like I was something worth saving, worth fighting for.

This keeps me strong, I told myself. Strong enough to save him. Strong enough to fix whatever the resurrection broke.

I approached the sleeping man. Placed my hand on his chest, feeling the warmth of him, the life pulsing beneath muscle and bone. A healthy heart. A heart that would beat for years if I let it.

This time, there was no hesitation. No horror. No moment of doubt.

I pulled.

His essence tasted different than the first—younger, brighter, like spring water instead of earth. Mint and morning dew and something clean. But it dissolved just as easily. Filled me just as completely. His heart stopped beneath my palm, and I barely noticed. Just felt the strength flooding back, the exhaustion receding, the cracks sealing over with stolen life.

When I stepped back, he looked peaceful. Like he'd simply stopped breathing in his sleep. A gentle death.

I'd given him that much, at least.

The plants wilted further. The bioluminescent moss died completely in a circle around me, leaving only darkness pressing in from all sides. Everything living retreated from my presence, recognizing death when it stood among them. Even the air felt thinner, colder.

I walked toward the door on steady feet. Strong feet. The exhaustion was gone. The spectral guardians no longer felt like a burden—just a tool I wielded with ease.

Two souls. That's all it took.

But I didn't feel like myself. I felt like something hollow and hungry. Something that could take life and call it mercy. Something that could justify murder as maintenance, as necessity, as fuel for a greater purpose.

For him, I told myself. This is for him.

I paused in the doorway, looking back at the two bodies. Two people who'd trusted the bone court to protect them, to heal them.

"This is temporary," I whispered. "Just until I'm stronger. Just until I can fix everything."

The lie tasted like ash and old blood. Or maybe that was just the residue of souls on my tongue.

I left before Cressa could return. The corridor stretched ahead of me, bioluminescent moss dimming as I passed, leaving darkness in my wake. Life retreating from death. The natural order recognizing the wrongness of what I'd become.

And I walked through it all, stronger than I'd been in weeks, telling myself this was necessary. Telling myself I'd stop once I didn't need it anymore.

Knowing I never would.

Chapter Sixteen

Alaira's First Contact

Nokoa

The medic's hands were cold against my chest. Professional. She pressed two fingers below my collarbone, feeling for something I couldn't name, then moved to my wrist. Counting heartbeats. Measuring death.

"Your eyes," she said quietly. "They're turning."

I knew. Could see it myself in the reflection of water, in the polished metal of borrowed blades. The gold was fading to yellow. Not the warm amber I'd been born with—something paler, sicker. Jaundiced, like old bruises or failing organs.

"How long?" I asked.

She didn't answer immediately. Just moved her examination to my ribs, pressing gently against bone that felt too prominent beneath skin. I winced. Everything hurt lately. Like my body couldn't decide what shape it was supposed to be and was trying all of them at once.

"The witch runes are spreading," she said finally. "Under your skin. I can see them when you move. They're not supposed to move."

"I know."

"And the chest pains?"

"Constant." I breathed shallowly, each inhale careful. Deep breaths felt like drowning. "Worse when I sleep. Worse when I'm awake. Just... worse."

She pulled back, wiping her hands on her apron. "I'm sorry," she said, and I heard genuine regret in her voice. "I don't know what else to do."

"You've done enough." She'd splinted my broken fingers, wrapped my ribs, given me something bitter to drink that dulled the pain for a few hours at a time. More than I deserved. "Thank you."

She left quickly, like they all did.

I sat on the edge of the cot, staring at my hands. Three fingers still splinted, wrapped in strips of cloth that had once been white but were now grey with dirt and use. The witch runes visible beneath the skin of my forearms, dark lines moving like living things. Crawling up toward my shoulders, spreading across my chest, taking emotion piece by piece, leaving only hollow echoes behind.

The resurrection was failing. Again. My body knew the truth: I was supposed to be dead. Had been dead. Should have stayed dead.

"Nokoa."

I looked up. Priestess Alaira stood in the tent's entrance—older than I remembered, with patchy hair and exhaustion written in every line of her face. White robes stained with travel and time, yellowed at the edges. The scent of incense and old paper clung to her.

"Why are you here?" I managed, my voice rough.

"Because I can help stabilize your resurrection." She stepped inside, her movements careful, measured. "I helped bring you back. I can keep you alive."

The offer landed like a physical thing. Hope, sharp and painful, lodging itself between my ribs where the constant ache lived.

"What do you want in return?" Because there was always a price. Always. Nothing came free, especially not life.

"Nothing." She smiled, but it didn't reach her eyes. "I want to help, Nokoa. I made mistakes—terrible mistakes—with the crown. Let me help fix at least one thing I've broken."

I wanted to believe her. Wanted it so badly my chest ached worse than usual. But I'd known Priestess Alaira my entire life, and I'd never known her to do something out of guilt. Never knew she felt the emotion at all.

"Tell me about the resurrection," I said. "About what's happening to me."

Alaira settled onto the stool the medic had vacated, her robes rustling. "You and Renata are soul-bound now. The first successful paired binding in recorded history. When she brought you back, she didn't just resurrect your body—she tied your soul to hers. Made you dependent on each other in ways that shouldn't be possible."

"The bond." I touched my chest, where the pain lived like a second heart. "It punishes us for wanting each other."

"Physical cost for emotional connection," she confirmed. She gestured at my arms, at the witch runes crawling beneath my skin. "Those marks—they're the binding made visible. They're spreading because the bond is unstable. Growing. Trying to complete itself but unable to because you're separated."

"Complete itself how?"

"I don't know." The admission seemed to cost her something. Her shoulders sagged slightly. "You're unprecedented. The rituals I designed, the magic involved—none of it was meant to work like this. You should have stayed dead. The fact that you're alive at all is..."

"Impossible," I finished.

"Miraculous," she corrected, and something flickered in her expression. Pride, maybe. Or fear. "And dangerous. Because impossible things have a way of breaking reality around them."

I looked at my hands again. At the runes crawling through my veins, visible beneath skin that had grown too thin. At my yellowing eyes reflected in the tent's polished metal—a stranger's eyes staring back.

"Can you stop it?" I asked quietly. "The spreading. The failing. Can you make it stop?"

"I can slow it." She pulled something from her robes—a small vial filled with liquid that looked like starlight and ash mixed together. It swirled in the glass, luminescent and dark at once. "This will ease the symptoms. Buy you time. Let me teach you how to manage the bond without it destroying you both."

I stared at the vial. Wanted to take it. Wanted to drink it down and feel relief—even temporary relief, even for just an hour without this constant grinding pain.

"Why should I trust you?" The question came out harsher than I meant, but I couldn't soften it. "You created the thing that's eating Renata alive. Why would you help us now?"

Alaira's face crumpled. Just for a moment, then she smoothed it away with visible effort. But I saw it. The genuine pain there. The regret that went deeper than words, carved into bone.

"Because I loved someone once," she said quietly. "Before the crown. Before everything went wrong. And I lost them because I made choices I didn't fully understand." She met my eyes, and hers were wet. "I see that same desperate love in you. In her. And I know where it leads."

The tent felt too small. I could smell the herbs the medic had used—something astringent and green. Could hear the camp sounds outside—children playing, someone hammering tent stakes, a baby crying. Normal sounds. Human sounds. Life continuing despite everything.

And here I was, dying slowly, listening to the woman who'd helped create this nightmare offer to save me from it.

"Renata is struggling," Alaira continued, leaning forward. "The hollow crown is overwhelming her. She's making choices she wouldn't normally make, becoming someone she wouldn't recognize. You've seen it. I know you have."

I had. In her letters. In the hollowness behind her words, the way sentences trailed off. In the way she couldn't remember things she should remember—promises made, dresses worn, the woman she'd been before bone fused to skull.

"I can teach you how to support her without adding to her burden," Alaira said. "How to use the bond instead of letting it use you. How to be her anchor instead of her weight."

"How?"

"By understanding the magic. By learning the rituals. By knowing what the bond can and can't do." She set the vial on the cot between us. It caught the light, glowing softly. "You're the anchor, Nokoa. If you stay stable, she stays grounded. But if you fail, if you die again, she'll lose the last thing keeping her human."

The words hit too close to truth. If I died again—really died, permanently—what would be left when the last piece of her humanity burned away?

"The hollow crown judges her," Alaira said softly. "The bone council judges her. The outer cities judge her. But you—you love her. That's worth protecting. That's worth fighting for."

I picked up the vial. Held it up to the light filtering through the tent's canvas. The liquid inside swirled like it was alive, stars caught in oil, darkness and light chasing each other.

"What is it?"

"Stabilization serum. Made from bone dust and heartfire and witch runes. It won't cure you—nothing can—but it'll ease the pain. Slow the spread. Give you time."

Time. That's all any of us wanted, really.

"Wait." Alaira's hand on my wrist stopped me. "Before you drink it, you should know—it'll tie you more closely to the magic. Make you more sensitive to the bond. You'll feel her more clearly, feel what she's feeling. The distance will hurt worse, but you'll understand her better."

"Will it help her?"

"Yes." No hesitation. "If you're stable, she can draw on that stability. Use it to resist the crown's influence. You'll be her compass when she loses direction."

I brought the vial to my lips. Hesitated, the rim cold against skin.

"Why now?" I asked. "Why show up now, after all this time?"

Alaira's expression shifted. Something flickered behind her eyes—calculation, maybe. Or fear. Or both, intertwined.

"Because things are accelerating," she said, her voice dropping. "The unsealing is happening faster than I expected. The guardians are waking. The prison is cracking. And you two are at the center of it all, whether you meant to be or not." She leaned closer. "I can't fix what I did. Can't undo the crown. But I can try to help you survive what's coming."

I drank.

The liquid burned going down. Not painful, exactly. Just intense. Like swallowing lightning and ice and fire all at once. It spread through my chest, through my arms, down into my legs. Everywhere it went, the pain eased. Not gone—never gone—but dulled. Manageable.

The witch runes under my skin flared bright for a moment, illuminating the tent's interior with sickly yellow-green light. Then they settled. Still there, still spreading, but slower now. Controlled. Contained.

"Better?" Alaira asked, watching me carefully.

"Yes." I gasped it out, my breath coming easier. "Thank you."

She stood, gathering her robes. "I'll return. Bring more. Teach you what you need to know." She paused at the tent's entrance, silhouetted against the afternoon light. "You don't have to trust me, Nokoa. You just have to let me help. For her sake, if not your own."

Then she was gone.

I sat alone in the tent, feeling the serum work through my system. The pain had dulled to a manageable ache. I could breathe deeply without wanting to scream.

But underneath the relief, something else stirred. Awareness. Connection. Like a door opening somewhere I couldn't see.

Renata.

I could feel her suddenly. Not just the bond's pain—something deeper. Her exhaustion. Her confusion. Her hollow, desperate love wrapped in thorns and bone.

She was thinking of me.

I doubled over, vomiting blood onto the tent floor. The taste of copper flooded my mouth. Three of my fingers snapped—clean breaks, one after another, each one a distinct crack of bone. The splints did nothing. The pain was double what it normally was, sharp and immediate and overwhelming.

I wanted to blame the serum. Wanted to curse Alaira for making it worse.

But I knew the truth.

She was thinking of me. Missing me so badly it was destroying her body, and mine along with it. And I was paying for it, bones breaking, blood rising, both of us trapped in this cycle of love and punishment that had no end.

I cleaned up the blood with shaking hands. Reset the broken fingers as best I could, biting down on leather to keep from screaming. Added new splints to the old ones.

And somewhere, in the bone court's depths, Renata probably sat in her grey chambers, bleeding from her nose, wondering why thinking of me hurt so much.

The serum burned in my veins. The bond ached in my chest.

I sat in a tent in the outer cities camp, dying slowly, loving her desperately, and hoping that somehow, impossibly, we'd both survive what we were becoming.

Chapter Seventeen

BROKEN NAILS

Renata

The letter arrived on purple wings. I watched the butterfly land on my windowsill, already knowing what it carried. Could feel it somehow—the weight of emotion pressed into parchment, waiting to unfold. The air in my chambers seemed to shift, growing heavier.

I approached slowly. My hands were steadier than they'd been in days. The souls I'd consumed had done that much, at least. Given me strength enough to walk without trembling, to hold things without dropping them. Borrowed life humming through my veins.

The butterfly dissolved at my touch, wings crumbling to ash that smelled faintly of death and distance. The letter uncurled in my palm, and his handwriting stopped me cold.

The words were messy. Rushed in some places, careful in others. Like he'd started writing and couldn't stop, emotions bleeding onto the page faster than his hand could keep up. Ink smudged where his fingers had dragged through wet letters.

Renata,

Sometimes I miss you so badly I hurt without the bond's help. Sometimes I hate you for what you've done to me. For bringing me back when you should have let me stay dead. For tying us together in a way that makes love feel like punishment.

But mostly I just miss you. Miss your voice. Miss the way you looked at me before everything broke. Miss believing we had a future that wasn't this.

I don't know who you're becoming. Don't know who I'm becoming either. The witch runes are spreading. My body is failing.

Are you still in there? Is the woman I loved still somewhere beneath the crown? Or have I been holding onto a ghost this whole time?

I need to know. I need—

The writing broke off there. Started again lower, shakier, the letters barely legible.

I love you. Whatever you're becoming, whatever I'm becoming, I love you. That's the only thing I'm sure of anymore.

—N

I read it three times. Each word cutting deeper than the last, opening wounds I didn't know I had.

Sometimes he hated me. Sometimes he missed me. Sometimes he didn't know who I was anymore.

I could feel the emotion bleeding through the parchment. Raw and desperate and real. More real than anything I'd felt in weeks. The hollow crown had hollowed out so much of me, taken so many pieces, but this—his pain, his love, his confusion—this reached through all of it. Cut straight to whatever remained beneath the bone and whispers.

My hands started shaking. Not from weakness this time. From something else. Something the crown couldn't quite suppress.

Grief, maybe. Or recognition. Or just the horrible understanding that I was hurting him. Not through the bond, not through separation, but through my choices. Through becoming something he couldn't recognize. Something that made him wonder if I was still there at all.

Are you still in there?

Was I?

I set the letter on my desk carefully, smoothing the creases. Pulled out fresh parchment. Dipped my quill in ink. The scratch of metal on paper was too loud in the silent chamber.

Started writing without planning what I'd say.

Nokoa,

I'm still here. I think I'm still here. It's hard to tell anymore. The crown takes things—memories, feelings, pieces of who I was. And I don't always notice what's missing until someone reminds me it was there.

You asked if I'm becoming something else. I think I am. I think I have been since the moment I put on this crown. Since the moment I chose to bring you back instead of letting you go.

I don't regret it. Even when I should. Even when the rational part of me knows I've broken something fundamental by refusing to accept your death. I'd do it again. I'd choose you again. Every time.

That probably makes me a monster. Maybe I am one. Maybe that's what love does—turns you into something willing to destroy the world just to keep one person in it.

I miss you too. Miss you so much it bleeds. Miss the cottage and the garden plans and the version of us that believed we could have something simple. Something good.

But we can't go back. I can't undo what I've done. Can only move forward and hope that whatever I'm becoming, you'll still recognize something worth loving in it.

I'm sorry. For the pain. For the bond. For everything this has cost you.

But I'm not sorry for keeping you alive.

—R

I tried to seal it. Pressed my thumb to the wax, reached for my signet ring with my other hand.

Pain lanced through my hand. Sharp and sudden, like someone had driven a nail through each finger. I gasped, dropped the ring. It clattered against stone. I watched as my fingernails started cracking—not breaking, cracking like porcelain, spiderweb fractures spreading from cuticle to tip. Black veins pulsed beneath them.

One nail snapped off completely. Then another. Blood welled up, bright against my bone-pale skin, dripping onto the parchment and staining the words I'd written.

"Hollow Queen!" The voice came from the doorway, sharp with panic.

I turned, trying to focus through the pain. One of the rattlemaids stood there, horror written across what remained of her face. Her joints clattered as she rushed forward, but I waved her back with bleeding fingers.

"Don't—" My voice came out strangled. "Don't touch me."

Another nail snapped, the sound loud as breaking bone. The pain was spreading now, up my hands, into my wrists. Fire racing along nerve endings. My body convulsed. Once. Twice. I tried to stay upright, failed. Hit the floor hard, stone cold against my cheek. The impact made my teeth clack together, filling my mouth with the taste of blood.

"Get Cressa!" The maid's voice, distant and panicked. "The hollow queen is reacting to the bond again!"

Footsteps. Running. Multiple people. Their voices blurred together, meaningless sound washing over me like water over stone.

The pain peaked. My spine arched, muscles seizing so hard I heard something pop in my back. I could feel the hollow crown's bone digging deeper into my skull, could feel the witch runes beneath my skin burning like brands. Everything was fire and agony and the horrible awareness that somewhere, in the outer cities, Nokoa was thinking of me.

Missing me so badly it was destroying us both.

Stop, I wanted to scream. Stop thinking of me. Stop loving me. It's killing us.

But the bond didn't work that way. Just punished us for wanting each other. Just made love into a weapon we couldn't put down, couldn't escape, couldn't survive.

Darkness crept in at the edges of my vision. Welcomed. Merciful. I let it take me, let consciousness slip away.

The last thing I heard was a voice. Deep. Gentle. Familiar in a way I couldn't place.

The Bone God.

"You're going to understand in time," he whispered, his voice resonating through my skull. "All of this. Every choice. Every sacrifice. You'll see why it had to be this way."

Then nothing.

I woke in my chambers. Still on the floor where I'd fallen, cold stone beneath me. The bioluminescent light from beyond my window was unchanged, giving no indication of how much time had passed.

Cressa knelt beside me. Her green eyes were tired, worried, ringed with shadows that spoke of too many nights spent tending to impossible patients. She pressed a cool cloth to my forehead, and I realized I was burning up—fever from the bond reaction. My body trying to process whatever Nokoa had put me through by simply thinking of me too hard.

"Your nails," she said quietly.

I looked at my hands. All ten fingernails were gone. Just raw, bloody nail beds remaining, weeping clear fluid. The pain had dulled to a constant throb.

"He must have been thinking of you," Cressa continued, wringing out the cloth with practiced efficiency. "The bond reaction was worse than I've ever seen."

I tried to sit up. Failed, my muscles weak. Tried again. Cressa helped me, supporting my weight until I could lean against the wall. The stone was cool against my spine, grounding.

"How long was I out?"

"An hour. Maybe less." She gestured to a basin of water and clean cloths on my desk. "I cleaned your hands. Wrapped them. You'll need to be careful until they heal."

I stared at the bandages. White cloth spotted with red, already soaking through. The black veins wrapped around my fingers like mourning ribbons.

"Did I say anything?" I asked, my throat raw. "While I was unconscious?"

Cressa's expression shifted. "You asked for him," she said finally. "Just his name. Over and over. Like he was the only thing keeping you tethered to consciousness."

Maybe he was.

I looked at my desk. The letter I'd been writing was still there, unsealed. Blood-stained where I'd bled on it. The words I'd poured out, raw and honest, sitting exposed.

"Can you seal it for me?" I asked.

Cressa followed my gaze. Hesitated. I watched her read it—the words visible from where she stood, everything I'd written, the apology and the admission and the refusal to regret. Something moved across her face that I couldn't quite name. Then she moved to the desk without a word, melted wax with a small flame, pressed my signet ring to it.

She handed it back to me without comment. It was the kindest thing she'd done for me in weeks, and we both knew it, and neither of us said so.

"I'll send it with a butterfly," Cressa said softly.

"Thank you."

She called one—purple wings, already dead, already serving. It landed on the sealed letter, and I watched his words and mine dissolve together into the butterfly's body. Message and messenger becoming one, bound by death and distance.

"Find him," Cressa whispered to it. "Show him she's still fighting."

The butterfly lifted off. Disappeared through the window crack. Gone to wherever Nokoa waited in the outer cities camp, dying slowly, hating me and loving me in equal measure.

Cressa turned back to me. "You need to rest. Your body can't take many more reactions like this."

"I need to work." I tried to stand. Made it halfway before my legs gave out.

Cressa caught me. She guided me toward the bed, and I was too exhausted to protest. My chambers spun, grey walls blurring into shadows.

"Rest," she said firmly. "Everything can wait."

I lay back on cold sheets that smelled of stone and emptiness. Stared at the ceiling. Bare stone, grey and unchanging. When had I stripped away everything that made these chambers feel like mine? The pressed flowers, the sketches, the colors—all gone.

"Cressa," I said quietly. "Am I becoming a monster?"

She didn't answer immediately. Just sat on the edge of the bed, her hands folded in her lap. When she finally spoke, her voice was careful.

"You're becoming something," she said. "Whether that's a monster or something else, I don't know. But you're changing, Renata. In ways that frighten people. In ways that should probably frighten you."

"But they don't," I finished. "I should be terrified. Should be horrified by what I'm doing. And I just... feel nothing."

"The crown—"

"The crown takes things. I know. Everyone keeps telling me that." I closed my eyes against tears that wouldn't come. "But it can't take him. It can't take how I feel about him. That's the only thing left that feels real."

Cressa was quiet for a long moment. Then, so softly I almost didn't hear it: "What if the crown isn't taking that feeling? What if it's using it?"

I opened my eyes. "What?"

"Every terrible choice you make, you justify through him." Cressa met my gaze, unflinching. "Every soul consumed, every mercy abandoned, every line crossed—you tell yourself it's for him. To keep him alive. To bring him home. What if the crown isn't taking your love for him? What if it's amplifying it? Making it so large, so all-consuming, that it drowns out everything else?"

I couldn't breathe. Couldn't think. The words circled in my mind, trying to find purchase, but my thoughts kept sliding away from them.

Was she right? Was my love for Nokoa the thing destroying me? Not the crown taking everything else—but the crown making him so important that nothing else mattered?

"No," I whispered. "No, that's not—he's the only good thing. The only reason to keep fighting."

"Or the only excuse to stop caring about anything else."

Cressa stood. Moved toward the door. Paused with her hand on the frame, silhouetted against the bioluminescent glow from the corridor.

"I'm not saying stop loving him," she said quietly. "I'm saying be careful how you love him. Because right now, your love looks a lot like destruction."

She left, the door closing with a soft thud that echoed in the empty chamber.

I lay in my bed, bandaged hands resting on my chest. Could feel my heart beating beneath them. Slow. Steady. Mechanical.

Was Cressa right? Was I using Nokoa as justification? As excuse?

No. I loved him. Genuinely. Completely. He was my anchor, my reason, my—

My excuse.

The thought came unbidden. Once it arrived, I couldn't dislodge it. It settled into my mind, heavy and cold.

Every terrible thing I'd done, I'd told myself it was for him. Every soul consumed. Every mercy abandoned. Every promise forgotten. All of it justified because it kept me strong enough to save him.

But what if I was just telling myself that? What if the hollow crown had found the perfect weapon—not by taking my love, but by making it so absolute that it excused everything else?

I thought of him deliberately. Let the pain come. Sharp spikes through my temples, pressure building behind my eyes. Blood started flowing from my nose again, warm and copper, dripping onto the pillow.

Worth it. The pain was worth it to think of him. To hold his image in my mind. Golden eyes and brown curls and the way he looked at me like I was something worth saving. To remember that somewhere beyond these chambers, he was alive because I'd refused to let him go.

Even if refusing to let him go was destroying us both.

The blood kept flowing. I didn't wipe it away. Just let it run down my face, tasting salt and copper, feeling the bond punish me for wanting what I couldn't have.

Outside my window, the bone court hummed with life and death. And I lay in my grey chambers, bleeding for love, wondering if love was the thing killing me.

Or if love was the only thing I'd chosen to keep while the crown took everything else.

I didn't know anymore.

Maybe the hollow crown didn't need to take my love for Nokoa. Maybe it just needed to make sure that love was the only thing I had left, so large it consumed everything else, so absolute it justified any atrocity.

"He's worth it," I whispered to the empty room.

The crown hummed against my skull.

And somewhere in its depths, the Bone God whispered back:

"Yes. Keep telling yourself that."

Chapter Eighteen

Valdic Returns

Renata

Valdic appeared in the bone court like he'd never left. One moment the throne room was empty save for me and the spectral guardians standing silent watch in the shadows. The next, he was there—purple eyes glowing in his emaciated wolf frame, patches of dark fur clinging to half-skeletal ribs. The scent of decay rolled off him, familiar and wrong all at once.

I blinked, uncertain if he was real or if exhaustion was making me see things. The bioluminescent light played tricks sometimes, made shadows look like movement, made stillness look like life.

"How was your nap?" I asked, and my voice sounded strange even to my own ears. Flat. Distant.

Valdic tilted his head, studying me with those violet eyes that saw too much. Confusion flickered across his features before settling into something sadder. "What are you saying?"

I frowned. Had I said something wrong? "You've been gone. Sleeping. Haven't you?"

"Renata." He moved closer, careful and slow. Like approaching something wild that might bolt or bite. "I wasn't sleeping. I've been with Nokoa. In the outer cities. You knew that."

Had I? The memory felt slippery, kept shifting every time I tried to fix it in place. I could see Valdic leaving—could remember him saying something about staying with Nokoa, about being needed there. But the details wouldn't come into focus. Just vague impressions, like trying to remember something told to you by someone else, secondhand and faded.

"Oh," I said. Then, because something else felt more important, more urgent: "He's back. I brought Nokoa back. It worked."

The words came out proud. Triumphant. Like I was announcing a great victory instead of stating something Valdic obviously already knew. Like I'd forgotten I'd already told him this, weeks ago, in the chaos after the resurrection.

Valdic's expression crumpled. Just for a moment—grief and horror and pity all mixed together—before he smoothed it away. But I'd seen it. That look of someone watching a tragedy unfold and being powerless to stop it.

"I know," he said quietly. "I've been helping care for him. You remember that, don't you?"

Did I? The memory wouldn't surface. Just emptiness where knowledge should be.

"Then why did you come back?" Not accusatory. Just genuinely confused. "He needs you there."

"I needed to see you." Valdic sat, his skeletal frame folding with the particular grace DirgeWolves had, joints clicking softly. "I miss you."

The words hit differently than they should have. Not with warmth or affection—I couldn't quite feel those anymore, they'd been taken or buried too deep to reach. But with something else. Recognition, maybe. Or the ghost of what recognition used to feel like.

"I'm right here," I said.

"Are you?" He watched me with those purple eyes that glowed faintly in the dim light. "I'm not sure anymore."

I wanted to argue. Wanted to insist that yes, I was here, I was present, I was myself. But the words wouldn't come. I was growing tired of having to prove to people that I hadn't disappeared entirely beneath the bone and whispers.

Valdic stood, moved closer, his claws clicking against stone. "I need to remind you of something. Of before."

"Before what?"

"Before the crown. Before everything broke." He pulled something from the satchel at his side—worn leather that smelled of travel and earth. A piece of fabric emerged—bright yellow, sun-faded but still vibrant. Almost painful to look at in the grey chamber. "Remember the gardens you wanted to plant?"

I stared at the fabric. It meant nothing to me. Just cloth. Pretty, I supposed, in an impractical way.

"Gardens?" I repeated, the word feeling foreign in my mouth.

"You talked about Orchids. Yellow ones, you said. To match this dress." He spread the fabric across his paws with careful reverence. It was a dress. Or had been. Now just a crumpled reminder of something I couldn't quite grasp. "You were going to plant them when Nokoa came home. Make the bone court beautiful instead of terrifying."

Orchids. The word stirred something. Faint. Distant. Like hearing music from another room and not quite being able to make out the melody.

"I don't..." I started, then stopped. Tried again. "I don't remember caring about that."

Valdic's face fell, his ears flattening against his skull. But he pressed on, pulling more items from his satchel. A journal—leather-bound, well-worn. Pressed flowers in various colors spilled out. Each one carefully preserved, labeled in handwriting I vaguely recognized as my own.

"Your clothes," he continued, his voice gaining urgency. "Bright colors everywhere. You said grey was for people who'd given up. That you'd never wear grey." He gestured at what I was wearing—black gown, simple and severe. "You said you wanted color. Life. Beauty in places of death."

I looked down at my dress. Black fabric, no adornment. Practical. Appropriate for a queen. When had I started wearing this? When had I stopped wearing... what? Yellow? The timeline wouldn't form. Just fragments scattered across a void.

"And your hair—you used to braid it every morning. Fill it with flowers. You said it made you feel alive." Valdic's voice cracked. "When did you stop braiding your hair?"

I touched my hair—white turned black by the hollow crown, hanging loose and uncombed. The answer wouldn't come. Just more emptiness, more absence where memory should live.

"I don't remember," I whispered.

Valdic's ears flattened. "You did. You cared so much. About beauty. About making things grow instead of watching them die. You had plans—detailed plans—for gardens throughout the bone court. You used to paint your nails just to change their color the next day. You drew sketches." He held up the journal with gentle paws. "This is yours. Your handwriting. Your dreams."

I took the journal with bandaged hands. Opened it carefully. The binding cracked slightly, stiff from disuse. Pages of sketches met my eyes—intricate drawings of garden layouts, plant species labeled in the margins, notes about sunlight and soil and growth patterns. Calculations for how deep the bioluminescent light could penetrate. Which plants might thrive in eternal twilight.

All in my handwriting. Undeniably mine. The loops and curves exactly as I still wrote them.

But I felt nothing looking at them. Just vague confusion, like examining artifacts from a civilization I'd only read about. Had I really cared about this? Had I really spent time drawing flowers and planning gardens?

It seemed impossible. Frivolous. Who had time for gardens when the world was starving and Nokoa was dying and everything was breaking? Who could afford to care about beauty when survival took everything you had?

"I don't remember caring about this," I said again. Firmer this time.

"You did." Valdic moved closer, close enough that I could smell the decay that clung to him. All DirgeWolves carried that scent—death and earth mixed together. Usually it bothered me. Now it just felt familiar. Comforting, even. "You were going to make the bone court beautiful. That's what you said. 'Beautiful instead of terrifying. Growing instead of dying.'"

I closed the journal. Set it aside on the throne's armrest. The pressed flowers scattered across the floor, bright spots of color against grey stone. Purple, yellow, white, red—a rainbow of death preserved.

"That sounds naive," I said. "Childish."

"It sounded hopeful." Valdic's voice cracked slightly. "It sounded like someone who believed things could be better."

"Things can't be better." The words came automatically. True in a way that needed no examination. "Things are what they are. We just survive them."

"You didn't always think that."

"Then I was wrong before." I stood, moved away from him. Away from the journal and the flowers and the yellow dress that meant nothing. My footsteps echoed in the empty throne room. "I'm right now."

Valdic followed, his claws clicking against stone. "Nokoa loved that about you. Your brightness."

And there it was. The only word that mattered anymore. Nokoa. I stopped, turned back to face Valdic, something stirring in my hollow chest.

"What about me did he love?"

"Your hope. Your determination to make things better instead of just accepting how they were. Your belief that beauty mattered even in places of death." Valdic gestured at the scattered flowers with his muzzle. "He said you made him want to be better. Made him believe in futures where things grew instead of withered."

I tried to picture it. Nokoa and me, planning gardens. Both of us covered in dirt, laughing about something. The bioluminescent glow around us, life growing instead of dying.

The image wouldn't form. Just fragments. Impressions. Nothing solid enough to hold.

"Did he like flowers?" I asked. "Did I pick them for him?"

"Yes." Valdic's voice was gentle. "You pressed flowers from every walk you took together. Kept them in that journal. Each one labeled with where you found it and what you were talking about that day."

I opened the journal again. Looked at the pressed flowers more carefully, running bandaged fingers over brittle petals. There—a note beside a dried violet: Found near the cottage. N said it matched my eyes. And another, beside a yellow wildflower: N laughed so hard he couldn't breathe. I can't remember why but I remember the sound.

Nokoa. Every page mentioned him. Every flower connected to a moment with him. This journal wasn't about gardens at all. It was about us. About the life we were building together, one flower at a time. About preserving moments in petals and ink because we'd believed we'd have forever to collect them.

"He loved you," Valdic said quietly. "That version of you. The one who pressed flowers and planned gardens and wore yellow dresses that made you look like sunshine."

"I'm not her anymore."

"I know." Valdic's agreement hurt worse than argument would have. "But you could be again. Maybe."

I laughed. The sound came out bitter, hollow, echoing off stone walls. "I can't go back, Valdic. The crown has taken too much. I can't even remember why I cared about flowers, let alone feel it."

"Then let me remember for you." He moved closer, pressed his muzzle against my bandaged hand. The gesture was tender. Familiar. Like something he'd done a hundred times before, though I couldn't recall when. His breath was warm against my cold skin. "Let me hold those memories until you can hold them yourself again."

I wanted to pull away. Wanted to tell him it was pointless, that the woman who cared about gardens was gone and wasn't coming back. That I preferred being what I was now—harder, unburdened by things like beauty and growth and color.

But I couldn't quite say it. Because somewhere, buried deep beneath the hollow crown's bone and the spectral guardians' drain and the hollow exhaustion, something stirred. Not memory—not quite. Just feeling. The ghost of caring about yellow dresses and pressed flowers. The echo of a person who'd believed beauty mattered.

"I can't be her again," I whispered.

"Maybe not today," Valdic agreed, his voice soft. "But maybe eventually. When this is over. When you and Nokoa are together again and the crown's power settles. Maybe then you'll remember Orchids."

When this is over. The phrase felt impossible. This—the crown, the power, the slow transformation—wasn't something that ended. It was something you became. Something that consumed until there was nothing left to consume.

But I didn't say that. Just stood there with Valdic's muzzle against my hand, surrounded by scattered flowers and forgotten dreams, feeling the faint warmth of his breath against my skin.

"Thank you," I said finally. "For trying."

"I'll keep trying." Valdic pulled back, meeting my eyes with his glowing purple gaze. "As many times as it takes. Until you remember or until there's nothing left to remember. Whichever comes first."

The words should have comforted me. Instead they felt like a countdown. A race between recovery and complete dissolution. And I didn't know which one would win.

I looked at the journal again. At the yellow dress. At the evidence of a person who'd existed once.

That girl—the one who drew gardens and pressed flowers and believed in beauty—she felt like a stranger. Someone I'd heard stories about but never actually met. Someone naive and hopeful and doomed from the start.

But Nokoa had loved her. Had loved her brightness, her hope, her determination to make things grow in places of death.

Did he still love what I'd become? This hollow thing that wore black and consumed souls and forgot about gardens?

Or was he holding onto the memory of her, waiting for her to return, not realizing she was already gone?

"I should send you away," I said quietly. "You're seeing something that isn't here anymore. It would be kinder to stop looking."

"I'd rather keep looking," Valdic said, and his voice was firm. "Even if all I see is absence. Because absence means something was there once. And if it was there once, maybe it can be again."

The hollow crown tightened. Just slightly. A gentle correction, bone pressing into bone. A reminder that this conversation was veering somewhere dangerous. Somewhere that made me question what I was becoming.

The voices stirred—Oriana, Alaric, Lyanna. All of them preparing to speak, to steer me back, to remind me what mattered.

But before they could, I made a choice.

"Leave the journal," I said. "And the dress. Leave them here."

Valdic's ears perked up, his tail moving slightly. "You'll keep them?"

"I'll keep them." I didn't know why. Couldn't explain the impulse. Just knew that throwing them away felt like giving up on something I couldn't quite name. Like closing a door I might someday need to open again. "Maybe I'll remember eventually. Maybe I won't. But they can stay."

"Thank you." Valdic backed toward the door, his movement careful, reverent. "I'll come back. Keep reminding you. As many times as it takes."

"Go back to Nokoa," I said. "He needs you more than I do."

"You both need me." Valdic paused at the threshold, silhouetted against the bioluminescent glow from the corridor. "You're both drowning. He's just louder about it."

Then he was gone, the sound of his claws fading down the corridor, leaving me alone.

I picked up the journal. Opened it to a random page, letting it fall where it would. A sketch of Orchids caught my eye—detailed, careful, clearly drawn over hours. Each petal shaded, each thorn precisely placed. Beneath it, a note: For N. Because he deserves sunshine.

For Nokoa. It was always for Nokoa. Even the gardens. Even the flowers. Even the brightness I'd wanted to bring to the bone court.

All of it for him.

The hollow crown seized on that thought. Amplified it. Made it fill my entire consciousness until there was no room for anything else.

"See?" Oriana whispered. "Everything you were, you were for him. Nothing's changed. You're still fighting for him. Just in different ways."

"The flowers don't matter," Alaric added. "What matters is keeping him alive."

"He won't care what color your dress is when he comes home," Lyanna finished. "He'll just care that you saved him."

The voices were right. Had to be right. The gardens and the flowers and the brightness—those were just decorations. Surface things. What mattered was deeper. More fundamental.

Keeping him alive. Bringing him home. Surviving long enough to be together.

That's what real love looked like. Not pressed flowers and yellow dresses. But sacrifice and strength and the willingness to become something terrible if it meant protecting what mattered most.

I closed the journal. Set it on my desk beside Nokoa's letters. Kept the yellow dress too, folded carefully, tucked into a drawer where I wouldn't have to look at it but wouldn't lose it either.

Maybe someday I'd remember why it mattered. Why gardens and Orchids and brightness had seemed important enough to fill pages of sketches.

Or maybe I wouldn't. Maybe that girl was gone forever.

Either way, I had the journal. Had the evidence. Had proof that once, briefly, I'd been someone who believed in growing things instead of killing them.

That had to count for something.

Even if I couldn't remember what.

Chapter Ninteen

THE REPORT

Nokoa

Valdic returned at dawn. I knew it was him before I opened my eyes—could smell the death-and-earth scent that clung to all DirgeWolves, could hear his particular breathing pattern, slow and measured like he was always choosing his words before he spoke them. The sound of his claws against packed earth, careful and quiet.

I opened my eyes. He sat at the entrance of my tent, purple eyes dim with exhaustion or grief or both. Patches of fur hung loose on his skeletal frame, revealing bone beneath. He looked like he'd aged years in the hours he'd been gone.

"How is she?" I asked.

The question came automatically. Always the first thing I wanted to know. How was Renata? Was she eating? Sleeping? Still herself? The answers were always terrible, but I needed to hear them anyway. Needed to track her descent so I could measure my own against it. Needed to know if there was still something left worth fighting for.

Valdic was quiet for a long moment. Then, carefully: "She's far."

"Far from what?"

"From everything. From who she was. From understanding what she's becoming." He moved into the tent properly, settling beside my cot with a soft thud. "She didn't recognize me at first. Thought I'd been sleeping instead of with you. The hollow crown is taking her memory in real time now. Not just old memories—recent ones. Things that happened weeks ago."

My chest tightened. Not the resurrection pain—something else. Something worse. "What did you show her?"

"The journal. The yellow dress. Pressed flowers." Valdic's voice was flat. Defeated in a way I'd never heard from him before. "Everything she used to care about. Everything that made her her instead of just the crown's vessel."

"Did she remember?"

"No." The word hung between us, acrid and choking. "She looked at her own handwriting and felt nothing. Saw sketches she'd spent hours drawing and couldn't connect them to herself. It was like showing a stranger someone else's dreams."

I tried to picture it. Renata holding that journal—the one she'd shown me once, pages filled with garden plans and pressed flowers and hopes for a future where things grew instead of died. Her looking at it with empty eyes. No recognition. No spark. Just void.

The image made my stomach turn.

"She kept it though," Valdic added, and there was desperate hope in his voice. "The journal and the dress. Didn't throw them away. That has to mean something."

"Or it means she's hoarding evidence of a person who doesn't exist anymore." The words came out bitter. Too harsh. But I couldn't soften them. Couldn't pretend this was anything but catastrophic. "Like keeping a corpse because you can't accept it's dead."

Valdic's ears flattened. "Nokoa—"

"Of all the ways I saw the future going when Renata's brother died, this wasn't it." I sat up, ignoring the way my ribs screamed protest. The witch runes under my skin burned hotter lately. Spreading faster, consuming more emotion with each passing day. "I thought we'd have problems. Thought the crown would be difficult. Thought there'd be political complications and power struggles and all the normal terrible things that come with ruling."

"You couldn't have known—"

"But I should have stayed away from her." The confession burst out before I could stop it, raw and jagged. "I didn't need to know the outcome to know her and I could only lead to ruin. I should have never confessed that I loved her."

The tent was too quiet. Outside, the camp was waking—cooking fires being lit, children asking for breakfast that might not exist, the low murmur of people trying to survive another day. Normal sounds. Human sounds. Everything we weren't anymore.

"You loved her," Valdic said simply. "Love doesn't calculate outcomes."

"It should." I looked at my hands. Three fingers still splinted, witch runes crawling up my arms. "If I'd stayed away—if I'd never sworn myself to her, never let her love me back—maybe she would have been different. Maybe she would have worn the crown and stayed herself."

"Or maybe she would have spiraled faster without you." Valdic moved closer, pressed his muzzle against my shoulder. "You're not responsible for the crown's corruption. You're not responsible for what it takes from her."

"I'm responsible for being the reason she won't let go." My voice cracked. "Every terrible thing she does, she justifies through me. Every mercy abandoned—it's all for me. To keep me alive. To bring me home. I'm the excuse she uses to become a monster."

"That's the crown twisting her love—"

"It's still love!" I shouted. Then quieter, broken: "It's still her loving me. Still her choosing me over everything else. Over the outer cities she promised to help. Over her own humanity. Over the world itself. And I can't—I can't fix it. Can't stop it. Can't even tell her to let me die because the bond won't let us communicate anything except pain."

Valdic was silent. What could he say? There was no comfort for this. No words that would change what we both knew was true.

"She's becoming someone else," I whispered, my throat tight. "And the worst part is, she's becoming someone else for me. Because she loves me too much to let me go. Because I'm her anchor and her excuse and her justification for everything terrible."

"She's still in there," Valdic said. But he didn't sound convinced. Just desperate. "Somewhere beneath the crown and the power and the hollow certainty, she's still Renata. Still the woman who pressed flowers and planned gardens."

"Is she?" I met his purple eyes. "Or are we holding onto a ghost? Waiting for someone to come back who's already gone?"

Valdic looked away first. "I don't know."

The honesty was worse than lies would have been. Because it meant even Valdic—loyal, steadfast Valdic who never gave up on anyone—was starting to doubt.

I lay back on the cot. Stared at the tent's canvas ceiling, watching shadows play across it from the fire outside. Tried to find something to hold onto.

Found nothing but exhaustion and the slow burn of witch runes stealing what little emotion I had left.

"I dream about the world covered in bone dust," I said after a while. "The seas run dry. The sky turns grey. Everything dead or dying. And she's there, in the center of it all, wearing her crown and telling herself it was worth it. That keeping me alive was worth destroying everything. In the dreams where I die again, she keeps my body preserved at her side."

"That won't happen," Valdic said. But again—no conviction. Just words filling silence.

"Won't it?" I closed my eyes. "Every step she takes leads closer to that future. Every choice she makes pushes her further from humanity. And I can't stop her. Can't reach her. Can't do anything but survive and watch her destroy herself trying to save me."

The resurrection burned through my chest. Constant now. No relief even with Alaira's serum. My body knew the truth even if magic kept it functioning—I was meant to be dead. Every breath I took was borrowed time.

"Maybe you're right," I said quietly. "Maybe I couldn't have known. Maybe love doesn't calculate outcomes." I opened my eyes, looked at Valdic through the dim light. "But I know now. And knowing doesn't change anything. She's still destroying herself for me. And all I can do is watch."

"You can survive," Valdic said, his voice gaining strength. "You can stay alive until we find a way to fix the bond and free her from the crown. That's something."

"Is it? Surviving so she has a reason to keep destroying herself?"

Valdic didn't argue. Just sat with me in the grey morning light filtering through canvas, two creatures that shouldn't exist discussing the woman who'd made us impossible.

"She sent a letter," he said finally. "Before I left. She was writing to you. Trying to explain what she's becoming. I didn't read it, but I saw her face. She knows, Nokoa. On some level, beneath everything the crown has taken, she knows she's losing herself."

"Does knowing matter if she can't stop?"

"I don't know." Valdic stood, shook himself, fur and fragments falling loose. "But it's something. It's proof that part of her still cares about being more than what she's becoming."

He left me alone after that. The sound of his claws faded into the general noise of the camp.

I lay on my cot, feeling the witch runes burn beneath my skin. Feeling the resurrection magic slowly unraveling. Feeling the bond pulse with every beat of my failing heart.

And I thought about Renata. About the woman I'd loved—bright and determined and convinced she could make the world better. About the woman she was becoming—hollow and powerful and convinced that keeping me alive was worth any cost.

Was she still worth loving? This version of her? This hollow queen who consumed souls and forgot her promises and justified everything through devotion to me?

Yes.

The answer came without hesitation. Without doubt.

I still loved her. Would always love her. Even if she became a monster. Even if she destroyed the world. Even if she forgot everything except my name.

But I also knew something else, something I'd been circling without wanting to look at directly.

If it were her dying and me with the power to stop it, I'd become a monster too.

The thought settled into me like a stone dropped into still water. Not comforting. Not condemning. Just true.

I fell asleep to the sounds of the camp—children's voices, cooking fires, someone's low laughter—and dreamed of bone dust and dry seas and Renata standing in the center of it all, wearing her crown and her black dress, telling me it was worth it.

Telling me she'd do it all again.

Telling me she loved me too much to let me die.

When I woke, I called for paper. Wrote until my splinted fingers ached.

Renata,

I need you to know something. If the situation were reversed—if you were dying and I had the power to stop it—I would become a monster too.

I'm not saying that to excuse what you've done. I'm saying it because I think you need to hear that I understand. That the thing driving you isn't madness. It's love. And love makes monsters of everyone, given enough time and enough grief.

I still love you. Whatever you're becoming. Whatever I'm becoming.

Don't let that be the reason you stop fighting to stay yourself.

—N

I folded it. Pressed it to the butterfly Valdic had left sleeping at the tent's entrance, its purple wings folded still as death.

"Find her," I told it.

It lifted off into the morning light.

And I lay back down, feeling the witch runes burn, and hoped she'd receive it before the crown took whatever was left of the woman who used to press flowers.

Chapter Twenty

PERLA WAKES

Renata

The magic lashed out before I could control it. Raw. Desperate. Wild in ways that magic shouldn't be. I'd been trying to strengthen the bond connection to Nokoa—another ritual, another attempt to stabilize what was killing us both—and the power had surged beyond my grasp, slipping through my fingers like a current I couldn't hold.

The spectral guardians responded to my panic, their forms flickering and intensifying. Seven dead souls pulling energy through me, channeling it into something I hadn't intended. Something dangerous.

The magic cracked something deep underground.

I felt it through the soles of my feet—a fracture spreading through ancient stone, through layers of bone and earth and time. Something that had been sealed breaking open. The floor trembled. Dust rained from the ceiling.

"What have you done?" The voice came from everywhere at once. "What have you DONE?"

I spun. Hivro stood in the doorway of my chambers. She'd been hovering at the edges of the court for weeks—I'd seen her in corridors, watching, never speaking. But now she was here, her star-covered skin glowing with distress. Butterflies swarmed around her frantically, dead wings beating in patterns that looked almost like words.

"Defended myself," I said. My heart was racing, each beat painful against my ribs. The magic still hummed through my veins, looking for an outlet. "Why do you care?"

Hivro stared at me. Her constellation face shifted—stars rearranging themselves into expressions of horror and grief. "You've woken flames."

"What are you talking about?"

She didn't answer. Just turned and ran. I'd never seen her run before. Never seen her move with anything but careful deliberation. But now she fled like something was chasing her, her robes streaming behind her.

Or like she was racing toward something she couldn't prevent.

I followed.

Through corridors lit by bioluminescent blue-green light. Down stairs carved from vertebrae. Into the deeper levels of the bone court where few people ventured. The walls here were older—made of bone arranged in patterns that predated the skull castle above. Femurs interlocking like puzzle pieces. Ribs forming arched ceilings that curved like cathedral vaults.

Everything bone. Everything ancient. Everything wrong.

Heat rose from below. Not the cold of tombs. Not the neutral temperature of deep earth. But warmth. Growing warmer with each step down, like approaching a forge.

Fire.

We emerged into the catacombs. The deepest level. Where the guardians slept in their alcoves, preserved by magic and time and the weight of their sacrifice.

Two remained. I'd seen them before, during rituals. Mummified figures covered in witch runes, sleeping in their bone cradles.

One alcove was empty now. Scorched. The witch runes that had bound the guardian inside were broken, burned away from the inside out. Ash coated the floor. The bones themselves had melted, running like wax.

And in the center of the chamber stood a small figure wreathed in flames.

Perla.

I knew her name without being told. Knew she was a pyreling—one of the elemental beings created by the Goddess of Magic herself. Knew she'd been sleeping for centuries, holding the seal on the bone god's prison while the world forgot her.

She was barely taller than a child. Her body looked like it was made of embers and ash, constantly smoldering. Where skin should be, there was flame. Where hair should flow, there was fire—orange and gold and white-hot at the tips. Her eyes burned blue—not with heat, but with grief so deep it had turned cold.

"We tried to stop the crown!" Her voice cracked like burning wood, like logs splitting in a bonfire. "We WARNED Alaira!"

The flames around her flared red. Anger replacing grief. The temperature in the chamber spiked—I felt sweat bead on my forehead despite the cool air of the catacombs. My skin tightened, drying in the sudden heat.

"We locked the bone god away to save you!" Perla gestured wildly, and fire followed her movements like living ribbons. The flames danced, responding to emotion instead of physics.

Blue flames now. Sorrow so deep it burned cold.

"We slept so the prison would hold!" The fire shifted through colors—red, blue, white, orange—each one matching the emotion pouring through her. "And you—you're breaking everything we sacrificed for!"

I stepped back. The spectral guardians moved with me, positioning themselves between me and this furious, heartbroken pyreling.

"I'm saving someone I love," I said.

The words came automatically. The justification I'd used a hundred times. A thousand. The truth that made everything else acceptable.

I thought of Nokoa. Deliberately. Actively. Let his face fill my mind—golden eyes, brown curls, the way he looked at me like I was worth saving. Pain lanced through my skull, sharp and immediate. Blood started flowing from my nose, hot against my lips. Worth it. Always worth it.

"We ALL loved!" Perla screamed. The flames around her exploded outward, scorching the ancient bones that made up the walls. They blackened, cracked, filled the air with the smell of burning calcium. "We gave up our worlds to protect yours!"

She moved closer. Fast. Faster than something made of fire should be able to move. The heat intensified—my skin felt like it was blistering even from feet away. I could feel my hair curling, singeing at the ends.

"Your love doesn't justify destroying everyone else's!"

She attacked.

Fire and grief and fury all mixed together, aimed at my chest. The spectral guardians intercepted—souls throwing themselves between me and the flames. They absorbed some of the heat, but not all. Not enough. The air itself seemed to ignite.

I called on bone magic. Pulled it up from the marrow-deep place where it lived. The catacomb floor cracked—femurs and ribs and skulls rising to form a barrier. Ancient bones responding to my will.

Perla burned through them. Her fire was divine—a gift from the Goddess of Magic herself. It consumed everything it touched. Bone turned to ash. Stone melted.

"We gave up EVERYTHING!" She was crying now. Blue flames streaming down her ember-face like tears made of sorrow. "Our homes! Our people! Our goddesses!"

The emotion in her voice was overwhelming. Centuries of sacrifice. Centuries of sleeping in the dark, holding a prison together, waiting for goddesses who never answered. All of it pouring out in fire and grief.

I felt something crack in my chest. Not physical. Something else. Something the hollow crown had been protecting me from.

Guilt.

She was right. They—the guardians—had given up everything to protect this world. Had locked away the bone god, sealed themselves in tombs, slept through centuries while the world forgot them. All to prevent exactly what I was doing.

And I was destroying their sacrifice. Piece by piece. Soul by soul. All because I couldn't let one person go.

"I'm sorry," I whispered.

Perla heard it. The fire flickered—shifting from red to blue to something softer. Gold, maybe. Hope, or just the desire to believe someone understood.

"Then stop," she said, and her voice was pleading now. "Please. Before you break everything we died to protect."

I wanted to. In that moment, looking at her grief and her desperation and the divine fire that was burning her up from the inside, I wanted to stop. Wanted to lay down the crown and the power and walk away from all of it.

But then I thought of Nokoa.

Thought of him in the outer cities camp, dying slowly. Thought of the witch runes spreading under his skin like poison. Thought of his resurrection failing despite everything I'd done to keep him alive.

He was dying. I was the only thing keeping him alive. If I stopped—if I honored these ancient sacrifices—he would die.

And I couldn't let him die.

Wouldn't.

The guilt the crown couldn't take—I could take it myself.

"No," I said.

Perla's fire flared red. Pure rage. "Then I'll stop you!"

She attacked again. This time with everything she had. Flames that could melt stone. Heat that could boil blood. Divine fire that had been sleeping for centuries, finally unleashed.

I met her with death.

Bone magic. Spectral guardians. The power of a thousand consumed souls. I wasn't as old as she was. Wasn't divine. Wasn't blessed by any goddess.

But I was desperate. And desperation made me relentless.

We fought across the catacombs. Fire against bone. Life against death. Passion against cold calculation. She fought with emotion—every attack colored by grief or rage or hope. Her flames shifted colors with each strike, unstable, beautiful, deadly. I fought with nothing. Just empty purpose. Just the hollow certainty that this was necessary.

I was winning.

Not because I was stronger. But because she cared too much and I cared too little. Because her emotions made her fire unstable—shifting between colors, between intensities, between wanting to destroy me and wanting to save me.

I had no such conflict.

The spectral guardians overwhelmed her. Dead souls that couldn't be burned. They swarmed around her, pulling at her fire, draining the divine energy that kept her form solid. She tried to fight them off, but there were too many.

"Fern will stop you," Perla gasped. Her fire was dimming. Blue now. All sorrow. No rage left. "Or Sevi. Or Hivro."

She was dying. I could see it happening. See her ember-flesh crumbling like paper exposed to too much heat. See the fire that made her who she was guttering out like a candle in wind.

"Someone has to," she whispered. "The goddesses may be silent but we're NOT."

A final burst of flame. Not red with anger. Blue with grief. She wasn't trying to kill me anymore. Just mourning. Mourning her failure. Mourning the world she couldn't save. Mourning the goddesses who never answered her calls.

Then nothing.

Her body crumbled to ash and ember. The fire went out completely. What remained looked almost like a person's outline, traced in grey ash on scorched bone.

I stood over her remains. Breathing hard. Skin blistered from heat, red and painful. Hands shaking.

I'd killed a guardian. A divine being. Something created by a goddess to protect the world.

I'd killed her.

For him.

The guilt tried to surface again. Tried to make me feel the weight of what I'd done. But the hollow crown was ready this time. The bone around my skull tightened, and the feeling disappeared. Not suppressed—just gone. Eaten before it could take root.

"Perla was part of an older world." Oriana's voice, quiet and almost reverent. "Like Alaira. From the original sisters of creation's first line. Created by the

Goddess of Magic herself—an elemental gifted divine power to protect the universe."

"And you killed her." Alaric sounded impressed. Almost proud. "A divine being. That shouldn't be possible."

"It shouldn't be," Lyanna agreed. "But you did it anyway. You're stronger than they are. Stronger than their sacrifices. Stronger than their gods."

The crown voices were celebrating. Genuinely pleased with what I'd accomplished. And I—

I felt nothing.

Should feel horror. Should feel grief. Should feel something about killing a being who'd given up everything to protect a world I was destroying.

But there was just emptiness where emotion should be.

"She was weak," I said aloud. Testing the words. Seeing if they felt true.

They did.

Perla had been weak. Ruled by emotion. Unable to separate what she wanted from what she needed to do. She'd loved too much, cared too much, let her feelings make her fire unstable.

I wouldn't make that mistake.

The crown whispered. Told me to eat the ashes. To consume what remained of Perla's divine fire, make it part of myself.

"Why?" I asked.

"It's an important part of your future," Oriana said. "Divine essence. Power from the goddesses themselves. If you consume it, you'll be stronger. Strong enough for what's coming."

I stared at the ash. At what remained of a being who'd loved and sacrificed and tried to save the world. Grey powder traced in the shape of loss.

"What power does it give me?"

"We don't know exactly," Alaric admitted. "But it's divine. That means it matters."

I knelt beside the ashes. They were still warm. Still smoldering slightly. The heat felt good against my blistered skin, soothing somehow.

I gathered them in my hands. They were soft, like flour. Brought them to my mouth.

Ate them.

They tasted like fire and grief and centuries of lonely sacrifice. Like divine purpose corrupted into fuel. Like everything wrong with what I was becoming, distilled into ash and ember.

I ate all of it.

And for a moment—just one bright, terrible moment—I felt emotion again.

Everything Perla had felt. All her grief and rage and hope and love and desperate determination to protect a world that had forgotten her. It flooded through me, overwhelming, unstoppable. Centuries compressed into seconds.

I gasped. Doubled over. Felt tears streaming down my face—not mine, hers. Felt her centuries of loneliness. Felt her calling to a goddess who never answered. Felt her watching the world she'd sacrificed for spiral toward destruction.

Felt her love for that world anyway. Despite everything. Despite the silence. Despite the forgetting.

Then it was gone.

The hollow crown took it. Consumed it. Turned divine emotion into nothing but power coursing through my veins.

I stood. Steadier than before. Stronger. The blisters on my skin were healing—divine fire from inside working to repair what divine fire from outside had damaged.

Hivro stood in the doorway still. Watching. Her constellation face showed only sorrow now—stars arranged in patterns of grief so profound they seemed to pull light into themselves.

"You ate her," she whispered. "You consumed a guardian."

"She attacked me," I said. "I defended myself."

"She tried to save you." Hivro's voice cracked, stars flickering. "She died trying to save you from yourself."

"Then she died for nothing." The words came out cold. Empty. "Because I'm not stopping. Not for her. Not for you. Not for anyone."

Hivro stared at me for a long moment. Then, quietly: "What have you become?"

I walked past her without answering.

Back toward my chambers. Back toward the rituals that would keep Nokoa alive another day. With each step, I felt the divine fire settling into my bones. Changing me. Making me something more than human. Something less than divine.

Something that could consume gods and call it love.

Chapter Twenty-One

FORGETTING THE PROMISE

Renata

The council chamber felt too large. Or maybe I felt too small. Hard to tell anymore when space and self kept shifting in ways I couldn't quite track. The walls seemed to breathe, expanding and contracting with each beat of my heart.

Ancelin sat across from me, his serpentine dreadlocks coiled beneath withered horns. His silver-sheen obsidian eyes watched me with something that looked like pity. I hated pity. Hated the way it made people look at you like you were already lost, already beyond saving.

Praxis stood near the wall, bleached bones gleaming in the bioluminescent light. Silent. Observing.

Maxin was dying. I could see it in the way he held himself—careful, like moving too quickly would make him fall apart. His blonde hair had started falling out in patches, leaving pale scalp exposed. His eyes were dimmer than they'd been weeks ago, clouded. The hollow crown's corruption was taking him, slowly.

He'd set parchments on the table between us. Documents covered in cramped handwriting and official seals. The paper was old, yellowed at the edges.

"The outer cities sent a formal complaint," Maxin said. His voice was steady despite his deteriorating state. "They're starving. The tithe system is still brutal. They want to know—where are the reforms you promised?"

I stared at the parchments. The words swam together, refusing to resolve into meaning.

"What reforms?" I asked.

The silence that followed was absolute. Heavy enough to feel. I could hear my own breathing, too loud in the sudden quiet.

"Hollow Queen," Ancelin said carefully. "The negotiations. Before Nokoa's death. You promised them fair treatment. Changes to the tithe system."

"I never promised anything." The words came easily. Certain. "Why would I promise them reforms? They're outer cities. They exist to serve the bone court."

Maxin pushed the documents closer, the parchment scraping against stone. "This is the written agreement. Your signature. The terms you negotiated."

I looked at where he pointed. There—my handwriting. Definitely mine. The loops and curves distinctive, the way I made my R with that extra flourish. My signature at the bottom, sealed with my personal mark pressed into red wax.

But I didn't recognize any of it.

"This isn't—" I started, then stopped. Stared harder at the parchment. "I wouldn't have agreed to this."

"You did agree to it." Maxin's voice was gentle. "You negotiated for hours. You and Nokoa both. You wanted fairness. You wanted to change how the tithe worked. No children taken. Volunteers only, paid for their service. No one forced against their will."

The words meant nothing. Just sounds. Concepts that didn't connect to any memory I could access.

"When?" I demanded. "When did I supposedly promise this?"

"Before Nokoa died." Ancelin leaned forward, joints grinding softly. "Maybe two weeks before. You were still hopeful then. Still believing you could make things better. Nokoa stood behind you during the negotiation. You kept look-ing back at him for reassurance."

I tried to remember. Tried to pull up any image of sitting across from outer cities representatives. Tried to see Nokoa behind me, his hand on my shoulder, his pride warming me from the inside.

Nothing.

Just empty space where memory should be. A void. A hole.

"I remember Nokoa dying," I said slowly. "I remember the coronation. I remember everything after. But before—"

"Before is gone," Maxin finished quietly. "The crown has eaten it. The promise. The negotiation. The reasons you cared. All of it consumed to fuel your power."

"That's not possible." But even as I said it, I knew it was. The hollow crown took things. Everyone said so. Valdic said so. Cressa said so. Even the crown's own voices sometimes acknowledged it.

But this felt different. This wasn't just a memory. This was an entire piece of who I'd been—someone who cared about outer cities, who wanted fairness, who believed in changing systems instead of just surviving them.

That person felt like a stranger.

"Show me again." I grabbed the parchment. Read it more carefully this time. Every line. Every clause. The paper was rough under my fingers, real.

Article I: No children shall be taken for tithe without express written permission from legal guardians, and only in cases of willing sacrifice.

Article II: All tithe volunteers shall receive fair compensation in food, shelter, and coin for their service to the bone court.

Article III: No citizen shall be forced to give heartfire or bone marrow against their will. All tithe must be freely given.

Article IV: Quarterly reviews shall be conducted to ensure compliance and address grievances.

My handwriting. My signature. My seal.

But I couldn't remember writing it. Couldn't remember caring enough to write it.

"You were trying to be better than the system," Maxin said. "Better than previous rulers. You wanted to prove that the bone court could be fair. That power didn't require cruelty."

"That's naive." The words came automatically. "Power requires whatever it requires. Fairness is a luxury."

"You didn't think so then," Ancelin said. His voice was sad. Disappointed.

I set the parchment down. "Even if I did promise this—which I don't remember—why should I honor it now? The outer cities are rebelling. They stole from the guardian tombs. They're attacking the bone court with death magic. Why should I give them anything?"

"Because you gave your word," Maxin said simply. "Because the woman you were believed in keeping her word more than she believed in power."

The woman you were. Past tense. Like I was dead and they were talking about a corpse.

Maybe they were.

"I don't believe you." I stood, pushing away from the table. "This is manipulation. You're showing me false documents to make me doubt myself."

"Hollow Queen—" Ancelin started. "The bone council was in charge before you. We created the brutal system. Why would we fabricate documents asking you to change it?"

"No." I cut him off. "The outer cities are lying. They want me to remember promises I never made so I'll give them power I shouldn't give them."

"Renata." Maxin stood too, moving carefully, one hand on the table for support. "The crown is taking your past. Piece by piece. You made this promise. Nokoa was there. He remembers. He wrote to you about it."

Nokoa. I thought of him deliberately. His face. His golden eyes. His presence at a negotiation I couldn't remember.

Pain lanced through my skull. Blood started flowing from my nose, hot and immediate. But underneath the pain—something. Some fragment. Some ghost of a memory.

Him standing behind me. His hand on my shoulder. The weight of it grounding me. Making me brave enough to say things I wasn't sure I believed yet.

A table. People across from it. Desperate people. Starving people. Hollow-eyed children clinging to their parents. People who needed help I could give, and the particular way that had felt—not like power, but like purpose.

Me wanting to deserve the way he was looking at me.

The memory crumbled even as I tried to hold it. Dissolved like ash in water. Gone before I could examine it properly, slipping through my mental fingers.

But it had been there. Briefly. Proof that Maxin and Ancelin were telling the truth.

I had promised them. Had negotiated in good faith. Had believed I could make things better.

And now I couldn't even remember why I'd cared.

"The crown is eating you alive," Ancelin said softly. "Everything you were. Everything that made you you. It's taking all of it to fuel its power. Soon there'll be nothing left but the crown wearing your face."

"That's not true." But my voice wavered.

"Look at us." Maxin gestured at himself and Ancelin. "We were human once. Or close enough. We made bargains with the crown. Gave it pieces of ourselves for power and immortality. And now look what we've become."

I looked at them. Really looked. Ancelin—entirely bone except for stretched skin over his jaw, joints grinding with every movement. Maxin—hair falling out, skin graying, slowly transforming from mortal man to something skeletal. Both of them corrupted. Both of them hollow versions of whoever they'd been before.

Was that my future?

"I remember Nokoa," I said. Desperate. "I still remember him. That proves the crown hasn't taken everything."

"Does it?" Maxin's voice was unbearably gentle. "Or has it just learned that Nokoa is useful? That your love for him makes you more controllable? That keeping that one feeling makes you lose sight of everything else?"

Cressa's words echoed in my mind: What if the crown isn't taking that feeling? What if it's using it?

"No," I whispered. "He's the only real thing left. The only thing that matters."

"That's the problem," Ancelin said, his silver eyes sad. "You've made him the only thing that matters. The outer cities don't matter. Your promises don't matter. Your own humanity doesn't matter. Just him. And the crown is using that obsession to hollow you out."

I wanted to argue. Wanted to prove they were wrong.

But I couldn't remember the promise. Couldn't remember caring about the outer cities. Couldn't remember being the woman who sat across from desperate people and wanted to help them.

All I could remember was Nokoa.

"Even if I did promise them," I said slowly, "I can't honor it now. They're rebelling. They have to be stopped."

"They're rebelling because you forgot them," Maxin said. "Because you broke your word. Because the woman they trusted disappeared and left someone else wearing her face."

"Then that's their problem." The words came out cold. Certain. Empty. "I have more important things to worry about."

"Like keeping Nokoa alive," Ancelin said. Not a question. Just sad certainty.

"Yes." No hesitation. "Like keeping him alive. Like bringing him home. Like fixing the bond that's killing us both. Not promises I can't remember making to people who are trying to destroy me."

The silence was damning. Both council members looking at me like I'd just proven their point.

"Dismiss their complaint," I said. "Tell them the bone court doesn't negotiate with rebels. Tell them they'll get nothing until they submit completely."

"Hollow Queen—" Maxin started.

"That's an order." I moved toward the door. "And send extra forces to the outer cities borders. I want them contained. And if they attack again, I want them destroyed."

I left before they could argue further.

The corridor outside was blessedly empty. Cool. Quiet. I leaned against the wall, feeling my heart race.

I'd made a promise. Had cared about fairness and justice and proving I could be better.

And now I couldn't even remember why.

The hollow crown's bone tightened slightly.

"They were trying to manipulate you," Oriana said. "The outer cities want to exploit you. They'll take any concession and demand more."

"We can show you the truth about what they plan," she added, her voice dropping to something almost conspiratorial. "Would you like to see?"

Before I could answer, the hollow crown began to play a memory behind my eyelids. Nalla and other outer city members stood in what looked like a war tent. Their voices carried clearly despite the distance. Too clearly.

"Once she gives in to our demands, we kill her," Nalla said, her voice cold. "We can't let her live. She's too dangerous."

"Agreed. We use the reforms as leverage, get her to weaken the bone court's defenses, then we strike. Kill the hollow queen, destroy the council, end this whole corrupt system."

"And Nokoa?"

"He dies too. Both of them have to die."

The memory faded. I opened my eyes, breathing hard.

Something about it nagged at me. The edges were too sharp. Real memories blurred at the edges—they smelled of something, or tasted of time, or arrived incomplete. This one had arrived whole and perfect, like a painting rather than a recollection.

The crown's bone pressed against my skull, and the feeling dissolved before I could examine it further.

They were planning to kill me. Planning to use my own promises against me.

I'd been right to forget. Right to dismiss their complaints. Right to order their containment.

I walked back toward my chambers on unsteady legs.

I'd make the same choice again. Forget the same promises. Become the same monster.

For him.

Always for him.

The crown hummed with approval, and I let it guide me back to the rituals that would keep him alive another day.

Back to forgetting who I'd been, one promise at a time.

Chapter Twenty-Two

The Camp

Nokoa

The dressings on my arm itched. Wrong word—they burned. Constant fire beneath the bandages where the witch runes had spread so aggressively that the medic had wrapped them to keep me from scratching the skin raw. My broken fingers throbbed in their splints. Three of them still. They weren't healing. Wouldn't heal, probably. Just more proof that my body knew the truth even when magic tried to deny it.

I was supposed to be dead.

The camp smelled like burning today. Not cooking fires—those were carefully managed, fuel too precious to waste. This was something else. Bodies. They were burning bodies at the edge of camp. People who'd died from starvation or sickness or just giving up. Too many bodies to bury properly anymore. The ground was too hard, the living too weak, the dead too numerous.

So they burned them. And the smoke carried across the camp, coating everything in the smell of char and mortality. It settled in my throat, in my clothes, in my lungs with each breath.

I tried to help anyway. Had to do something. Had to be useful instead of just a burden they were keeping alive for leverage. The children needed food—what little food existed—and someone had to help distribute it fairly.

Nalla had set up a system. Careful rationing. Everyone got something, but children got more. Pregnant women got priority. The elderly got what was left. It was brutal math. Life-and-death arithmetic. But it was better than chaos.

I stood at the distribution point, counting out portions with my good hand. Dried meat that was more gristle than protein, tough as leather. Hard bread that could break teeth if you weren't careful. Water that tasted like metal and desperation, drawn from wells that were running dry.

A child approached. Maybe six years old. Hollow eyes too large for her face. Ribs visible through her thin shirt. She held out her hands without speaking, palms cupped together like a prayer.

I gave her the child's portion. Watched her clutch it to her chest like treasure, like something that might disappear if she didn't hold tight enough. She didn't eat it immediately—probably saving it to share with family. Or saving it because eating too fast on an empty stomach would make her sick.

She whispered "thank you" and disappeared into the camp, her bare feet silent against packed earth.

I tried to ignore the smell of burning bodies.

Tried to ignore the fact that this was Renata's doing. Her broken promise. Her forgotten negotiation. Her choice to let them starve while she consolidated power in the bone court.

Tried to ignore it and failed.

Valdic found me an hour later. I was sitting on a crate near the cooking fires, staring at my bandaged hands. The witch runes underneath were moving. I could feel them crawling. Spreading like roots through soil. Soon they'd cover everything and there'd be nothing left that looked human.

"How are you doing?" Valdic asked, his voice gentle.

The question was almost funny. How was I doing? I was dying. Slowly. Painfully. While the woman I loved destroyed herself and everyone around her trying to keep me alive.

"I've been better," I said.

Valdic settled beside me, his skeletal wolf frame folding gracefully, joints clicking softly. His purple eyes were sad. Tired in a way that went beyond physical exhaustion. He'd just returned from the bone court—from trying to reach Renata, from watching her become something else, from failing to help her remember who she'd been.

"She's getting worse," he said quietly. Not a question. Just a statement of fact.

"I know."

"She ordered another purge. Smaller this time. More targeted. But still—" He trailed off, ears drooping. "Still her. Still choosing violence. Still forgetting why she ever wanted to be better."

I didn't know what to say. What comfort could I offer? What words would make it hurt less?

"I'm sorry," I said finally. "I know you care about her. I know watching her become this—"

"I love her." Valdic's voice was soft but certain. "Not the way you love her. But I love her. She was kind to me when I was just a dying wolf. She saw something worth saving. And now I'm watching her forget how to see anything worth saving in anyone."

The grief in his voice was almost unbearable. Raw. Honest.

"I don't know how to help her," he continued. "Don't know how to reach her. The crown has taken so much. And every time I think I'm making progress, every time she shows a flicker of who she was, the crown takes it. Eats it. Leaves her more hollow."

"I hate standing by doing nothing," I said, my voice rough. "Hate hoping she'll remember when every day makes it clearer she won't. Hate being the reason she gives for becoming what she's becoming."

"You're not the reason." Valdic's tone was firm. "The crown is the reason. The resurrection magic is the reason. The impossible situation is the reason. You're just the person she loves enough to destroy herself for."

"That doesn't make me feel better."

"It's not supposed to." He looked at me. "It's just supposed to be true."

We sat in silence for a while. Watching the camp. Watching people move through their routines of survival. Children playing with sticks and stones because there were no toys, their laughter thin and brittle. Women mending clothes that were more patches than fabric, fingers working by firelight. Men sitting idle because there was no work, no purpose, no future worth building toward.

The sun was setting—what little of it penetrated the perpetual grey of this place. Shadows lengthened. The temperature dropped. People began retreating to their tents, seeking whatever warmth they could find.

"What if she never remembers?" Valdic asked quietly. "What if the crown has taken so much that she can't remember why she cared about these people? Can't remember making promises? Can't remember who she was before it consumed her?"

"Then I'm watching the woman I love become someone else." My voice split on the last word. "And I can't do anything to stop it."

"Neither can I." Valdic's ears flattened against his skull. "And it's killing me. Watching her forget how to be kind. Watching her justify cruelty. Watching her look at me like I'm a tool instead of someone who cares about her."

"Does she know you care?"

"I don't think so. I don't think she can see it anymore. Can't see that people love her beyond just you. That we're all grieving what she's becoming." He paused, looking at the smoke rising from the camp's edge. "Sometimes I wonder if telling her would help. If knowing that more people than just you are watching her descend would change anything."

"Would it?"

"Probably not. The crown would just take that too. Turn it into another weight to carry. Another reason to be strong. Another justification for be-coming monstrous." His voice was bitter, edged with exhaustion. "Everything becomes justification. Nothing becomes reason to stop."

I thought about that. About how every attempt to reach her seemed to fail. About how every letter I sent was answered with apologies that never changed anything. About how Valdic kept trying despite knowing it was probably hope-less.

"Why do you keep going back?" I asked.

"Because someone has to." Valdic looked at me, and there was steel beneath the sadness. "Because if everyone gives up on her, if everyone stops trying, then the crown wins completely. And I'm not ready to let that happen yet."

"Even knowing it might be pointless?"

"Even then." He stood, stretched, his spine popping audibly. "I'm going back. Someone needs to keep trying. Someone needs to keep reminding her who she was, even if she can't remember."

"Will you tell her—" I stopped. What could I say? What message could possibly matter?

"What?" Valdic prompted gently.

"Tell her I'm still here. Still loving her. Still hoping she finds her way back." The words felt insufficient. Like trying to hold the dam with your hands while the water rises. "Tell her that even watching her become this, I can't stop."

"She knows. On some level, beneath everything the crown has taken, she knows." Valdic's expression softened. "But I'll tell her anyway. Sometimes hearing it helps, even when nothing else does."

He left me alone with the smoke and the dying light and the weight of loving someone who was becoming unrecognizable.

I sat there for a long time. Thinking about Renata. About the woman who'd pressed flowers and planned gardens and worn yellow like armor against the darkness. About the woman who consumed souls and killed guardians and forgot her own promises.

Were they both her? Different versions of the same person, shaped by different circumstances? Or had one replaced the other so completely that the bright woman was just a memory, just a ghost that haunted those of us who remembered?

I didn't know. Wasn't sure it mattered. All I knew was that tomorrow would be the same as today. Her becoming more monstrous. Me becoming more dead. Both of us trapped in a spiral neither could escape.

The smoke from the burning bodies rose into the darkening sky. Each one had been someone's child, someone's parent, someone's hope for the future.

Each one was proof that the woman I loved had forgotten how to care about anything except keeping me alive.

A woman approached the distribution point. Old, bent, her face a map of wrinkles and hardship. She held out trembling hands.

I gave her what was left. Watched her shuffle away into the gathering darkness.

Tomorrow I'd help distribute food again. I'd ignore the smell of burning bodies. I'd exist in this camp of starving, desperate people who were suffering because the woman I loved had forgotten how to care about anyone except me.

I couldn't do anything except endure and hope and break a little more each day.

Just like she was breaking.

Just like we were all breaking.

The witch runes burned beneath my bandages. The resurrection magic flickered, unstable. My body counted down to death while hers counted down to something worse.

And somewhere, in the bone court's depths, she sat in her grey chambers, convinced she was doing this for love.

Convinced she was saving me.

Never salvation. Never peace. Never an end to this slow catastrophe we called devotion.

Chapter Twenty-Three

SMALL CRUELTIES

Renata

The tray hit the floor with a crash that echoed through the throne room. Porcelain shattering, sharp and final. Food scattering across ancient stone—bread, dried fruit, precious protein. A servant girl—couldn't have been more than twelve—stood frozen in the spreading mess, her face pale with terror. Her hands still held the phantom weight of the tray.

I watched her from the throne. Waited for her to speak. To explain. To offer some reason why she'd wasted food when people were starving. The silence stretched, thick and choking.

"I'm sorry, Hollow Queen." Her voice shook. "I didn't mean—the tray was slippery, and I—"

"Clumsiness wastes food." The words came out cold. "Food is scarce. Wasting it is unacceptable."

She started crying. Silent tears streaming down her cheeks, making tracks through the dust on her face. "Please, I'm sorry. It won't happen again."

"You're right. It won't." I gestured to the guards standing at attention along the walls. "Five lashes."

The authority in my voice felt right. Natural. This was leadership. This was maintaining order in chaos.

The girl's face went from pale to grey. "Hollow Queen—"

"Five lashes," I repeated. "In the courtyard. Tomorrow at dawn. So everyone can see what happens to carelessness."

The guards moved forward. One of them—older, with scars across his face and grey threading his hair—hesitated. "Hollow Queen, she's just a child."

I looked at him. Let him see the certainty in my eyes. "Are you questioning my judgment?"

He stepped back, boots scraping against stone. "No, Hollow Queen."

"Good." I leaned forward slightly, the hollow crown's weight shifting against my skull. "Because questioning authority creates weakness. And weakness creates chaos. And chaos kills more children than discipline ever will."

The logic was perfect. Unassailable.

Well done, Oriana whispered through the crown. Authority must be absolute, or it means nothing.

They took the girl. Still crying. Still apologizing. Still failing to understand that her carelessness had consequences that extended beyond just a broken tray. Her small frame disappeared between the guards, swallowed by shadow.

I watched them go and felt certain. This was the correct choice. The only choice. Anything else would have shown weakness, and weakness would spread like rot through the entire court.

She'll learn, Alaric murmured. And others will learn from watching her learn. That's how order is maintained.

A rattlemaid came with a broom and dustpan. Started cleaning the mess without looking at me, her joints clattering softly. Good. She understood hierarchy. Understood her place.

I turned back to the documents on my lap. Reports from the outer cities borders. Complaints from citizens. Requests for audience. All of it requiring decisions, requiring attention, requiring me to care enough to read them properly.

Most of it was noise. Complaints from people who didn't understand what leadership required. Who thought mercy and kindness could maintain order in times of crisis.

They were wrong. The crown had shown me the truth: strength maintained order. Fear enforced strength. And order kept everyone alive.

Even if individuals had to suffer for it.

Especially then.

I thought of Nokoa deliberately. Let his face fill my mind—golden eyes, brown curls, the way he'd looked at me with such trust before everything broke. Pain lanced through my skull immediately. Sharp. Familiar. Expected.

I smiled through it. Let the pain remind me why these choices mattered. Why being strong mattered.

He needed me powerful. Needed me certain. Needed me unwavering in my decisions so that when he came home, there would be stability waiting instead of chaos.

Exactly, Lyanna's voice, warm with approval. Everything you do, you do for him.

The prisoner came that afternoon. Brought before me in chains, already beaten by guards who'd caught him stealing. A man, maybe thirty, with hollow eyes and bruises blooming across his face—purple and yellow, fresh and old. His lip was split. His hands were bound so tight the rope had cut into his wrists.

"Found him stealing bread from the market, Hollow Queen." The guard captain pushed him forward. He stumbled, barely catching himself on knees that hit stone with an audible crack. "Third offense this month."

Third offense. That made it simple. Clear. The law existed for a reason, and the law said three strikes meant death.

"What do you have to say for yourself?" I asked, though I already knew the answer. They always had excuses. Always had reasons why laws shouldn't apply to them.

The man looked up at me. Those hollow eyes trying to find sympathy where none existed. "My children. They haven't eaten in three days. I couldn't—I had to—"

"You had to steal," I finished for him. "Because feeding your children is more important than following laws."

"Yes." No apology. Just desperate defiance. "I'd do it again. I'd steal every day if it meant they ate."

There it was. The admission. The proof that mercy would be wasted on him.

"How many children?"

"Three. Two girls and a boy. The youngest is four." His voice cracked on the last word, breaking like old wood.

Numbers. Just numbers. Mouths to feed in a court that couldn't feed everyone. The math was brutal but simple: one death now or four deaths later from starvation.

Better to make an example. Better to show everyone that laws applied equally. Better to demonstrate that even sympathetic circumstances didn't excuse disobedience.

"The law is clear," I said, my voice steady. "Third offense is death."

The man's face crumbled. Something breaking behind his eyes. "Please. Please, Hollow Queen. Kill me tomorrow if you must, but let me see them one more time. Let me explain why I won't come home."

"Appeal denied." The words came without hesitation. "Execute him at dawn. Public."

"Hollow Queen—" The guard captain started.

"His children will starve anyway," I said, cutting him off. My voice was calm. Reasonable. "Whether he lives or dies. At least his death sends a message: theft will not be tolerated. Not for any reason. Not under any circumstances."

"They're children." The guard captain's voice held something dangerous. Not quite rebellion. But close. "You're sentencing children to death by starvation."

I stood. Let my full authority fill the throne room. Let them all feel the weight of my power. The spectral guardians shifted in the shadows, responding to my will.

"I'm enforcing laws," I said, each word deliberate. "What happens to his children is the consequence of his choices, not mine. He chose to steal. He chose to break laws. He chose to put his family at risk. Those consequences are his responsibility."

You are queen, Oriana said. You maintain order. His choices created this situation, not yours.

The prisoner started screaming. Not words. Just raw sound. Horror and grief and rage all mixed together, echoing off bone walls. They dragged him away still screaming, his voice echoing through the corridors until someone shut a door and muffled it to nothing.

I sat back down. Listened to the fading screams without flinching. This was leadership. This was strength. This was what keeping order required.

You held firm, Lyanna said softly. That's what matters.

I looked at my hands. They were shaking. Slight tremor, barely visible. But there.

Just adrenaline. Just the body's response to confrontation. Nothing that indicated doubt or uncertainty.

I steadied my hands through force of will. Placed them flat on the armrests. Let the tremor fade.

Between decisions—between ordering the child beaten and the man executed—I thought of Nokoa. Let his image fill my mind completely. Let the bond pain come and accepted it as proof of connection.

This keeps me strong, I thought with perfect clarity. Strong enough to save him. Strong enough to bring him home.

Mercy would create weakness. Weakness would create chaos. Chaos would endanger him.

Therefore these choices—hard choices, necessary choices—were actually protecting him.

The logic was flawless. The justification absolute. The crown's voices agreed.

And I agreed with them.

You understand, Oriana said, and I could hear the satisfaction in her voice. You finally understand what it means to rule.

That night, alone in my chambers, I stared at my hands. They'd stopped shaking hours ago. Now they were just still. Steady. The hands of someone who knew what needed to be done and did it without hesitation.

The fingernails had grown back—sort of. Thin. Brittle. More like claws than nails, yellowed and ridged. The skin across my knuckles looked translucent. I could see bone beneath. Not metaphorically. Literally. My skeleton showing through skin that had worn too thin to hide it.

I was becoming something else. Something stronger. Something that didn't flinch from hard choices or second-guess necessary cruelty.

I was becoming what a queen should be.

The child's face flashed in my mind. Twelve years old. Terrified. About to be beaten for dropping a tray.

She'd learn. They'd all learn.

The prisoner's voice echoed in memory. My children. They haven't eaten in three days.

His problem. His responsibility. His consequences to face.

Nokoa. I thought of Nokoa with perfect focus. Pictured his face. His smile. The way he'd looked at me like I was worth believing in.

Pain lanced through my skull. Blood started flowing from my nose. I wiped it away calmly. Just the bond. Just proof that he was thinking of me too.

He'd understand eventually. He'd see that every hard choice had been necessary. That love sometimes required being harder than anyone else could be.

They'd all understand eventually.

You are queen, the crown whispered, all three voices merging into one. You are right. You are strong.

I believed them.

I believed them completely, without question, because believing anything else would mean admitting I'd become the monster everyone feared.

And I wasn't a monster.

I was just strong enough to let a child be beaten and a father be killed and call it justice.

The bioluminescent light dimmed in my chambers.

Or maybe my eyes were just adjusting to a new kind of darkness.

Chapter Twenty-Four

VALDIC'S SECOND ATTEMPT

Renata

Valdic appeared in my chambers without knocking. His emaciated wolf frame stepped from the shadows—one moment empty space, the next his presence filling the room, purple eyes glowing in the dim light.

"Come with me," he said.

Not a request. Just a statement. An expectation.

"I have work—"

"It can wait." His purple eyes were determined. "Nokoa asked me to try again. Asked me to show you something different. Something the crown might not have eaten yet."

Something different. The journal and the dress hadn't worked—not really. I'd looked at them and felt nothing except vague confusion about who that person had been. A stranger's belongings.

"Where?" I asked.

"You'll see."

I followed him through the bone court's corridors. Past the throne room where I'd ordered cruelties. Past the council chambers where I'd forgotten promises. Down, always down, into the lower levels where natural caves twisted through limestone like ancient veins.

The bioluminescence here was dimmer. Older. Blue-green light that seemed to come from the stone itself. Like these tunnels had been part of the bone court since the beginning, long before anyone had carved thrones or arranged femurs into mosaics.

We stopped in front of a door I didn't recognize. Carved wood, worn smooth by centuries of hands pushing it open. The grain was visible, polished by touch. Witch runes traced the frame—not the corrupted ones I'd been using, but older. Simpler. The kind meant to preserve and protect rather than control.

"Do you remember this place?" Valdic asked.

I stared at the door. Felt something stir. Not memory, exactly. More like the ghost of familiarity. Like seeing a face you know you should recognize but can't quite place.

"I don't know."

"Then let's find out."

He pushed the door open. The hinges didn't creak—well-maintained, still cared for.

The room beyond was circular. Carved entirely from the cave's natural stone. Stalactites hung from the ceiling like frozen teardrops, catching the bioluminescent light. The floor was worn smooth in patches—places where feet had walked the same paths over and over until the stone remembered.

Desks. Small ones. Child-sized. Arranged in a semicircle facing what must have been the instructor's platform. The air smelled of old stone and chalk dust.

A schoolroom.

"This is where noble children were taught," Valdic said quietly, his voice echoing slightly in the circular space. "History. Manners. Court protocol. Magic theory. Everything a young noble needed to know to survive in the bone court."

I moved into the room slowly. Touched one of the desks. The stone was cool beneath my skeletal fingers, smooth from years of young hands resting on it.

"You sat here." Valdic pointed to a desk near the front. "You, Nokoa, your brother Theron, and Cressa. The four of you. Always together. Always causing trouble."

Theron. The name sent a spike of pain through my chest. My brother. Dead now. Killed by—

The memory skittered away before I could grasp it. Just pain remaining. Just the knowledge that he was gone and it was somehow my fault.

"What kind of trouble?" I asked, trying to focus on something else.

"Do you see that alcove?" Valdic gestured to a small nook carved into the wall, partially hidden behind a stalactite. "Hide and seek. You four would play during lessons when you were supposed to be studying. The instructor would turn to write on the board, and one of you would disappear. Then another. Then another. By the time they turned back around, the entire front row was empty."

I stared at the alcove. Tried to imagine hiding there. Tried to picture myself small enough to fit, young enough to think it was worth the trouble.

Nothing came.

"You were caught every time," Valdic continued. "The instructor always knew where you'd gone. But they let you do it anyway. Let you have those moments of being children instead of future court members."

He moved to another desk, his claws clicking softly against stone. "Cressa sat here. She failed her manners class three times. Kept forgetting which fork to use, kept speaking out of turn, kept laughing at inappropriate moments."

"Cressa?" I couldn't imagine the quiet, competent healer failing anything.

"She was different then. Loud. Irreverent. Couldn't understand why manners mattered when there were more important things to learn." Valdic's expression softened with memory, his ears perking slightly. "You three helped her pass. Nokoa would quiz her during breaks. Theron would act out scenarios so she could practice responses. And you—you wrote out all the rules on cards so she could study them."

Cards. Rules. A girl with green eyes struggling to remember which hand held which fork.

Something flickered. Not quite memory. But close. Like light through a keyhole.

"Why would I do that?" I asked.

"Because she was your friend." Valdic said it simply. Like it explained everything. "Because you cared about her. About all of them. You wanted them to succeed."

I tried to imagine caring about someone that way. About wanting their success enough to spend time helping them. About friendship meaning more than just strategic alliance. About caring being its own reward rather than a means to an end.

Couldn't quite manage it. The concept felt foreign.

"There." Valdic pointed to the wall behind the instructor's platform. Carved into the stone: names. Dozens of them. Maybe hundreds. Generations of students who'd sat in this room. Some deep and clear, others worn shallow by time.

I moved closer. Ran my fingers over the carvings. The stone was cool, uneven where names had been etched.

Renata. Age 9.

My handwriting. Childish. Uneven. But definitely mine. I recognized the way I formed my R, even then.

Beside it: Nokoa. Age 9.

Theron. Age 11.

Cressa. Age 8.

All four of us. Carved into stone. Proof we'd existed here together.

"You did that on the last day of lessons," Valdic said. "Right before you were all considered old enough to join formal court life. The instructor caught you carving and just smiled. Said every student added their name eventually. That it was tradition."

I touched Nokoa's name. Traced the letters with one skeletal finger. The grooves were deep—he'd carved with determination.

He'd been nine. So young. So small. Had his handwriting looked like this? Uneven and enthusiastic? Had he stood beside me while we carved our names illegally, laughing about getting caught?

"You were happy here," Valdic said quietly. "All of you. This was before responsibilities. Before crowns and resurrections and impossible choices. Just four children learning together. Playing together. Caring about each other in simple ways."

"I don't remember." The words came out frustrated. "I see the names. I see the desks. I understand what you're telling me. But I don't remember feeling it."

"Then let me tell you." Valdic moved to stand beside me, his warmth a contrast to the cool stone. "There was this game you four played. During lessons on the bone god. The instructor would talk about death and transitions and the eternal cycle. Heavy topics. Scary for children. So you four would kick each other under the desks."

He demonstrated, tapping my leg gently with his paw.

"Just little taps. Reminders you weren't alone. That someone was there. Someone understood that the lessons were frightening. That death was frightening. That growing up in a court made of bones was frightening."

I looked at the desks again. Tried to imagine four children kicking each other. Finding comfort in simple contact. In knowing they weren't facing scary things alone.

"Who started it?" I asked.

"You did." Valdic's voice was gentle. "You saw Cressa getting pale during a particularly graphic lesson about soul harvesting. Saw her hands shaking. So you kicked her under the desk. Just a little tap. She looked at you, and you smiled. And she knew: it's okay to be scared. We're all scared. But we're scared together."

"That seems—" I struggled for the word. "Small."

"It was small," Valdic agreed. "But it mattered. Those small gestures of care. Those tiny reminders that you weren't alone. They built something. Built friendship. Built trust. Built the foundation for four people who loved each other enough to face impossible things."

I thought about that. About small gestures mattering. About caring being built from tiny moments rather than grand declarations. About love being accumulated through kicks under desks and carved names and study cards.

"Does Nokoa remember this place?" I asked.

"Yes." Valdic moved to Nokoa's desk. Sat beside it. "He talks about it sometimes. About lessons here. About the four of you being inseparable. About Theron making jokes during history lessons. About Cressa accidentally setting her notes on fire during magic practice. About you—" He paused. "About you being the one who held everyone together."

"I don't hold anything together now." The observation was factual. "I tear things apart."

"You did then." Valdic's purple eyes met mine. "You were the one who noticed when Theron was struggling with something. Who helped Cressa with manners. Who made sure Nokoa didn't get in too much trouble for his pranks. You saw people and cared about what you saw."

"I can't do that anymore." I looked at my skeletal hands, bone visible through translucent skin. "I can't see people. Just obstacles or tools or threats. Just things to manage or remove."

"I know." Valdic's voice was sad, ears drooping. "That's why I brought you here. To show you that once, you did see people. Once, you cared about more than just Nokoa. You cared about your brother. About Cressa. About random students struggling with lessons."

He stood, moved to the alcove where we'd apparently played hide and seek.

"There's a carving here too. Hidden. You four did it together one day when you were supposed to be studying."

I followed him. Peered into the alcove. The space was small, intimate, hidden from view.

Carved into the stone, small and careful:

The Four of Us Against the World.

Underneath, a date. Years ago. When we were all still children. Still innocent. Still believing we could face anything together.

"You were ten when you carved this," Valdic said. "Theron had just found out he'd be king someday. Was terrified. Didn't want the responsibility. So you four came here after lessons and carved this. A promise. That no matter what came, you'd face it together."

I stared at the words. At the childish optimism. At the belief that four people could stand against an entire world if they just stayed together.

"We didn't stay together," I said.

"No." Valdic's voice was gentle. "Theron is dead. You're wearing a crown that's eating you alive. Nokoa is resurrected and dying. Cressa watches everything fall apart from the sidelines. The four of you are scattered. Broken. Changed beyond recognition."

He pressed his muzzle against my hand, warm and solid and real.

"But this place remembers. The carvings remember. The stone remembers four children who loved each other enough to make promises. Who believed in simple things like friendship and loyalty and facing fear together."

I touched the carving. The Four of Us Against the World. The stone was smooth where fingers had traced these words over the years.

"I killed Theron," I said. The words came out flat. "Or I let him die. I can't remember which. The crown took that memory. But I know it's my fault he's gone."

"I know." Valdic didn't argue. Didn't try to absolve me. "And Cressa knows. And Nokoa knows. And they're all still here anyway. Still trying to reach you. Still hoping the woman who carved these promises is still somewhere inside."

"Why?" I looked at him. "Why keep trying? Why not just accept that she's gone?"

"Because giving up on you means accepting that love dies," Valdic said simply. "That friendship dies. That promises carved in stone don't mean anything. And if we accept that—if we let you disappear completely—then what was the point of any of it?"

I had no answer for that.

We stood in the schoolroom. In this place where children had learned and played and made promises they believed they'd keep forever.

A place I didn't remember but that remembered me.

"Can I stay here?" I asked. Not sure why. Just needing to remain in this space a little longer.

"As long as you want." Valdic settled onto the floor, patient. "I'll wait."

I moved through the room slowly. Touching each desk. Reading each carving. Finding names of students I didn't remember. Finding traces of a girl who'd existed here.

At Cressa's desk, I found something carved into the underside. Had to crouch to see it, pressing my cheek against cold stone.

C is brave even when she doesn't feel brave. - R

My handwriting. My words. Written to a friend who needed reassurance.

I sat on the floor. Stared at the carving.

"I wrote that," I said. Not a question. Just acknowledgment.

"Yes." Valdic's voice came from across the room. "After Cressa failed her manners exam the second time. She was crying. Thought she'd never pass. You took her to her desk and showed her that carving. Told her you'd written it months earlier. That you'd always known she was brave."

"Did it help?"

"She stopped crying." Valdic moved closer. "And she passed the third time. Because you all believed she could."

I touched the carving again. Traced the letters with skeletal fingers. Tried to feel connected to the person who'd written them.

Couldn't quite manage it. But something stirred. Something small and buried. Something that whispered: You were this once. You cared this once. You saw people's pain and tried to ease it once.

"I ordered a child beaten yesterday," I said. "She dropped a tray. Wasted food. I didn't think about whether she needed reassurance or help. Just thought about discipline and consequences."

"I know." Valdic's tone held no judgment. Just sadness. "That's not who you were in this room. But it's who the crown has made you."

"Or who I've chosen to become." I stood slowly, bones creaking. "The crown doesn't control me. It influences. It takes. It whispers. But ultimately, I'm making choices. Even when I don't remember my reasons, I'm choosing."

"Then choose to remember this place." Valdic stood beside me. "Choose to remember that you once cared about more than just one person. Choose to carry these carvings with you even if you can't remember making them."

I looked at the room one more time. At the desks and the alcove and the names carved in stone. At evidence of four children who'd believed in each other enough to make promises.

"I'll try," I said. Not a promise. Just an acknowledgment that trying mattered.

"That's enough." Valdic moved toward the door. "For now, that's enough."

We left the schoolroom. Walked back through the corridors toward my chambers. The bioluminescence seemed brighter after the dimness of that ancient room.

At my door, Valdic paused.

"Nokoa wanted me to tell you something."

"What?"

"He remembers this room. Remembers all of it. The hide and seek. The kicked shins. The promises carved in stone." Valdic's purple eyes were gentle. "And he says that even if you don't remember, he's holding those memories for both of you. Waiting for when you're ready to share them again."

"What if I'm never ready?"

"Then he'll hold them forever." Valdic's voice was certain. "Because that's what the four of you promised. To face things together. And he's not ready to break that promise, even if the crown makes you forget you made it."

He left me at my door.

I entered my chambers. Stared at the yellow dress still hanging there. The journal in my drawer. And now: a schoolroom. Names in stone. Carvings under desks. Four children who'd believed friendship mattered enough to make promises.

The crown whispered. Tried to take it.

"No," I said aloud. "Not this one. Let me keep this one."

And the crown, perhaps surprised by resistance, went quiet.

I sat on my bed. Closed my eyes. Held onto the image of that room. Of desks and carvings and evidence that I'd once seen people's pain and tried to ease it.

Couldn't remember feeling it. Couldn't access the emotions that had driven that girl.

But I could remember that she'd existed. That she'd made promises. That she'd believed in caring about people.

And maybe—just maybe—that was enough to start with.

The hollow crown pulsed against my skull, waiting.

But I held firm.

Not this memory.

Not yet.

Chapter Twenty-Five

The Outer Cities Attack

Nokoa

The attack was planned for dawn. When the bone court would be least prepared. When guards were changing shifts. When the spectral guardians might be at their weakest.

I watched them prepare from my tent. Couldn't help—could barely stand without support—but I could watch. Could bear witness to desperation sharpening itself into action.

Nalla moved through the camp like a general. Quiet commands. Efficient movements. Organizing people who had no business being soldiers into something that resembled an army. Most of them had never held weapons before. Had never fought anything more dangerous than hunger and despair.

Now they were going to attack the bone court. Were going to march on the skull castle with its bridges and caves and spectral defenders. Were going to fight death magic with stolen divine weapons and desperate hope.

They were going to die.

I could see it in their faces. They knew it too. These weren't soldiers convinced of victory. These were people who'd decided dying while fighting was better than dying while starving. At least fighting meant something. At least resistance left a mark.

"You shouldn't watch this," Valdic said from behind me.

I didn't turn. Couldn't look away from the grim parade. "They're doing this because of her. Because she forgot them. Because she broke her promise."

"They're doing this because they're starving." Valdic moved beside me, his warmth a contrast to the cold morning air. "Because the tithe is killing them. Because they have nothing left to lose."

A woman walked past my tent. Maybe twenty-five, though starvation made age hard to judge. Her ribs showed through her shirt. Her eyes were sunken, shadowed. Her hands shook as she carried a rusted sword that looked older than she was.

Behind her, a man—older, grey-haired, moving with the careful deliberation of someone whose body was failing. He carried the bone weapon. The one they'd stolen from the guardian tomb. It pulsed with pale light, hungry for death magic it could channel.

"They're already dead," I said quietly. "They just haven't stopped moving yet."

More people gathered. Thirty. Forty. Fifty. Not an army. Just a collection of desperate, starving survivors who'd been pushed past the point where self-preservation mattered. Some wore armor—scraps of leather, bent metal, anything that might stop a blade. Most wore nothing but threadbare clothes and determination.

Children watched from the edges of camp. Too young to fight. Too weak to be useful. Just witnesses to their parents' last stand.

I saw the girl I'd given food to yesterday. The six-year-old with hollow eyes. She clutched something to her chest—probably the dried meat and hard bread I'd handed her. Still saving it. Still trying to make resources last.

She was watching her mother prepare to die.

"Nokoa." Nalla's voice cut through my thoughts. I turned. She stood at my tent's entrance, fully armed. Leather armor reinforced with bone fragments. The stolen weapon strapped to her back. "You're coming with us."

"What?" Valdic stepped between us, hackles rising. "He can barely stand. He's dying. You can't—"

"I can." Nalla's voice was flat. Final. "He's our insurance. If the hollow queen sees him in danger, maybe she'll hesitate. Maybe she'll remember something. Maybe we can use that."

"You want to use me as a hostage." Not a question. Just tired understanding.

"I want to use every advantage we have." Nalla met my eyes. No apology in hers. No guilt. Just cold pragmatism born from desperation. "You're the only thing she still cares about. That makes you valuable."

She was right. Renata would hesitate if she saw me in danger. Would second-guess her spectral guardians if I stood among the outer cities fighters. Might even negotiate if she thought my life hung in the balance.

Or she'd kill everyone to get to me. Hard to say which anymore.

"Fine," I said. "I'll come."

"Nokoa—" Valdic started.

"It's fine." I grabbed his shoulder for support. Stood on shaking legs. "Maybe seeing me will break through. Maybe she'll remember something worth remembering."

"Or maybe you'll die," Valdic said quietly.

"I'm already dying." I gestured at my bandaged arms, at my yellowing eyes, at everything the resurrection had made me. "At least this way it might mean something."

Nalla nodded. Turned away to finish preparations, barking orders to people too weak to follow them properly.

Valdic helped me walk to where the others were gathering. Each step hurt. Each breath felt like work. The witch runes under my skin burned hotter with every movement, spreading faster, consuming more of me. I could feel them crawling up my neck now, reaching for my jaw.

The outer cities army—if you could call it that—stood ready. Fifty people. Maybe sixty. All of them starving. Most of them already half-dead. Armed with rust and desperation and one stolen divine weapon.

They were going to march on the bone court.

They were going to die fighting a queen who'd forgotten she promised to help them.

And I was going with them. Because maybe—impossibly, desperately—maybe seeing me would remind her of who she'd been.

* * *

The march to the bone court took hours. We moved slowly—had to. Half the people could barely walk. Some collapsed and had to be helped up. Some collapsed and couldn't get up, had to be left behind to die in the wasteland.

The famine's effects were visible everywhere. Not just in the people—in the land itself. Dead earth stretched in all directions. Grey soil that had once supported crops, now cracked and lifeless. Withered forests now just skeletal remains. Streams showing only muddy trickles of poisoned water that smelled of rot and death.

Bones protruded from grey earth like accusations.

This was Renata's doing. Not directly—she hadn't killed the land with her hands. But her death magic had done it. Her spectral guardians had drained life from everything they touched. Her power had spread like corruption.

For me. She'd done this to keep me alive.

"I did this," I said to Valdic.

He walked beside me, paws sinking in mud that sucked at every step. "You didn't."

"I died. She brought me back. Everything after is consequence of that choice." I stared at the dead land. "If I'd stayed dead, none of this happens. The outer cities still have their promise. The land still grows food. The guardians still sleep peacefully."

"You didn't ask to be resurrected."

"Didn't stop her either." I nearly fell. Caught myself against Valdic, fingers digging into his fur. "Could have refused. Could have found a way to die permanently. Could have ended this before it started."

"You love her," Valdic said simply. "Love doesn't refuse. Love doesn't end itself to prove a point."

Maybe. But maybe love should. Maybe loving someone enough to let them destroy the world was wrong. Maybe being willing to live while everything else died was the real monstrosity.

The bone court appeared on the horizon. Skull-shaped castle rising from dead earth like a monument to death itself. Bridges spanning dark water that looked more like oil than liquid. Caves glowing with bioluminescent light—blue and green against the grey wasteland. Home to death magic and spectral armies and one hollow queen who'd forgotten everyone except me.

The outer cities army halted. Stared at what they were about to attack.

"We're really doing this," someone whispered.

Nalla raised the bone weapon. It caught the weak sunlight, pulsing with its own inner glow. "We're doing this. For our children. For the promise she broke. For a chance to make her remember what fairness looks like."

Noble words. Brave words. Words that couldn't disguise the fact that they were all about to die.

"Forward," Nalla commanded.

They moved. Slow. Steady. Toward the skull castle and the bridges and the death that waited beyond. Their footsteps made no sound on the dead earth. Like ghosts marching toward their final rest.

I moved with them. Each step agony. Each breath a negotiation with failing lungs. Valdic supported me, kept me upright, kept me moving when everything in my body screamed to stop.

"This is suicide," Valdic said quietly.

"I know."

"You'll die if we attack. The resurrection is barely holding. Combat will finish it."

"I know." I kept walking. "But maybe she'll see me. Maybe she'll remember. Maybe something will break through."

"And if it doesn't?"

Then I'd die. Really die. Permanently die. And maybe that was better. Maybe being dead was better than being the excuse she used to justify everything terrible.

Maybe my death would free her. Let her stop. Let the crown lose its grip. Let the woman who'd pressed flowers and planned gardens come back from wherever she'd gone.

Or maybe she'd just get worse. Maybe losing me would break her completely. Maybe my death would be the final push that transformed her from hollow queen into something truly monstrous.

No way to know. Just had to move forward and see what happened.

The bridges came into view. Ancient bone architecture spanning dark water. Spectral guardians stood watch—the seven previous hollow rulers, their forms towering and terrible. Behind them, spectral soldiers filled every space. Dead souls bound to Renata's will, ready to defend the bone court against anything.

Against us. Against this collection of starving, desperate people who just wanted her to remember what she'd promised them.

Nalla raised the bone weapon higher. It blazed with light—pale and cold and hungry. Death magic channeling through stolen divine architecture. Wrong in every way that mattered. But powerful.

"For our children!" Nalla's voice rang out across the dead land. "For the promise! For fairness!"

The outer cities army charged.

Not really a charge. More like a shambling advance. But they moved forward with whatever strength remained. Moved toward the spectral guardians and the skull castle and the queen who'd forgotten them.

I moved with them. Felt the resurrection magic flaring, burning, trying to keep up with demands my body couldn't meet. Felt witch runes spreading across my chest, my neck, reaching for my face. Felt death approaching.

The spectral guardians met them at the bridges. Seven towering forms with empty eyes and absolute purpose. They moved with perfect coordination—Renata's will made manifest.

People died immediately. Not from wounds—from exhaustion, from starvation, from bodies too weak to sustain combat even for seconds. They just collapsed. Stopped breathing. Became corpses among the other corpses.

Others fought. Swung rusted weapons with desperate strength. Managed to damage spectral forms, make dead souls falter, create small openings.

Nalla wielded the bone weapon with terrible precision. Each strike dissolved spectral soldiers completely. Divine death magic against regular death magic. Where the weapon passed, spectral forms simply ceased to exist.

She was winning her small battles. Creating space. Pushing forward.

But they were losing the war. There were too many spectral soldiers. Too many dead souls bound to Renata's will. And the outer cities fighters were too weak, too starving, too desperate.

This wasn't a battle. It was a slaughter.

I stumbled forward anyway. Let Valdic half-carry me toward the skull castle. Toward where Renata would be watching. Toward where maybe—impossibly—she might see me and remember something worth saving.

"Renata!" I shouted. Not sure if she could hear. Not sure if it mattered. "I'm here! I'm alive! You don't have to do this!"

No response. Just spectral guardians moving like waves of death. Just outer cities fighters dying like candles in wind.

I collapsed. Couldn't keep standing. The resurrection failed—not completely, but enough. My legs gave out. I hit the bridge hard, stone cold against my cheek. The impact knocked the air from my lungs.

Valdic stood over me. Protecting me.

Above, the skull castle loomed. Silent. Watching with empty eye sockets large enough to swallow the sun.

And inside, Renata sat on her throne, forgetting us all.

Around me, people screamed. Died. Fought impossible battles with their last breaths.

The bone weapon blazed. Nalla pushed forward, carving a path through death itself.

But she'd forgotten how to hear anything except the crown's whispers.

Forgotten everything except my name.

Chapter Twenty-Six

Blood on Marble

Renata

The alarm reached me in my chambers. Bells ringing, sharp and insistent. Guards shouting. The bone court under attack.

I felt it through the spectral guardians before I heard it through my ears. Seven dead souls registering threat. Coordinated assault on the bridges. Outer cities fighters wielding the stolen bone weapon.

They'd actually done it. Actually attacked.

I should have felt something. Surprise, maybe. Or anger. Or even just the strategic calculation of threat assessment.

Nothing came. Just cold acknowledgment: they were attacking, therefore they needed to be stopped.

I walked toward the throne room without hurrying. No need to rush. The spectral guardians would hold. They always held. Death didn't tire. Didn't fear. Didn't hesitate.

Maxin met me in the corridor. He looked worse than yesterday—more hair gone, skin greyer, the slow transformation accelerating. "Hollow Queen, the outer cities—"

"I know." I moved past him. "Assemble the council. I'll handle this from the throne room."

"Handle it how?" He followed, his footsteps uneven. "They're starving. Desperate. This is suicide for them."

"Then let them commit suicide." The words came easy. Automatic. "They made their choice."

The throne room opened before me. High ceiling made of interlocking ribs. Floor of polished vertebrae forming spiral designs. Walls covered in the court's history—bones carved with names and dates and deeds.

I sat on the throne. Felt it connect to me—bone to bone, magic to magic. The hollow crown tightened, its bone pressing deeper into my skull, and I could see through the spectral guardians' eyes.

The bridges. Blood already staining ancient stone. Bodies in the water—some outer cities, some spectral soldiers they'd managed to destroy. Not many. The outer cities fighters were too weak. Too starving. Too desperate to fight effectively.

But that bone weapon. That was dangerous. I watched through dead eyes as Nalla wielded it. Each strike dissolved spectral soldiers completely. Divine magic cutting through death magic like it was paper.

She had to be stopped. Contained. Killed.

I called the full force of the spectral guardians to the bridges. Every dead soul I commanded. Every piece of death magic I could channel. They poured out of the bone court like a flood finding the lowest ground.

The outer cities fighters didn't stand a chance.

I watched through a thousand dead eyes as my army overwhelmed them. Surrounded them. Cut them down with bone weapons and cold efficiency.

They tried to fight back. Some of them were brave. Some of them managed to destroy multiple spectral soldiers before being overwhelmed.

It didn't matter. There were too many of us. Too few of them. And they were already dying before they arrived.

This was just finishing what hunger had started.

Blood on marble. Blood on bridges. Blood in water turning it dark and viscous. Bodies everywhere—collapsed from starvation and exhaustion as much as from combat wounds.

Nalla still fought. Desperate. Precise. Destroying spectral soldiers faster than seemed possible. But even she was slowing. Exhaustion catching up. The weapon burning through energy faster than her starving body could provide. She stumbled. Caught herself. Kept fighting.

She would die soon. They would all die soon.

And I felt nothing watching it happen.

Then I saw him.

Through spectral eyes on the bridge. Through the chaos and blood and fighting. A figure collapsed on stone. Too thin. Too pale. Dying.

Nokoa.

Everything stopped.

Not metaphorically. Actually stopped. The world contracted to a single point: him, collapsed, barely breathing, my army advancing toward him.

"STOP!" The word tore out of me. Not a command. A scream.

The spectral guardians froze. Every dead soul. Every guardian. Every soldier. All of them halting mid-strike as my will crashed through them.

"Pull back! All of you! NOW!"

They retreated. Immediately. Without question. Creating space around Nokoa's collapsed form and Valdic standing guard over him.

The outer cities fighters stopped too. Stared. Not at the spectral guardians withdrawing—at me. At the sudden, absolute cessation of violence the moment I'd seen him.

Nalla lowered the bone weapon slowly. Her face showed something between horror and understanding.

They'd brought him as leverage. As insurance. As a way to make me hesitate.

They hadn't expected this. Hadn't expected me to abandon the entire battle instantly. Completely. Without calculation or strategy or thought.

"Hollow Queen—" Maxin started from beside the throne.

"Quiet." I stood. Moved toward the balcony. Needed to see him with my own eyes.

There. On the main bridge. Valdic standing over him protectively. Nokoa's chest rising and falling. Shallow breaths. Barely alive. But alive.

"Spectral guardians," I said, my voice steady now. Cold. "Form a perimeter. Protect the collapsed figure. Nothing touches him. Nothing approaches him. If anyone tries, destroy them."

The guardians moved. Not toward the outer cities fighters—toward Nokoa. Creating a wall of death around him. Protecting him even from his own allies.

Nalla's eyes widened. "You're—you're protecting him? Even though he's with us?"

"I'm protecting him," I confirmed, "because he's HIM. He doesn't come to attack me. He comes out of guilt and force. He's not on your side—you took his choices away from him."

I would always choose him. Always. Without thought. Without calculation. Without hesitation.

"This is insane," Nalla whispered, but she was backing away. They all were.

"Let them go," I said to Maxin. To Praxis, who'd appeared during the chaos. "All of them. Let them retreat."

"They attacked—" Praxis started.

"I don't care." My voice was flat. Final. "He's with them. They retreat safely or the guardians will ensure it. Those are the only options."

"You're letting them escape," Maxin said slowly. "You're letting rebels who attacked the bone court just... leave. Because he's there."

"Yes." No shame in it. No doubt. "Valdic, get him out of here. Take him back to their camp. Keep him safe."

Valdic stared up at me. Even from the distance, I could see the grief in his purple eyes. The horror of understanding what I'd become.

I'd just proven I cared about nothing except Nokoa. Not the bone court. Not victory. Not strategy or consequences or sending messages about rebellion.

Just him.

"This is what you wanted," I called down to Nalla. "You brought him thinking it would make me hesitate. You were wrong. I didn't hesitate. I chose him immediately. Over everything. Over everyone. Remember that next time you think about using him as leverage."

The threat was clear: bringing him into danger would make me more unpredictable, not less. Would make me abandon strategy entirely. Would make me protect him with such absolute focus that anyone near him would be caught in the crossfire.

Nalla's face went pale. She understood. They all understood.

They'd wanted to prove I could be reasoned with. Instead, they'd proven I couldn't. Not when it came to him.

"Go," I said. "Before I change my mind about mercy."

They went. Valdic helping Nokoa up, half-carrying him toward the retreating forces. Nalla covering the retreat with the bone weapon, her movements mechanical. Shocked.

The outer cities fighters fled back into the wasteland. Carrying their wounded. Dragging their dead. Moving as fast as starvation allowed.

And my spectral guardians held position. Watching them go. Protecting Nokoa's retreat even as he left with my enemies.

"That was a mistake," Praxis said quietly.

"No." I turned away from the balcony. "That was the only choice. The only one I'll ever make."

"You just showed them your weakness." Maxin's voice held despair. "Showed them exactly how to control you."

"They already knew," I said. "Everyone knows."

I walked back to the throne. Sat down.

"Execute the prisoners," I said calmly. "The ones too wounded to retreat. Dawn. Public. Make it brutal."

"Hollow Queen—" Maxin protested.

"They're not him." My voice was empty. Hollow. "So they don't matter. Execute them all."

Praxis nodded slowly. "As you command."

I sat on the throne and watched through spectral eyes as Nokoa disappeared into the wasteland. Watched until I couldn't see him anymore.

My hands shook.

Not from guilt. Not from doubt about choosing him.

From rage. From the pain of seeing him with them. From the agony of watching him stand with rebels who'd attacked my home. From the bond that punished me for loving him while he'd been carried here by people who wanted me dead.

He'd been so close. Close enough that I'd felt him through the bond as clearly as my own heartbeat. And then he was gone again, back into the wasteland, and every inch of distance between us was another thread of the bond pulled taut.

I'd chosen him immediately. Without thought. Over everything.

And he'd left anyway.

"You did well," Oriana whispered, but the words felt distant, thin. Like something said at a great remove. "He'll come home. He has to."

I didn't answer.

Just sat on the throne with my shaking hands and watched the wasteland through spectral eyes, waiting for something that might never come.

Act Three

Hollowed

Chapter Twenty-Seven

PUBLIC EXECUTION

Renata

Dawn came grey and cold. I stood outside the skull castle, where the outer cities camp could see. Where what remained of them—twenty survivors, maybe less—could watch from the wasteland and understand what rebellion cost.

The prisoners knelt in a line. Five of them. Too wounded to retreat. Too weak to fight. Captured during the battle and held overnight in cells that smelled like death and despair and old blood.

They were already dying. I could see it in their faces. Starvation had hollowed their cheeks, made their eyes sink deep into skulls. Blood loss from yesterday's wounds. Exhaustion so profound it looked like they'd forgotten how to breathe properly.

Executing them was mercy. Really. Ending their suffering instead of letting them waste away in cells.

That's what I told myself.

The bone court citizens gathered to watch. Forced assembly. Everyone had to see. Had to witness. Had to understand that this is what happened when you attacked the queen.

Children in the crowd. I could see them between adult bodies. Wide eyes. Scared faces. They shouldn't be here. Shouldn't have to watch this.

But they needed to learn.

A man near the front flinched when I stepped forward, pulling his daughter behind him as if my shadow could strike. Others refused to meet my eyes. That tremor of fear moved through the crowd—and for a heartbeat, I almost felt it.

Almost felt what it meant to inspire such terror.

The logic lined up neatly in my mind, cold and sharp. But the more perfect the reasoning became, the sicker it should have made me.

Should have. Didn't.

I walked forward. The prisoners watched me approach. No begging. No pleading. Just tired acceptance. They knew this was coming. Had known since they attacked.

"You breached the bone court," I said. My voice carried across the silent crowd, echoing off bone walls. "Used stolen weapons. Threatened the council. Attacked spectral guardians. The penalty is death."

One of them—a woman, maybe forty—met my eyes. "We were starving. You forgot us. Forgot your promise."

"I made no promise." The lie came easily. Automatic. "And starvation doesn't justify treason."

"You did promise." Her voice was weak but certain, each word costing her. "You sat across from us and promised fairness. Promised our children would be safe. Promised the tithe would change." She coughed. Blood on her lips, bright against pale skin. "You promised, and you forgot."

I stared at her. Tried to remember. Tried to access any memory of sitting across a table from outer cities representatives and promising anything.

Nothing came. Just empty space where memory should be.

"Stop reaching for these memories," Oriana said, her voice sharp. "They aren't there. You don't need to allow these people to keep using this line against you."

"Even if I did promise," I said slowly, "you broke that promise by attacking. By stealing. By threatening everything I'm trying to protect."

"What are you protecting?" Another prisoner. Young. Maybe twenty. "We're all dying anyway. The land is dead. The food is gone. You're not protecting anything. You're just making sure we all suffer equally."

The crowd shifted. Uncomfortable murmuring. Guards tensing, hands moving to weapons.

But they were arguing. Making me defend myself. Making me sound like—

Like what I was. A queen who'd forgotten her people. Who'd broken promises she couldn't remember making. Who was killing desperate, starving rebels for the crime of reminding her she'd once cared.

"Enough." I raised my hand. Called bone magic to the surface. It came easily now, like breathing. "You attacked the bone court. That is the only fact that matters. The only truth that needs speaking."

The first prisoner—the woman who remembered my promise—started to speak. I didn't let her finish.

Bone magic lanced through her. Not quickly. Not mercifully. I broke her bones methodically. One by one. Starting with fingers. Moving to hands. Then arms. Working my way through her skeleton while she screamed.

The crowd watched. Silent. Horrified. Children buried their faces in parents' clothing. Adults stood frozen, unable to look away even as their stomachs turned.

I kept going. Ribs. Spine. Pelvis. Each bone breaking with precision. With control. Each crack audible. Each break deliberate.

She stopped screaming eventually. Went silent. Went still. Just a broken body that used to be a person who'd wanted her children to eat.

"This is justice," I said to the silent crowd. "This is what happens to rebellion."

I moved to the second prisoner. The young one who'd asked what I was protecting.

He didn't scream. Just stared at me while I broke him. While I demonstrated exactly what the bone court's power looked like. His eyes never left mine. Accusing until the very end.

The crown voices stirred. Not concerned. Pleased.

"Power is beautiful when you claim it," Alaric said, warmth in his voice. "They'll remember this. They'll understand."

"Legacy matters." Lyanna's voice was almost reverent. "This moment defines you. Defines your reign. Let them see strength."

"Whatever it takes to protect him," Oriana said, always bringing it back. Always. "This keeps you strong enough. This keeps him safe."

All three of them genuinely celebrating. All three convinced this was right and necessary and good.

And I—

I felt nothing.

Should feel horror. Should feel guilt. Should feel the weight of breaking living people's bones while crowds watched and children cried and the last pieces of my humanity crumbled to dust.

But there was just methodology. Just the work of demonstrating power. Just the cold certainty that this was necessary for survival.

Third prisoner. Fourth. Fifth. All of them broken slowly. All of them dying in stages. All of them turned into examples that would haunt the bone court's nightmares for years.

When it was done, I stood among the bodies. Blood on my hands—theirs, not mine. Bone dust in my hair, white against black. The smell of death and fear coating everything, thick enough to taste.

The crowd was completely silent. Not even children crying anymore. Just shocked, horrified silence that pressed down like physical weight.

"Let this be remembered," I said. "Attack the bone court and this is what awaits you. Question my authority and this is what happens. Choose rebellion and this is how you die."

I walked away. Back toward the skull castle. Back toward my chambers. Back toward the isolation that came with being someone who broke people's bones in public and called it justice.

The crowd parted before me. No one wanted to be close.

Valdic stood in my doorway. I hadn't seen him arrive. But he was there now, purple eyes dim with grief.

"That wasn't you," he said quietly.

"Wasn't it?" I moved past him into my chambers. "Seems like it was very much me. My hands. My magic. My choice."

"The Renata I knew would have helped them. Would have fed them. Would have kept her promise even when it was hard."

"The Renata you knew is dead." I washed blood off my hands in the basin. Watched it swirl pink in the water, then darker. "This is what remains. This is what the crown made. This is what Nokoa needs me to be."

"He doesn't want this." Valdic followed me inside, claws clicking on stone. "He'd be horrified. You know that."

"He doesn't have to want it." I dried my hands, the cloth coming away stained. "He just has to be alive. That's all that matters. Keeping him alive. Keeping him safe. Everything else is just noise."

"Everything else is your humanity." Valdic's voice cracked. "Everything else is what made him love you in the first place. What made you worth saving."

"Then he loved a weakness." The words came easy. Too easy. "Loved something that would have gotten us both killed. Better to be strong and hollow than weak and dead."

Valdic stared at me. Long silence. His purple eyes seeing something that made his skeletal frame slump, defeated.

"You're already dead," he said finally. "You just haven't stopped moving yet."

He left.

I stood alone in my chambers. Blood still under my fingernails despite washing. The memory of breaking bones still fresh—the sound, the feel, the resistance giving way. The screaming still echoing in the hollow spaces of my skull.

And I felt nothing.

That was the worst part. Not that I'd done it. Not that I'd broken people slowly while crowds watched. But that I'd done it and felt nothing except the cold satisfaction of work completed.

The woman who would have been horrified was gone. The woman who would have wept was gone. The woman who would have found another way was gone.

Just this remained.

I pulled out the journal. Opened it to that entry about violets. About growing in impossible places. About Nokoa comparing me to flowers that survived where nothing should survive.

Would he compare me to flowers now? Would he look at me—blood under my nails, death in my eyes, cruelty in my hands—and see anything worth comparing to beauty?

No. He'd see a monster. He'd see what I'd become. He'd see the woman who broke people's bones in public and justified it through love for him.

He'd be horrified.

And I'd tell him it was necessary.

The journal pages blurred. Not from tears—the crown had taken those too. Just exhaustion. The weight of being someone who did terrible things and felt nothing.

Tomorrow I'd be queen again. Would make more hard choices. Would justify more cruelty. Would forget the faces of the people I'd broken today.

Tomorrow I'd be a little less human. A little more hollow.

But tonight, I'd sit with the journal. With the pressed flowers. With the evidence of who I'd been.

And I'd know—really know, in the parts of me the crown hadn't quite reached—that Valdic was right.

I was already dead.

Just hadn't stopped moving yet.

Chapter Twenty-Eight

Nokoa's Collapse

Nokoa

The screaming reached the camp before the survivors did. Not from the executed—they were already dead. But from those who'd watched. From outer cities people who'd witnessed what their queen had become. Their voices carried across the wasteland, raw and broken.

What I'd made her become.

I sat in my tent, listening. Couldn't move. Couldn't stand. The resurrection had failed during the battle—not completely, but enough. My legs wouldn't hold weight anymore. My arms barely functioned. The witch runes had spread across my chest, up my neck, reaching the edges of my jaw. Dark lines visible against pale skin.

Soon they'd cover my face. Soon there'd be nothing left that looked human. Just a walking corpse. Just death refusing to stay dead.

The survivors stumbled into camp. Twenty of them. Maybe less. Out of sixty who'd attacked. The rest were dead on the bridges or dying in the wasteland or captured and—

And executed. Publicly. Slowly. While crowds watched and children cried.

I'd heard about it from the survivors who'd witnessed from the wasteland. Heard their descriptions. Heard their horror. Heard them try to explain what it looked like when someone you'd trusted broke prisoners' bones one by one and called it justice.

My skin felt like it was burning. Not metaphor—actual sensation spreading from my chest outward, the witch runes blazing beneath bandages. Everything tangled through the bond—her cruelty, my horror, both of us connected in ways that made separation impossible.

"Nokoa." Valdic's voice. He'd appeared in my tent without me noticing. "You need to eat something."

"Can't." My voice rasped, throat raw. "Can't hold anything down anymore."

It was true. Everything I ate came back up within minutes. My body rejecting sustenance because corpses didn't need food. Because I was supposed to be dead and my stomach knew it even if magic kept me moving.

"You need to try." Valdic set down a bowl of something—broth, maybe, or warm water with herbs. "You're dying."

"I know."

"Faster than before." He moved closer, his warmth a small comfort against the cold creeping through me. "The attack. The battle. It accelerated everything. You need—"

I screamed.

Didn't mean to. Couldn't stop it. Pain lanced through me, every nerve ending igniting. Every bone cracking under pressure that had nothing to do with physical force.

The witch runes weren't just spreading anymore. They were burning. Moving under my skin. Crawling. Burrowing. Rewriting everything they touched into something that shouldn't exist.

Valdic held me down. Kept me from thrashing. Kept me from breaking myself further.

"She's thinking of you," he said. Quiet. Sad. "The bond is destroying you."

Of course she was thinking of me. She always thought of me. Between every terrible choice. Between every cruelty. Between breaking prisoners' bones, she probably thought of me. Justified it through me. Made it all about keeping me safe.

And every time she did, we both paid for it.

"Make it stop," I gasped. "Please. Make it—"

Another wave. Worse than before. My spine arched, vertebrae grinding against each other. Three more fingers broke—clean snaps, one after another. My left arm twisted at an angle arms shouldn't twist. Something in my chest tore, wet and final.

Valdic held me through it. Steady. Speaking words I couldn't quite hear through the roar of agony filling my skull.

When it ended—never really ended, just dulled to manageable torture—I lay gasping on the cot.

"Alaira sent a message," Valdic said after a moment. "She says she can stabilize you. Completely this time. Stop the deterioration. Give you time."

"What does she want?" Because there was always a cost.

"She wants you to come to her. Says there's a ritual she needs to perform in person."

I stared at the tent's ceiling. Canvas stretched tight overhead, stained with smoke and time. "She's using me."

"I know."

"She wants something specific. This isn't just about helping."

"I know." Valdic's purple eyes were dim. "But she's also the only one who might actually help. The only one who understands the magic that brought you back."

I tried to laugh. Failed. Just coughed blood instead, tasting copper and rot. "Everyone's using everyone. At least she offers relief."

"She offers survival." Valdic wiped blood from my mouth with gentle paws. "That's not nothing. Nokoa, you're dying. Really dying. Days, maybe. Hours if the bond reactions continue. If you want more time, she's the only option."

Time. For what? To watch Renata become worse? To be the excuse she used for more atrocities? To exist as the justification for everything terrible?

But also—time with her. Time to maybe reach her. Time to find some way to break through the crown's influence and remind her who she'd been.

Time to try. Even if trying was pointless. Even if she was already gone.

"Tell her I'll come," I said.

Valdic nodded. "I'll arrange it. She's waiting at the wasteland's edge."

"Nalla won't like this."

Another pain spike. Smaller this time. Just my body reminding me it was falling apart.

"Nalla isn't in charge of whether you live or die," Valdic said quietly. "Only you get to decide that. Only you get to choose if you want more time or if you're ready to let go."

Let go. The phrase hung in the air. Heavy. Final. True.

I could let go. Could stop fighting the resurrection's failure. Could just die—really die, permanently—and maybe that would free Renata. Maybe losing me would break the crown's hold.

Or maybe it would destroy her completely.

No way to know. No way to calculate. No way to choose the right path when every path led to ruin.

"I'll go to Alaira," I said. "I'll take whatever time she can give me. Because maybe—impossibly—maybe I can still reach Renata. Maybe I can still remind her who she was."

"She broke people's bones in public." Valdic's voice was gentle but firm. "Slowly. Methodically. While crowds watched. While children cried. That's what she's become."

"I know." I did know. Understood it completely. "But I have to try anyway. Have to believe there's something left worth reaching. Because if there's not—if she's truly gone—then everything we went through, everything we sacrificed, it was all for nothing."

He left to arrange the meeting.

I lay on the cot and thought of her deliberately. Let the pain come. Let the bond punish me for missing her. Let everything burn because at least burning meant feeling something.

Her face. Grey eyes I'd loved since we were children. The way she'd looked at me before everything broke—like I was sunshine instead of shadow.

Did she still look at me that way? When she thought of me between atrocities? Or did she just see justification?

The pain peaked. My body convulsed. More bones breaking—ribs this time, two of them cracking like dry branches. More witch runes spreading, crawling up toward my ear.

Worth it. The pain was worth it to hold her image. To believe—despite everything—that she was still in there somewhere.

That the woman who'd pressed flowers and planned gardens wasn't completely gone.

Even if saving each other meant dying first.

Even if love had become the thing destroying us both.

Even as we destroyed everything trying.

Chapter Twenty-Nine

Into the Catacombs

Renata

Alaira's message arrived on dead wings. A butterfly messenger, ash-grey and deteriorating, its body crumbling even as it landed. The letter it carried was brief. Almost desperate.

The ritual. Now. He's failing faster than expected. If you want him to survive, come to the deepest chamber. Bring bone dust from the sealed box. Bring water from the underground lake. Come alone.

I read it three times. Trying to find the trap. Trying to see the manipulation hidden in urgent words.

Found nothing. Just desperation. Just the priestess who'd created the crown trying to fix what she'd broken.

Or make it worse. Hard to tell which anymore.

The pain hit without warning. Sharp spike through my temples. Nokoa thinking of me. Missing me so badly it was destroying his body. I gasped, pressed my hands to my head, felt blood start flowing from my nose. Hot against my lips.

He was dying. Really dying this time. The resurrection finally failing. And I could feel it through the bond—his body giving up, his witch runes spreading out of control, everything unraveling.

I had to go.

The hollow crown's bone tightened as I stood. Not quite pain. Just pressure.

"Be careful," Oriana whispered. "The catacombs hold old magic."

"Small ritual only," Alaric added. "Don't disturb too much. Don't wake what's sleeping."

"He needs you," Lyanna finished. "Do what's necessary."

I descended alone. Through corridors I barely saw, my vision tunneling. Down stairs carved from vertebrae and ribs, each step echoing in the silence. Into the depths where few people ventured and fewer returned unchanged.

The catacombs opened before me. Ancient. Sacred. Wrong in ways I couldn't articulate but felt in my bones.

The walls were mosaics of femurs—thousands of them, arranged in patterns that seemed almost like writing. Spirals and symbols that hurt to look at directly. The ceiling was interlocking ribs forming gothic arches that shouldn't be structurally possible but were. The floor was vertebrae inlaid in spiral designs that drew the eye inward, deeper, toward the center where something waited.

Everything bone. Everything beautiful in its wrongness.

The carved bone box sat where it always had. Seal anchor. Prison focus. The thing that kept the bone god contained—or had, before I'd started breaking it piece by piece.

It was covered in warnings carved repeatedly around its surface: Don't touch. Don't open. Don't disturb.

I'd disturbed it already. Had cracked it during previous rituals. Had weakened the seal with every desperate attempt to save Nokoa.

Now I needed to disturb it more.

The box had a small opening at its base. Just large enough to reach inside. I pulled out a handful of dust that glowed faintly in the dim light. It felt aware. Conscious. Like holding ground-up pieces of something that still remembered being alive.

I put it in a vial. Sealed it with wax. Tried not to think about what I was carrying.

The underground lake waited beyond. Black water, perfectly still, reflecting nothing. Not even the bioluminescent light penetrated its surface. It smelled like time and darkness and things that shouldn't exist.

I filled a second vial. The water was cold—colder than water should be. It burned my hand even through the crown's numbness, like touching winter itself concentrated into liquid form.

When I pulled my hand back, the water where I'd touched had frozen. Just that spot. Ice spreading in crystalline patterns.

The lake was aware. Something that knew I was there.

I backed away carefully.

The two alcoves still held their sleeping guardians. Fern and Sevi. Mummified figures covered in witch runes. Perla's alcove was empty. Scorched. Just empty space where a pyreling guardian had slept for centuries before I woke her and killed her and consumed her ashes.

Fern stirred.

Just slightly. Just a rustling of petals. Like she was dreaming. Like my presence was disturbing her sleep.

I froze. Barely breathing. Watching.

She settled. Went still. Didn't wake.

Not yet.

But soon. I could feel it. The prison was weakening. The seal was cracking. The guardians were starting to respond to the magic I kept pouring into this chamber.

Soon they'd all wake. And I'd have to kill them like I'd killed Perla.

I gathered my vials and prepared to leave.

"You're breaking the prison." The voice came from everywhere. From the bones in the walls. From the water in the lake. From the air itself.

The bone god.

I spun. Saw nothing. Just empty chamber. Just ancient architecture and sleeping guardians and the carved box with its cracking seal.

"Every ritual you perform," the voice continued. Gentle. Almost concerned. "Every time you pull magic through this chamber. Every desperate attempt to save him. You're not strengthening the seal. You're breaking it."

"I know." The admission came easily. "I'm breaking it slowly. Piece by piece. But he's alive. That's what matters."

"Is it?" A pause. "You've killed one guardian. The other two stir in their sleep. The prison has gone from wall to door. Soon it will be nothing at all. And when that happens—when I'm free—what then?"

"Then I'll deal with it." I moved toward the exit. "One crisis at a time."

"You're not afraid of me." Not a question. Just observation. "Everyone else fears me. The guardians locked me away because they feared what I'd do. The priestess who made your crown feared my influence. But you—you don't fear me at all."

"Should I?" I stopped. Turned back toward the empty chamber. "You haven't done anything to me yet. The crown does worse."

Silence. Long enough that I thought maybe he'd gone. Then:

"I don't need to threaten you. You're already doing exactly what I want." The voice was warm. Almost affectionate. "Breaking the prison. Killing the guardians. Becoming something powerful enough to free me completely. All while thinking you're just trying to save him."

The words should have terrified me. Should have made me reconsider everything.

Just tired acceptance. Because he was right. I was breaking the prison. Was killing guardians. Was becoming something powerful and hollow and wrong.

And I was doing it all for Nokoa.

"What do you want?" I asked. "Really want? Not the freedom—I know you want that. But what comes after?"

"I want to fix what's broken." The voice was sincere. Genuine in a way that felt dangerous. "The world is dying. The famine spreads. Life drains away because death has no balance. Your crown disrupted the natural order. I want to restore it."

"By doing what?"

"By having proper deaths again. Proper transitions. Proper balance between life and ending." A pause. "Your love is beautiful. Desperate. All-consuming. But it's also breaking the world. When he dies—really dies—things will balance again. Life will return. The famine will end."

"He's not dying." My voice was flat. Final. "I won't let him."

"I know." The bone god's voice was impossibly gentle. "That's why you're breaking the prison. That's why you'll free me eventually. Because keeping him alive requires power you don't have. Power only I can provide."

He was offering. Not threatening. Not manipulating. Just offering truth.

"What's the cost?" I asked.

"The world continues dying. The famine spreads. Everyone else suffers so you two can have each other." Matter-of-fact. No judgment. "But you knew that already. You've known for a while. You just keep choosing him anyway."

I did know. Had known since killing Perla. Had known since breaking the promise to the outer cities.

I was choosing Nokoa over the world. Over everything. Over everyone.

And I'd keep choosing him.

"I should go," I said. "The ritual won't wait."

"Go." The voice faded. "Perform your ritual. Strengthen the bond. Break the prison further. I'll be here. Patient. Waiting. For when you finally need what only I can offer."

He was gone.

I stood alone in the catacombs. Holding vials of bone dust and dark water. Surrounded by sleeping guardians and the slowly cracking prison of something that wanted to help me destroy the world.

And I felt nothing.

Should feel horror. Should feel the weight of understanding that I was the villain in this story. That I was the thing breaking reality. That everyone who tried to stop me was right.

But there was just determination. Just cold certainty. Just the knowledge that I'd made my choice and would keep making it.

Nokoa needed this ritual. So I'd do it. Would mix bone dust and dark water. Would speak whatever words Alaira gave me. Would break the prison further if it meant keeping him alive.

The vials felt warm in my hands. The bone dust pulsing. The dark water moving even though I held it still.

I left the catacombs. Climbed back toward light and air and the surface world that was slowly dying because of choices I kept making.

One desperate choice at a time.

Chapter Thirty

Alaira's Teachings

Alaira waited at the wasteland's edge, exactly where Valdic said she'd be. White robes stained with travel and time, grey at the hems. Patchy hair falling out in clumps, revealing pale scalp. Face that had aged decades since I'd seen her last—leathery now, ancient. Like she was aging in fast-forward while the world died around her.

She looked powerful anyway. Experienced. Patient.

I approached slowly. Valdic half-carried me, supporting weight my legs couldn't bear anymore. Each step hurt. Each breath was negotiation with failing lungs. The witch runes had spread across my jaw now, dark lines visible against pale skin.

"Nokoa." Alaira's voice was steady. Calm. Like greeting an old friend instead of a dying man she'd helped create. "You came."

"You said you could stabilize me." I collapsed onto a rock, rough and cold beneath me. "Completely this time. Stop the deterioration."

"I can." She pulled items from her satchel. Vials and herbs and things I didn't recognize. Glass clinked against glass. "The ritual Renata just performed—gathering bone dust and dark water—it helped you, yes?"

I did feel newer. Stronger than I had since the battle. The constant burning had dulled to manageable ache. The witch runes had stopped their aggressive spread. Something had given me relief.

"How did you know about that?" I asked.

"Because I told her to do it." Alaira smiled. Not quite kind. Not quite cruel. Just knowing. "Sent her a message. Told her where to go, what to gather, how to perform the stabilization. She did exactly as instructed."

The words settled heavy in my chest. "You're manipulating her."

"I'm helping you both navigate this safely." She corrected gently, hands never stopping their work. "You're the first successful paired binding in recorded history. That makes you valuable. That makes you worth preserving. Worth studying. Worth keeping alive to see what happens."

"We're experiments." Not a question. Just tired understanding.

"You're unprecedented." Alaira began mixing components. "The rituals I designed, the magic involved—none of it was meant to work like this. You should have stayed dead. The fact that you're alive at all is miraculous. And dangerous. And fascinating."

She was being honest. More honest than she'd been before. Maybe because I was dying and honesty didn't cost her anything anymore.

"Tell me about the Bone God," I said.

She stopped mixing. Looked at me with those ancient eyes. "What about him?"

"Everything. Why he was sealed. Why you created the crown. Why the guardians gave up their worlds to keep him contained." I met her gaze. "I want real answers. Not manipulation disguised as teaching."

Alaira studied me for a long moment. Then nodded. Sat across from me, her joints creaking. Set aside her ritual components.

"The Bone God was obsessed with balance," she began. "With transitions. With the space between life and death. He had the ability to create the most marvelous abilities but he didn't have the ability to use them himself—he could only gift them."

"That upset him," I said.

"Constantly." Alaira's voice held something like sympathy. "He wanted to merge with the crown I created. Wanted to hold extra power so he could stand beside his sister as equal. But we didn't trust him. The crown was already dangerous—corrupted from its original purpose. Adding the bone god to it would have been catastrophic."

"So you locked him away."

"Out of distrust, we denied the merge. We almost allowed it—almost gave him what he wanted after listening to his promises. Many people were on opposite sides." She looked down at her weathered hands. "In the end his bones were locked away in the catacombs. His prison sealed by guardians who gave up the life they had in their worlds to protect ours."

She looked toward the bone court, toward the skull castle rising from wasteland. "But if Renata is on the cusp of desperation—and she is—he has a chance. His chance to merge after all. His chance to make a deal."

"What kind of deal?" I asked.

"You for the crown." Simple. Direct. "One soul erased, one goes free. The Midnight Oath. Ancient. Dangerous. Often backfires spectacularly. But it exists."

Midnight Oath. The phrase settled into my bones. Felt important. Felt true.

"Tell me about it," I said.

Alaira hesitated. Just briefly. Then: "It's a ritual. Blood moon required. One person willingly sacrifices themselves to free another from magical binding. The sacrifice must be genuine—no coercion, no manipulation, true willingness to die. If performed correctly, the bound person goes free."

"And if it's wrong?"

"Both die. And usually the thing they were trying to escape gets stronger." She met my eyes. "It's a last resort. A desperate gamble when nothing else works. It has a high failure rate because true willingness is rare. Most people think they're willing but aren't. Not really. Not when it comes to actually dying."

I thought about it. Really thought. Tried to imagine willingly dying—permanently, finally—to free Renata from the crown.

Could I do it? Could I be willing enough? Could I mean it so completely that the magic would accept my sacrifice?

Maybe. Probably. Yes.

"What's in it for you?" I asked.

Alaira's expression shifted. Something flickered behind her eyes—hope, maybe. Or desperation. Or fanatic certainty.

"I want the Goddess to appear," she said quietly. "The Goddess of Fate. She created me, my sisters. My coven. She taught me. Guided me. I was devoted to her. Then she went silent. Won't answer prayers. Won't appear. Won't tell me if I failed Her gift or if this was Her plan all along."

"You think the Midnight Oath will make Her appear."

"I think something this significant—a paired binding attempting to break itself, a crown possibly being freed, the bone god's prison at its weakest—I think She'd notice. I think She might finally answer." Alaira's voice cracked, showing her age. "I need to know. Need to understand if everything I did was failure or purpose."

I stared at her. This ancient, powerful priestess who'd created the crown that was destroying Renata. Who'd spent centuries wondering if she'd failed her goddess or served her.

She wasn't manipulating me. Not really. She was just desperate. Just another broken person trying to fix what couldn't be fixed.

"Renata would never agree," I said. "She'd never willingly let me die to save her."

"She might." Alaira's voice was soft. "If she's pushed far enough. If she sees clearly enough what she's becoming. If she understands that keeping you alive is destroying her. She might choose your death over her continued transformation."

Maybe. But I doubted it. Renata had proven again and again that my survival mattered more than anything.

"The stabilization ritual," I said. "You said you could complete it."

"Yes." Alaira returned to her components, relief visible in her movements. "What Renata gathered will help. What I add will complete it. Together they'll give you weeks. Maybe months."

She worked quickly. Mixing bone dust and dark water with herbs and blood and things that smelled like time itself—old parchment and decay. Chanting in languages I didn't recognize.

The witch runes under my skin responded. Burning. Moving. But differently than before. Not spreading. Consolidating. Becoming stable instead of chaotic. The pain shifted from sharp to dull, from chaos to order.

When she finished, I felt better. Stronger. The constant burning dulled to almost nothing. The witch runes settled into patterns instead of crawling chaos. My breathing came easier, lungs expanding fully for the first time in days.

"There." Alaira sat back. Exhausted. Aged further—new lines around her eyes. "That should hold you. Long enough to matter."

"Thank you." I meant it. Despite her manipulation. Despite her hidden agenda. She'd given me time.

"Remember," she said as Valdic helped me stand. "The Midnight Oath exists. But only use it if there's no other choice. Only attempt it if everything else has failed. Because failure means both of you die and the crown wins completely."

I nodded. Started to leave. Stopped.

"What do you hope She tells you?" I asked. "The Goddess. If She appears. What answer are you hoping for?"

Alaira was quiet for a long moment. Then: "That it was all part of Her plan. That corrupting Her gift was necessary somehow. That I didn't fail Her—I served Her." She looked at me with ancient, tired eyes. "But honestly? I think I just want Her to acknowledge I exist. That after centuries of silence, She remembers I'm here. That would be enough."

I left her there. Old and desperate and waiting for a goddess who might never answer.

Valdic helped me back toward camp. Each step easier than before. The stabilization had worked.

But the knowledge Alaira had given me weighed heavier than any physical burden.

The Midnight Oath. One soul erased, one goes free.

A way to break the crown's hold. A way to free Renata. A way that required me to die.

And I knew—already knew, deep in my bones—that if it came to that, I'd do it. Would sacrifice myself willingly. Would give her back herself even if it cost me everything.

Because that's what love was. Not holding on. Not forcing survival. But being willing to let go when letting go was the only mercy left.

Somewhere in the bone court, Renata sat breaking herself to keep me alive.

Not knowing the cost would be me.

Chapter Thirty-One

Reading

Renata

The butterfly found me in my chambers. Purple wings, delicate and dead. It landed on my desk where I sat staring at reports I couldn't quite focus on. Numbers and complaints and requests that all blurred together into meaningless noise.

Only one thing cut through the fog anymore. Only one name.

I touched the butterfly. It dissolved into parchment and his handwriting.

His handwriting. Always his handwriting. The only thing that felt real anymore.

I unfolded the letter carefully. My skeletal hands shaking slightly. When had they started doing that? When had I become someone whose hands trembled holding paper?

Renata,

I found something. A possible solution. A way out of this—the bond, the crown, all of it.

My heart stuttered. A way out. Something that could fix this impossible situation. Something that could free us both.

It's called the Midnight Oath. Ancient ritual. Dangerous. But it exists.

One person willingly sacrifices themselves to free another from magical binding. If performed correctly, the bound person goes free. Completely free. The crown would lose its hold on you.

The words swam. I read them again. Then again.

Sacrifice. Willingly. One person dying to free another.

If it comes to that, I want to be the one who—

The sentence broke off. Unfinished. Like he'd started writing and couldn't complete the thought. Like the words were too heavy to fully form.

But I understood anyway.

He was offering to die. To sacrifice himself. To perform this Midnight Oath and free me from the crown even if it cost him everything.

"No." I said it aloud. To the empty room. To the letter. To him even though he couldn't hear me. "No, absolutely not."

I thought of him actively. Deliberately. Let his face fill my mind—golden eyes turning yellow, brown curls, the way he looked at me like I was worth saving even when all evidence suggested I wasn't.

Pain lanced through my skull immediately. Sharp. Familiar. The bond punishing me for missing him. For loving him. For wanting him with intensity that destroyed us both.

Blood started flowing from my nose. Hot against my lips. I let it. Let the pain anchor me. Let it remind me he was real and alive and absolutely not sacrificing himself for me.

The hollow crown's bone tightened. Not quite pain. Just pressure.

"He's trying to help," Oriana whispered. "But he doesn't understand—you need the crown. Without it, you're just human. Weak. Mortal."

"He can't die," Alaric added. "Not after everything you've done to keep him alive. That would make it all meaningless."

"Write back," Lyanna urged. "Tell him you'll find another way."

I pulled out parchment. Dipped my quill in ink. Started writing before the crown could stop me. Before the voices could guide my words into something they wanted instead of what I needed to say.

Nokoa,

Whatever it takes. We'll survive this. Together.

If this Midnight Oath is a real option, we'll find a way to make it work. We'll find a way to both survive. Because I'm not losing you. Not after everything. Not when you're the only thing keeping me tethered to anything that matters.

Don't sacrifice yourself. Don't even think it. We find another way. We always find another way.

Wait for me. Keep surviving. Keep fighting. I'll figure this out. I'll find a solution that doesn't require your death.

I love you. I love you more than the crown. More than power. More than everything. And I'm not letting you go.

—R

I tried to seal it. Pressed my thumb to the wax. Reached for my signet ring.

The crown stopped me.

Not violently. Not with pain. Just... stopped me. Made my hand freeze mid-motion. Made the letter suddenly feel wrong.

"You can't promise him that," Oriana said quietly. "Can't promise you'll find another way. Because you might not. And then what?"

"He needs to know all options are open," Alaric added. "Needs to understand that his death might be necessary."

"Don't close that door," Lyanna finished. "Don't make promises you can't keep."

I stared at the letter. At the desperate words I'd written. At the promises I couldn't keep.

The crown was right. Wasn't it? I couldn't promise we'd both survive. Couldn't promise I'd find another way.

But telling him his death was an option? That felt like giving up. That felt like admitting defeat before we'd tried everything else.

I crumpled the letter. Threw it aside. Started again.

Nokoa,

I received your letter about the Midnight Oath. I understand what you're offering. I understand what it would cost.

But I need you to understand something too: I'm not ready to consider that option yet. Not while other possibilities exist. Not while we're both still fighting.

Keep searching. Keep surviving. We'll find something that doesn't require sacrifice. Something that lets us both live.

Don't give up on me. Don't decide your death is the answer before we've exhausted everything else.

I love you. Stay alive. That's all I ask.

—R

Better. More honest. Less desperate promise and more realistic hope.

I sealed it this time. The crown didn't stop me.

It just let me do it. Watched me fold the letter and press the wax and call for a butterfly. Didn't argue. Didn't interfere. Just went quiet in a way that felt more deliberate than silence—the kind of quiet that means I've already won this, so let her think she's choosing.

I tried not to think about that.

Purple wings. Already dead. It landed on my outstretched hand, its body cold and light as nothing. I pressed the letter to its body. Watched ink and parchment dissolve into the butterfly's form.

"Find him," I whispered. "Tell him I'm not giving up. Tell him we're not done yet."

The butterfly lifted off. Disappeared through my window. Gone to wherever Nokoa waited in the outer cities camp.

I sat back in my chair. Blood still flowing from my nose. The pain in my skull had dulled to constant ache. Manageable. Familiar.

The bond punishing me for thinking of him. For loving him with the kind of intensity that destroyed everything it touched.

But I'd written back. Had told him no. Had refused his sacrifice—for now, at least. Had bought us time to find another solution.

The crown's voices were quiet. Not arguing. Not interfering. Just watching.

They thought I'd accept his death eventually. Thought I'd reach a point where his sacrifice seemed reasonable. Necessary. The only option left.

Maybe they were right. Maybe I would. Maybe desperation would push me there.

But not yet. Not today. Not while I still had any chance of finding another way.

I pulled out the journal Valdic had left. Opened it to that entry about violets. About growing in impossible places.

He said they reminded him of me.

I touched the pressed violet on the page. Dried. Faded. Dead but preserved. Like me. Like what I was becoming. Dead but still moving. Still pretending to be alive.

The petals crumbled slightly under my skeletal fingers. Turning to dust.

Everything I touched turned to dust eventually.

"We'll find another way," I whispered to the flower. "I'll figure this out."

The crown hummed. Not agreeing. Not disagreeing. Just present.

I sat with his letter. His offer of sacrifice. His love.

And refused to let him go.

Chapter Thirty-Two

FERN WAKES

Renata

The ritual was supposed to be routine. Another attempt to channel magic. Another desperate push to strengthen the bond without thinking of Nokoa directly. Another way to stay powerful enough to matter.

I called the spectral guardians to me. Seven dead souls responding to my will. Let their power flow through me, let death magic pool in my hands like cold water, ready to be shaped into whatever I needed.

The magic surged. Too much. Too fast. I tried to contain it but it poured through me, around me, into places it shouldn't reach.

I felt weaker suddenly. Drained in ways that had nothing to do with using power. Like something was pulling life from me even as I tried to channel death. My knees buckled slightly.

I needed to recharge. Needed essence. Needed—

I left the bone court without deciding to. My feet knew where to go even when my mind was fog. Out through the skull castle's mouth. Across the bridges. Into the wasteland beyond.

A body lay there. Already dying. Already so close to gone that taking him would be mercy. His breathing was shallow, rattling in his chest.

I didn't hesitate. Didn't pause. Just knelt and pulled.

His essence dissolved into me. Tasted like dirt and copper and the last desperate hope of someone who'd already given up. It filled the cracks, sealed the leaks, made me whole again.

For a moment. Just a moment.

Then the drain started again. Faster than before. Like I was a vessel with holes that kept growing. Like no amount of consumed souls could fill what the spectral guardians and the bond and the crown were taking from me.

I needed more. The magic flared. Wild. Out of control. It escaped my grasp and poured down—through earth, through stone, through layers of bone court architecture into the catacombs below.

Something cracked. Deep underground. Fundamental. Final. The sound echoed up through my bones.

"No." I gasped the word. "No, not yet. Not—"

Too late.

I felt it through the ground beneath my feet. Felt something waking that had slept for centuries. Felt divine magic stirring in response to my corruption.

Fern.

The floraithe guardian. The second of three remaining. Created by the Goddess of Nature to protect life itself.

I ran. Back across the bridges. Into the bone court. Down stairs and corridors toward the catacombs. Maybe I could stop her. Maybe I could explain. Maybe—

The courtyard stopped me.

Not the one inside the skull castle. My courtyard. The one I'd grown a garden in once, back when I was someone who believed in growing things instead of killing them.

It was dead now. Had been dead for weeks. Grey earth. Withered plants, their stems brittle and black. Everything poisoned by my death magic spreading like corruption through soil that used to support life.

But standing in the center of that dead garden was Fern.

She was large. Praxis-sized. Made of petals and stems and living flowers in colors that shouldn't exist together—blues and purples and greens all flowing into each other like she was made of spring itself.

But she was wrong too. Her petals were browning at the edges. Her stems looked brittle. Her colors were fading even as I watched. Like being in my presence was killing her slowly.

Like the wasteland was killing her just by existing.

She stared at me. Then at the dead earth around her. Then back at me.

"I'm from the Goddess of Nature's world." Her voice was like wind through leaves. Gentle. Horrified. "I left my world, gave up my life, to protect THIS?"

She gestured at the wasteland. At miles of dead earth stretching away. At grey soil and poisoned water and withered forests visible through the courtyard's broken walls.

"You've killed all of Thiros! Nothing will grow here!" Her petals started falling. Drifting down like tears made of flowers. "My goddess gave LIFE—you've made WASTELAND!"

"I didn't mean—" I started.

"MEANING DOESN'T MATTER! ONLY CONSEQUENCES!" Her voice cracked like breaking branches. "We locked the bone god away to save nature itself! And you're freeing him with every spell you cast!"

She was right. I knew she was right. Could see the evidence in the dead earth. Could see what my magic had done.

All of it my doing. All of it consequence of choices I kept making. All of it the cost of keeping one person alive.

Fern tried to heal the land. Raised her hands and called on divine magic. Nature power from the Goddess of Nature herself, trying to restore what I'd destroyed.

Vines grew from her petal-flesh. Green and alive and desperate. They reached for the dead soil, trying to take root, trying to spread life back into corruption.

They withered on contact.

Brown within seconds. Dead within minutes. The soil rejected them. The earth itself was too poisoned. Too corrupted. Too fundamentally changed by death magic to accept life anymore.

Fern wept. Actual tears streaming down her petal face, clear drops falling onto dead earth. "It's already dead. It's all dead."

I wanted to tell her I was sorry. Wanted to explain that I hadn't meant for this. Hadn't intended to kill the world. Had just been trying to save one person and lost track of the cost.

"I didn't mean for this," I whispered anyway.

Fern looked at me. Really looked. Saw through the hollow queen to whatever remained underneath.

"Then stop," she said, her voice breaking. "Please. Before you break everything we died to protect."

I thought of Nokoa. Deliberately. Actively. Let his face fill my mind—golden eyes, brown curls, the way he'd looked at me like I was worth saving.

He's alive. That matters more.

The thought came automatically. Reflexively. The justification I'd used a thousand times.

But looking at Fern—looking at the divine being weeping over dead earth, at the gardens that would never grow, at the wasteland spreading in all directions—the justification felt hollow.

He was alive. But the world was dying. Nature itself was being destroyed.

Was his life worth that?

"Of course," Oriana whispered.

Yes. The answer came immediate. Certain. True in ways I couldn't question.

"No," I said aloud. "I can't stop. Won't stop. He's dying and I'm the only thing keeping him alive."

"He's ONE PERSON!" Fern screamed. Her petals exploded outward in a burst of desperate nature magic. "We are BILLIONS! The world is BILLIONS! And you're destroying all of us for ONE!"

She attacked.

Not with violence. With life. With desperate, beautiful, terrible life magic trying to restore what I'd broken. Trying to force growth back into dead earth. Trying to make me feel the weight of every plant I'd killed, every forest I'd withered, every piece of nature I'd corrupted.

I felt it. All of it. Every blade of grass. Every tree. Every flower that would never bloom because I'd chosen him over them.

It hurt. Actually hurt. The weight of all that death pressing down on me. The knowledge of what I'd destroyed.

I raised bone magic anyway. Called spectral soldiers to defend me. Met her life with death.

We fought across the dead courtyard. Life against death. Growth against decay. Her desperation against my cold certainty.

Every vine she grew, I withered. Every flower she called, I killed. Every attempt at restoration met with corruption.

She was losing.

Not because I was stronger. But because the land itself was already dead. Because there was nothing for her magic to draw from. Because my corruption had spread so deep that even divine power couldn't restore it.

The spectral soldiers overwhelmed her. Dead souls that couldn't be killed again. They swarmed around her, pulling at her divine essence, draining the nature magic that kept her form solid.

"Sevi will show you," Fern gasped. Her petals were falling faster now. Her colors fading to grey. "What comes next. You'll see the future. And you'll wish you'd stopped."

She was dying. I could see it happening. See her petal-flesh crumbling. See the divine light guttering out.

"I'm sorry," I said. Meant it. "I'm so sorry."

"Sorry doesn't matter." Her voice was barely a whisper. "Only consequences. Only what you've done. Only—"

She crumbled. Petals and stems and soil. Body dissolving into what looked like dirt and dead flowers.

I stood in the remains. In what was left of Fern. In the garden that would never grow again.

Should feel something. Should feel horror or guilt or at least acknowledgment of what I'd done.

Nothing came. Just emptiness.

The crown's voices stirred.

"She was weak," Oriana said. Almost pitying. "Ruled by emotion. Couldn't separate sentiment from necessity."

"Divine beings aren't stronger than you," Alaric added. "You've proven that twice now."

"For him," Lyanna finished. "You did this for him. To stay strong enough. To keep him safe."

For him. Always for him.

I looked at the ashes that used to be Fern.

"You need to consume the ashes," Oriana said quietly.

I knelt. Gathered them in skeletal hands. They felt different than Perla's had—softer, cooler, like soil after rain. Like potential that would never be realized.

I ate them.

They tasted like spring and growth and every garden I'd never plant. Like life itself turned to ash. Like hope corrupted into fuel.

And for a moment—one bright, terrible moment—I felt emotion again.

Everything Fern had felt. Her love for nature. Her dedication to life. Her desperate hope that growth could overcome destruction. Her grief watching the world die. Her determination to protect it anyway.

All of it flooding through me. Overwhelming. Unstoppable.

I felt the weight of every plant I'd killed. Felt the earth itself mourning. Felt nature crying out for restoration that would never come.

Then the hollow crown took it.

Consumed it. Turned divine emotion into nothing but power coursing through my veins like liquid fire.

I stood. Stronger than before. Fuller. The drain from the spectral guardians felt less intense. The bond's pull felt more manageable.

I left the courtyard. Left the ashes. Left the dead garden where flowers would never bloom.

One guardian remained. Sevi. The last one standing between me and the bone god's complete freedom.

And when she woke—when my magic inevitably cracked that final seal—I'd kill her too.

For him.

I was killing the world to keep one person alive.

Chapter Thirty-Three

The Bone God's Comfort

Renata

I sat in what used to be my garden. Surrounded by ash and dead earth and the weight of what I'd done. The courtyard walls were broken—had been broken for weeks, maybe months. I couldn't remember when. Just knew they let me see the wasteland beyond.

Miles of grey soil. Dead forests, their skeletal branches reaching toward empty sky. Poisoned streams that smelled of rot and metal. Everything dying because of magic I kept using. Everything destroyed because I wouldn't stop.

Because I couldn't stop.

Because stopping meant losing him.

The sun set somewhere beyond the wasteland. Grey light fading to darker grey. No colors anymore. No beauty. Just varying shades of death and decay.

I'd done this. Not directly—hadn't walked through the land killing plants individually. But my magic had. My death magic spreading like poison through soil and water and air. My spectral guardians draining life from everything they touched. My desperate attempts to stay powerful enough to save Nokoa corrupting the natural order.

Fern had shown me. Had tried to heal the land and failed because the corruption went too deep. Because I'd broken something fundamental. Because nature itself rejected my presence now.

"You did what you had to." The voice was gentle. Compassionate. Coming from everywhere and nowhere at once.

The Bone God.

I didn't look for him. Knew I wouldn't see anything. He was still sealed—barely, but sealed. Still contained in his prison below. Still speaking through cracks I'd made.

"Did I?" My voice was hollow. Empty as the dead earth around me. "Fern said I killed billions for one person. She was right."

"Fern saw things in absolutes." He moved closer—I could feel his presence even without seeing him. Warmth in the grey cold. "Life or death. Growth or decay. She couldn't understand that sometimes love requires sacrifice. That sometimes keeping one person alive is worth any cost."

"Even this?" I gestured at the wasteland. "Even killing the world?"

"The world was always dying." His voice was matter-of-fact. Not cruel. Just honest. "Everything dies eventually. Everything transitions. You're not destroying—you're accelerating. Hastening what was always coming."

"That's not comfort," I said.

"No." He agreed. "But it's truth. And sometimes truth is all we have."

Silence settled. Heavy.

"Survival isn't cruelty," he continued after a moment. "It's just survival. Everything fights to live. Everything fights to keep what it loves alive. You're not monstrous for wanting that. You're just honest about the cost."

"The cost is everything." I looked at my hands. Skeletal. Translucent skin showing bone beneath. "The cost is the world."

"The cost is change." He corrected. "The world changes. Life becomes death. Death becomes life. The cycle continues. You're part of that cycle. Not breaking it—participating in it."

I wanted to believe him. Wanted to accept that what I was doing was natural instead of monstrous. That choosing Nokoa over billions wasn't evil—just love pushed to its logical conclusion.

But Fern's face haunted me. Her weeping. Her desperate attempt to heal land that rejected healing. Her understanding that I'd destroyed something sacred and wouldn't stop.

"The crown judges you," the Bone God said. "The guardians judge you. Everyone looks at your choices and calls them wrong. But I don't judge. I only understand."

"Why?" The question came out broken. Raw. "Why don't you judge? Why don't you condemn me for what I've done?"

"Because I know what it's like to love something impossible." His voice softened into something I hadn't expected from him—genuine sorrow. "To want something so badly you'd break the world to have it. To be willing to destroy everything for one thing that matters."

"What did you love?" I asked.

Silence. Long enough I thought maybe he wouldn't answer. Then:

"Balance. The space between life and death where everything changes." His voice held grief. "My sister created life. Made things grow and thrive and flourish. I could only help them end. Help them transition to whatever comes after. And I loved that work. Loved being necessary. Loved being the other half of her gift."

"But it wasn't enough," I said. Understanding without knowing how.

"It was never enough." He agreed. "She was celebrated. Worshipped. Loved for creating. And I was feared. Avoided. Locked away for ending. Even though ending is just as necessary as beginning. Even though death is just life's transition."

I understood. Actually understood. The Bone God wanted to be valued. Wanted to matter. Wanted to be more than just the thing people locked away.

He wanted what I wanted. To be necessary to someone. To matter so much that destroying everything else seemed worth it.

"You're not the monster they claim," he continued. "You're just desperate. And desperation is the most human thing there is."

The words hit different than they should. Not comfort exactly. Just acknowledgment. Someone seeing what I'd become and not flinching. Not condemning.

Just understanding.

"When there's nothing left," he said quietly, "when you've consumed the last guardian and broken the final seal, when the crown has taken everything except his name—I'll still be here. No demands. No payment. Just presence."

"There's always a price." I'd learned that. Known it bone-deep. "Everyone always wants something."

"I want freedom." He admitted it easily. No deception. "Want to walk in the world again instead of being sealed away. Want to restore balance instead of watching everything decay. But I won't demand it. Won't force you. Will just offer: when you have nothing else left, when everyone has abandoned you—I'll be here."

"Why?" I asked again. "Why help me? Why offer anything?"

"Because you're doing what no one else would." His voice held something I couldn't quite name. "Refusing to give up. Refusing to let go. Refusing to accept that sometimes love means letting someone die. That takes strength. That takes courage everyone calls monstrosity."

I sat with that. Trying to decide if he was manipulating me or being genuine. Trying to understand if this was comfort or trap.

Couldn't tell. Could only feel the relief of someone not judging. Someone not condemning. Someone understanding that I'd made terrible choices and would keep making them.

"You and I are different," I said slowly. "I love a person. You love an abstract concept."

"Does the object of love matter?" He asked. "Or just the depth of it? Just the willingness to sacrifice anything to protect it?"

Good question. Uncomfortable question. Question I didn't want to answer because the answer revealed too much.

"I should go," I said. Standing. Brushing ash from my black dress. Fern's remains coating my hands like grey snow. "Nokoa needs—"

"Nokoa needs you stable," the Bone God interrupted. "Needs you functional. Needs you strong enough to keep fighting. Does he need you guilty? Does he need you breaking under the weight of judgment?"

"No," I admitted.

"Then take what I offer. Not as payment. Not as bargain. Just as gift: someone who understands. Someone who doesn't judge. Someone who sees what you're becoming and doesn't flinch."

He was gone as gently as he'd come. Just voice fading into wind. Just presence dissolving into nothing.

I stood alone in the dead courtyard. Surrounded by ashes that used to be a divine guardian. Surrounded by earth that would never grow again.

And I felt lighter. Just slightly. Just enough to notice.

The Bone God had offered understanding without judgment. Had seen my choices and called them strength instead of monstrosity. Had acknowledged cost without condemning payment.

That should terrify me. Should make me understand I was being groomed. Being prepared. Being shaped into someone who'd free him willingly because he was the only one who didn't judge.

But the comfort remained anyway. Because judgment was exhausting. Because everyone looking at me with horror was exhausting. Because carrying guilt for choices I'd keep making anyway was exhausting.

I walked back toward the skull castle. Left the dead courtyard. Left the ashes. Left the proof of sacred things destroyed.

One guardian remained. Sevi. I'd kill her too when the time came.

And the Bone God would understand when I did.

Even if comfort was just another form of manipulation.

Even then.

The hollow crown pulsed against my skull, warm and approving.

And I walked back into the bone court.

Chapter Thirty-Four

Nokoa's Vision

Nokoa

The visions started small. Just flashes. Moments that might be memory or might be prophecy or might be the resurrection magic finally breaking my mind along with my body.

I saw Renata dying. Over and over. Different deaths. Different circumstances. But always dying.

In one, she crumbled to ash like the guardians she'd killed. In another, the crown consumed her completely—just hollow bone wearing her face. In another, she stood in wasteland that stretched forever, alone, calling my name to emptiness that swallowed the sound whole.

All of them felt real. All of them felt true. All of them felt inevitable.

I couldn't tell which was memory, which was present, which was future. They bled together, mixed, became one terrible certainty: she was dying, I was dying, we were both dying, and nothing could stop it.

The witch runes burned. Not spreading anymore—Alaira's stabilization had stopped that. But burning anyway. Like they were trying to show me something. Like they carried messages carved in languages my conscious mind couldn't quite read but my bones understood perfectly.

I saw myself. Not as I was—broken, skeletal, barely alive. But as I would be. Bones exposed completely, pushing through skin like tree roots through pavement. Eyes gone, just empty sockets weeping darkness. Just death walking. Still moving because the resurrection wouldn't let me stop. Still breathing because magic said I had to.

And in that vision, Renata stood beside me. Also bone. Also hollow. Both of us transformed into what we'd been fighting to avoid.

Monsters. Together. Forever.

The image tasted like copper and grave dirt.

"Nokoa." Valdic's voice pulled me back, distant at first, then closer. "You're having another episode."

I blinked. Focused. The tent canvas swam into view above me, bioluminescent moss casting sickly green shadows. I was on the ground. When had I fallen? Couldn't remember. Couldn't separate vision from reality anymore—the line between them had worn thin.

"How long?" My voice rasped.

"Ten minutes. Maybe more." Valdic helped me sit up, his decay-scent strong in my nostrils. "You were speaking. Saying things I couldn't understand. Languages that don't exist."

Languages that don't exist. The witch runes talking through me. The resurrection magic trying to communicate. Or maybe just my mind breaking under pressure it was never meant to bear.

"I saw her," I managed. "Saw Renata with runes crawling across her face like mine. Saw myself as skeleton reaching for her. Saw—"

The vision hit again. Stronger this time. Overwhelming.

The Bone God. Beautiful. Terrible. Standing in flesh instead of sealed in prison, and the wrongness of it made my stomach clench. His skin was white as bone, smooth and perfect in a way that felt obscene. His eyes were shadow-dark, depths that went down and down forever. His heart was visible through translucent chest—still beating, impossibly alive, pumping something that wasn't quite blood through veins that weren't quite real.

And beside him stood Renata. Transformed. Powerful. Wrong in ways I couldn't articulate but felt in my soul.

She looked at me. Through me. Past me. Like I was already dead and she was seeing my ghost, seeing through to whatever came after.

"It's the only way," she said. But her voice was layered—multiple voices speaking in unison. The crown's voices and hers mixed together until I couldn't tell which was which, couldn't find her in the chorus.

The vision shifted. Showed me the goddess of fate. Distant. Silent. Turning away from something I couldn't see, her back a rejection more complete than words.

Showed me Alaira weeping, her ancient face crumpling. Calling to the goddess who wouldn't answer. Praying to silence that echoed back empty.

Showed me Hivro surrounded by butterflies. All of them dying. All of them falling from the sky like ash, like snow, like the end of small beautiful things.

Showed me the world. Not dying. Already dead. Just wasteland and bone and the slow ending of everything, the final gasp stretched into eternity.

And in the center of it all—Renata and me. Together. Transformed. No longer human but not quite dead either. Just existing in the space between. Just transition made permanent, just becoming without end.

"Can you see it?" The Bone God's voice, deliberate and cold. Not to me. To Renata. "The future where you both survive? Where you're together forever? Where love doesn't hurt anymore?"

"Yes," Renata answered, and the longing in her voice made something crack inside my chest. "I see it."

"Then come to me. Accept what I offer. Free me and I'll free you both."

The vision shattered.

I gasped. Fell forward. Vomited blood onto the tent floor, the copper taste flooding my mouth. My body rejecting everything—the visions, the magic, the impossible truth they revealed.

"Nokoa!" Valdic held me. Kept me from collapsing completely. "What did you see?"

"Him." I couldn't say more. Couldn't explain. Just: "The Bone God. He's offering her something. Showing her a future where we're together. Where we survive."

"What kind of future?"

"Wrong." The word came out strangled, desperate. "Wrong in every way. We're together but we're not us anymore. We're something else. Something that shouldn't exist."

Valdic was quiet. Then: "Is she going to accept?"

"I don't know." I wiped blood from my mouth with shaking fingers. "The vision felt true. Felt inevitable. But maybe it was just possibility. Maybe it's something that could happen but won't if we make different choices."

"Can you make different choices?" Valdic asked gently. "Can she?"

I didn't have an answer. Every choice we made led toward that future. Every attempt to survive pushed us closer to transformation. Every day we refused to give up was another step down a path that only led one direction.

The witch runes flared hot against my skin.

"I keep seeing her die," I whispered. "In a thousand different ways. All of them feel real."

"Maybe they're all possible," Valdic offered. "Maybe you're seeing every way it could end. Every branch of future."

"Or maybe I'm just going insane." I laughed, the sound hollow and broken as old bells. "Maybe the resurrection is breaking my mind and these are just hallucinations given meaning by desperation."

"Do they feel like hallucinations?"

"No." I met his purple eyes, saw my own reflection in them—gaunt, dying, marked by magic I couldn't control. "They feel like prophecy. Like warnings. Like the universe trying to show me what comes next so I can stop it."

"Can you stop it?"

"I don't know." The honest answer. The only answer. "Every vision shows different ending. But they all end badly. We die. She dies. We both transform into something monstrous. The world ends. All of it terrible. All of it consequence of choices we're still making."

Another flash. Briefer. Just image without context.

Renata standing in the catacombs. Holding something dark and terrible, something that pulsed with wrongness. Speaking words in languages older than thought. And the carved bone box—the prison—shattering completely, fragments spinning through air like deadly snow.

The Bone God walking free.

And Renata beside him. Transformed. Powerful. His.

"We have to stop her," I said. "Have to reach her before she goes too far. Before she frees him completely."

"How?" Valdic's voice was gentle but firm. "She's in the bone court. You can barely stand. The outer cities are broken, scattered. What can we possibly do?"

"The Midnight Oath," I said. Not planning to. Just knowing it was true, knowing it the way I knew my own heartbeat. "That's the answer. That's how we stop this. One of us sacrifices willingly to break the crown's hold. To free her before she becomes what the visions show."

"You can't know that," Valdic argued. "The visions might be wrong. Might be just possibilities. Might not even be real."

"They're real." I was certain. Completely certain. The certainty sat in my bones like truth carved in stone. "They're showing me what happens if we don't act. Showing me the cost of hesitation. Showing me that the Midnight Oath is the only solution left."

"It requires blood moon," Valdic reminded me. "Those are rare. Could be months before the next one."

"Soon," I said. Knowing it like I knew my own name, like I knew Renata's face in darkness. "There's one coming soon. The visions show it. Red moon rising over wasteland. The universe offering one chance to fix this before it's too late."

Valdic stared at me, purple eyes wide. "You're certain?"

"I'm certain." I couldn't explain how. Just knew. The witch runes knew. The resurrection magic knew. The visions knew. "And when it comes, I'll perform the ritual. Will sacrifice myself to free her. Will end this before she transforms completely."

"She won't let you." Valdic's voice was sad, heavy with grief for something not yet lost. "She'll refuse. Will fight you. Will choose keeping you alive over being freed."

"I know." I closed my eyes, exhaustion pulling at me. "But I have to try anyway. Have to offer her the choice. Have to make her see that my death is better than what she's becoming."

"What if she can't see it?" Valdic pressed. "What if the crown has taken so much that she can't understand why your death would save her?"

Then we'd both die anyway. Both transform. Both become what the visions showed. Just monsters wearing familiar faces, just shells pretending at humanity we'd already lost.

But at least trying gave us chance. At least offering sacrifice meant I'd done everything possible. At least dying on purpose was better than dying from giving up.

"I'll make her understand," I said. "When the blood moon rises, when the Midnight Oath becomes possible, I'll convince her."

Another vision. Stronger. Longer. It dragged me under.

Renata and me. Standing under red moon that painted everything the color of old blood. Ancient words between us, heavy as stones, sharp as glass. Witch runes blazing on both our skins, identical marks binding us together. The ritual beginning, power rising like water, like flood, like ending.

And the look in her eyes—desperate, terrified, determined. Like she knew what was happening but couldn't stop it. Like she understood and refused and accepted all at once, emotions warring across her face.

"I love you," I heard myself say in the vision, voice breaking. "This is how I save you."

"This is how you kill me," she answered, and her voice was raw as open wound.

The vision ended.

I lay on the tent floor, gasping. Everything hurt. Everything burned. The witch runes were moving again despite Alaira's stabilization, crawling up my neck. Reaching for my face, hungry and inevitable.

Soon they'd cover everything. Soon I'd look as monstrous as the visions showed.

But maybe—impossibly—maybe I'd last long enough to reach the blood moon. Long enough to perform the Midnight Oath. Long enough to sacrifice myself and free her before she became what the Bone God wanted.

"Rest," Valdic murmured, pressing his muzzle gently against my shoulder. "Save your strength. If the blood moon is coming, you'll need everything you have left."

I closed my eyes. Let exhaustion take me. Fell into dreams that might be visions might be prophecy might be just my mind breaking under weight it was never meant to carry.

Dreamed of Renata dying. Of me dying. Of us both transformed into something wrong, something that hurt to look at.

Dreamed of red moon rising like an eye opening. Of ancient words spoken with blood on our tongues. Of sacrifice offered and accepted and refused all at once, all three possibilities existing in the same moment.

Dreamed of endings. So many endings.

And wondered which one would claim us first.

Chapter Thirty-Five

The Council Falls

Renata

The council meeting was routine. Reports. Assessments. Logistics of maintaining a dying court in a dying world. The bioluminescence cast everything in sickly blue-green, made the bone council look more skeletal than usual. The air was thick with the scent of damp stone and something else—something like rot, like endings.

Ancelin sat across from me, his serpentine dreadlocks coiled beneath withered horns. Every movement brought the sound of joints grinding, bone on bone. Maxin stood near the wall, looking worse than yesterday—more skeletal, more grey, the bone pressing through skin more visibly than it had yesterday. Praxis was there too. Always there. Watching with crimson eyes that missed nothing.

"The outer cities remain quiet," Praxis reported. "No activity since the attack. They're likely starving. Too weak to organize another assault."

"Good," I murmured. Not really listening. Thinking about Nokoa instead. About his letter. About the Midnight Oath. About solutions that didn't require his death. There had to be another way.

"The tithe is failing," Maxin added. His voice was strained, thin as paper. "Not enough volunteers. Those who do give heartfire or marrow don't survive it anymore. The bone court's power is—"

Ancelin collapsed.

Not dramatic. Not violent. Just stopped mid-breath and fell forward. His bone body hitting the table with a dry, final sound. His silver-sheen obsidian eyes going dark.

I stared. The moment stretched, became something suspended and strange. Maxin rushed forward, his deteriorating form moving faster than I expected. Praxis didn't move—just watched, like he was observing an experiment.

"Ancelin?" Maxin checked for pulse. For breath. Found nothing. "He's gone."

"Gone?" I repeated. The word felt wrong in my mouth. Strange. Heavy. "He was just... he was talking yesterday. He was fine."

But had he been fine? I tried to remember. The memory slipped away. The crown took so much. Made everything blur together until I couldn't separate yesterday from last week from last month.

"He wasn't fine." Maxin looked up at me, and something in his expression made my stomach clench. "None of us are fine. The famine—it's not just affecting mortals. It's affecting us. Council members. Those of us who gave pieces of ourselves to the crown for immortality. We're dying too. Slowly. Inevitably."

Ancelin's body was just bones now. The stretched skin that had clung to his jaw was gone, dissolved or fallen away. No movement. No breath. Just skeleton in council robes, collapsed on ancient table.

I should feel something. Should feel grief or shock or at least acknowledgment that someone I'd known for months was dead. Someone who'd argued with me, who'd had opinions and thoughts and existence.

Nothing came.

Just cold observation. Just noting the facts: Ancelin dead, council reduced, one less voice to argue with.

"He opposed you," Oriana whispered, her voice settling into my thoughts. Not gloating. Just stating fact. "Questioned your martial law. Tried to convince you to show mercy. Now he's gone. Obstacles remove themselves when you're strong enough."

"The weak fall," Alaric added, his voice resonating with authority that felt ancient. "The strong endure. That's natural order. That's how power works."

"You're still here," Lyanna finished. "That's what's important. You're strong enough to survive what kills others. Strong enough to protect him."

"The weak fall, the strong endure," I repeated to Maxin. The words felt right in my mouth. True. Simple.

Maxin stood slowly. Each movement looked painful, like his bones didn't quite fit together anymore. He looked at me with those dimming brown eyes, and I saw something I couldn't quite name. Something that looked like grief. Like pity. Like loss for something not yet gone but already mourned. "This is what serving the crown means. It eats everyone around you until you're alone. Ancelin gave himself to the crown for immortality. And now it's killed him anyway. We all die eventually. The crown just chooses when."

"He was weak," I said again, needing it to be true.

"He was old," Maxin corrected gently. "And tired. And dying from lack of tithe just like the rest of us. The heartfire he needed to survive stopped coming. That's not weakness—that's consequence."

The word hung between us. Consequence. Like cause and effect. Like actions leading to results.

"Consequence of what?"

"Of you." Maxin's voice was gentle but firm. "Of your choices. Of the famine spreading across the land. Of the tithe system failing because the outer cities are starving and the volunteers are dying faster than we can replace them. Of everything you've done to keep one person alive while everyone else dies around you."

The words just settled. Heavy. True. Undeniable as stone.

Ancelin had died because the bone court was failing. The bone court was failing because the famine was spreading. The famine was spreading because my death magic was corrupting everything. My death magic was corrupting everything because I kept using it to save Nokoa.

Linear. Logical. My fault from start to finish.

I tried to feel something about that. Tried to summon guilt or regret or at least acknowledgment of responsibility.

But there was just hollow space where they should live.

"I helped create this," Maxin continued. Quieter now. "Helped Alaira make the crown. Helped design the system that's eating you alive. And now I'm paying for it. Transforming. Dying slowly. Becoming what Ancelin became—bones and corruption and hollow service to power that consumes everything."

He touched his face. His patchy hair that fell out in clumps, leaving bare patches of grey skin. The grey skin stretched tight over increasingly visible bone, ribs showing through his chest like bars.

"I'm next," he said, and the certainty in his voice made something twist in my chest. One of the few emotions that still reached me—fear of being alone. "Maybe weeks. Maybe days. But I'm next. And after me, Praxis will be last. And then you'll be alone. Just you and the crown and whatever's left of your humanity."

Alone. The word bounced around inside my skull.

"I'm not alone," I said. "I have Nokoa."

"Do you?" Maxin's voice held something like pity, and I hated the sound of it. "Or do you have the idea of him? The memory of him? The justification you use to make everything else acceptable?"

"He's alive." My voice was flat. "That's not idea. That's fact."

"He's dying." Maxin gestured toward where the outer cities camp would be. "Deteriorating despite every ritual. Despite Alaira's help. Despite everything you've sacrificed to keep him breathing. You're not saving him, Renata. You're just prolonging his dying while destroying everything else."

"That's not true." But the words felt hollow. Felt like something I was supposed to say rather than something I believed.

"Isn't it?" Maxin moved closer. "Ancelin died today. I'll die soon. The bone court is collapsing. The world is wasteland. And Nokoa is a witch-rune-covered skeleton who can't even stand without help. What have you saved? What have you actually preserved except suffering?"

I wanted to argue. Wanted to defend myself. Wanted to prove that everything I'd done mattered.

But Ancelin's body lay between us. Silent proof.

The bioluminescence flickered, casting dancing shadows across his bones. Made them look like they were moving. Like he might sit up and argue with me one more time.

"We need to remove the body," Praxis announced. Practical. Emotionless. "And adjust council procedures. Three members now instead of five."

He moved forward. Started organizing Ancelin's removal like it was furniture being relocated instead of a person being discarded.

Efficient. Cold. Exactly what the bone court required.

Exactly what I was becoming.

Maxin watched Praxis work, and something in his expression crumpled. The careful control falling away. Then he looked at me. "I'm sorry. For all of it. For helping create the crown. For teaching you how to use it. For not stopping this before it started." He touched the table where Ancelin had fallen. "I thought I could control the corruption. I was wrong."

"You tried to help," I said. Not sure why I was defending him. Maybe because he was dying too. Maybe because soon there'd be no one left who remembered what I'd been before the crown.

"Trying is just failing slowly." He smiled. Sad. Tired. Broken. "And I'm done failing. When my time comes—when the transformation finishes—I won't fight it. Will just let go and hope the next person who wears this crown learns from my mistakes." He paused, met my eyes. "At least give me a burial. Treat me with more dignity than you're treating Ancelin."

The request hung in the air. A plea for basic respect. For acknowledgment that he'd been a person instead of just obstacle or tool or casualty.

"I will," I heard myself say. "When the time comes, I'll make sure you're buried properly."

Maxin's expression shifted. Something like relief crossing his deteriorating features. "Thank you."

He left. His footsteps echoing away down the tunnel. Getting quieter. Fading. Until there was just silence and the drip of water and Praxis organizing Ancelin's removal.

The guards arrived. Started lifting Ancelin's body. His bones clattered slightly, the sound too casual for what it was. They carried him toward the door, and I watched his dreadlocks drag across the stone floor.

"Where will they take him?" I asked Praxis.

"The catacombs." Praxis didn't look up from his notes. "With the other failed immortals. The ones who couldn't sustain themselves on diminishing tithe."

Failed immortals. Like it was a grade they'd received. Like death was just a performance review.

"How many others?"

"Seven so far. Ancelin makes eight. At this rate, the entire council will be gone within the year."

"Can we increase the tithe?"

"From where?" Praxis looked at me with those crimson eyes. "The outer cities are starving. The agricultural city can't grow food anymore—you killed the floraithe guardian. The mining city is collapsing because workers keep dying. There's nothing left to tithe. The system is eating itself."

The system is eating itself. My system. My choices. My consequences.

I watched them carry Ancelin away. Watched the council chamber empty. Watched Praxis make notes with crimson eyes that reflected bioluminescent light.

And still felt nothing.

Just the crown humming approval. Just the voices whispering that this was natural, was right, was how power worked.

Just the knowledge that I'd do it all again.

I stood. My legs felt strange—hollow, lightweight. The black veins wrapped around my jaw pulsed slightly. "Send word if Maxin's condition worsens," I said. "I want to know when he's close."

Praxis nodded. "Of course, Hollow Queen."

I left the council chamber. Walked through tunnels lit by bioluminescence. My skeletal hands caught the glow strangely—bone showing through translucent skin.

The voices whispered as I walked. Oriana soft and motherly. Alaric strong and certain. Lyanna always bringing it back to him.

"You did well," Oriana murmured. "Stayed strong. Didn't let his words shake you."

"The weak fall away," Alaric added. "That's how power purifies itself."

"Nokoa needs you strong," Lyanna finished. "And you are. You always are."

I reached my chambers. Valdic was waiting, purple eyes watching me with that look he got. The one that said he knew.

"Ancelin died," I told him.

"I heard." Valdic moved closer. "How do you feel about it?"

"I don't." The honest answer. "I know I should. But there's just nothing there."

Valdic was quiet for a long moment. Then: "The crown takes the feelings first. Then the memories. Then everything else until there's just the crown and whatever it decides you need."

"Maxin said I'll be alone soon. That everyone's dying and I'll be the last one left."

"Will you?" Valdic asked gently.

"I'll have Nokoa."

"Will you?" Valdic repeated. Different emphasis. Different meaning.

I looked at him. At my friend who'd stayed loyal through everything. "You think he'll die too."

"I think everyone dies eventually," Valdic said. "Even with all your rituals. Even with everything you've sacrificed. Death is patient. Death always wins."

"Not this time." I lay back. Stared at the cave ceiling above me. "I'll find a way. Will keep him alive. Will do whatever it takes."

"I know," Valdic said softly. "That's what I'm afraid of."

He curled up beside the bed. And I lay there thinking about Ancelin's body being carried to the catacombs. About Maxin dying. About Praxis eventually falling. About being alone except for Nokoa in a world I'd destroyed.

And felt nothing.

Just the crown humming. Just the voices whispering. Just the certainty that this was all worth it.

Nokoa was alive.

That was the only fact that mattered.

Chapter Thirty-Six

Burn the Archives

Renata

I needed answers. Needed solutions that didn't require Nokoa's death. Needed something—anything—that would let us both survive this without sacrifice, without the Midnight Oath, without choosing which one of us got to live.

The ancient temple at the forest's edge held records. Archives. Documentation from the original priestesses who'd received witch runes from the Goddess of Fate. History of the hollow crown's creation, every mistake and triumph carved into parchment. Records of previous wearers and how they'd struggled. Information about rituals and bindings and ways to break curses that seemed unbreakable.

If answers existed anywhere in this dying world, they'd be there.

The problem was the temple also housed refugees. People sheltering in its halls because they had nowhere else to go. Families camping in rooms meant for worship. Children sleeping where priestesses once prayed to gods who'd long since stopped listening.

And beneath, in lower levels—food stores. Grain silos. The last significant reserves in the bone court's territory. Carefully rationed. Desperately needed.

I couldn't search with people there. Couldn't risk them interfering or questioning or trying to stop me from taking what I needed. Couldn't let them slow me down when time was running out and Nokoa was dying and answers might be buried in those ancient texts.

So I set fire to the upper levels.

Not planning it. Not considering consequences. Just acting. Just channeling bone magic into the ancient wood, feeling it catch like dry kindling. Watching flames spread across beams that had stood for centuries. The heat felt good against my translucent skin, felt alive in a way most things didn't anymore.

The fire forced evacuation. People running. Screaming. Grabbing children and whatever possessions they could carry. Flooding out into the wasteland beyond.

Good. That's what I needed. Empty temple. Clear access. Space to search without interruption or judgment.

I descended into the archives while smoke filled the air above, while ash drifted down like black snow. Stone stairs worn smooth by centuries of footsteps. Underground chambers cool and dry. Rooms lined with scrolls and books and parchments preserved for longer than some kingdoms had existed.

The documentation was extensive. Beautiful. Irreplaceable.

Witch rune manuscripts from the original coven, their handwriting still visible after all these years. Detailed instructions on how to receive divine gifts from the Goddess of Fate. How to use them properly, with respect and restraint. How to maintain balance between power and purpose.

I skimmed them. Looking for anything about bindings. About paired souls. About breaking curses without sacrifice.

Found nothing useful. Just theory. Just philosophy. Just priestesses writing about ideal circumstances that no longer existed, about a world where magic worked the way it was supposed to and gods still answered prayers.

The hollow crown records were more promising. Every wearer documented. Their struggles laid bare. Their failures catalogued.

Queen Oriana's journal. Detailed. Desperate. Pages and pages about trying to save her lover through the Midnight Oath. Pages about how it failed. How they both ended up sealed in the crown instead of freed, their voices becoming part of the chorus that haunted every wearer after.

I read it three times. Looking for what went wrong. Looking for how to avoid her mistakes.

But the writing was fragmented. Desperate. Half the pages torn out, leaving ragged edges. Like she'd documented everything and then destroyed the crucial parts in a fit of rage or despair. Like she'd hidden the truth even in her own records, like she couldn't bear to leave evidence of her failure complete and whole.

King Alaric's notes. Military strategy. How to use the crown's power for conquest. How to suppress dissent with calculated brutality. Nothing about bindings or salvation or love. Just power and control and the efficient application of force.

Queen Lyanna's writings. Obsessed with legacy. Page after page of failed attempts, each one more desperate than the last. Each one ending in disappointment and the slow realization that the crown couldn't be controlled, only survived.

All of them documented how they'd tried to resist. How they'd fought the consumption. How they'd ultimately failed and been absorbed into the crown's collective consciousness.

Not helpful. Not solutions. Just proof that everyone who'd tried to break free had ended up more trapped.

Hours passed. The smoke above grew thicker, seeping down through cracks in the stone. I barely noticed. Just kept searching. Kept reading. Kept looking for answers that didn't exist.

My hands left ash prints on ancient pages.

The spine forge records. Ancient weapons made by previous councils. Witch rune blades that could cut through death itself, that could sever bindings thought permanent.

Nothing about breaking soul-bindings. Nothing about surviving paired resurrection. Nothing useful.

I was wasting time. Smoke was getting worse, burning my throat when I breathed. The fire was spreading faster than I'd anticipated.

And I'd found nothing. No solution. No answer. No way to save us both without sacrifice.

The realization hit like a physical blow. Made me stumble. Made me press my skeletal hand against ancient stone to stay upright.

There was no other way. The archives contained centuries of knowledge. Generations of desperate people documenting every attempt to break the crown's power. All searching for the same thing I was searching for now. And none of them had succeeded.

The Midnight Oath was the only option. Nokoa's sacrifice was inevitable. And I'd destroyed irreplaceable records for nothing.

Nothing came. Just hollow acknowledgment. Just the crown humming its approval.

"You tried," Oriana whispered, almost gentle. "That's what matters. You searched for another way. Now you know there isn't one."

"The strong make hard choices," Alaric added. "Accept what must be done."

"He'll understand," Lyanna finished. "He loves you. He'll accept the sacrifice."

I heard shouting above. Distant. Panicked. The fire had spread further than I'd intended.

I climbed back up. Emerged into chaos.

The temple was burning. Not just the upper levels I'd lit—everything. The ancient wood caught faster than expected, dry from centuries and hungry for destruction. The fire spread down stone corridors that should have contained it. Into rooms I hadn't touched. Into spaces I hadn't even known existed.

Into the lower levels.

Into the food storage.

I stared. Understanding slowly, the emotion reaching me through layers of crown-induced numbness.

The grain silos were burning. Supplies carefully rationed to keep the bone court alive were turning to ash and smoke. The smell of burning wheat filled the air, acrid and wrong. Three people were trapped inside—had been checking inventory when the fire spread. Their screaming echoed through the stone halls.

Then stopped.

The silence was worse than the screaming.

Guards ran toward the inferno. Trying to save something. Anything. But the fire was too intense, a wall of heat that drove them back. Flames licking up walls and across ceiling beams, devouring everything.

Everything was burning.

Maxin appeared beside me. Coughing through smoke, his grey skin darker with ash. "Those were irreplaceable. Archives from the original priestesses. Hollow crown history spanning centuries. Celeste's writings before her sacrifice." He stared at the flames. "You've destroyed our entire history."

"There could have been something that might save him," I said. Not quite defending. Just explaining.

"Was there?" His voice was flat.

"No." The admission lodged in my chest like a sharp thing. "Nothing. Just documentation of failure. Just proof that no one's ever broken the crown's power without dying."

"Three people died in that fire." Maxin's voice held something dangerous. Simmering beneath the surface. "Checking inventory. Trying to keep the court fed. They burned to death because you were looking for information you didn't find."

"I didn't mean—"

"Their children will starve anyway." He cut me off, each word deliberate. "Whether they're alive or dead. The grain silos are destroyed. Dozens lost their only food source. You've sentenced them to starvation because you needed to search empty archives."

The numbers settled. Heavy. True.

Three people dead. Dozens more sentenced to starvation. Archives destroyed—centuries of knowledge turned to ash. History lost forever.

Nothing came. Just cold calculation. Just weighing costs.

"They wouldn't have helped anyway," I said. Testing the words. They felt true. "The archives. They wouldn't have saved him."

Maxin's face shifted from anger to something worse—pity mixed with grief. "You're not even pretending anymore. Not even trying to justify it or make it sound necessary. Just... accepting that you did this. That three lives for information you didn't gain was acceptable trade."

"Three lives for his life." The equation was simple. "Worth it."

"Their children," Maxin's voice broke. "You're sentencing children to death by starvation. Their parents died trying to feed them. And now they'll starve anyway because you burned the food they needed."

"Children die." The words came out flat, easy as fact. "Everyone dies. At least their parents died trying to help. At least it meant something."

Maxin stared at me. Long silence broken only by the crackling of flames and the distant sound of people weeping. His brown eyes seeing something that made him step back, physically recoiling.

"You're destroying everything," he whispered. "History. Food. People. All for knowledge you didn't gain. All for answers that don't exist. All for one person who's dying anyway."

"He's not dying." My voice was automatic. Defensive. "I'm keeping him alive. That's what matters."

"Is it?" Maxin gestured at the burning temple, at the ash falling around us. "History, food, people—you said it yourself. All for his life. That's worth more than grain. More than three deaths. More than irreplaceable knowledge."

He was throwing my justifications back at me. Making me hear how they sounded.

"Yes," I said. Refusing to flinch. "Yes, his life is worth more. Worth all of it. Worth everything."

"Then you've already lost." Maxin turned away, his shoulders sagging. "Because valuing one life over everything else isn't love. It's obsession. It's madness. It's exactly what the crown wants you to believe."

He left. Walking away from the burning temple. From the destruction. From me. His footsteps fading into smoke and distance.

I stood in the smoke and ash. Watching the temple collapse, beams falling in showers of sparks. Watching centuries of knowledge turn to nothing. Watching food stores burn while people who needed them watched helplessly.

I refused to feel guilt. I'd eliminated a possibility. Confirmed the archives held no solutions. Confirmed the Midnight Oath was the only option left.

That was worth something. Wasn't it?

Later that night, back in my chambers, I learned the death count. Three in the fire.

That was low. Hardly worth thinking twice about.

"Three lives were easy to replace," Queen Oriana agreed, her voice warm with approval.

"Yes," I said aloud. "The confirmation was worth that."

Valdic lay beside my bed, purple eyes watching me.

"Three people," he said quietly. "Their names were Merin, Kolva, and Jess. Merin had two children. Kolva was pregnant. Jess was sixteen."

Names. Details. Things that should make them real, make them matter.

"They were in the way," I said. Not defensive. Just factual. "I needed to search. The archives might have held answers."

"Did they?"

"No." I lay back on my bed, the honey-scent from my last bath faint on the sheets. "But I had to check. Had to know for certain."

"And the children who'll starve?"

"Everyone's starving." I closed my eyes. "At least this served purpose. At least their deaths meant something."

Valdic was quiet for a long time. Then: "Do you hear yourself?"

"I hear the truth." I pulled the blanket up, suddenly cold despite the bone magic warming my veins. "I hear that sometimes sacrifices are necessary. That Nokoa's life is worth more than three people checking inventory."

"What about the children who'll starve?"

"Unfortunate." The word felt right. Clinical. "But not my fault. They would have died anyway. I just accelerated the inevitable."

"You burned their food supply."

"I needed the archives empty." My voice was getting sharper. "They were in the way."

"So you killed them."

"I set a fire." The distinction mattered somehow. "They died because they didn't evacuate fast enough. That's not the same as killing them."

Valdic's purple eyes reflected the low light from the bioluminescent fungi growing in the corner. "You're becoming something I don't recognize."

"I'm becoming what I need to be." I looked at him. At my friend who stayed loyal even as I transformed into something monstrous. "I'm becoming strong enough to save him. That's what matters."

"Is it?"

"Yes." Simple. Final. True.

Valdic laid his head on his paws, but his eyes never left me. Watching. Grieving. Unable to stop what I was becoming.

I closed my eyes again. Let exhaustion take me. Fell asleep thinking about burning temples and empty archives and the Midnight Oath that was looking more inevitable with every passing day.

Three lives seemed like a small price. Barely worth mentioning.

The crown hummed its agreement, and the voices sang me to sleep.

Chapter Thirty-Seven

Valdic's Third Attempt

Renata

Valdic returned permanently this time. I knew because he came to my chambers without announcement, without permission, without the careful distance he'd maintained before. Just appeared in the doorway like he belonged there, like he'd always belonged there.

But he wasn't alone.

Cressa stood beside him. Green eyes tired but determined. And Hivro—the butterfly keeper, his hands still stained with nectar and pollen from tending creatures that were slowly dying like everything else.

"We brought breakfast," Cressa said. Not asking permission. Just stating fact. She carried a tray—boiled eggs, honey tea, bread that looked fresh despite the famine. "You haven't been eating."

I stared at them. At this strange delegation that had invaded my space. "I'm not hungry."

"You're never hungry," Valdic said, moving closer. "But you need to eat anyway. Need to remember what it feels like to care about sustaining yourself."

Cressa set the tray on my desk. Pushed the reports aside—death counts and resource inventories scattering. The honey tea's scent filled the air, sweet and warm and wrong in a room that smelled like bone dust and decay.

"Boiled eggs," she said quietly. "Valdic said they're your favorite. Or were, before—" She stopped. Started again. "Before the crown."

I looked at the eggs. Tried to remember if I'd ever liked them. Tried to access that preference, that taste, that small human thing.

Nothing came. Just the knowledge that I should eat them because Cressa had brought them, because refusing would be inefficient, because maintaining this body required fuel even if I couldn't taste it anymore.

"Your fingertips," Hivro said suddenly. His voice was soft, always soft, like he was afraid of startling butterflies. "They're turning to bone. No flesh left. Just skeleton showing through."

I looked at my hands. He was right. The translucent skin that had covered my fingers was gone now. Just bone. White and clean and dead. The transformation spreading faster than I'd realized.

"Soon it'll be your whole hand," Cressa said. Not accusing. Just observing with healer's precision. "Then your arms. Then everything. The crown is consuming you faster now."

"I know." I picked up an egg. Felt nothing through the bone of my fingertips. "It doesn't matter."

"It does matter," Valdic insisted. "You're dying. Not slowly anymore. Not over months. Quickly. Maybe weeks before there's nothing left but bone and crown."

"Then I have weeks." I cracked the egg. Peeled it with skeletal fingers that left no warmth on the shell. "Weeks to keep him alive. Weeks to find another solution. Weeks before I have to accept the Midnight Oath."

"Is that all you care about?" Cressa's voice held something dangerous. "Time? Calculations? How many days you have left before you're completely consumed?"

"Yes." Simple. Honest. "That's all that matters. How long I can maintain this. How long before everything collapses."

"We were friends once," Cressa said quietly. "Do you remember? We studied together in the schoolroom. You, me, Nokoa, Theron. We were children together. We carved our names in that desk. We made promises about making the bone court better."

I bit into the egg. Tasted nothing. Just the mechanical process of chewing and swallowing. "I remember that it happened. But I can't feel it. Can't access what it meant."

"Try," Hivro urged. "Please. Just try to remember what it felt like to care about something other than him."

I closed my eyes. Reached for memories of the schoolroom. Of friendship. Of caring about Cressa and Theron and futures that didn't revolve around Nokoa.

Found nothing. Just hollow space. Just the crown humming. Just voices whispering that those memories didn't matter, weren't important, weren't worth preserving.

"I can't." I opened my eyes. "It's gone. Whatever I felt then—friendship, hope, belief in making things better—the crown has taken it. Or maybe I gave it willingly. I don't know anymore."

"The crown protects you," Valdic said. Not a question. An observation. "Doesn't it? When you start to feel too much—when guilt or grief or horror starts to surface—the crown steps in. Takes it away. Keeps you numb."

The words hit true. I hadn't articulated it but had known. Had felt it happening every time emotion threatened to overwhelm me.

"Yes." The admission came slowly. "Every time I start to feel something—start to question what I'm doing or regret what I've done—the crown intervenes. Makes it distant. Makes it matter less. Protects me from the weight of my choices."

"That's not protection," Cressa said. "That's prison. That's the crown making sure you can't stop. Making sure guilt won't slow you down."

"I know." I picked up the honey tea. Held the cup with bone fingers that couldn't feel its warmth. "But I need it. Need that protection. Because if I let myself feel everything—every death, every destroyed life, every consequence—I'd break. I'd stop. And if I stop—"

"Everything you've done would be for nothing," Valdic finished. "That's what you're afraid of. Not that you've become monster. That you've become monster for no reason. That all the destruction and death and suffering might not save him anyway."

The fear crystallized. Sharp. Clear. Undeniable.

"Yes." My voice was barely audible. "I'm terrified that if I try to stop—if I try to turn back, try to be better, try to remember how to care about anything else—it'll mean admitting that everything I've done was wrong. Was pointless. Was just destruction without purpose."

"So you keep going," Hivro said. "Keep destroying. Keep letting the crown consume you. Because stopping would mean facing what you've become."

"Because stopping would mean it was all for nothing," I corrected. "At least if I keep going, there's chance it meant something. Chance that his survival justifies everything. Chance that love—even twisted, destructive love—was worth the price."

Cressa sat down across from me. Met my grey eyes with her green ones. "I watched you become this. Watched the crown hollow you out piece by piece. Watched you forget who you were and why any of it mattered. And I kept hoping—desperately hoping—that you'd stop. That you'd remember. That you'd choose to be human again."

"I can't." The words hurt to say. "Even if I wanted to—even if I could access those feelings, remember who I was, care about anything else—I'm too far gone. Too much done. Too many people dead. I can't go back."

"You're scared," Valdic said softly. "Scared that trying to change would make everything you've suffered meaningless. Scared that becoming human again would mean facing the full weight of what you've done. So you let the crown keep you numb. Let it protect you from feeling. Let it justify everything so you don't have to."

"Yes." I drank the honey tea. Tasted nothing but knew intellectually it was sweet. "I'm scared. Terrified. Because if I stop now—if I try to be better—I have to admit that I destroyed the world for nothing. That I burned temples and killed people and consumed guardians and none of it mattered. That I'm just monster who broke everything and can't fix it."

"But if you keep going," Cressa said, "you become worse. You destroy more. You kill more. And eventually, when Nokoa dies anyway—because he will die,

Renata, the resurrection is failing—you'll have destroyed everything for nothing anyway. You'll just have more blood on your hands when it ends."

The logic was sound. Undeniable. True in ways I couldn't argue against.

But the fear was stronger.

"I can't stop," I whispered. "Can't face what I've done. Can't admit it was all wrong. Can't—" My voice broke. "Can't let it be for nothing."

Hivro moved closer. His butterfly-stained hands gentle on my skeletal ones. "The butterflies are dying. All of them. Because the famine you're creating is killing the flowers they need. Soon there won't be any left. And when they're gone, that's one more beautiful thing destroyed. One more piece of the world ended because you couldn't stop."

"I'm sorry." The words felt hollow. "I'm sorry about the butterflies. Sorry about the flowers. Sorry about everything dying. But I can't—I can't prioritize butterflies over him. Can't choose beauty over his survival. Can't stop just because the world is ending."

"What if he asked you to?" Cressa's voice was very quiet. "What if Nokoa—your Nokoa, the person you're destroying everything for—what if he begged you to stop? To let him die? To choose the world over him?"

I thought of his letter. About the Midnight Oath. About his willingness to sacrifice himself.

"He has asked," I admitted. "Has offered the Midnight Oath. Has said he'd rather die than watch me become this. But I can't accept it. Can't let him go. Can't—" I closed my eyes. "Can't face a world without him. Even if that world is beautiful and full of butterflies and growing things. Even if stopping would save everyone else. I can't lose him."

"So everyone else loses instead," Valdic said. Not accusing. Just sad.

"Yes." I opened my eyes. Looked at my bone fingertips. At the tea I couldn't taste. At the eggs I couldn't enjoy. At the friends who'd brought breakfast to a monster. "Everyone else loses. The butterflies die. The flowers wither. The world ends. All so I don't have to face losing him. All so I don't have to admit that everything I've done was wrong."

"The crown whispers, doesn't it?" Hivro asked. "When you start to feel guilty. When you start to question. It steps in. Tells you it's worth it. Tells you to keep going. Protects you from the full weight of what you're doing."

"Every time." I touched my chest where the crown's influence pulsed through bone and what remained of flesh. "Every time I start to break—start to feel the horror of what I've become—the voices come. Oriana soft and understanding. Alaric firm and certain. Lyanna always bringing it back to Nokoa. They tell me it's necessary. Tell me I'm strong. Tell me that love justifies everything."

"And you believe them," Cressa said.

"I need to believe them." The distinction mattered. "Because if they're wrong—if the crown is just using me, just manipulating me, just feeding my obsession to serve its own purposes—then I'm not saving him. I'm just destroying everything while the crown laughs and consumes me. And I can't—I can't face that possibility."

Silence. Just us sitting. Just me holding tea I couldn't taste while my friends watched me admit my fears.

"I brought boiled eggs because Nokoa said they were your favorite," Cressa said finally. "He remembered. Even dying, even covered in witch runes, even barely human anymore—he remembered what you loved. Remembered who you were before the crown. Holds onto those details while you forget them."

"I know." I looked at the eggs. At evidence of love I couldn't feel, couldn't remember, couldn't access. "He holds my memories while I destroy his world. He loves who I was while I become something he'd hate. He offers to die for me while I kill everything to keep him alive."

"It's cruelty," Valdic said gently. "Prolonging his dying while destroying everything he cares about—that's not love. That's possession. That's fear. That's the crown using your love as excuse to consume everything."

"I know." The admission hurt. "I know it's cruelty. Know it's wrong. Know it's destroying him as much as everything else. But I'm too afraid to stop. Too afraid that stopping means admitting it was all pointless. Too afraid of facing a world where I've destroyed everything and he's still dead and nothing mattered."

"So you'll keep going," Hivro said. "Keep destroying butterflies and flowers and people and worlds. Keep letting the crown consume you until there's nothing left but bone. Keep calling it love while everyone who actually loves you watches you disappear."

"Yes." Simple. Final. True. "Because the alternative—stopping, facing what I've done, admitting it was wrong—that's worse. That's impossible. That's an ending I can't survive."

Cressa stood. Touched my skeletal hand with her warm one. The contrast stark—my bone cold and dead, her flesh alive and human. "We love you. All of us. Valdic and Hivro and Nokoa and me. We love you even though you're destroying everything. Even though you've become this. Even though you're choosing him over the world. We love you anyway."

The words should comfort. Should prove that love survived my transformation.

They just made the fear worse. Because if they loved me unconditionally—if Nokoa loved me despite everything—then I was using their devotion to excuse my cruelty. Using their belief in me to destroy everything they believed I could be.

"I'm sorry," I whispered. "I'm sorry I can't be better. Sorry I can't stop. Sorry I'm choosing him over everything else. Sorry the butterflies are dying. Sorry about all of it. But I'm too scared to change."

"We know," Valdic said. "That's why we came. Not to change your mind. We know we can't. But to make sure you remember—while you still can—that people love you. That you're destroying people who care about you. That every choice has faces attached. Names. Butterflies and flowers and boiled eggs and memories of schoolrooms."

They left. Took the tray but left one egg. Left the honey tea growing cold. Left me sitting with skeletal fingertips and fears I couldn't face and the slow realization that I'd chosen this. That the crown protected me because I wanted protection. That I stayed numb because feeling was too terrible. That I kept destroying because stopping meant admitting it was all wrong.

And I still couldn't stop.

The crown hummed its approval, and the voices whispered that I was strong, and Lyanna brought it back to Nokoa like she always did.

And I sat in the dark with an egg I couldn't taste and tea I couldn't feel.

And then—and this was the worst part—I thought of the Bone God. Of how he didn't judge. Of how he understood. Of how his comfort, even if it was manipulation, was the only kind that didn't ask me to stop.

The thought settled. Comfortable.

The crown pulsed warm against my skull.

And I ate the egg, and tasted nothing, and chose to keep going.

Act Four

Chapter Thirty-Eight

The Journal

Renata

I couldn't sleep. Hadn't been able to for days. Time blurred together when consciousness was just varying degrees of numbness, when daylight and darkness meant nothing beyond the bioluminescence that never changed.

The reports sat on my desk. Death counts. Resource inventories. Patrol schedules. Everything documented with efficient precision. Fifteen children dead defending bridges during the last outer cities attack. Grain supplies depleted from the temple fire. Water sources contaminated by death magic seeping into aquifers. The bone court collapsing in measurable increments.

All of it my doing. All of it consequence of choices I kept making. All of it documented in neat columns that made atrocity look like accounting.

I should review the reports. Should plan next moves. Should calculate how many children I'd need to conscript to make up bone court losses, how much longer the spectral guardians could maintain defense, how many days until complete collapse.

But I couldn't focus on the numbers. Couldn't make them matter. Couldn't find the energy to care about logistics when everything was ending anyway, when every choice led to the same destination.

I was too tired to pretend. The crown didn't need to hollow me out anymore—I was doing that all on my own.

The journal sat where Valdic had left it. Garden sketches and pressed flowers and evidence of someone I didn't recognize. It caught the dim bioluminescent light, the leather cover worn soft with handling.

I pulled it toward me. Opened it slowly. Afraid of what I'd see. Afraid of what I wouldn't feel.

The first page was dated. Three months before Nokoa's death. Before everything broke.

Started planning the courtyard garden today. Nokoa says I'm being optimistic—trying to grow things in a place made of death and bone. But that's exactly why it matters. If I can make something beautiful here, maybe I can make the whole bone court beautiful. Maybe I can prove that life and death can coexist.

The handwriting was mine. Undeniably. The loops and curves familiar even if the sentiment wasn't. But the words felt foreign. Strange. Like finding my name in someone else's diary, finding my hand forming letters that spelled out thoughts I couldn't recognize.

I turned the page. A sketch. Careful. Detailed. Orchids arranged in circular pattern, each bloom rendered with precision. Notes in the margins about soil composition, sunlight angles, water requirements. Someone had spent hours on this. Someone had believed this mattered.

Nokoa helped me measure today. He pretended to understand what I was talking about—nodded along while I explained drainage systems and root depth. But I could tell he had no idea. He just wanted me to be happy. Just wanted to support this impossible project because I cared about it.

That's what love looks like, I think. Not understanding but supporting anyway. Not sharing the dream but helping build it. Not seeing the point but caring because I care.

I closed my eyes. Tried to remember that moment. Tried to picture Nokoa standing beside me, measuring string between his hands, pretending to understand drainage systems.

Couldn't reach it. Couldn't access that feeling. Just knew from reading these words that it had happened. That once, briefly, we'd measured garden beds together and been happy about it. That once, his lack of understanding hadn't mattered because his support had been enough.

Next page. More sketches. Herbs this time. Notes about which ones were medicinal, which ones decorative, which ones would thrive in the bone court's strange environment.

Cressa is excited about the medicinal herbs. Says if I can grow them successfully, it would help her healing work. Says having fresh herbs instead of dried ones would save lives. Says she's tired of watching people die from infections she could prevent if she just had better supplies.

I want that. Want to grow things that help. Want to prove the bone court can nurture instead of just consume. Want to show everyone that death doesn't have to mean ending—sometimes it can mean transformation. Sometimes what looks dead can still grow.

The optimism hurt to read. The naive belief that growing herbs would make a difference. That small acts of creation could balance out the constant destruction.

That woman—the one who wrote these words—she believed in small victories. Believed in incremental change. Believed that making one corner beautiful was worth the effort even if the rest stayed ugly.

I'd destroyed that corner completely. Had stood there and watched Fern try to heal dead earth. Had killed her when she failed. Had consumed her ashes and moved on like that garden had never mattered.

That garden would never exist. Those herbs would never grow. Cressa would keep losing patients to infections, would keep watching people die because I'd prioritized Nokoa's resurrection over her healing supplies.

More pages. More sketches. Trees that would provide shade and fruit and shelter for birds that no longer nested in the bone court's dead branches.

Nokoa says the birds matter. Says if we can get birds to nest in the bone court, it means we've made something worth staying for. Something worth building life around. Something that draws living things instead of repelling them.

I love how he thinks about these things. How he sees beyond the immediate. How he understands that gardens aren't just about plants—they're about creating space where life wants to exist. About making death less lonely.

I wish I could tell him that. Tell him how much I admire the way his mind works. Tell him that loving him makes me want to be better, makes me want to create instead of destroy, makes me believe in futures I'd never imagined before.

I touched the page. Traced the sketch with skeletal fingers. Tried to understand why any of this had mattered. Why I'd spent hours planning gardens that would never grow. Why I'd believed in futures that would never happen.

Couldn't reach it. Just knew that once, these sketches represented hope. Represented the woman Nokoa had loved before the crown consumed her, before she became something that destroyed gardens instead of planting them.

Theron thinks I'm wasting time. Says the bone court doesn't need gardens, needs stronger defenses. Says I should be thinking about military strategy instead of which Orchids bloom longest.

But that's exactly why gardens matter. Because Theron is right—the bone court thinks like that. Thinks in terms of defense and strategy and control. And maybe if I can grow something beautiful here, maybe if I can prove that creation matters as much as protection, the whole place could change.

Nokoa understands. Says gardens are quiet rebellion. Says every flower I plant is proof that the bone court doesn't have to be what it's always been.

I flipped to the last entry. Day before I was banished from the bone court.

I was called into a meeting today. Told that I'd be leaving. Sent away to a cottage in the northern burrows to live out the rest of my days. I had been expecting it. Had been hoping it would happen, if I'm honest.

My brother was chosen for the crown—not by the crown itself, but by the Bone Council. It was the first time they'd ever tried to pick the wearer instead of listening to who it called for. They wanted Theron. Thought he'd be easier to control. I didn't argue. Didn't resist. Let my brother take the weight of the Hollow Crown and accepted my fate gladly. I wanted to run as far away as I could.

I only stopped for a brief moment to look at myself in a mirror. To consider what kind of person I was to leave Nokoa and my brother behind. To abandon them to the bone court while I escaped to safety.

But I looked in that mirror, and I didn't feel guilty. I felt relieved. Free. Like I was finally allowed to breathe after years of holding my breath.

The gardens will never happen now. The orchids won't get planted. The herbs won't grow. The birds won't nest. All those careful plans and sketches and dreams—they'll stay in this journal, evidence of futures that won't arrive.

Maybe that's okay. Maybe some dreams are meant to stay dreams.

I'm leaving tomorrow. Nokoa doesn't know yet. I haven't told him. Don't know how to explain that I'm choosing to leave, choosing to abandon him, choosing my own freedom over our friendship.

I hope he understands. I hope he forgives me. I hope someday he sees that leaving was the only choice that made sense.

But I doubt he will. I'm not sure I'd forgive me either.

The entry ended there. Abrupt. Final. No resolution.

The orchids never got planted. And the garden never got made.

But I had left. Had escaped to the northern burrows. Had abandoned Nokoa and Theron and the bone court. Had chosen my own peace over everything else.

And then Theron died. And the crown called for me anyway. And everything I'd run from found me in the cottage where I'd thought I was safe.

I closed the journal carefully. Set it back where Valdic had left it.

The woman who wrote those entries had believed in gardens. Had believed in creation. Had believed leaving was the right choice, that abandoning the people she loved was acceptable if it meant her own freedom.

And now that woman was dead. Replaced by someone who'd come back. Who'd taken the crown willingly. Who'd destroyed everything in the name of love instead of running away from it.

I didn't know which version was worse. The one who abandoned people for peace, or the one who destroyed the world for love.

Maybe they were both monsters. Just different kinds.

The crown hummed. Oriana whispered about strength. Alaric about necessity. Lyanna about Nokoa.

But for once, I didn't want to hear them. Didn't want their approval or their justifications or their promises that what I was doing was right.

I just wanted to understand why that woman in the journal had believed gardens mattered. Why she'd thought beauty was worth the effort.

And why I'd come back.

Valdic stirred beside the bed. Looked at me with purple eyes that saw too much.

"Did you read it?" he asked quietly.

"Yes."

"Did it help?"

"No." I touched the journal's cover. "Just proved that whoever I was then, she's gone. She left before the crown ever touched me. She abandoned everyone and called it freedom. And when I came back, when I took the crown, when I became this—maybe I was just finishing what she started."

"What do you mean?"

"She wanted to escape." I traced the leather binding. "Wanted nothing to do with the bone court or the crown or the responsibility. And maybe becoming the hollow queen is just another kind of escape. Maybe losing myself to the crown is just running away with extra steps."

Valdic was quiet. Then: "That's not the same thing."

"Isn't it?" I looked at him. "She ran from the bone court. I ran into the crown. Both of us just trying to escape what we were supposed to be. Both of us destroying things in the process."

"You came back," Valdic said. "That matters."

"I came back because the crown called me. Not because I chose it. Because when Theron died, the crown needed a new wearer, and I was the only option left. I didn't choose this. It chose me. Just like she tried to run from."

"But you're still here."

"Because I'm too afraid to leave again." The confession hurt. "Too afraid of what happens if I run. Too afraid of losing Nokoa. Too afraid of being alone.

So I stay and I destroy and I call it love when really it's just cowardice. Just fear of facing what I am without the crown giving me purpose."

Valdic moved closer. Pressed his muzzle against my hand. "You're not a coward."

"Then what am I?"

He didn't answer. Couldn't answer. Because there wasn't a word for what I'd become. Just hollow queen and monster and something in between. Just the woman who'd run from the crown and the woman who'd embraced it, somehow existing in the same body, destroying everything either version touched.

I left the journal on the desk.

Both of us monsters. Both of us destroyers. Both of us just trying to survive in ways that killed everything else.

Chapter Thirty-Nine

Sevi Wakes

Renata

The third ritual felt different from the start. Heavier. Like the magic itself knew something I didn't.

I needed to stabilize Nokoa again. Alaira's instructions were specific—bone dust, dark water, ancient words. The same ritual I'd performed before. The same desperate attempt to keep him alive while everything else died.

The spectral guardians responded to my call. Seven raised previous hollow rulers channeling power through me. More than before. Stronger than before. The guardians I'd consumed had made me powerful—Perla's fire, Fern's nature magic, both corrupted into fuel for resurrection that shouldn't exist.

The magic flowed. Down. Through. Into the catacombs where the last guardian slept.

I felt something shift. Deep underground. Fundamental. The final protection crumbling.

No. Not yet. Not until I finished the ritual. Not until Nokoa was stable.

But it was too late.

The magic had gone too far. Touched too much. Woken what should have stayed sleeping.

Sevi.

The clockworker guardian. The last of three. Created by the Goddess of Time to protect the prison through patience and prophecy.

I ran. Down stairs worn smooth by centuries. Through corridors that smelled like old stone and older magic. Maybe I could stop her. Maybe I could explain. Maybe—

She was already awake.

Standing in the chamber. Not like Perla's fire or Fern's petals. Sevi was mechanisms. Gears and blood and oil all mixed together. Her body clicked and whirred with each movement, precise and calculated. Like she was made of clockwork given divine consciousness.

But she was deteriorating. The gears were grinding, metal on metal making sounds that hurt to hear. The oil was dark, thick as tar. The blood was wrong—too slow, moving through transparent tubes like sludge. Like she'd been sleeping so long that even divine construction couldn't maintain itself perfectly.

She turned to me. Her eyes were clock faces. Literally. Showing different times. Different moments. Past, present, future all visible at once, hands spinning at different speeds.

"I see what you become." Her voice was like gears meshing. Precise. Terrible. Each word clicking into place with mechanical certainty. "All versions."

"What?" I stopped. Ready to defend if necessary.

"I can consume time," Sevi explained. "See futures clearly. Watch possible timelines unfold like threads in a tapestry." Her gears clicked faster. "I've been watching you. Watching all the ways this ends."

She gestured. The air rippled. Images appeared—not solid, not quite real, but visible. Prophetic visions hovering in the space between us.

I saw myself. Multiple versions. Different futures. Different choices. Different endings.

In one, I was transformed completely. Bone and shadow. Standing beside the Bone God as he walked free. Powerful. Terrible. Wrong in every way that mattered.

In another, I was dead. Just corpse on the floor. Crown shattered beside me. Nokoa weeping over my body, his face covered in witch runes.

In another, I was alone. Completely alone. The bone court empty. The world wasteland. Just me and the crown and endless grey stretching forever.

Different paths. Different outcomes. But all of them—every single one—ended in either unsealing, transformation, or apocalypse.

"All of them end terrible," Sevi said. Her clock-face eyes ticked through possibilities. "In some futures you realize what you're doing. In others you don't. Doesn't matter—result is same."

"That can't be true." I stared at the visions. "There has to be a path where we both survive. Where we're together and free and—"

"There is." She showed me. One future among many. Nokoa and me. To-gether. Transformed. Powerful. Standing in ruins of everything we'd ever cared about.

We looked monstrous. Wrong. Our humanity completely gone. Just power and corruption given flesh.

"That's not surviving," I whispered. "That's just existing. That's not us any-more."

"But you're together." Sevi's gears clicked in rhythm with my heartbeat. "Alive. Bound. Forever. Isn't that what you wanted? Isn't that what all of this was for?"

It was. She was right. I'd wanted us alive and together. Had sacrificed every-thing for that outcome.

And here it was. The future where we both survived. Where we were together forever.

We just weren't human anymore. Just weren't ourselves. Just weren't any-thing worth being.

"I'm from the Goddess of Time's world!" Sevi said. Her voice cracked, gears grinding wrong. "You're not just breaking the prison—you're breaking the world you live in! The veil between realms! The boundaries that keep gods contained!"

She showed me more visions. Flashes of futures. Each one worse than the last. The Bone God rising free. The world dying completely. Time itself distorting under the weight of corrupted magic, moments bleeding into each other.

"Every choice you make leads HERE!" She pointed at the unsealing. At the transformation. At the future where I became what the Bone God wanted. "You think you're choosing him. You're choosing THIS."

The vision focused. The moment of transformation in sharp detail. And Nokoa was there. Beside me. Equally changed. Both of us together in the worst possible way.

"That future—you think you'll be happy," Sevi said. "But you won't feel anything. Won't be anything. Just power wearing familiar faces. Just corruption pretending to be love."

I stared at the vision. In that future, we touched. Held hands. Looked at each other. But our eyes were empty. Our expressions were blank. We were together but we weren't us anymore. Just hollow things occupying the same space, proximity without connection.

"That's not love," Sevi said quietly. "That's just proximity. That's not what you wanted. Not really."

She was right. I knew she was right. Could see it in the vision. The future where we survived wasn't the future where we were happy. Wasn't the future where love meant anything.

"Then what do I do?" I asked. "Every path leads to ruin. Every choice makes it worse. How do I save him without destroying everything?"

"You don't." Her clock-face eyes showed all possible futures simultaneously. "There is no path where everything works. No future where you both survive as yourselves. No timeline where love doesn't require sacrifice."

"The Midnight Oath," I said. Understanding dawning cold and terrible. "That's the answer."

"It's an answer," Sevi corrected. "One person dies. One person goes free. Clean sacrifice. Clear outcome. But it requires genuine willingness. Requires both of you accepting it completely. No coercion. No manipulation. Just choice."

"I won't let him die for me."

"Then you choose transformation." Sevi showed me that future again. Monstrous. Together. Empty. "You choose becoming what the Bone God wants. You choose losing everything that makes you human. You choose proximity over actual connection."

"There has to be another way."

"There isn't." Her gears slowed, distressed. "I've seen every possibility. Every branch. Every choice. They all lead to variations of same endings. Transformation or sacrifice or apocalypse. Those are your options."

I thought of Nokoa actively. Deliberately. Let his face fill my mind—his golden eyes turning yellow, his brown curls falling out in patches, his skin covered in witch runes. Let pain lance through my skull as punishment for thinking of him.

Worth it. Worth anything to keep him alive. To keep him existing. Even if existing meant transformation. Even if transformation meant losing humanity.

At least we'd be together. At least we'd survive. At least—

"You're doing it right now," Sevi said. Watching my thoughts through prophetic sight. "Choosing him over sense. Choosing transformation over wisdom. Choosing the future where you're together and hollow instead of the future where one of you is free."

"Because I love him." Simple. Final. "Because that's what love means. Choosing him. Always choosing him. No matter the cost."

"Then you've already lost." Sevi's gears slowed further. "Because love that destroys everything isn't love. It's obsession pretending to be devotion. It's fear wearing love's face. It's exactly what the Bone God wanted you to believe."

She attacked then. Not with violence. With time. With visions. With the weight of every possible future crashing down at once.

I felt it all. Saw it all. Every ending. Every choice. Every consequence. All of it real and happening and inevitable.

The pain was overwhelming. Temporal. Prophetic. The burden of knowing exactly what came next and being powerless to change it.

But I had death magic. Had consumed guardians. Had power that even divine gifts couldn't overcome completely.

I met her time with death. Met her visions with spectral guardians. Met her prophecy with cold certainty.

We fought across the catacombs. Time against death. Prophecy against power. Her desperate attempt to show me truth against my desperate refusal to accept it.

I was winning. Not because I was stronger. But because I'd already chosen. Already decided. Already accepted that transformation was worth it if it meant keeping him.

Sevi's time magic was finite. Running down. Her gears slowed. Her clockwork failed. The divine gift from the Goddess of Time couldn't sustain itself forever.

"Hivro is last," she gasped. "She'll show you. Not futures. But who you WERE. Before crown. Before corruption. Before you chose this."

"I don't want to remember." The truth came easy. "Remembering just makes it harder. Makes the weight heavier. Makes the choices more painful."

"Exactly." Sevi smiled. Sad. Understanding. "That's why she'll show you anyway. Because you need to understand what you're destroying. Need to see who you were before you can accept who you've become."

Her gears stopped. Oil and blood spilling across stone floor. What remained looked almost human. Almost peaceful. Just divine being laid to rest after centuries of service.

I stood over her remains. Breathing hard. Skin blistered from temporal magic backfire.

I'd killed a guardian. Another one. Third of three. Divine being created by goddess to protect the world.

All of them dead by my hand. All of them obstacles to keeping Nokoa alive.

The hollow crown pulsed. Not tightening. Just satisfied. Pleased.

"She was wrong," Oriana whispered. "About the futures. About transformation. You're not losing yourself—you're becoming stronger."

"Prophecy doesn't account for will," Alaric added. "Doesn't account for determination. You can change futures."

"Nokoa is alive because you chose," Lyanna finished. "Keep choosing. Keep becoming what you need to be."

But underneath their voices—underneath their reassurance—I heard something else.

The Bone God. Laughing. Gentle. Approving.

"Three guardians," he said. Voice barely whisper. "Three divine beings. Three gifts from goddesses. All dead. All consumed. All used to fuel your power."

"You did this," I said. "Manipulated me. Guided me. Made this happen."

"I offered understanding." He corrected gently. "Offered comfort. Offered truth. You chose to act on it. You chose to become this. I just... made sure you didn't feel guilty about it."

"I should feel guilty." I stared at Sevi's remains.

"Would guilt change anything?" He asked. "Would remorse bring them back? Would horror undo your choices?"

No. It wouldn't.

"Consume the ashes," the crown urged. All three voices together. "Divine essence. Time magic. Power you need."

I knelt. Gathered what remained of Sevi. Gears and blood and oil mixed with ash. Divine construction reduced to fuel.

Brought it to my mouth.

Hesitated.

For just a moment—one brief, terrible moment—I felt something real. Not the crown numbing me. Not the voices justifying. Just me, alone with what I was doing, understanding with terrible clarity that killing all three guardians meant the prison was completely unprotected. That nothing stood between the Bone God and freedom except my choice to stop.

I could stop.

Right now. This moment. I could stop.

I ate the ashes anyway.

They tasted like time itself. Like every moment I'd lost. Like all the futures I'd destroyed. Like prophecy corrupted into power. Metallic and bitter and wrong.

For one bright moment, I felt emotion again.

Everything Sevi had felt. Her devotion to time. Her dedication to showing truth. Her desperate hope that prophecy would change outcomes. Her grief watching all futures end in ruin. Her love for the Goddess of Time who'd created her. Her sorrow at failing her purpose.

All of it flooding through me. Overwhelming. Unstoppable.

I felt the weight of every possible future. Felt them all ending. Felt the certainty that nothing I did would save us. Felt Sevi's knowledge—absolute and prophetic—that I was choosing wrong.

Then it was gone.

The crown took it. Consumed it. Turned divine emotion into nothing but power.

I stood. Stronger. Fuller. Three guardians consumed. Three divine gifts corrupted.

All for him.

Even knowing Sevi was right. Even knowing every path led to transformation and I'd just chosen which version.

I left the catacombs. Climbed back up. Back to chambers that smelled like honey and death. Back to reports about children dying and supplies dwindling and the world ending in increments.

Back to the crown humming approval and the voices whispering justification and the Bone God laughing somewhere deep in his prison that was barely prison anymore.

Three guardians dead.

And Hivro waiting. Not a guardian of the prison. Just the butterfly keeper. Just someone who would show me who I'd been before all this.

I didn't want to see. Didn't want to remember. Didn't want to face the person I'd destroyed to become this.

But Sevi had said it would happen anyway.

And after everything—after three guardian deaths and consumed ashes and the moment I could have stopped and didn't—I was starting to think she might have been right about the other things too.

Chapter Fourty

Declare Martial Law

Renata

The council chamber held only three of us now. Me. Maxin—barely holding together, more skeletal each day, his blonde hair reduced to a few brittle strands. And Praxis—immortal, watching everything with those crimson eyes that never blinked, that saw everything and judged nothing.

"The outer cities are organizing again," Praxis reported. "Not attacks. Movements. Gathering. Planning something."

"Let them plan." I stared at reports documenting the bone court's collapse. Food stores destroyed in the temple fire. Population decimated by famine and conscription. Guards reduced to conscripted children who could barely lift their weapons. "They're too weak to matter."

"They have the bone weapon still," Maxin reminded me. His voice was thin. Strained. "Nalla survived. She still wields it. That makes them dangerous."

"Everything is dangerous." I set down the reports, heard the papers rustle. "The outer cities. The famine. The collapsing infrastructure. The bond slowly killing me and Nokoa. All of it dangerous. All of it ending. The only question is whether we maintain control while it ends."

"Then maintain control," Praxis said simply. "Declare martial law. Suspend all rights. Make questioning you punishable by death. Use fear to maintain order while everything collapses."

The suggestion was logical. Exactly what the situation required.

Also monstrous. Obviously monstrous. The kind of thing that would make me tyrant instead of queen, that would erase any pretense of legitimacy I still maintained.

"Do it," I said.

Maxin looked at me. Something flickered in his dimming eyes. Tired acceptance that I'd become exactly what he'd feared. What he'd helped create.

"Martial law requires enforcement," he said quietly. "Requires making examples. Requires public demonstrations of power. Are you prepared for that?"

"I've already made examples." The public executions. The conscripted children. The burned temple. "What's a few more?"

"A few hundred more," Praxis corrected. "Anyone who questions gets punished. Anyone who resists gets executed. Anyone who even looks at you wrong becomes an example. That's not a few. That's organized coercion."

"Then organized coercion is what we'll have." I stood, felt my skeletal spine shift. "Draft the proclamation. Effective immediately. Anyone who questions my authority dies without trial. Anyone who resists bone court edicts dies without trial. Anyone who spreads dissent dies without trial."

"You'll be killing your own people," Maxin said.

"They're dying anyway." The justification came automatic. "Starvation is killing them. Famine is killing them. The wasteland is killing them. At least this way they die knowing there are rules. Knowing there's order. Knowing rebellion means immediate consequence."

"That's not order," Maxin whispered. "That's tyranny."

"Is there a difference?" I asked. "When everything is collapsing? When the only choices are controlled descent or chaotic free-fall? Maybe tyranny is just what order looks like when everything else has failed."

Maxin stared at me for long moment. Then nodded. Slow. Defeated. "I'll help implement it. Will create the enforcement structures. Will make sure it's at least organized instead of random violence."

"Why?" The question was genuine. "Why help me do this? Why not resist?"

"Because I'm dying," he said simply. "Because resisting takes energy I don't have. Because I helped create the crown that's destroying you and this is my penance. Because someone has to administrate the apocalypse and it might as well be me."

He left to draft proclamations. Left to create systems of oppression. Left to help me become tyrant.

Praxis remained. Watching. His tentacles shifting slightly.

"The food," he said. "That's the real weapon. Not executions. Not fear. Food."

"Explain."

"Distribute rations only to compliant citizens," he said, pulling maps from his robes. "Those who obey eat. Those who question starve. Those who resist die—not from execution, but from hunger. Let starvation do the work for you. Let people watch their families waste away and understand: obedience means survival."

The strategy was brilliant. Terrible, but brilliant. More efficient than execution, more pervasive than fear.

"The outer cities guerrilla forces get nothing," I said. "They're already starving. Cutting them off completely ensures they can't sustain resistance."

"Exactly." Praxis spread the maps across the table. "Those who arrive at bone court to serve receive food. Those who stay in wasteland receive nothing. Make compliance the price of survival. Make obedience the only path to eating."

I studied the maps. Saw the logic. Saw how hunger would do what terror couldn't—break people completely, make them choose survival over resistance, make them complicit in their own oppression.

"Implement it," I said.

"It will kill thousands," Praxis warned. Not arguing. Just stating fact. "Maybe more. The outer cities. The resisters. The questioners. All of them will starve."

"They're starving already." I couldn't feel the weight of it anymore. "This just makes it official. Makes it policy instead of consequence."

"This makes it weapon," Praxis corrected. "Makes it choice instead of circumstance. Makes you responsible instead of just complicit."

"If I let the Hollow Crown have its way entirely, they'd all be dead right now." I looked at him, at those crimson eyes. "I'm giving them choice. Obey and eat. Resist and starve. That's more than the crown wants to give them."

Praxis nodded. Started organizing. Started creating infrastructure of oppression with his usual efficiency.

I watched him work and felt nothing.

He'd been useful. But that didn't make him safe. Didn't make him loyal beyond utility. He was too willing to let his council members die as if they weren't his equals. Too comfortable with all of this.

The bone court members—what remained of them—gathered for the announcement. Maybe fifty people. Most of them skeletal, bones visible through translucent skin. All of them starving, hollow-eyed and weak.

I stood before them. Felt nothing looking at their hollow faces. Felt nothing seeing children too weak to stand, held up by parents too weak to carry them.

"Martial law is now in effect," I said. Voice carrying across silent crowd. "All rights are suspended. Questioning my authority is punishable by death. Resisting bone court edicts is punishable by death. Spreading dissent is punishable by death."

They stared at me. Too weak to protest. Too scared to argue. Too hungry to care about anything except survival.

"Food will be distributed only to compliant citizens," I continued. "Those who serve the bone court will eat. Those who question will starve. Those who resist will die. Choose obedience. Choose survival. Choose wisely."

"Witch runes will be carved," I added. "Obedient citizens will receive marks showing their compliance. Traitors will receive marks showing their status. Everyone will be categorized. Everyone will be visible. Everyone will know where they stand."

Maxin stood beside me. His expertise with witch runes making him essential despite his deterioration. He'd carve the marks. He'd burn them into foreheads with iron and magic. He'd make obedience and treason visible for everyone to see.

He'd helped create the crown. Now he'd help me use it to create something I didn't have a better word for than what it was.

The crowd dispersed. Slowly. Weakly. Accepting martial law because what choice did they have? Fight and starve? Resist and die? Better to be marked obedient. Better to eat than to resist.

That's what tyranny looked like. Not dramatic. Not violent. Just slow acceptance that obedience was the only path to survival. Just quiet capitulation born of hunger and fear and exhaustion.

I watched them leave. Watched them shuffle away to receive their marks. Watched them become complicit in their own oppression.

And felt nothing.

"You're creating the conditions for uprising," Maxin said quietly. "Oppression always breeds resistance. Always creates martyrs."

"Let it breed resistance," I said. "By the time those seeds grow, everything will be over anyway. Nokoa will be stable or dead. Either way, their resistance won't matter."

"So you're just postponing collapse."

"I'm maintaining control while I find solution. That's all I can do. Control the descent. Make it last long enough for me to save him."

"And if you can't save him?" Maxin asked. "If he dies anyway? What happens to all this terror you're creating? What happens to the people you've marked as traitors?"

"Then it doesn't matter." Simple. Final. "If he dies, none of this matters. The bone court can collapse. Everyone can starve or rise up or do whatever they want. Without him, there's no point to any of it."

Maxin was quiet for long moment. Then: "That's what I feared most. Not that you'd become tyrant. But that you'd become tyrant for nothing. That you'd destroy everything and he'd die anyway and you'd have built all this suffering for no reason."

"Then hope I save him," I said. "Hope something changes. Because if he dies, I guarantee your fear comes true. I guarantee all of this was for nothing."

I returned to my chambers. Sat at my desk. Stared at the proclamations Maxin had drafted. Organized tyranny documented in careful script.

Thought of Nokoa. Deliberately. Let his face fill my mind. Let pain lance through my skull as punishment for missing him.

Between every order. Between every choice. Between declaring martial law and weaponizing starvation—I thought of him.

But underneath the cold efficiency, doubt stirred again. The same doubt that had surfaced when I'd held Sevi's ashes.

Was I keeping him alive? Or just keeping him dying slowly? Was I maintaining power for him? Or using him as excuse to avoid facing truth—that I'd become tyrant because becoming tyrant was easier than accepting I'd already failed?

I didn't know. Couldn't tell anymore.

Just knew I'd declared martial law. Just knew I'd weaponized starvation. Just knew I'd crossed another line I couldn't uncross.

The crown hummed approval. And for once, that approval felt less like comfort and more like confirmation.

Chapter Forty-One

MAXIN'S SACRIFICE

Renata

The days blurred together. Each one bled into the next until I couldn't tell dawn from dusk, couldn't remember if I'd slept or simply stood staring at walls made of bone while my mind wandered somewhere far away.

The prisoners had stopped screaming. That much I knew. Their bodies still hung in the courtyard, marked with witch runes that glowed faintly in the bioluminescent light, but the sounds had stopped three days ago.

Or was it four?

Time felt slippery lately.

I stood in the throne room because that's where I always stood now. The spectral guardians hummed behind me—seven raised previous hollow rulers, a constant presence that had become as natural as breathing. More natural, maybe. Breathing required thought sometimes. The spectral guardians just existed, always there, always waiting.

Praxis sat in his usual seat, managing logistics with the same impassive ef-ficiency he brought to everything. Supply lines. Patrol schedules. Execution orders. All of it handled with the careful precision of someone who'd done this before. Many times before.

The throne room was cold. Had it always been this cold? I pulled my black gown tighter, but it didn't help. The cold came from inside, from the hollow places where something warmer used to live.

"Hollow Queen."

I turned. Maxin stood in the doorway, and something about seeing him made my chest tighten in a way I couldn't explain.

He looked terrible. Worse than I'd ever seen him. His patchy blonde hair hung limp around his face, unwashed and tangled. His brown eyes were sunken, ringed with dark circles that spoke of sleepless nights and desperate calculations. But it was his skin that made me stare.

Where once he'd looked mortal—human and warm and alive—now patches of bone showed through. His left hand was nearly skeletal, the flesh worn away to reveal white metacarpals and delicate phalanges. His cheekbone on one side had broken through the skin, creating a death's-head grin that never changed no matter his expression.

"You look unwell," I said, and wondered when I'd stopped caring about such things. When had concern become just an observation?

"I need to speak with you." His voice was rough, like he'd been screaming. Or crying. "Alone."

I glanced at Praxis. The massive skeletal figure rose without being asked, his bleached bones clicking, tentacles flowing behind him as he exited the chamber. The door closed.

"What is it?" I asked, but part of me already knew.

Maxin walked toward me slowly, his skeletal hand trembling. When he was close enough that I could see the individual threads of corruption spreading through his remaining flesh, he stopped.

"I made a mistake," he said.

"We've all made mistakes."

"No." His voice cracked. "Not like mine. I helped Alaira create the crown. I used the Goddess's gift—the witch runes She gave us to help the world—and I helped corrupt them into this." He gestured at my head, at the hollow crown fused to my skull. "I thought we were helping. I thought we were easing suffering, managing death, protecting people."

I wanted to tell him it wasn't his fault. Wanted to offer comfort. But the words wouldn't come. They felt too far away, like something I'd once known how to do but had forgotten the mechanics of.

"And then I was sealed away," he continued. "Locked up for refusing to aid the corruption any further. And I thought—I thought that was my punishment. My penance. Centuries of darkness, alone with what I'd done."

"The council brought you back."

"Yes." He laughed, and it sounded like something breaking. "They brought me back because they thought I could help. Because I understood the system's design. And I did help, didn't I? I taught you. I showed you how to push the magic further, how to bend the rules, how to combine things that should never be combined."

The spectral guardians hummed. I felt their presence like a weight on my shoulders.

"I've been architect of this disaster twice over," Maxin said, and tears were running down his face now, cutting tracks through the thin layer of flesh that remained. "Every time I try to help, I make it worse. Every time I think I'm fixing something, I'm actually destroying it."

"You helped me save Nokoa."

"Did I?" He moved closer, and I could smell the decay on him. Not rot, exactly. More like the absence of life. "Or did I help you break the world for one person? Did I teach you how to justify anything as long as you loved him enough?"

The crown pulsed. Warning. Danger. But I didn't feel threatened by Maxin. I felt—

What did I feel?

Sad, maybe. Like watching something precious shatter and being unable to catch the pieces.

"There's a pattern," he said, his voice dropping to barely above a whisper. "The Goddess gave us tools. Divine magic. Witch runes. A gift meant to help, to heal, to guide. And we keep using them wrong. We keep corrupting them.

Alaira did it with the crown. I did it by helping her. You're doing it now with every spell you cast."

"I'm surviving."

"You're destroying." He reached up with his skeletal hand and touched my face. His finger bones were cold against my skin. "And I can't watch it anymore. I can't be the one who taught you how to do this."

Something in his tone made me focus. Made me look at him—really look at him—and see the determination behind the despair.

"What are you going to do?" I asked.

"Fix it." He stepped back. "Or try to. One last time."

"Maxin—"

"The crown was a mistake," he said, speaking faster now, words tumbling over each other. "The whole system is wrong. We thought we were managing death, easing transitions, helping souls find peace. But we were just controlling. Enslaving. Using divine gifts for power instead of mercy."

He pulled something from his robes. A bone knife, carved with witch runes that glowed with soft golden light. The runes were backwards. Inverted. Wrong in a way that made my eyes hurt to look at them directly.

"What is that?"

"Divine magic backwards," he explained. "If the crown was made by corrupting the Goddess's gift, maybe it can be unmade by inverting it. Running the ritual in reverse. Using the same power that created the curse to destroy it."

The crown pulsed harder. All three voices spoke at once, overlapping in panic.

Stop him!

He's dangerous!

Don't let him—

But I couldn't move. Couldn't speak. Just watched as Maxin began carving runes into his own remaining flesh.

He carved them into his arms first. Long, careful lines that split skin and exposed bone beneath. The inverted witch runes glowed as blood welled around them, golden light mixing with red until I couldn't tell where one ended and the other began.

"Maybe the system itself is wrong," he whispered, his voice shaking. "Maybe trying to control death at all is the mistake. Maybe we were never meant to have this power."

The crown screamed. Not in my head—physically screamed, a sound like metal scraping against bone, like thorns dragging across stone. The sound made my teeth ache, made my vision blur, made the spectral guardians surge forward in defense.

But Maxin was already speaking. Words in a language I didn't know. Old words. Divine words. The same words Alaira must have spoken when she created the crown, but backwards now. Reversed. Unmade.

The crown lashed out.

Not at Maxin.

Through me.

My hands moved without my permission. The spectral guardians surged forward at my command—a command I didn't remember giving. Bone spikes erupted from the floor, sharp and sudden, aimed at Maxin's heart.

"No!" I tried to stop it, tried to pull back the magic, but my body wasn't mine anymore. The crown had taken control, using me like a puppet, using my power to defend itself.

The bone spikes drove into Maxin's chest. Pierced through his ribs. Shattered the runes he'd so carefully carved.

He gasped. Stumbled forward. The golden light flickered but didn't die.

"Keep... going..." he whispered, blood bubbling on his lips. "Almost... there..."

He carved another rune. Into his own skull. The knife scraped against bone, carving divine symbols into his forehead, between his eyes, down his nose. Blood ran into his mouth, but he kept speaking those backwards words, kept pushing the ritual forward even as his body failed.

And then something changed.

The prison. The Bone God's prison, deep underground. I felt it shift. Felt the structure of it transform from solid wall to—

Door.

A door where there should have been a wall. An opening where there should have been seal.

Maxin's spell hadn't destroyed the crown. Hadn't saved us. Hadn't fixed anything.

It had made everything worse.

"No," Maxin whispered, his eyes widening as he felt it too. The change. The shift. The terrible, irreversible transformation. "No, that wasn't supposed to—I didn't mean to—"

His legs gave out. He collapsed forward, and I caught him without thinking. My skeletal hands wrapped around his shoulders as he fell into my arms, his weight dragging us both down until we were kneeling on the cold stone floor.

Blood soaked into my black gown. His blood, bright red against the darkness.

"I'm sorry," he gasped, looking up at me. His brown eyes were already going dim. "I tried to fix it. I thought—I thought if I inverted the magic, if I used the Goddess's gift the right way for once—"

"Shh." I held him closer, cradling his head against my chest. "Don't speak. Save your strength."

"No strength left." He coughed, and blood bubbled on his lips. "Used it all. For nothing. Made it worse again. Always worse."

The crown pulsed. I felt it reaching, felt it trying to take something—

His memory. The crown wanted to take the memory of this moment, wanted to erase him the way it had erased so many other things.

"No," I said out loud. "Not him. Not this."

The voices whispered urgently.

He hurt you.

He made things worse.

Better to forget.

Easier without the pain.

Maxin's skeletal hand reached up and touched my face. His fingers were so cold. When had they gotten so cold?

"Find another way," he whispered. "Not Alaira's way. Not the crown's. Something... new..."

"What way? There is no other way."

"There has to be." Another cough. More blood. "The Goddess wouldn't have... given us gifts... just to watch us... destroy ourselves..."

"Maxin—"

"Remember me." His voice was barely audible now, just a thread of sound unwinding into nothing. "Please. Someone has to remember. Someone has to know... what I tried to do... even if I failed..."

His hand fell away from my face.

His eyes closed.

His chest stopped moving.

And I knelt there holding a body that was still warm, still real, still someone who'd mattered—

The crown pulsed.

The memory began to slip.

I fought it. Dug my mental heels in. Tried to hold onto this moment, this person, this terrible weight of loss.

The details went first. The exact words he'd said. The way his blood had felt soaking into my gown. The golden light of the inverted runes.

Then the emotions. The grief. The horror. The realization that I'd killed him—that the crown had used my hands to murder someone trying to help.

Then his face. His name. The fact that he'd been important at all.

I stood up—when had I stood up?—and looked down at the body at my feet.

A body. Just a body. Someone had died here. Recently. The blood was still warm.

Did I care?

I tried to remember why I would care. But it slipped away—memory after memory—until there was nothing but the ache of something missing, and no way to name what it was.

The body was heavy. I should have someone move it.

The door opened. Praxis entered, his crimson eyes taking in the scene with his usual impassiveness.

"There's been a death," I said, gesturing at the body. My voice sounded strange. Distant. Like I was reading lines from a script.

"So I see."

Praxis moved closer, studying the corpse with clinical interest. The inverted witch runes were still visible in the flesh and bone, still glowing faintly with golden light.

"That's Maxin," he said. "Was Maxin. Your teacher."

Maxin. The name meant nothing to me. Should it?

I looked at the body, trying to find recognition. Trying to understand why there was an ache in my chest that had no source, a grief that had no object, tears on my face that I didn't remember crying.

"He taught you," Praxis continued. "Helped you develop your magic. Was sealed away for centuries and only recently resurrected to aid the bone court."

"Oh." I wiped at my face, my skeletal fingers coming away wet. "That's why I'm crying?"

"I couldn't say."

I stared at the tears on my fingers, watching them catch the bioluminescent light.

"Remove the body," I said, my voice steadying. "Proper burial. He was—" I struggled to find the word. "Important. Somehow. I think he was important."

"As you command, Hollow Queen."

Praxis lifted the body easily, cradling it in his massive skeletal arms. He carried it toward the door, leaving small drops of blood behind on the stone.

"Praxis," I called out, and he stopped. "What was his name again?"

"Maxin."

"Maxin." I repeated it, trying to commit it to memory. Trying to hold onto at least that much. "I should remember that. Shouldn't I?"

"Does it matter?"

The question hung in the air between us.

Did it matter? Did any of it matter? Names, faces, the people we'd been, the things we'd lost—did any of it change what we had to do to survive?

"No," I said finally. "I suppose it doesn't."

Praxis nodded and continued out the door. It closed behind him, and I was alone again except for the spectral guardians.

Always alone except for the dead.

I looked down at the blood on my gown. There was so much of it. Someone had died right here, in my arms, and I couldn't remember who or why or if I should be devastated.

The crown pulsed. Warmth flooded through me, chasing away the cold ache, the sourceless grief, the phantom pain of a loss I couldn't name.

It's better this way, Oriana whispered.

You're stronger without the weight, Alaric added.

Think of Nokoa, Lyanna finished. Think of him. That's all that matters.

I touched my chest, feeling the struggle of my heart beneath bone and crown. Still beating. Still fighting.

Someone had died here.

I was crying about it.

But I couldn't remember why.

The crown whispered comfort, and I let it wash over me. Let it take the confusion and the grief and the terrible ache of knowing I should feel more than I did.

Let it take everything except the one thing it could never have—
Nokoa.

The pain was immediate and blinding. My skull split with it. My vision whited out. I tasted copper, felt warmth on my face.

Bleeding again. Nose and eyes, the bond punishing me for daring to love.

I collapsed where I stood, my skeletal hands pressed against my temples.

Worth it. Worth the pain. Worth everything.

For him.

I pushed myself up, leaving handprints of blood on the stone floor. My head throbbed. My eyes burned. Everything hurt in a way that felt both familiar and wrong.

I walked to my chambers because there was nowhere else to go. The route was familiar, worn smooth by repetition.

My chambers were dark and cold and exactly as I'd left them. Everything black. Everything empty. Everything the color of forgetting.

I collapsed onto the bed without removing my blood-stained gown. The honey-scent from old baths had faded completely. The pressed flowers in my journal were just dead plants now, no memory attached to why I'd kept them.

Sleep came slowly.

And when it came, I dreamed not of Nokoa but of someone else. Someone with patchy blonde hair and brown eyes and a skeletal hand that touched my face with gentleness I didn't deserve.

Someone who'd said something important. Something I needed to remember.

But the dream faded before I could grasp it.

Dawn came. I rose and prepared myself. Changed into a fresh black gown. Stared at my reflection and tried to recognize the creature looking back.

Skeletal fingertips. Black veins wrapped around my jaw. Hollow crown fused to skull. Grey eyes that held nothing but emptiness.

Praxis was waiting in the throne room when I arrived. He'd taken the seat beside mine—the seat that used to belong to someone. I couldn't remember who.

"The burial is complete," he announced.

"Burial?"

"For the council member who died yesterday. Maxin."

The name tugged at something. A memory that wouldn't form. A grief that had no shape.

"Did I know him?"

Praxis studied me with those crimson eyes. "You did. He taught you a great deal."

"Oh." I settled onto my throne, feeling the weight of the crown press down. "That's unfortunate then. Losing a teacher."

"Indeed."

"How did he die?"

"In your arms. You killed him, though not intentionally. The crown used your hands to defend itself when he attempted to destroy it."

I stared at Praxis, waiting to feel something. Horror. Guilt. Remorse. But there was only a hollow curiosity, like hearing about something that had happened to someone else in another life.

"Did I care about him?"

"Very much, I believe. For a few moments before the crown took the memory."

"How efficient." The words came out flat. "Is there anything else I should know?"

"The prison has changed. Maxin's spell—his attempt to invert the divine magic—it didn't destroy the crown, but it altered the seal. The prison is no longer a wall. It's a door now."

I sat up straighter. "What does that mean?"

"It means the Bone God has access he didn't have before. Not freedom, but possibility. A way through if the right ritual is performed."

The crown pulsed. The voices were quiet, but I could feel them listening. Waiting. Almost pleased.

"I see." I folded my skeletal hands in my lap. "And what ritual would that be?"

"I don't know. But Alaira might. Or the Bone God himself, if he chose to share."

"Send word to Alaira," I said. "I want to speak with her. About rituals. About possibilities. About doors that used to be walls."

"As you command, Hollow Queen."

Praxis rose and left me alone in the throne room.

Alone with my dead and my crown and the blood-stained memory I couldn't quite grasp.

Someone had died yesterday.

Someone important.

Someone who'd tried to help me and failed.

And I had killed them without meaning to.

The crown whispered comfort.

And I believed it.

Because believing was easier than remembering.

Because forgetting was easier than grief.

Because the hollow spaces inside me were all that remained, and filling them with memory would only make the emptiness more obvious.

I sat on my throne and waited.

Just waited.

Because waiting was all I had left.

Chapter Forty-Two

THE PURGE

Renata

The word came to me in the middle of the night, whispered by voices that might have been the crown or might have been my own thoughts. I'd stopped being able to tell the difference.

Traitors.

They were everywhere. In the bone court, among the skeletal figures who served me. In the outer cities, among the starving rebels who still thought they could win. Even among those who claimed loyalty—I could see it in the way they looked at me. The fear that wasn't quite respect. The obedience that wasn't quite willing.

Traitors, all of them. Or they would be, eventually.

Better to act first.

I rose from my bed and dressed in the same black gown I always wore now. I couldn't remember the last time I'd worn color.

Had I ever worn color?

The thought felt important somehow, like a door I couldn't quite open, but the crown pulsed and the feeling faded and I finished dressing without questioning further.

The throne room was dark when I entered. The bioluminescence had dimmed overnight, giving everything a shadowy quality that made the bone mosaics look like they were moving.

Praxis was already there. "Hollow Queen. You're awake early."

"I need to give an order."

"I'm listening."

I moved to my throne and sat, feeling the weight of the crown settle more firmly against my skull. The bone fused to bone, inseparable now. It should have frightened me. It didn't.

"A purge," I said, and the word felt right on my tongue. "Clear the bone court of traitors."

Praxis's posture didn't change, but something in the quality of his attention sharpened. "That's extensive. How do you define traitor?"

"Anyone who might oppose. Anyone who questions. Anyone who looks at me with doubt." I leaned forward. "I can see it in them."

"Hollow Queen, with respect—paranoia can—"

"It's not paranoia if they're actually planning something." The crown pulsed, warming me. "Better to be safe. Better to act first."

Praxis studied me for a long moment. "You want me to arrest anyone who might potentially oppose you at some theoretical point in the future."

"Yes."

"That could be hundreds of people."

"Then arrest hundreds." My voice was steady. Calm. Reasonable. "We'll sort through them. Mark them as we marked the prisoners—witch runes carved into bone. Let everyone see who's been judged and found wanting."

"This will create terror," Praxis said.

"Good. Terror creates order. Order keeps—" I reached for the justification. "Order keeps him safe."

The crown pulsed agreement.

"Begin immediately," I said. "I want this done before dawn tomorrow."

He left to prepare.

I sat on the throne and waited, alone with my dead.

Dawn arrived, and with it, the sound of screaming.

I watched from a balcony overlooking the main courtyard. Below me, the purge arranged itself in rows—skeletal figures in tattered clothing, some still wearing the remnants of court finery, others in simple servant wrappings. Maybe a hundred of them. Forced to their knees, hands bound, waiting.

Praxis worked through them methodically. Bone carving tools inscribed with inverted witch runes, divine magic corrupted into brand. Each prisoner brought forward, each one marked.

T-R-A-I-T-O-R.

Some died during the carving. Their bodies simply gave out, hearts stopping. Those were left where they fell.

The teenagers he'd conscripted to hold the tools—I noticed some of them were shaking, their hands burning from the inside where the rune-carved handles touched their skin. The corrupted magic was eating them too. Another cost I hadn't calculated.

I noted it distantly. Told myself I'd think about it later.

"Hollow Queen."

Valdic stood beside me on the balcony, his purple eyes fixed on the scene below.

"You shouldn't be here," I said.

"Neither should you."

"They're threats. Potential threats, at least."

"Safe." Valdic's voice was flat. "You call this safe?"

"I call it necessary."

"For him?" He moved closer. "You think this is what he wants?"

The crown pulsed. Anger flooded through me. The spectral guardians surged forward in response, ready to defend.

"Don't presume to know what he wants."

"I know he doesn't want this." Valdic gestured at the courtyard. "This isn't protection. This is paranoia."

"Control," I said. "This is control. Order. Stability."

"He sent me to remind you of who you were," Valdic said quietly.

The anger stuttered. Caught on something.

"But I don't remember who I was," I said, the heat draining as quickly as it had come. "The crown took it. All those memories, all those feelings, all that person I used to be—gone. Eaten. So all I can do is what seems necessary in the moment."

"He's going to hate this. When he finds out—and he will—he's going to hate what you've become."

The words just felt like information. Facts to be noted and filed away.

"Then I'll deal with that when it happens," I said. "But at least he'll be alive to hate me. That's all that matters."

Valdic walked away without answering. I watched the purge continue through the day and into the night.

By the time it was done, nearly half the remaining bone court had been marked or killed. The walls were lined with bodies. The courtyard smelled like death and burnt flesh and corrupted divine magic.

Praxis gave his report with the same impassive precision he applied to everything. One hundred and forty-seven arrested. Eighty-three marked and chained. Sixty-four died during processing.

"The teenagers we conscripted," he added. "Most won't survive another day of this work. The rune-carved tools are corrupting them from the inside."

"Replace them when they die," I said. "There are always more."

Something crossed Praxis's skeletal face. Gone before I could name it.

"As you command, Hollow Queen. Though I want you to understand something."

"What?"

"History will remember this. What you're doing right now—it will be written down. Recorded. Studied by future rulers who'll try to understand how a queen went from promising reforms to ordering mass purges in the span of months."

"I don't care about history."

"You should. History is all that remains when we're gone." He paused at the door. "I'll continue serving you. But I want that acknowledgment on record somewhere, even if only in my own accounting."

He left before I could respond.

I sat alone on the throne and tried to feel the satisfaction I'd felt earlier. It was fading. Being replaced by something colder. Emptier.

Somewhere deep inside, a small voice was screaming.

This is wrong. This is wrong. This is wrong.

I pressed my skeletal hands to my temples and tried to make it stop.

Night fell. I walked through the corridors because I couldn't sit still.

I found myself in the lower levels without choosing to go there. The walls here were older, the bone mosaics more elaborate. Stories carved in femur and vertebrae, tales of deals made and prices paid.

I stopped in front of one particular mosaic. It showed a figure kneeling before a crown, offering something—a heart? A soul?—in exchange for power.

"That's the story of the first hollow ruler," Valdic said behind me. "Queen Oriana. You and her walk the same lines."

I hadn't heard him follow me. I'd stopped being surprised by this.

"Did it work for her?"

"No. The ritual failed—he wasn't as willing as he claimed. Both of them became the first voices in the crown. Trapped forever, neither alive nor dead. Helping every wearer after make the same mistakes."

The words settled slowly. I turned them over.

"She's the voice that calls herself Oriana," I said. "The one who tells me it's worth it. The one who brought it back to love and necessity and him."

"Yes."

"She's trapped in my crown. Helping me repeat what she did. Watching me walk toward the same failure."

"Yes."

The grief hit then. Not the distant ache I'd been carrying. Something sharper. I touched the mosaic with skeletal fingers, Oriana's kneeling figure cold beneath them.

"Does she regret it?"

"Does she sound like she regrets it?"

I thought about her voice. Soft. Motherly. Always bringing everything back to love. Always whispering that it was worth it.

"No," I admitted. "She sounds satisfied. Like she got what she wanted even though it destroyed her."

"Maybe that's what the crown does. Makes you satisfied with your own destruction."

"I don't want to be her," I whispered. "I don't want to end up trapped here, whispering to the next hollow queen, helping her destroy herself the same way."

"Then stop."

"I can't."

"Why not?"

"Because he's dying. Because without my power, without everything I've become, he'll die."

"Even if he'd rather die than watch you become this?"

I stumbled back from the mosaic. My skeletal hands shaking.

"He wouldn't—"

"He would," Valdic said. "He's told me so. Multiple times. He'd rather die than watch you destroy yourself trying to save him."

"Then he doesn't understand." My voice went sharp. "He doesn't understand that losing him is worse than becoming monster."

"Maybe. But you've already lost yourself. The woman who planned gardens is gone. The woman who believed in beauty is gone. The woman Nokoa fell in love with—she's gone."

Tears ran down my face. I didn't remember starting to cry.

"He remembers the gardens," Valdic continued softly. "The orchids. The plans you made together. He's holding onto those dreams for both of you."

Orchids. Gardens. Words without meaning now. Just sounds.

But something in my chest ached at them.

"I don't remember that," I whispered.

"He knows. He remembers anyway. Someone has to remember who you were. Someone has to believe you can be that person again."

The ache spread. Became grief. Real grief, for the person I'd been. For the gardens I'd planned. For the woman who'd believed beauty could coexist with death.

"I don't know how to be that person anymore," I said, and my voice cracked.

"Then be this person who knows she's lost. That's a start."

"A start to what?"

"I don't know. But it's more than nothing."

I walked away without answering. Back up through the levels. Past the marked prisoners and the dying teenagers.

I returned to my chambers and stood in the darkness, feeling the grief I couldn't let the crown take. It refused to be consumed. Refused to be made distant.

The bond pulsed. Nokoa, thinking of me. Missing me. Loving me despite everything.

Pain lanced through my skull. My nose bled. I fell to my knees, pressing my hands to my temples.

Stop, I thought. Please stop thinking of me.

But he couldn't hear me. He never could.

When it subsided, I lay on the bed. The spectral guardians formed a protective circle around me.

"I'm doing this for him," I told them.

They didn't respond. They never did. The dead don't lie.

I closed my eyes and waited for sleep.

When it came, I dreamed of orchids in gardens I couldn't remember, tended by a woman who used to be me. In the dream, Nokoa stood beside her, smiling.

When I woke, the grief was still there.

Still raw. Still refusing to be taken.

The crown pulsed, trying to consume it. Trying to make it distant.

But for once—just this once—I didn't let it.

I held onto the grief. Let it hurt. Let it remind me that somewhere underneath the hollow queen, underneath everything I'd become, there was still someone who could feel.

Even if all she could feel was loss.

Chapter Forty-Three

THE LAST TOUCH

Nokoa

The outer cities camp smelled like smoke and desperation. Like unwashed bodies and rotting food and the particular stench of hope dying slowly.

I sat outside the tent Nalla had assigned me, watching the survivors move through their daily routines. Children with hollow eyes and protruding ribs. Adults who looked like they'd aged decades in months, backs bent under invisible weight. Everyone marked by the same grey pallor, the same defeated slouch, the same knowledge that they were losing a war they'd never had a chance of winning.

My right hand throbbed. Three of the fingers were splinted—broken two days ago when I'd tried to write a letter and my bones had simply snapped under the pressure of holding the pen. The witch runes under my skin had flared bright gold, and I'd screamed loud enough that Valdic had come running.

But Valdic was gone now. Back to Renata. Back to trying to save a woman who might already be beyond saving.

I flexed my left hand carefully, feeling the joints grind against each other. That one was still mostly functional. For now. The resurrection was failing again, eating through my body piece by piece, breaking me down into component parts that no longer wanted to work together.

Sometimes I couldn't tell if the pain was from the resurrection or from the bond. They'd become so tangled up together that one fed into the other in a constant loop of suffering.

A butterfly landed on my splinted fingers. Purple wings, iridescent in the afternoon light. One of Hivro's messengers, carrying a letter wrapped around its delicate body.

From Renata.

My heart did something complicated in my chest. Joy and dread mixing together until I couldn't separate hope from fear.

I unwrapped the letter carefully, trying not to break any more bones. Her handwriting was shakier than it used to be, the letters uneven and smudged in places like she'd been bleeding while she wrote.

Nokoa,

The only time I feel like myself is in my dreams. I dream of us at the cottage. When I'm awake I still feel like I'm dreaming even when I'm awake. Like I'm outside of myself. Watching what should be my body or in a prison cell.

I don't remember who I was before. The crown has taken so much. But I remember you. Always you. Your face. Your voice. The way you looked at me like I was something precious.

I'm trying. I don't know if I'm succeeding. I don't know if there's enough of me left to save. But I'm trying.

For you. For us. For the dreams I can't remember but you're holding for both of us.

Wait for me. Please. I'm coming back.

I love you.

R.

The letter ended there, her signature trailing off into an ink blot like she'd collapsed mid-word.

I read it three times. Then a fourth. Trying to find hope in the words, trying to convince myself they meant she was getting better, that Valdic's visits were working, that the woman I loved was still in there somewhere fighting her way back to me.

But all I could think about was the report that had reached the camp two days ago. Mass purge. Hundreds arrested. Children marked with witch runes that burned them alive from the inside. Bodies lining the courtyard walls, displaying their traitor brands for everyone to see.

And Renata—my Renata, the woman who'd pressed flowers and dreamed of gardens—had ordered all of it without hesitation.

"You okay?"

I looked up. Nalla stood nearby, her arms crossed. She'd grown thinner in the months since I'd known her, her face gaunt and hard.

"Reading old letters?"

"New one." I held it up. "From her."

Nalla's expression hardened. "Saying what? That she's sorry for systematically destroying everything we are? I lost fifteen people in her last purge. People I'd known for years. Marked as traitors and chained to walls to die slowly while their families watched."

I didn't have an answer. What could I say? That Renata loved me so much she'd lost herself? That every terrible thing she did was somehow for me? That I was the justification for all of it, the excuse that made atrocity acceptable?

It sounded hollow even in my own head.

"The weapon," Nalla said after a moment. "We're planning another strike."

"You'll die."

"Probably." She shrugged, the gesture weary. "But at least we'll die fighting instead of starving while she picks us off one by one."

"There has to be another way."

"If there is, we haven't found it." Nalla studied me. "You're her weakness. Everyone knows it. So maybe... maybe if you weren't alive anymore, she'd stop."

The suggestion hung in the air between us.

She wasn't wrong. If I died—really died, permanently—Renata would have no reason to continue. No justification for the purges, the executions, the destruction.

"I've thought about it," I admitted. "About finding a way to die that she can't undo. About removing myself so she has to face what she's become without me as an excuse."

"Why haven't you?"

"Because I'm selfish." The words tasted bitter. "Because even knowing what she's done, I still want to see her again. Touch her again. Tell her I love her even if it hurts us both."

"That's not selfish. That's human."

"Is there a difference anymore?"

Nalla was quiet for a moment. "For what it's worth, I don't think killing you would stop her. I think it would break her completely. Turn her into something we wouldn't recognize as human at all."

"So I'm trapped. Living keeps her destroying the world. Dying makes it worse."

"Seems like it."

A cough wracked through me suddenly. Deep and violent, rattling my ribs. I tasted copper, felt warmth on my lips. When I pulled my hand away from my mouth, it was covered in blood.

Nalla helped me sit down. "You need to rest."

"Resting doesn't help."

"Neither does standing."

She was right. I let myself slump against the tent pole, feeling the exhaustion settle into my bones.

"Valdic said she's struggling," I said once the coughing subsided. "That she's starting to question what she's become."

"Do you believe that?"

"I don't know." I looked at my splinted fingers. "Sometimes I think she's too far gone. That the crown has eaten too much. But other times I remember her laugh. How she looked in yellow dresses. How excited she got about garden plans. And I think maybe that person is just buried. Maybe she's waiting for someone to dig her out."

"You can't save someone who doesn't want to be saved."

"I know." I looked at the blood on my hand. "But I can't stop trying either."

Nalla nodded slowly. "That's love, I guess. Stupid and painful and completely irrational."

"Yeah."

She left me there with Renata's letter and my bleeding hands.

* * *

Night fell. The camp settled into uneasy quiet punctuated by coughing and the sound of children crying from hunger.

I lay in my tent staring at the canvas ceiling, unable to sleep. The witch runes under my skin were glowing faintly, casting golden light across the darkness. They'd been spreading faster lately, winding up my arms, across my chest, down my legs.

What happened when they covered everything? Did I become something else? Something not quite Nokoa anymore?

I was too tired to be terrified.

Instead I thought of Renata. Was she thinking about me? About the letter she'd sent?

The pain came slowly. Building gradually instead of spiking suddenly. My head began to ache. My vision blurred. I tasted copper.

She was thinking about me too. We were caught in the same loop, thinking about each other despite the cost, unable to stop even when we knew we should.

I pressed my hands to my temples and endured it. Let the pain remind me that I was still alive, still connected to her despite everything.

When it finally faded, I was left gasping and bleeding and more exhausted than before.

A sound outside the tent made me look up. Nalla pushed through the entrance, her expression grim.

"We need to talk. The next attack. We're moving it up. Tomorrow night instead of next week."

"Why?"

"We got word. She's planning something. Another purge, bigger than the last. We attack first or we don't get another chance."

My stomach dropped. I thought about her letter. About her saying she was trying.

Had she written that before or after ordering the new purge?

"I want to go with you," I heard myself say.

Nalla stared at me. "That's suicide. You can barely stand."

"I know. But I need to see her. Need to try one more time before it's too late."

"You understand we're planning to kill her if we get the chance. The bone weapon might even be able to destroy the crown."

"I know."

"And you still want to come?"

I couldn't stand the thought of her dying without seeing her one more time. Without touching her. Without telling her that despite everything—all the terrible choices, all the blood, all the destruction—I still loved her.

"Yes," I said. "I still want to come."

"You're going to get yourself killed."

"Probably."

She left with her guards, and I was alone again. I pulled out parchment and began writing with my left hand.

Renata,

I'm coming to see you. I don't know if this is smart or stupid or somewhere in between. But I need to be near you again, even if it hurts.

Valdic told me what you've become. The purges, the executions, the children marked with burning runes. And I should hate you for it. I should be able to look at what you've done and feel nothing but horror.

But I can't. Because under all of that, I still see the woman who pressed flowers. Who dreamed of gardens. Who looked at me like I was her whole world.

I don't know if that woman still exists. Maybe she's gone. Maybe the crown ate her completely.

But if there's any part of her left—if you're still in there somewhere, fighting—

I'm coming to help you fight.

Wait for me.

I love you. I've always loved you. Even when loving you hurt. Even when it was the stupidest possible choice.

Forever yours,

N.

I folded the letter and gave it to a purple butterfly that had landed on my tent pole. It took off into the night, carrying my words toward the bone court.

Would she read it before I arrived? Would it matter?

I lay back down and tried to rest. But sleep wouldn't come. Just thoughts of her.

Her face in sunlight. Her laugh echoing through cottage rooms. Her hands covered in dirt from planting flowers.

And then: Her face gaunt and skeletal. Her hands bone-white and deadly. Her eyes hollow and grey.

Both versions were real. Both existed simultaneously. The woman I loved and the monster she'd become, occupying the same body, fighting for control.

Which one would I find tomorrow?

I closed my eyes and tried not to think about the answer.

* * *

Dawn came too quickly.

The outer cities fighters gathered at the edge of camp, armed with whatever weapons they could scavenge. Most of them looked half-dead from starvation. The bone weapon Nalla carried glowed faintly.

Nalla looked at me. "Last chance to stay behind."

"I'm coming."

She turned to address the fighters, her voice low and fierce.

"We've been starving. Dying. Watching our children waste away while she sits in her bone court and orders purges. Today we fight back. Today we remind her that we're not broken yet."

A murmur went through the crowd.

"We probably won't win," Nalla continued. "She's too powerful. But we'll make her remember us. Make her see what her choices have cost."

She raised the bone weapon. "For our dead. For our children. For a future where we're not just fuel for her resurrection magic."

A ragged cheer went up, more defiant than hopeful.

We began the march toward the bone court.

The wasteland stretched around us, grey and dead. Nothing grew here. The bone coral in scattered patches was the only thing that thrived where death magic had touched.

I walked among the fighters, my body protesting every step. Twice I stumbled and had to catch myself on someone's shoulder. But I kept moving.

The skull castle came into view as we crested a ridge. Massive and terrible and beautiful in its way, carved from bone and stone, the entrance a gaping mouth that seemed to swallow light.

She was in there.

My heart did something complicated in my chest.

"Ready?" Nalla asked quietly.

I nodded, not trusting my voice.

"Then let's go remind a queen what it means to break promises."

We descended toward the bone court. I thought of orchids and garden plans and a future where we were just people who loved each other.

That future felt impossibly far away.

But I held onto it anyway.

An alarm sounded from the ramparts. The bone horn's cry echoed across the wasteland.

And somewhere inside those walls, Renata would hear it. Would know we were coming.

The bond pulsed. Pain lanced through my skull, sharp and sudden. She was thinking of me. Even now.

And it hurt us both.

"Nokoa?" Nalla caught my arm.

"I'm fine. Just the bond."

We reached the outer walls. Guards poured out to meet us. Behind them, the spectral guardians formed ranks.

"For the outer cities!" Nalla screamed, and charged.

I hung back as promised, watching the battle unfold. Watching fighters fall. Watching blood and bone dust mix in the courtyard.

And through it all, I searched for her.

The entrance to the bone court stood open. Unguarded in the chaos.

I pushed forward, leaving the battle behind, and descended into the bone court's depths.

Toward her.

Always toward her.

Chapter Forty-Four

HIVRO

Renata

The yellow dress hung in my chambers like an accusation.

I'd placed it carefully on a hook near the bone mirror, and every time I passed it, I felt something twist in my chest. Recognition maybe. Or grief. Or the ghost of an emotion I couldn't quite name anymore.

It had been three days since Valdic showed me the storage room. Three days since I'd allowed myself to consider—even briefly—that maybe I was wrong. That maybe there was another way.

But nothing had changed. Not really.

The purge was still ongoing. The marked prisoners still hung in the courtyard. The spectral guardians still hummed behind me constantly. And Nokoa was still dying slowly, somewhere out there in the wasteland, suffering because I loved him too much to let him go.

I touched the dress fabric with my skeletal fingers. Soft. Bright. So yellow it hurt to look at.

Had I really worn this once? Had I really been someone who chose sunshine over shadows?

The crown pulsed, and the thought scattered.

A sound at my door made me turn. One of the rattlemaids stood there, her skeletal frame trembling slightly.

"Hollow Queen. The butterfly oracle requests an audience."

My heart did something complicated in my chest. "Hivro?"

"Yes, Hollow Queen. She's waiting in the oracle chambers."

Hivro. The butterfly oracle. The woman who'd helped raise me after my parents died. Who'd taught me to read the stars, who'd sung to me when I couldn't sleep.

When was the last time I'd seen her? Weeks? Months? The timeline was slippery, made worse by the crown taking memories.

"Tell her I'm coming."

* * *

The oracle chambers were in the eastern wing, far from the throne room, far from the courtyard where bodies hung. A place that had always felt separate from the rest of the bone court—quieter, gentler, touched by something the death magic couldn't quite corrupt.

I remembered coming here as a child. Hivro showing me butterflies, explaining how they were the souls of the dead, how each color meant something different.

The door was open. Purple butterflies swarmed in and out.

I stepped inside.

Hivro stood by the windows, her paper-white skin glowing softly in the afternoon light. The constellations that covered her entire body—her face, her arms, every visible inch of skin—were shifting and changing, stars dying and being born in real-time across her flesh. Her face was made of stars, a constantly moving map of the heavens that made it impossible to focus on any single feature.

She wore simple white robes, the same style she'd always worn. Purple butterflies covered her shoulders, her hair, landing and taking off in a rhythm that seemed almost like breathing.

"Renata." Her voice was distant and beautiful and sad. "Thank you for coming."

"You requested an audience. Of course I came." The formality felt wrong. This was Hivro. The woman who'd braided my hair and held me when I cried about my parents.

When had we become strangers who requested audiences?

"Sit with me?" She gestured to the cushions on the sofa—the same ones we'd sat on countless times when I was young.

I sat carefully, my skeletal spine making the movement awkward. The spectral guardians remained by the door, giving us space but never truly leaving.

Hivro sat across from me. The butterflies settled into a purple halo around her.

"You look tired," she said softly.

"I'm always tired now."

"The crown is taking more."

"The crown always takes more." I touched the bone fused to my skull. "That's what it does."

"I've been watching you, child. Through the butterflies. Through the messages they carry. I've seen what you're becoming."

The words should have made me defensive. But this was Hivro. The woman who'd known me since I was born.

"I know what I'm becoming," I said quietly.

"Do you?" Her face shifted, stars rearranging into patterns I recognized—the ones she used to trace on my forehead when I couldn't sleep. "Or has the crown taken so much you can't see clearly anymore?"

"I see clearly enough. I see that Nokoa is dying. I see that I have power to stop it."

"And the cost of those choices?"

I thought about the purges. The executions. The children marked with burning runes. "Necessary."

"Necessary." Hivro repeated the word like it tasted bitter. "That's what the crown tells you, isn't it? That all of it is necessary. That love justifies destruction. That keeping one person alive is worth destroying everyone else."

"You don't understand—"

"I understand perfectly." Her voice was gentle but firm. "I helped raise you, Renata. I know how you love. How deeply you feel. How desperately you hold onto the people you care about. And I know how easily that love can be twisted into something toxic when you're afraid of losing them."

The crown pulsed. Warning. But I pushed back against it, wanting to hear this.

"The guardians—Perla, Fern, Sevi. You killed them all."

"They were in my way."

"They were trying to help you." Hivro leaned forward, and I caught her scent—butterflies and starlight. "Perla tried to save what was burning. Fern tried to heal what was dying. Sevi tried to show you what would come. And you consumed them like they were nothing."

"I needed their power."

"You needed their wisdom. But the crown wouldn't let you see that."

I wanted to argue. But sitting here with Hivro—the woman who'd taught me to braid my hair, who'd explained death magic with patience and care—I couldn't find the words.

"I can show you something," Hivro said quietly. "Not the future. But the past. Who you were before the crown took so much."

"I don't want to see."

"I know, child. That's why you need to."

She raised her hand, and the space between us changed.

* * *

The oracle chamber didn't disappear. Just layered. Like reality became translucent, and I could see through it to something underneath.

A memory. My memory. Playing out in the air between us.

I saw myself—maybe nine years old, small and fragile-looking. Sitting in this very room, crying so hard I could barely breathe.

Hivro sat beside child-me, her face a gentle glow of shifting stars. She was singing. A lullaby about standing strong and remembering who you were even when the world tried to make you forget.

Child-me looked up at her with such trust. Such desperate love.

"You'll be alright," memory-Hivro said, her voice warm. "I know it doesn't feel like it now. But you're stronger than you know. Braver than you think. And you're not alone."

"Everyone leaves," child-me sobbed. "Everyone dies."

"Death is part of the bone court. But so is life. So is love. So is choosing to keep going even when it hurts." Hivro wiped tears from child-me's face. "You're going to do great things, Renata. You're going to change this place. Make it better. Make death mean something other than ending."

"Promise?"

"I promise to help you try."

The memory shifted.

I was older now. Thirteen, maybe. Standing in the oracle chambers, excited about something. Wearing a pink dress—bright and cheerful and so at odds with the bone court's usual darkness.

"Hivro, look!" Memory-me twirled, the dress flaring around me. "I made it myself. It's not practical for court but I don't care. I'm tired of wearing grey all the time."

"It's beautiful." Hivro's face brightened with approval, stars shifting into warmer patterns. "Sunshine in a place that needs it."

"That's what I thought! Death doesn't have to mean darkness, right? You taught me that. So I'm going to wear pink and prove that the bone court can be beautiful."

"That's my girl." Hivro pulled me into a hug, butterflies swarming around us both. "Never let them make you forget that. Never let this place make you grey inside."

The memory shifted again.

I was sixteen. Sitting with Hivro, learning to read the butterfly messages. She was teaching me patience, showing me how to let the dead speak through their wings.

"Every soul has a story," she explained. "Every death means something. Your job—as someone who understands death magic—is to remember that. To treat each soul with dignity. To never let power make you forget they were people once."

"I won't forget," memory-me promised.

"I believe you will."

The memory shifted one last time.

I was eighteen. Standing in the oracle chambers, crying again. But not from grief this time. From joy.

"I love him, Hivro. I really love him."

"I know, child. I can see it written on your cheeks."

"Is that foolish? To love someone this much?"

"Love is never foolish. Love is the bravest thing we do. But remember—love shouldn't consume you. Shouldn't make you forget who you are. Real love makes you better, not smaller."

"I'll remember."

"Promise me, Renata. Promise that no matter what happens, you'll remember that love should make you grow, not shrink. That caring for him shouldn't mean forgetting to care for yourself or others."

"I promise," memory-me said, smiling. "I promise I'll remember."

The memories dissolved.

And I sat there in the oracle chambers, staring at Hivro with tears running down my face, the weight of broken promises crushing my chest.

"I didn't remember," I whispered. "I forgot all of it."

"The crown took it. Piece by piece. Every memory of who you were before, consumed to fuel its power." Her voice was soft. "But I remember, child. I've held those memories for you. Waiting for you to be ready to reclaim them."

"That girl—the one who wore bright colors and promised to be different—she's gone."

"Is she? Or is she just buried under months of trauma and crown manipulation and desperate love that turned toxic?"

I thought about the purges. The executions.

"I broke my promise. I let love make me smaller. I forgot to care about anything except keeping him alive."

"Yes."

The simple acknowledgment hurt worse than accusation would have.

"I killed the guardians. Perla and Fern and Sevi. They were trying to help and I—consumed them."

"Yes." Hivro's face dimmed with sorrow. "I watched it happen through the butterflies."

"Then why are you here? Why show me this? Why not just—give up?"

"Because I made a promise too. To that little girl who'd just lost her parents. I promised to help her be strong. To help her change this place. I can still see a glimpse of you in there."

"I've failed."

"You've lost your way. That's different." Hivro took my skeletal hands in hers, the contrast stark—my bone-white and dead, hers paper-white and alive. "Failure is permanent. Lost is temporary."

"I don't know how to find my way back."

"Start by remembering who you were. Not to become her again—you can't, too much has happened. But to understand what you've lost. What you've sacrificed on the altar of desperate love."

I looked at our joined hands. Felt the warmth of hers against the cold of mine.

"I've done terrible things."

"Yes."

"I've hurt people. Killed people. Destroyed things that can't be undone."

"Yes."

"And you still—you're still here."

"I raised you, Renata. I sang to you when you couldn't sleep. I watched you grow into someone bright and hopeful and kind." Her stars settled into a pattern of deep sadness. "I can't just abandon that person because she made terrible choices out of desperation."

"The crown wants me to kill you," I admitted. "Right now. It's screaming at me to summon the spectral guardians, to use bone magic, to end you before you weaken me further."

"I know."

"You're not afraid?"

"Terrified. But I came anyway." She squeezed my hands gently. "Because you're worth the risk. Because somewhere under that crown, under all the corruption and desperation, there's still a girl who wore yellow dresses and promised to plant gardens. And she deserves one more chance."

The crown pulsed. Hard. I gasped at the sudden pain.

The voices were panicking.

Kill her!

She's dangerous!

She'll destroy everything we've built!

"I can feel them fighting you," Hivro said quietly. "The previous hollow rulers. They don't want you to succeed where they failed."

"I don't know if I can break free. The crown has taken so much."

"Then start smaller. Don't break free. Just... resist. Just once. Show yourself that you can still make a choice they don't control."

I looked at Hivro. At the woman who'd raised me. Who'd taught me about stars and death and love that made you grow instead of shrink.

I could kill her. One command and she'd crumble like the other guardians.

The crown wanted it. Demanded it. Screamed for it.

But—

I thought of the child in the memories. The one who'd looked at Hivro with such trust. Such love. The one who'd promised to be different.

I thought of the teenager, determined to bring sunshine to dark places.

I thought of the young woman who'd promised that love would make her better, not smaller.

Were they really all gone? Every version of who I'd been, consumed completely?

Or were they just waiting for me to remember them?

"No," I whispered.

The bone magic dissipated. The spectral guardians fell back.

"No?" Her stars brightened with surprise.

"I won't kill you." The words came out stronger. "The crown can scream all it wants. But I won't—I can't—" My voice broke. "You raised me. You loved me. You taught me to be brave. I won't kill you just because it's efficient."

The crown fought back. Pain lanced through my skull. My nose bled. My vision blurred.

But I held on. Drew on reserves of will I didn't know I still had. Held onto those memories—the child, the teenager, the young woman, all of them choosing light over darkness.

"Leave," I gasped. "Please. I'm fighting them but I don't know how long I can hold out. Just go before they take control—"

"Renata—"

"Go!" The word came out desperate. "Please. Before I hurt you."

Hivro studied me for a long moment. Then she stood, butterflies swarming around her.

"I'm proud of you," she said softly. "That little girl would be proud too. You remembered something important today. You chose mercy over efficiency. You fought the crown and won, even if just for a moment."

"It doesn't feel like winning."

"It never does. But it matters anyway." She moved toward the door, then paused. "I'll be in the eastern gardens. The ones you planned to plant with Nokoa. When you're ready—if you're ready—come find me."

"The eastern section is all wasteland now. Nothing grows there."

"Not yet. But maybe someday." Her face brightened with something that might have been hope. "If someone brave enough decides to try."

Then she was gone.

I sat there in the oracle chambers, surrounded by purple butterflies, feeling the crown rage against my defiance.

I'd chosen mercy. I'd fought the crown. I'd remembered, even briefly, who I used to be.

It wasn't much.

But it was a start.

Chapter Forty-Five

Through the Wasteland

Nokoa

The entrance to the bone court gaped before us like a skull's open mouth, and I hesitated at the threshold.

Not from fear, exactly. More from the sudden, overwhelming knowledge that crossing this line meant everything changed. That there would be no going back after this, no more delays, no more waiting.

Whatever happened next happened now.

"You don't have to do this," Valdic said quietly beside me. "You could still stay with the fighters. Let Nalla handle it."

"No." I stepped forward, feeling the witch runes under my skin flare in response to the bone court's magic. "I have to see her."

The bridge across the underground lake stretched ahead, carved from vertebrae and femurs arranged in intricate patterns. The water beneath was clear but somehow wrong, reflecting nothing despite the bioluminescence that lit the cavern.

I started across, my legs shaking with each step.

The resurrection was failing worse than usual today. Maybe because of the proximity to Renata. Maybe because my body knew this was the end one way or another and had stopped bothering to hold itself together.

Halfway across the bridge, my right leg gave out completely.

I went down hard, catching myself on my one functional hand. The impact sent pain lancing through my arm, and I felt something crack. Not bones this time—something deeper. Something fundamental.

Valdic helped me up. "I've got you."

"I can walk."

"You can barely stand." But he didn't argue further, just supported my weight as we continued across the bridge.

Through the bond, I felt her. Closer now. So much closer. The pull was magnetic, irresistible.

The pain came in waves. Not the sharp spike of her thinking about me directly, but the constant low ache of proximity. Of two souls bound together being forced toward each other despite every magical barrier trying to keep them apart.

We reached the other side, and I had to stop and lean against the wall. My vision was blurring. Doubling.

"Nokoa." Valdic's voice. "Stay with me. Don't fade now."

"Not fading. Just... adjusting. The bond—it's stronger here. Everything's stronger here."

I pushed off the wall and kept moving. One foot in front of the other. One breath after another.

The corridor opened into a larger cavern, and I stopped.

Bodies.

Dozens of them. Chained to the walls, slumped in their restraints, marked with glowing runes carved into bone and flesh.

T-R-A-I-T-O-R.

The purge victims. Some of them were still alive. Barely. I could see the shallow rise and fall of their chests, hear the wet rasp of their breathing. But they were past saving. Past anything except the slow slide into death.

A few of them turned their heads as we passed. Hollow eyes following our movement. No hope in those gazes. Just the dull recognition that more people were walking through their suffering without helping.

I wanted to help. But I could barely keep myself upright.

"This is what she's done," I said, my voice rough.

"Yes."

"These are her orders. Her choices."

"Yes."

"And I still love her." The words came out quiet but certain. "Looking at this—at all the evidence of what she's become—and I still love her as much as I always did."

Valdic turned to look at me.

"That's shameful, isn't it?" I continued. "I should hate her for this. But I can't. I can't stop loving her."

"That doesn't make you shameful. That makes you human."

"Does it?" I gestured at the marked prisoners. "Because it feels like it makes me complicit. Like by loving her despite this, I'm saying it's acceptable."

"Your feelings don't make this acceptable. They just exist alongside it. Love doesn't require approval of every action. It just is."

I wanted to believe that. But standing here, looking at the evidence of systematic cruelty, it felt impossible to separate the two.

"She did this for me. Every terrible choice. Every execution. All of it—so I could keep breathing."

"I know."

"And knowing that—knowing I'm the reason, the justification, the excuse—I still want to see her. Still love her with the same desperate intensity I always have." I looked at Valdic. "What does that make me?"

"Someone who loves deeply enough that it doesn't stop when it should. That's not wrong. It's just complicated."

We continued through the cavern, past the marked prisoners, into another corridor that sloped upward.

The witch runes were spreading faster, burning brighter. I could see them glowing through my shirt now, golden lines winding up my arms, across my chest, down my legs.

What happened when they covered everything? Did I become something else?

I was too tired to be terrified.

We emerged into what must have been a courtyard once.

More bodies. Children this time. Teenagers. Their skeletal hands still gripping bone weapons inscribed with witch runes. They'd died holding them, the divine magic burning them from the inside out.

"The conscripts," Valdic said quietly. "The ones she promised food in exchange for service."

I knelt beside one of them. A girl, maybe fourteen. Her ribs were visible through torn clothing. The bone weapon in her hand had scorched her fingers black, the witch runes still glowing faintly with residual power.

She'd died trying to serve a queen who'd forgotten how to care about people like her.

"This is what saving me cost," I whispered.

"Nokoa—"

"Look at this. She did this for me. Every terrible choice. Every execution. Every child conscripted and burned alive. All of it—all of it—so I could keep breathing."

Valdic was quiet.

"Is my life worth this?" I looked up at him. "Is anyone's life worth this many deaths?"

"That's not a question I can answer."

"Then who can?" I stood slowly, legs shaking. "Because I need someone to tell me if I should be grateful she loves me this much or horrified by what that love has become."

"Maybe both." His expression was sad. "Love doesn't have to make sense. It just has to be real."

"And mine is real." The admission felt like confession and declaration simultaneously. "Standing here, looking at all this death, knowing what she's become—and I love her. Still. Always. As much as I did when she wore yellow dresses and planned gardens. Maybe more, because now I see the full price of that love and I still can't let it go."

"That's not shameful. That's honest."

"It feels shameful. It feels like I should be able to turn it off. To look at these children and decide that no, my feelings don't matter more than their lives." I touched the girl's cold hand gently. "But I can't make myself stop loving her."

"Would you want to? If you could?"

The question hit hard.

"No," I said finally. "Even knowing everything. Even standing here surrounded by the consequences. I wouldn't choose to stop loving her."

"Then that's your answer. Not shame. Choice. You're choosing to love her despite knowing the cost. That's different."

We continued through the courtyard, stepping carefully around the bodies. I tried not to look at their faces.

Failed. Looked anyway. Saw them all. Carried each face with me.

And loved Renata anyway.

That was the part I had to reckon with. Not the love itself. But the fact that it remained unchanged. That seeing this evidence of monstrosity didn't diminish my feelings even slightly.

Maybe that made me a monster too. Maybe that's what love did—made monsters of everyone it touched.

The corridor beyond sloped upward again, and my body decided it had had enough.

My legs gave out completely. I went down hard, unable to catch myself, and hit the bone-carved floor with an impact that drove the air from my lungs.

Valdic pulled me up, but I couldn't stand. Couldn't make my legs work.

"I've got you," he said, shifting his grip to support my full weight. "We're almost there."

"How do you know?"

"Because the bond is pulling you so hard you're practically vibrating. She's close."

He was right. Through the bond, I could feel her like a physical presence. Close enough that every breath hurt, every heartbeat was agony, every moment of separation felt like being pulled apart.

And I wanted to get closer. Wanted to close the distance despite the pain. Wanted to see her face, touch her hand, tell her that I loved her even though I shouldn't.

Especially because I shouldn't.

Valdic half-carried me up the corridor. I tried to help, tried to move my legs, but they wouldn't respond.

"Tell me I'm not wrong," I said suddenly. "Tell me it's not monstrous to love someone who's done monstrous things."

"You're not wrong."

"How can you know?"

"Because love isn't about deserving or earning. It just is. You love her. She loves you. Neither of those facts requires the other person to be good or right or acceptable. The monstrosity isn't in the loving. It's in what you do with that love."

"What do I do with it?"

"That's what you're about to find out."

We emerged into a great hall. Bone mosaics covered the walls.

More bodies. More marked prisoners. More evidence.

Renata had turned the bone court into a charnel house. Methodically. Efficiently. Without hesitation.

For me.

Always for me.

And I loved her anyway.

"I need to stand," I said suddenly.

"You can't."

"I need to. When I see her—when I finally see her—I need to be standing. Need to look her in the eyes like an equal."

"You are broken. You are something that needs saving."

"Then let me be broken on my feet."

Valdic studied me for a long moment. Then he nodded and helped me find my balance.

I stood, swaying, my legs shaking so hard I could hear my bones rattling. But I stood.

I took a step. Then another. Each one an act of will over body. Each one bringing me closer to her.

Through the bond, the pull intensified. She knew I was close.

The pain spiked suddenly. Sharp and blinding. I gasped, tasted copper, felt warmth on my face.

Bleeding. Nose, eyes, ears. All of them at once.

She was thinking about me. Missing me. The bond punishing us both for proximity and longing.

And I welcomed the pain. Because it meant she was there. Real and close and thinking of me.

"Almost there," Valdic said. "Just a little further."

I pushed forward, one hand on the wall for support. The corridor seemed to stretch forever, each step taking twice as long as it should.

But finally—finally—we reached the end.

A massive doorway. Carved from what looked like an entire spine, vertebrae fitted together into an arch. Beyond it, I could hear voices. Movement. The hum of spectral magic.

The throne room.

She was in there.

My Renata. My love. The woman who'd destroyed the world trying to save me. The woman I loved despite everything, because of everything, regardless of everything.

I stood at the threshold, bleeding and shaking and barely upright, and tried to find the words for what I wanted to say.

I love you.

I'm horrified by what you've done.

I want to hold you.

I understand why you did it.

You're everything I've ever wanted and everything I never wanted you to become.

And I love you anyway.

All of it true. All of it impossible to reconcile. All of it honest.

"Ready?" Valdic asked.

I thought about the children burning. The prisoners marked. The wasteland spreading. All of it done in my name, for my life, because she loved me too much to let me go.

And I thought about how none of it changed what I felt.

"Ready," I said. And meant it.

We crossed the threshold into the throne room.

And the world narrowed to a single point.

Her.

She stood before her throne, skeletal hands gripping the armrests, grey eyes fixed on the doorway like she'd been waiting. Like she'd known the exact moment I would arrive.

Her white-turned-black hair was pulled back severely. Her face was gaunt, hollow, more bone than flesh. The hollow crown fused so deep into her skull I could see where bone met bone across her temples.

The black veins wrapped around her jaw were darker than I remembered. Thicker. Spreading down her neck, across her collarbones.

She looked like death given form.

She looked like the woman I loved.

Both. Simultaneously. Impossibly.

My heart did the same thing it had always done when I saw her. It reached. It yearned. It loved without permission or qualification.

"Nokoa." My name on her lips.

"Renata." Her name in my mouth tasted like grief and hope and something that might have been absolution.

We stared at each other across the throne room, neither moving, both of us vibrating with the bond's proximity pain.

The spectral guardians hummed behind her. A wall of dead souls, watching with empty eyes.

Nalla and her fighters poured in behind me. I heard the bone weapon activate. Heard shouts. Heard the beginning of attack.

But I only saw her.

I took a step forward.

The bond screamed. Pain lanced through both of us. I saw her gasp, saw blood trickle from her nose, saw her hands tighten on the throne.

I took another step.

More pain. More blood. My vision whited out.

Another step.

We were twenty feet apart now. Close enough that I could see the patterns in her grey eyes. Close enough that I could see her chest rising and falling with rapid breaths.

"Don't," she said, her voice breaking. "Nokoa, don't come closer. It hurts. It hurts so much."

"I know." Another step. Fifteen feet. "I've come this far. I'm not stopping now."

"I still love you." Ten feet. The pain was constant now, no longer spiking. Just a steady, agonizing pressure. "I know how shameful that is. I've seen what you've done, and it doesn't change how I feel."

Her eyes widened. "You shouldn't—"

"I know I shouldn't. I've walked through corridors lined with bodies. I've seen the children you conscripted and burned. I've seen the prisoners you marked. I've seen the wasteland spreading for miles." Five feet. "And I love you exactly as much as I did when you ate boiled eggs all day in the bone garden."

"That's not love. That's—"

"It's love. Complicated and shameful and honest." I gestured at myself, at my failing body. "You've destroyed the world trying to save me. And I can't stop loving you for it."

Tears were streaming down her face, mixing with blood. "You should hate me."

"But I don't." Three feet. "I want everything to do with you. Want to hold your hand and tell you I understand even though understanding doesn't make it right."

"Nokoa—"

"I love you." The words came out fierce. "Not despite what you've become. Not separate from your choices. Just... completely. Entirely. The woman who planned gardens and the woman who destroyed them. The bright hopeful girl and the desperate hollow queen. All of it. All of you."

I reached out my hand.

She stared at it like I was offering poison.

"If I touch you," she whispered, "we'll both collapse. The pain—"

"I know." My hand stayed steady. "Touch me anyway."

"Nokoa—"

"Please." The word came out broken. "I've walked through wasteland and bodies and the evidence of what my life has cost. I've admitted that I love you despite it all. And all I want—all I've ever wanted—is to hold your hand."

"Even knowing what it means?"

"Especially knowing what it means."

She looked at my hand. At her own skeletal fingers. At the space between us.

"I don't deserve this," she whispered.

"Neither do I. But we're here anyway."

She lifted her hand slowly. Trembling. Hesitating.

"I love you too," she said. "I've destroyed everything for you. Become monster for you. And I'd do it again. I'd make every terrible choice again if it meant keeping you alive."

"I know."

"That's shameful too, isn't it? That I'm not sorry. That I'd choose you over the world again and again."

"Probably." I smiled despite the pain, despite everything. "We're both shameful. Both loving each other more than we should. Both choosing each other over what's right."

"What does that make us?"

"Human. Broken. Honest." My hand waited between us. "Ours."

And she took it.

The pain was immediate and overwhelming.

The bond didn't just hurt—it detonated. Every nerve ending lit up simultaneously. My vision went white then black then white again. I tasted copper and magic and something that might have been my own soul tearing.

I heard screaming. Mine? Hers? Both?

But I felt her hand in mine. Bone against bone. Cold and wrong and absolutely necessary.

I felt her.

And despite everything—despite the pain, despite the cost, despite the shameful admission that love didn't require deserving—

I held on.

Chapter Forty-Six

The Crown's Offer

Renata

His hand in mine was agony.

Pure, unfiltered agony that made every previous pain seem like a gentle warning. The bond didn't just hurt—it rewrote the definition of hurt. Expanded it. Made it encompass things I didn't have words for.

But I could feel him. His pulse. His warmth. His life.

And I didn't let go.

Around us, chaos erupted. Nalla's fighters poured into the throne room, the bone weapon glowing with stolen divine power. The spectral guardians surged forward to defend. Shouts. Screams. The clash of weapons against magic.

I didn't care about any of it.

All I could see was Nokoa. His golden eyes locked on mine. His skeletal hand gripping mine so tightly our bones creaked. Blood running from his nose, his eyes, his ears. The witch runes under his skin burning so bright they were visible through his clothes.

He was dying. Right here. Right now. Holding my hand while his resurrection failed completely.

"Let go," I gasped. "Nokoa, please. You're killing yourself."

"So are you." His voice was rough. Wet. "We're both dying. Might as well die holding hands."

"Don't—" The pain spiked, and I couldn't finish the sentence. Just held on. Just endured. Just existed in this moment where we were finally, finally touching despite everything.

Through the bond, I felt him. Not just the surface—but deeper. His memories flooding through where our magic connected.

I saw myself through his eyes. The woman in the yellow dress, laughing about something. The careful way he'd watched me plant flowers, like I was precious. The pride on his face when I'd negotiated with the outer cities, when I'd talked about making the bone court beautiful.

He'd loved that woman so much.

And then I saw what came after. Saw myself through his eyes as I descended. The first execution. The first purge. The systematic transformation from bright queen to hollow monster. Watched myself justify every terrible choice, watched myself forget who I'd been.

But through it all—through every awful moment—he'd kept loving me. Not because I deserved it. Not because it made sense. Just because he couldn't stop.

"I'm sorry," I whispered, tears mixing with blood. "I'm so sorry. For all of it. For bringing you back. For becoming this. For—"

"Stop." His grip tightened. "We don't have time for apologies. We need—"

He coughed. Blood sprayed from his lips. His legs gave out completely, and he collapsed, pulling me down with him.

We fell together, still holding hands, and hit the stone floor hard.

The throne room spun. I could hear Valdic shouting. Nalla barking orders. The bone weapon humming.

But the crown was louder.

The voices—Oriana, Alaric, Lyanna—were screaming. Not at me. At each other. Panicked. Desperate.

He's dying!

The bond is collapsing!

Tell her! Tell her now before it's too late!

"Tell me what?" I said aloud.

The ritual, Oriana's voice cut through clearly. Love's Bitter Bond. The final stabilization. The only thing that can save him now.

I tried to focus, but Nokoa was convulsing in my arms. His witch runes were flaring so bright I had to look away.

"What is it?" I demanded. "Tell me!"

The crown pulsed, and time seemed to slow. The fighters mid-charge. The spectral guardians mid-defense. Even Nokoa's convulsions slowed.

And the voices spoke. All three at once.

We should have told you sooner, Oriana said. But we were trying to protect you. From the final price.

The ritual completes what you started, Alaric began. You resurrected him, but the resurrection was never stable. The bond is destroying you both because it's incomplete.

This ritual finishes it, Oriana continued. Stops the pain. Stops the deterioration. Makes him permanently stable.

But it requires a willing death, Lyanna said. Someone who chooses to die knowing exactly what it means. Their life force becomes the anchor.

And you need Maxin's bones, Alaric added. His remains carry the specific resonance needed for the binding.

Divine magic to anchor mortal resurrection, Oriana explained. The guardian ash you consumed—Perla, Fern, Sevi—already inside you. That's the other component needed.

Perform it in the bone god's crypt, Alaric instructed. Where the barrier between worlds is thinnest.

The world snapped back into motion. And Nokoa's convulsions returned full force.

"Why didn't you tell me before?" I asked desperately.

Because it might kill you, Oriana finally admitted. The ritual requires immense power. You might burn out completely trying to channel it.

We were trying to find another way, Lyanna said. But there is no other way. This is it.

"And if I don't do it?"

He dies, all three voices said in unison. Within minutes.

I looked down at Nokoa. At his fading light. At his golden eyes rolled back.

Minutes. We had minutes.

"Why do you care so much?" I asked. "You're dead. You're trapped in the crown. Why does it matter to you if he lives or dies?"

The voices went quiet.

Too quiet.

"Tell me," I demanded.

Because we want you to succeed, Oriana said finally. Because we failed. All of us. We tried to save the people we loved and failed. We want you to succeed where we couldn't.

Their words should have reassured me.

They didn't.

But Nokoa's hand in mine was going cold. His grip was loosening. The golden light in his eyes was dimming.

"Renata." His voice was barely audible. "Let me go."

I looked down at him. At his face going grey.

"What?"

"Let me go." He coughed, and more blood came up. "Stop trying to save me. Stop destroying yourself. Just... let me die."

"No."

"Please." His skeletal hand squeezed mine weakly. "I've seen what my life costs. Walked through the bodies. Saw the wasteland. Counted the price. I'm not worth it. I never was."

"Don't say that."

"It's true." His eyes met mine. "You are so much more than this hollow crown. Than these choices in front of you. Let me go. We will see each other again. Somewhere it's not so hard."

"I can't. I love you."

"I know." He smiled, and it was heartbreaking.

I looked at the throne room. At the chaos. At Nalla fighting her way toward us with the bone weapon. At Valdic trying to reach us. At Cressa standing in the doorway, green eyes sad and knowing.

Everyone had opinions. Everyone had plans. Everyone thought they knew what should happen next.

But only I could choose.

Only I could decide if one more terrible decision was worth it.

"Tell me about the ritual," I said to the crown. "Every detail."

Yes, the voices breathed in relief. Yes. We'll tell you everything.

And they did.

They told me about the crypt. About the weakest point in the prison where magic flowed most freely. About grinding Maxin's bones to powder. About mixing them with the guardian essence already inside me. About using my blood to bind it all together.

About the witch runes I'd need to carve. The words I'd need to speak. The precise way to channel divine and mortal magic simultaneously until it became something new. Something that could anchor resurrection permanently.

About the sacrifice. How it had to be willing. How any coercion or force would backfire spectacularly.

They promised it would work. That this was the final thing. The last sacrifice. The end of the terrible choices.

"And the bone god?" I asked. "Performing this in his chamber—what does that do to the prison?"

A pause. Uncomfortable.

It weakens it further, Oriana admitted. Opens more pathways. Gives him more access.

But you're strong enough now, Alaric insisted. You've absorbed three guardians. Enough power to control the ritual. To direct the outcome.

I looked down at Nokoa. At his fading light. At his acceptance of death.

"I'll do it," I heard myself say.

"Renata, no—"

"I'll perform the ritual. I'll find a willing sacrifice. I'll save you." I looked down at him, at his horrified expression. "I'm sorry. I know you don't want this. But I can't watch you die. Not again. Not ever."

I released his hand—had to force my fingers to open—and stood. "Praxis!"

The massive skeletal figure rose.

"I need Maxin's remains. His bones."

Praxis's crimson eyes studied me. "And a sacrifice. Willing."

"Yes."

"Do you have someone in mind?"

I looked at Nalla. At her desperate fight. At her inevitable defeat.

"I will."

Praxis followed my gaze. Understanding crossed his skeletal face. "She'll never agree willingly."

"She will if I ask the right way." I turned to him. "Prepare what I need. Bring Maxin's bones to the crypt."

He nodded and left.

I looked down at Nokoa. He was unconscious now, his body still convulsing.

You're doing the right thing, Queen Oriana whispered.

Am I? I thought back.

But I pushed the doubt away. I'd come too far to question now.

The Crypt

I descended into darkness with Nokoa's dying body in my arms.

The spectral guardians had subdued the fighters. Not killed—I'd ordered restraint for once—just contained. Nalla was among them, the bone weapon wrenched from her hands.

Valdic walked beside me, his purple eyes fixed on Nokoa's unconscious face. He hadn't spoken since I'd announced my decision. Just followed silently, loyally, like he always did.

Cressa was there too, her green eyes sad and knowing. The healer who'd watched everything unfold without intervention. Just quiet witnessing.

And Praxis led the way, his massive skeletal frame navigating the corridors. His crimson eyes glowed in the darkness, lighting our path down into the bone court's deepest level.

"How much further?" I asked.

"We're here."

The corridor opened into the chamber I'd been to before. Where I'd performed rituals. Where I'd accidentally woken Fern. Where someone had died—someone important whose name the crown had eaten.

Walls made of femur mosaics, thousands arranged in patterns that might have been beautiful or might have been warnings. Ceiling of interlocking ribs forming gothic arches. Floor inlaid with vertebrae creating spiral designs that drew the eye toward the center.

And in the center: the carved bone box. Cracked now. The witch runes that covered it still pulsing with a rhythm that matched my heartbeat.

Beyond the box: the door that shouldn't exist. Wall turned to doorway. Prison seal broken.

I could feel it from here. The wrongness of it.

I set Nokoa down carefully on the stone floor. His breathing was so shallow I had to watch his chest closely to see it move. The witch runes under his skin had faded to barely visible lines.

Minutes. We had minutes.

Praxis set down a wrapped bundle. "Maxin's bones. Ground to powder."

The name meant nothing to me. Just bone dust from someone who had died recently — the crown had eaten even the grief of losing him.

I unwrapped the bundle. Fine white powder, still carrying residual warmth. The resonance needed for binding.

"Bring Nalla," I said.

Praxis gestured, and two spectral guardians dragged the outer cities leader into the chamber. She fought every step, her body thin from starvation but her will unbroken.

"Let me go! Whatever you're planning—I won't help you!"

"You don't have to help." I moved toward the bone powder. "You just have to choose."

"Choose what?"

"Death." The word came out flat. Honest. "Willing death. For a purpose. To save him." I gestured at Nokoa.

Nalla stared at me. Then she laughed. Brittle and broken. "You think I'd die willingly to save your lover? After everything you've done?" She spat at my feet. "I'd rather burn."

"I know." I knelt beside the powder. "That's why I'm going to offer you something in exchange."

"There's nothing you could offer—"

"Peace for your people." I looked up at her. "If you die willingly. Then I'll honor it. I'll end the purges. I'll establish the reforms I promised. Fair tithe. No children forced. Volunteers paid."

Nalla's eyes narrowed. "You're lying."

"Maybe." I didn't bother denying it. "Probably. But it's the only offer you'll get. Die for nothing, fighting. Or die for something. For the possibility that your people might eat again."

"The reforms—you won't remember. The crown will take the memory like it took everything else."

She was right. I knew she was right. I only needed her to believe long enough to be willing. I forced my voice to sound raw. "Valdic. If I make this promise. If she dies willingly for it. You'll remember. You'll hold me accountable."

His purple eyes met mine. Something passed between us.

Nalla was staring at us both. "You're serious."

"I'm desperate," I said. I began mixing the bone powder with my blood, feeling the guardian essence inside me flow into the mixture. Gold and green and silver light swirling together. "He's dying. I'll promise anything."

Silence in the chamber. Just the distant drip of water and Nokoa's labored breathing.

"How does the ritual work?" Nalla asked finally.

I told her. Told her about Love's Bitter Bond. About the mixture. About the witch runes. About how her willing death would power the spell, stabilize the resurrection permanently.

I didn't tell her about the Bone God. About the prison door already broken. About how many other things I had already broken in the name of the same desperate love.

Some truths were better left buried.

When I finished, Nalla was quiet for a long time. Then: "Will it hurt?"

"Probably."

"Will my people actually benefit?"

I looked at Valdic. At his loyal, patient, constant presence.

"He'll make sure," I said.

Nalla closed her eyes. When she opened them again, something had shifted. Acceptance, maybe. Or exhaustion so deep it looked like peace.

"Then I choose this death." Her voice was steady. "Not for you. Not for him. For my people. For the children who are starving."

"Thank you," I whispered.

"Don't thank me." She moved toward the center of the chamber, shaking off the spectral guards. "Promise me something else."

"What?"

"That you'll remember this moment. That when you forget everything else, you'll remember at least one person sacrificed themselves hoping you'd be better."

The crown pulsed. Warning. But I pushed back against it.

"I'll remember," I said. Even knowing I wouldn't. Even knowing the crown would eat this too.

Of all the things I had done, lying felt like nothing at all.

I brought the mixture to her. It glowed in the vial—gold and green and silver swirling with bone-white.

"Drink this," I said.

She took the vial. Stared at the glowing liquid. Then, without hesitation, drank it all.

The effect was immediate. She gasped, doubling over. The mixture burned through her from the inside. I could see it glowing in her veins, spreading through her body.

"The runes," Praxis said, handing me carving tools. "Now."

I moved to Nalla. She was on her knees now, shaking, the glow intensifying with each passing second.

"I'm sorry," I said.

"Don't be sorry. Be better." She looked up at me with eyes starting to glow gold. "Be the queen you promised to be. Be the woman he fell in love with. Be someone worth dying for."

I began carving the witch runes.

Into her skin. Into her bones where they showed through. Around her in a circle on the stone floor. Divine magic, the Goddess of Fate's gift, corrupted one more time.

Each rune I completed glowed. Connected to the others. Formed a web of power that was beautiful and terrible and absolutely wrong.

The crown whispered instructions. All three voices urgent, excited.

Yes, they breathed. Yes, like that. Perfect.

Something about their eagerness made my stomach turn.

But I kept carving. Because Nokoa was dying and this was the only way.

I carved the final symbol. The moment it was complete, the entire web ignited.

Light flooded the chamber. Golden and blinding.

And from inside Nalla: a scream.

Not pain exactly. Something beyond pain. Something that had no name. Her back arched. Her body convulsed. The witch runes around her exploded with light.

The prison opened.

Like a mouth. Like a wound.

And from inside: the Bone God.

The skeleton stood up. Bones clicking together, finding form. Flesh growing from marrow. Shadow becoming substance.

He took shape before my eyes. Tall. Beautiful. Terrible. Bone-white skin. Shadow-dark eyes. Heart visible through translucent chest, beating, pumping in a new body.

His voice: grinding stone and distant thunder.

"Thank you, priestess."

I turned. Alaira stood in the doorway. When had she arrived?

She was weeping. "Did I serve her well? Does the Goddess forgive the corruption?"

The Bone God looked at her with something like pity. "You failed, Alaira. Your Goddess is inside a locket, alone. Watching her sister and her lover die in a dream. Over and over."

"What?" Alaira's voice shook.

"She's silent because you didn't protect her. You didn't protect any of them."

Alaira's face crumbled. "No. No, you said—you promised if I helped—"

"I promised nothing." He dismissed her. Turned to me. "You, however. You I made very specific promises to."

"You said this would save us." I looked at Nokoa, still unconscious. At Nalla, dying in the circle of runes.

"I did say it would save you, and it will." He moved closer, and I could feel the power radiating off him. Ancient. Patient. Overwhelming. "Every step. Every sacrifice. Every guardian killed. Every piece of humanity you gave up. All of it leading here. To this moment."

He touched my face with fingers that felt like ice. "I won't abandon you now."

"This feels wrong," I whispered.

"My child." His voice went quiet. Almost kind. "She'll die. Her willing death will power the spell. Nokoa will be stabilized. Love's Bitter Bond will complete. And then—then you and I will speak of the future."

Something in me wanted to pull back. To stop what was already in motion. The small hairs on my body pricked in warning.

"Okay," I whispered. Because I had nothing else left to give.

Nalla's scream cut through the chamber. The ritual was completing. The witch runes burning brighter.

And then: I wanted to stop it. Felt it suddenly and completely. Not the crown's manipulation—something older, something the crown hadn't eaten yet. The understanding that one person was dying right now because I had maneuvered her there.

"No!" I lunged toward her. "Stop! I don't want this—"

The Bone God caught my arm. "The ritual is already in motion. Can't be stopped. She chose willingly. That makes it binding."

Nalla's body went rigid. Her back arched one final time.

And then—

Her soul ripped free.

A shimmer rising from her body, pulled toward the Bone God. He breathed it in. Her body collapsed. Hollow. Empty. Used up completely.

The witch runes around her pulsed once. Twice. Then the power redirected.

Toward Nokoa.

Golden light flooded into him. His body convulsed. The witch runes under his skin flared back to life. His breathing steadied. Deepened. The death pallor faded from his face.

Stabilizing. The ritual was working.

And the Bone God was free.

Nokoa's eyes opened. Golden and clear and confused.

"Renata?" His voice was steady for the first time in months. "What happened?"

I couldn't answer. Could only stare at him. At the life in his eyes.

I'd saved him.

"Now," The Bone God said, his voice carrying power that made the walls shake. "Now we discuss the Midnight Oath. It is the only path left in your future."

He gestured, and the chamber transformed. The walls fell away. We were suddenly in the throne room—or the throne room had come to us. Everyone was there.

Nokoa, sitting up now, alive and stable and whole. Valdic beside him, purple eyes wide with horror. Cressa standing silent. Alaira collapsed on the floor, broken.

Praxis in his seat, crimson eyes calculating the new reality.

And Hivro—when had she arrived?—her constellation-face flickering with distress, butterflies swarming in agitation.

The Bone God stood at the center of it all. Free. Powerful. Exactly where he'd wanted to be all along.

"Sit," he said, gesturing to my throne.

I sat. Not because he controlled me. But because my legs wouldn't hold me.

Nokoa struggled to his feet and moved to my side. His hand found mine.

This time—this time—it didn't hurt.

The bond was stable. We were bound properly. Together.

And it had cost everything.

"The Midnight Oath," the Bone God said, almost gentle now. "The ritual that unmakes what should never have been made. One soul erases, one goes free. It requires a blood moon. And a choice. One of you choosing to be erased completely so the other can be free."

"Free of what?" Nokoa asked.

"Of this." The Bone God gestured at us. At the bond. At the crown. "The resurrection. The curse. The corruption. All of it undone. But only for one of you. The other... ceases. Not death. Not imprisonment. Just gone. Erased from existence as if you never were."

"That's impossible," I said.

"No," he said calmly. "It isn't. Not for me."

He moved toward the throne. Placed himself beside it. Beside me.

Nokoa's hand tightened on mine. I felt his pulse. His warmth. His life finally, finally stable.

And I understood: I'd saved him. I'd actually saved him.

But the price—

The Bone God free. The world changed forever. One final, impossible choice waiting.

Choose which of us erases. Which of us survives. Which of us becomes nothing so the other can be free.

He spoke one more time. "I think, before we make any choices, we should start with a few truths."

www.ingramcontent.com/pod-product-compliance
Lightning Source LLC
Chambersburg PA
CBHW070312310726
48976CB00005B/1674